The Scales of Judgement

To Mandy—
Thank you for believing in me,
even when I didn't believe in myself.
For letting me bounce ideas off of you
and never complaining about it.
And for pushing me to tell this story.
This book wouldn't be here without you.

THE SCALES OF JUDGEMENT

MEREDITH C. ARMOLT

Chapter 1

BAXLEY

BAXLEY FELT LIKE THERE WAS A VICE CLAMPED AROUND his ribcage, restricting his lungs from expanding. When did breathing become so difficult? He tried to pull in a larger breath, chest struggling to inflate. It didn't seem to help. His nerves were jumping all over the place. This had to work. They already wasted too much time for it to fail. Checking his pocket watch for the hundredth time, he found that only thirty seconds had passed since he last looked. He snapped it closed, spinning it over and over in his hands. From his position ducked behind a display containing Vesperis' Proclamation of Independence, he glanced around to see if he could spot the others.

A team had been stationed in the most advantageous positions around the central circular room in the museum. He had spent the last three nights in the Museum of Aglar, waiting and hoping. Resting on a pedestal in the center of the room was the original crown of the first King of Vesperis. It was a priceless artifact for their kingdom, which usually never left the royal vault. This specific room was an exhibit dedicated to the origin of their country, making it the perfect place to display the crown. Baxley still couldn't believe that his father, King Oren Limorelli, allowed them to risk the relic for this; to try and use it as bait for *Skeleton Key*. They managed to catch several other lesser-known thieves in the process who hadn't made it as far as this central room; however, they weren't his goal. He needed Skeleton Key.

The soldier to his left was visible from this angle. Cain, who was crouched behind a display of maps depicting Vesperis' original borders, was recalled to the palace for his gift of being able to freeze a person for a few seconds. It was taxing on him to do so, leaving the man gasping for breath and shaking, but those seconds were often the difference between failure and success.

Their healers still weren't able to determine why some people were chosen and others weren't when it came to gifts — let alone what gift someone would develop. They believed that whether or not one could wield the minerals at all was linked to bloodlines. Parents who could both wield would produce offspring who also had the power. If only one parent could, there was less of a chance to have a magically inclined child. Still, it wasn't unheard of for non-magical parents to sometimes end up having a child who could wield. Generations ago, it became common in upper society to marry not for love, but to ensure their children would be wielders—and hope their child was special enough to present with a gift.

Baxley's gaze moved past Cain to continue his sweep, his eyes lingering on each entrance to the circular shaped room. There were six in total—five of which should be blocked as long as everyone did their jobs as assigned. The normal security had been shifted to funnel Skeleton Key through the entrance that was in front of Baxley off to the right. He couldn't see any of the other three soldiers hiding at present. Each of them was also chosen and brought in for the gifts they possessed. Luther could levitate objects, Felix moved twice as fast as anyone, and Arla could become invisible.

He didn't know any of them well, but he had been working with all four of them in the past week to strategize and come up with the best plan. All of them had risen up through the military ranks, and in society, within a few years of signing on as soldiers—as one does when they present with an exceptionally useful gift. It was quite common for entire families to climb the social ranks due to just one of their children manifesting a gift.

Outside the five blocked hallway entrances, Baxley also had soldiers posted who didn't have gifts; however, they were extremely powerful wielding certain minerals that could come in handy if they were required to assist in apprehending Skeleton Key. Some of the hallways branched off and he had more soldiers there waiting. He wanted nothing to go to chance. Every possibility needed to be covered. His stomach sank as the thought of Skeleton Key slipping through his fingers entered his mind despite all his planning. No, he couldn't think that way. Shaking his head, he opened his watch again. One more minute gone. His legs were cramping from being in the same position for over three hours.

A dark shape in his peripheral vision caught his attention. Whipping his eyes back up, he saw him. Standing in the targeted entrance was a man wearing a black cloak with his hood drawn up. Skeleton Key. Baxley's heart picked up in pace. Its beats were so strong, it felt like it might explode through his chest. Palms shaking, he clicked his watch closed and slipped it into his pocket. Skeleton Key's head turned, surveying the room. He still hadn't stepped farther past the threshold. Shit—did he hear the sound of the watch? Refusing to blink in case he was to disappear, Baxley chanted in his head: *Take the bait. Take the bait. Take the bait.*

Finally—Skeleton Key took the first step forward. He seemed on the shorter side for a man. Maybe that helped him avoid capture for all these years. Even with the help of moonlight from the windows lining the upper part of the room, he couldn't make out any facial features on the man thanks to the hood. Skeleton Key approached the pedestal, skulking around the stanchions that kept the crowds back from actually being able to touch the crown. After making a full loop around it, the thief moved to duck under the chain.

"Now!" Baxley yelled, surging out from behind his hiding place. He tilted to the side as his legs buckled from the blood flow returning to them.

Cain's right arm rose up, palm facing forward as he also stood. Skeleton Key froze in his stooped position, right hand still holding the chain he was about to duck under.

"Felix!" Baxley called.

A blur moved from the opposite side of the room, appearing at the thief's side within seconds. Felix clamped a cuff—made of copper, which cut off someone's access to magic—onto the wrist that was exposed from holding up the chain.

Cain groaned, his arm shaking, "I'm losing it."

Felix pulled a pair of chained manacles from his belt. He got one side locked onto that same exposed wrist before Cain's arm fell, releasing Skeleton Key. Not prepared for the thief to move again, Felix lost his grip on the second manacle, allowing Skeleton Key to finish slipping beneath the stanchion chain. In a blur of cloak, a glass vile smashed in front of Felix as he tried to follow. A plume of bluish smoke burst into existence and enveloped Felix. A second later, the soldier had fallen to the ground, where he now lay motionless.

Skeleton Key hadn't even paused to watch. Grabbing the crown in his right hand, he leaped over the other side of the stanchions and pivoted to run back the way he came. He got all of five steps before he was yanked off the ground. Luther had both palms outstretched, fingers spread wide, as he approached Skeleton Key, who was now floating several feet above the stone floor. Still not deterred, Skeleton Key whipped a knife in Luther's direction with his free hand.

Baxley reacted this time, using his magnetite magic to redirect the dagger towards himself instead. Plucking the dagger from the air, he moved in closer to help subdue the man. A second dagger appeared in Skeleton Key's hand, but before he could throw it, Luther made a circular motion with his arms. Skeleton Key was flipped upside down, his cloak tangling in his arms. The dagger and crown dropped to the ground as the thief fought to right himself. Giving up on the cloak, Skeleton Key unclasped it and let it fall, too. Baxley still couldn't make out his features as he wore a mask that covered the lower half of his face. His hair was much longer than expected, though, hanging down to brush the stone floor.

"Come peacefully and this will go easier for you," Baxley said as the soldiers stationed outside the room joined them in surrounding the apprehended man.

Skeleton Key responded by pulling another knife he had stashed by his ribs. Out of nowhere, Arla blinked into existence behind the thief, her sword resting against his neck. "Drop it," she growled.

That dagger joined the other one on the floor. Skeleton Key held out both hands in a surrendering gesture, the manacle still clasped on his right wrist, chain dangling. Baxley motioned one of the additional soldiers forward with a nod, who took the remaining manacle and clamped it closed around the unsecured left wrist. Arla removed her sword from Skeleton Key's neck, taking a step back. Luther rotated his arms the opposite way, which moved the secured man back into the upright position before he was lowered to the ground.

"Remove his mask, Arla," Baxley commanded as he kept his eyes pinned to his prize. She moved forward again to untie the strip of fabric. The mask fell away revealing— "You're a girl!"

Baxley squeaked. Shock rippled through him, his stomach plummeting. What if this wasn't Skeleton Key?

"A woman," the thief corrected, scoffing.

Raising the palm not currently holding the dagger that had been flung at Luther, Baxley sent a ball of light towards the ceiling, illuminating the space. Now that he could see her better, he noted that her hair was a dark brown and reached past her shoulders. Her almond skin tone and what appeared to be dark brown eyes were very standard to those found in the north. At first impressions, he thought her pretty, if somewhat plain. A face to be lost in a crowd. She had no visible tattoos and he didn't see any bracelets or necklaces with minerals, either. Could she somehow not be a wielder, and yet still be the only rumored thief to have successfully broken into the palace of Gleyra?

"You *are* Skeleton Key, correct?" He narrowed his eyes, studying her again from head to toe.

"If that's what you choose to call me." She smirked back at him.

Hope sparked to life in his chest. Still glaring, Baxley said, "Check her for other weapons, and someone check on Felix."

More light filled the room as the other soldiers joined them. One of them must have touched the small piece of quartz that controlled the much larger piece hanging from the middle of the ceiling. Baxley let his own light die out.

Arla stepped forward to pat down Skeleton Key. The woman was wearing a fitted black halter top vest that laced up in the front over a short-sleeved black shirt. Overtop was a leather harness with several sheaths for daggers. The two sheaths on either side of her ribs were empty, along with one by the shoulder. Arla removed another dagger from the other shoulder and two hidden behind her back before checking the rings the woman was wearing. Finding none of them contained minerals, Arla continued checking farther down.

"Felix is breathing steadily, but still unconscious," Cain reported.

"Is anyone decent at healing?" Baxley asked, still watching Arla as she removed the tactical weapons belt the woman was wearing. No one spoke up. "What was in that vial?" His eyes narrowed even more as he met Skeleton Key's gaze.

"Would you even believe me if I told you?" She cocked her head to one side.

"Probably not." His lips thinned. "Get him to the healers."

Three of the extra soldiers moved forward, lifting Felix off the ground.

"Here." Arla thrust the tactical belt to a fourth soldier nearby. "There are still vials left over. They might be the same thing she used on him—deliver them to the healers to help determine his treatment."

The soldier turned and followed the others carrying Felix out of the room.

Two more smaller daggers from the belt had been added to the growing pile along with what appeared to be some lock picking tools. The thief wore tight leather pants paired with sturdy boots. Arla found two daggers strapped on either side of her thighs and one slipped into the right boot. Once she was finished, she gave a nod. "She's clean."

Baxley tossed the dagger he still held into the pile with the others and then bent to retrieve the crown.

"Don't lose that. It'll be in my hands again soon enough." Skeleton Key grinned at him.

He scoffed at her arrogance. "I find that highly unlikely." Turning to address the remaining soldiers, he said, "I want three of you scouting ahead of us and three guarding from behind. The rest, spread out around us. Cain and Luther, you're on the prisoner with me. Arla, you know what to do. We get her to the carriage and straight to the palace. No deviations. One person ride ahead to alert the king. Any questions?" He glanced around the room. When no one spoke, he said, "Good. Let's move out."

His heart soared for the first time in weeks. All his patience had finally paid off. This was going to work—he knew it.

Chapter 2

SKELETON KEY

CAIN AND LUTHER HAD ESCORTED HER TO THE THRONE room after exiting the carriage. They now stood guard on either side of her while the walls were lined with the other soldiers who accompanied them from the museum. The prince had stormed off without a word when they arrived.

The carriage ride from the museum to the palace was tense. Trying to goad the prince into telling her why, exactly, she was being brought before the king, instead of going straight to the dungeon, had done no good.

"Do all women you put in cuffs get to meet the king?" Skeleton Key had asked the crown prince, studying him where he sat across from her. He was shorter than she expected. A couple inches under six feet, if she had to guess. But then, she had only ever viewed him from a distance before. His black hair and thick brows made his green eyes pop. The multicolored mandala-style tattoo winding up his neck had a falcon with its talons extended in the center. It glimmered in the light of the moon, making it stand out on his honey-colored skin. The tattoo disappeared beneath the collar of his shirt. She wasn't sure how far it went down. Most women gushed over how handsome he was; she would describe him as regal, which made her gag instead of swoon.

He had ignored her question and continued watching out the window.

"Oh, come now, you must have had a woman in cuffs before. Unless all the rumors about you are true." She fake-gasped and clutched her chest, the chains rattling. "My dear, Prince," her face melted into concern, "you're not really a virgin, are you?"

His cheeks tinted with a hint of pink at that comment. Cain, who was seated next to her, let out a small chuckle before turning it into a cough after getting kicked by Luther, who was opposite him.

"Is that why Princess Adelaide ran back to her country? Cause you couldn't please her?" She couldn't keep her smirk to herself after that one and covered her mouth with her hand.

"Enough!" Baxley roared, his nostrils flaring. "Sit there in silence or I swear I'll make you regret it." He finally met her eyes.

"Do you promise?" Her answering smile made him groan.

The amusement she'd felt in that moment still lingered with her now as she waited.

The palace at Aglar—the capital of Vesperis—was built with comfort and pleasure in mind. With a hot climate, where even their winters never truly cooled off and they never saw snow except on the peaks of the mountain range bordering their country to the south, everything was as open as possible for air flow. The outside of the palace was secure, but the inside had many courtyards and gardens that one could walk straight into without opening a door. Sheer curtains were hung for the illusion of privacy. One of the courtyards she caught a glimpse of even had a pool where people might lounge around to cool off from the oppressive heat.

Her gaze wandered around the large, gaudy throne room. "I love what they've done with the place. Very...loud." Cain snorted. Most of the decor in the room was dipped in gold—the three thrones on the dais, the Limorelli crest hanging on the wall, even the sheer curtains that led to the courtyards outside were all gold. One of the largest deposits of quartz she'd ever seen hung from the middle of the ceiling. It illuminated the entire room, making all the gold sparkle. She wrinkled her nose; she was more of a silver woman.

"Tell me, do they actually hold some of the smaller balls in here rather than the formal ballroom?" She turned towards Cain, picking him out as the more probable one to answer her out of the pair.

"Only for the more intimate ones," the soldier replied. Cain boasted a yellow sunburst mineral tattoo on his left cheek. He wore the other eight minerals in a thick bracelet around his wrist, making sure he maintained contact with them and could still wield their magic.

Her eyes traced the mandala-style pattern that was always somehow incorporated into the design when tattooing minerals. The tradition began when the process of grinding down minerals and adding them to tattoo ink was discovered thousands of years ago.

"You're lucky to have been deemed worthy enough to receive a tattoo," she said. Most of the time, it was only those wealthy enough to afford them that were tattooed. They were displayed on the face, neck, and sometimes the arms; anywhere on the body that they could be shown off easily.

"Most of us have them for any magic the crown determined is useful to our service," he explained.

Her gaze went to the soldiers posted around the room. The majority of them did have visible mineral tattoos. Luther seemed to have something tattooed on the back of his neck. She leaned back, trying to get a better look at it, but the soldier shifted, not letting her see what it was.

"There's nothing worse than a soldier getting cut off from their magic in a fight due to a broken bracelet or necklace," Cain continued.

Her eyes snapped back to him. "Do they give you a choice?"

"Why would we not want to?" He frowned at her.

"With the risks involved, it should be your choice," she said, head cocked to the side.

Mica was the binding agent required to mix the solution together for the tattooing process, and if the measurements were off even a little, the results could lead to death. Every so many years, an increase in deaths around smaller villages would crop up from fools who tried to tattoo themselves. Even if someone went to a trusted tattoo artist, some bodies ended up rejecting the tattoo on their own. Luckily, in those cases, most people survived, though they were left permanently scarred.

"I suppose if someone didn't want the tattoo, they'd be allowed to say no. Though, I've never heard of someone rejecting the offer. We consider it the highest privilege to be chosen. The benefit of not having to stay in contact with the minerals, and the power boost from it, outweighs the risks."

She hummed in response, not saying anything else.

The minutes dragged by at an unbearably slow pace. Skeleton Key was about to start counting the gold veined marble tiles out of boredom when the door to the right behind the thrones opened.

Prince Baxley Limorelli led the way, his chin held high. He still had on the tight, darker clothing from the museum that was worn by their soldiers. King Oren and Queen Mesra, however, were dressed as if it wasn't the middle of the night and they hadn't just been awoken, their flowy silk clothes drifting around them. Vesperis preferred a more modest style compared to some of their neighboring countries. The queen's dress had several slits in the skirt, but one would never see a hint of skin within the layers. Her hair was coiffed into an elaborate updo to fit the ensemble. No wonder it took them so long to get here. Skeleton Key huffed in annoyance.

Behind them trailed a surprise guest. He was middle aged and dressed in almost as fine of clothing as the king and queen. She didn't know who he was.

The three royals took their seats, leaving the man standing off to the side. The king stared her down for several seconds before turning to the prince, asking, "*This* is Skeleton Key?"

"Ouch," she muttered, low enough that only Luther and Cain could hear her.

Baxley simply nodded.

The king swung back to her. "What minerals have you been tattooed with?"

Whoever had painted the large portrait of him hanging behind the center throne had done a decent job capturing his likeness. She had rolled her eyes at it when she had first entered the room. King Oren was just an older, richer in color, version of the prince. He had the same strong jaw, straight nose, and green eyes as his son. The green that often ran in the Limorelli line. And his black hair was speckled with gray.

"What makes you think I've been tattooed?" She met his gaze, unflinching.

"You're wearing no minerals on your person. You're a well-known thief throughout all the northern countries, and if rumors are true, have even stolen from Voglar's royal family." He cocked one eyebrow. "Now, let's try again," he said, steepling his fingers and leaning forward. "What tattoos do you possess? Or, do we need to have you stripped?"

Skeleton Key studied King Oren's own tattoo, which was displayed on his face. The Limorelli family crest—a falcon holding a sword—was tattooed inside of a mandala design on his cheek. The tattoo carried on down his neck. Each individual color of the mandala shimmered in the light. "No need. I have them all," she said, after finishing her examination. She raised her chin, managing to look down her nose at him despite him being seated above her.

"Strip her," he commanded, signaling to Cain and Luther.

"What the hell?" Skeleton Key tried to shove the soldiers off as they moved to grab her arms.

"You'll learn fast not to lie to me, girl."

"Woman," she spat. "And I'm not lying!" She fought harder as two more soldiers from along the wall joined in their efforts. After she landed an elbow to someone's nose, they kicked the back of her knees, sending her tumbling to the floor. They forced her all the way down, someone's boot pressing against her neck. "My back! They're on my back," she gasped, her airway being restricted.

A knife cut through her vest before hands grasped her shirt, ripping it down the middle. They left her leather harness and bra intact. The boot from her neck was removed. Two sets of hands grabbed her upper arms, hoisting her to a standing position again and spinning her so her back faced the dais. She staggered with the force they used.

Running down her spine was a sword that speared through a mandala, with two scales hanging from either side of the guards on the hilt. Unlike most tattoos, hers was all in *white*. It stood out against her medium brown skin. The only indication that it held minerals within it was the gleam it gave off in the light from above.

Footsteps approached from behind her. "What is the meaning of this?" King Oren demanded.

It was established long ago that each of the nine minerals were to be mixed with a certain color when tattooed to identify them. Quartz was yellow to represent the light it gave off; magnetite was black and let people control metal, and fluorite controlled water and was blue. Gypsum was green for plants, while talc helped with healing and was orange. Olivine was turned gray for rocks. Feldspar was brown for soil and sand. Red was assigned to pyrite for fire, and zinc ended up being purple for air. Unlike normal tattoo ink on darker skin tones, it was possible to still make out the colors when they shimmered.

"I paid extra." She turned her neck to smirk at him. If people didn't know that she could wield and that she was tattooed on top of that, it gave her a leg up in her line of work.

The king grabbed a fist full of her hair, yanking her head backwards and down. "You'd do well to remember your life is in my hands now." His hot breath brushed over her face. Her nose wrinkled at the rank smell; the least he could have done was brush his teeth after making her wait for so long. "Are you strong in any of them?"

Everyone who could wield the minerals could use all nine to a certain extent. Most of the time, they ended up being more powerful in one or two of them. Historically, it was found that if someone grew up in close proximity to a mineral, they would specialize in it; however, as trade expanded and minerals were spread to other locations, it meant that children were exposed to all of them more.

"Why don't you take off the cuff and find out?" She couldn't help but taunt him.

He tilted her head back even farther, making her back arch. Gritting her teeth, she refused to cry out because of him.

"And your gift?" He trailed a finger from his other hand down her spine.

"Unfortunately, for you, there's no way to tell if I have one and I'm no longer in a sharing mood." She snapped her teeth in his direction as best she could.

He shoved her head away before turning and walking back towards his throne.

"Was that truly necessary?" asked the queen, her lips pursed.

Queen Mesra didn't resemble her son at all. The story goes that she joined her father touring the continent while he was part of a delegation representing Armarands—one of the southernmost countries. The then Prince of Vesperis—now king—took one look at her and declared his intentions. She never returned to her own country. Her skin was a deep olive, which made her stick out in the north. Her blonde hair was streaked with gray at her temples, the only revealing sign of her age. She bore her tattoo on the center of her neck. It was a delicate mandala design that made her look like she wore a choker necklace.

King Oren didn't respond as he took his seat once more. "We'd like to present you with a deal." The guards turned her back around to face them directly. "There's something that we'd like you to retrieve from Voglar, and, in exchange, you'll be granted your freedom."

Here it was. The real reason behind why they'd set an elaborate trap to capture her. She couldn't lie to herself that she was, indeed, intrigued. "And what is this object I'm to steal?"

"The Princess of Aswal was taken. We believe they're keeping her at the palace in Gleyra."

Skeleton Key burst out laughing, the sound reverberating around the chamber. "You expect me to not only break into their capital, but to rescue a *person*?" She scanned their grim faces. "You're *mad*. It's not possible."

"You've gotten into the palace before, have you not?" The man standing off to the side spoke up for the first time.

"And you are?"

"Daimian Ashford, the Ambassador of Aswal." He inclined his head her way. "Your reputation would imply that it's not impossible—for you."

"Fine. Not interested, then," she said, shrugging.

"We're willing to pay," he countered.

"Her freedom is payment enough," the king cut in, crossing his arms.

"And what makes you think I won't take off the first chance I get?" Skeleton Key pointed out.

"You need us to remove that cuff."

"Oh, please. You think I don't have the means to get this cuff removed? I'll be gone the minute you let me out of here. *You. Need. Me.* Clearly, you went through a lot of effort to capture me in the first place. Now surely, we can come to some sort of understanding." She smiled up at them, ignoring her cut and ripped clothes that kept sliding farther down her arms.

"What do you want?" Prince Baxley asked before his father could say anything else.

"The crown," she replied without hesitation.

"Agreed." The prince nodded.

While his father roared at the same time, "Absolutely not!"

The pair started arguing with each other.

"We need this—"

"I'll not have some thief carrying around the first—"

"There's no other—"

"There's always another—"

"There's no time! She doesn't have time. Who knows what's already—"

"Enough." The queen didn't raise her voice, but the two quieted down. Her gaze was fixed on the Skeleton Key, unwavering. No one spoke.

"You can do it?" Queen Mesra asked, breaking the silence. "Get in and get her out?"

Skeleton Key nodded. "It won't be easy, but yes. I could do it."

"Give her the crown," Queen Mesra said, turning to her husband.

"But—" he began.

"It's just a crown. This is your future daughter-in-law's life we're talking about." Their eyes were locked together, neither looking away. "Give it to her."

The king said nothing.

"If this was my life, what would you do?" she whispered.

"Fine." King Oren ducked his chin, pinching the bridge of his nose. "After your service is no longer required, you'll receive the crown as payment and be released."

"Agreed." Skeleton Key beamed. "I'd like that in writing of course. Can't be too careful." She tilted her head to the side. "And make sure I get a copy. Oh—and it's once the princess has been returned to the castle that I'll be released. Wording is everything, after all."

"Done." Prince Baxley rose to his feet.

"If you go back on our deal, it won't end well for you," she warned them, her eyes narrowing on the king.

"You don't trust the word of your king?" King Oren puffed out his chest.

"Who says you're my king?"

Baxley interrupted their stare down, saying, "We leave at first light."

"Not quite." She took a step forward, shaking off her guards. "I may be in chains, but you'll be following my lead on this one, Prince."

The prince straightened up. "I don't think so."

"If you want her back, we need a plan and not whatever half-cocked *thing* I'm sure you've concocted." Her lips pressed together. "Tomorrow, you tell me everything I want to know." She pushed her clothes back up her arms, trying to keep some of her dignity intact. "For now, you can show me to a room and replace the clothes you've ruined. I just bought this vest," she moaned.

The prince didn't react at first. "Fine," he bit out. "Cain, find her an acceptable room for the night."

"Wonderful." She clapped her hands together, chains clanking. Skeleton Key pivoted on her heel, whistling as she walked for the doors.

"I believe you've got your work cut out for you, Prince Baxley," she heard the ambassador say.

The corner of her mouth tilted upward. They had no idea what they'd gotten themselves into when they captured her.

Chapter 3

BAXLEY

THE NEXT MORNING, BAXLEY FOUND SKELETON KEY'S guards posted outside Adelaide's rooms. He'd originally gone to the room that Skeleton Key had been escorted to last night—a small interior room, with no window to escape from—only to find it empty and the guards also missing. No bodies or signs of a struggle indicated that someone else authorized her removal. Fury drove his footsteps as he stormed through the palace, searching for her. By chance, he happened across a servant who pointed him in this direction. She'd seen the Ambassador of Aswal and Skeleton Key strolling through the halls together, discussing the details of the princess' last week in Aglar.

That's how he'd come across the pair, standing together out on the balcony that overlooked a private enclosed garden. "What're you doing in here?" he demanded, not pleased that his betrothed's privacy was being invaded.

"Don't you find it odd that someone managed to kidnap her from here without being seen? Without her at least alerting someone?" Skeleton Key trailed her fingers along the balcony railing, the chain from the manacles she still wore clinking against the stone. "There are enough balconies that open up to the garden that someone should have seen or heard something. Accessing the roof wouldn't be unreasonably hard, but getting her back up there would be a challenge. And going down could be equally as difficult depending on the circumstances." She rubbed at her chin, eyes surveying the area.

"They must have someone gifted on their side," he reasoned.

"Possibly..." Her head tilted up towards the two balconies above them that someone would have to bypass before reaching the roof.

"What're you thinking?" Baxley asked.

She turned his way at the question. He noticed that someone had secured her similar clothing to those she wore yesterday. Her hair was braided back away from her face. She still wore her leather harness, despite it being empty of weapons. "Nice of you to finally grace us with your presence this morning, Prince." The sun was just beginning to lighten the sky behind her.

His fury sparked anew, rising up within him. Taking a deep breath, he grumbled, "I hadn't realized we'd scheduled a meeting."

"My apologies, Prince Baxley." Ambassador Daimian bowed his head. "I wanted to get an early start and forgot to notify you."

Skeleton Key pushed by Baxley to reenter the sitting room. "There's no sign of struggle. No sign that anyone broke in. No marks from them having climbed in. Her lady-in-waiting heard nothing. *Nothing* is out of place." Her fingertips tapped together while she took in the room. "Is there any secret passage out of these rooms? Any servant passageway?"

"No, none," Baxley replied. It was something he made sure of before having these rooms assigned to Adelaide. There was a sitting room, bedchamber, walk-in closet, and a bathing chamber. A door off the sitting room led to Adelaide's lady-in-waiting's room.

He watched Skeleton Key pace in a circle. "So, the only ways out would be through this entrance," she pointed to the door leading to the hallway, "the lady-in-waiting's entrance, or the balcony."

"What are you alluding to?" asked the ambassador.

"You really believe someone managed to take her from here without anyone knowing?"

"Well, what else could have happened? She wouldn't have left willingly with them," Baxley fumed, blood rushing to his cheeks.

"If you say so." She waved him off, not even glancing his way.

"I do." His fists clenched. "You don't know her."

"And how well do you really know her, Prince?" She wandered over to a small desk, leafing through the letters that were left there.

He stormed over, slamming his hand down on the one she was about to pick up. "Those are private." His eyes flashed, glaring down at her. "Can you even read?"

"Of course I can read, you twit." Her eyes pierced into him. "Nothing can be private if you want her back." She met him toe to toe. "How do you even know she's been taken by Voglar? Taken to Gleyra?"

"We received a letter the week after she went missing," Ambassador Daimian interjected. "It demanded new trade agreements with both countries...but they don't want to return her." He grimaced. "They want to keep Princess Adelaide as insurance that the agreements will be upheld."

"They'll be expecting you to try and get her back." She maintained eye contact with Baxley.

Baxley nodded. "That's why we have you."

"I should have asked for more than the crown," she groaned.

"Now, if you're done invading her privacy, might we go meet with the others to actually plan her rescue?"

"If you wish to miss something important in her correspondence, who am I to judge?" She raised one shoulder.

"I can assure you; these are simply personal letters of no importance." He crossed his arms, refusing to back down.

"How can you be sure?"

"Because they're all from me." His teeth ground together.

"Love letters." She smirked, her eyes darted down again, trying to get a peek at anything written on them.

His hand landed atop the letters once more.

"Fine," she whined. "Let's go—as long as breakfast is involved. I'm starving." She turned, walking towards the door. "Oh," she called back over her shoulder, "don't think I still haven't ruled out her running away due to your lack of *skills*, Prince."

His cheeks heated for a different reason.

***

They were situated in the council chamber. A large circular table took up most of the room. On it was a map of Vesperis, Aswal, and Voglar. Before they had entered the room, he sent the Commander of the Guard ahead to clear the map of any sensitive information—like the locations of their troops.

Now, the select few he had chosen to accompany him on the mission, along with the Master of Intelligence, the Commander of the Guard, and the Ambassador of Aswal, were seated around the table, all looking to him for direction. Skeleton Key slid into the seat next to him.

"You already know Daimian." Baxley motioned the man's way. "This is our Master of Intelligence, Edwin." A man in his mid-fifties inclined his head at the thief. "The Commander of the

Guard, Roland." The man next to Edwin also nodded. Roland was younger than Edwin by a few years and appeared to be in better physical condition. "Then we have those who will be traveling with us. Captain Luther Dunn, Major Arla Farbough, and Major Cain Hillcrag, you have already met." Baxley pointed out the three.

"Levitation, invisibility, and you," Skeleton Key's eyes tracked to Cain, "can freeze people. Though you need to work on your control." She clicked her tongue at him. "Such potential if you had any discipline."

Cain sat straighter in his chair. He opened his mouth to retort, but her gaze had already left him, moving down the table.

"And what gifts do you possess?" she asked the last two men.

"None," Baxley stepped in again. "Lieutenant Del Underwood is an extremely powerful rock wielder and Sergeant Wadyn Thorrig excels at fire." He held his hand out towards Skeleton Key, turning to address the group at large, saying, "Everyone, this is —"

Before he could finish, the door to the room burst open. "Bax, you didn't tell me you captured Skeleton Key!" His sister, Lumoz, whirled into the room, her airy dress floating around her. She was approaching her seventeenth birthday. Her birth had come as a surprise a little over a decade after he was born. His parents struggled for years after him to have another child until they had given up, then Lumoz was miraculously conceived. She had also inherited more of their father's features over their mother's, her long black hair reaching nearly to her waist. Her skin tone was almost a perfect match to Baxley's—though her eyes were more hazel than green. "I had to find out from court gossip of all things." She threw her hands up in the air. "Imagine my embarrassment when I sat down for morning tea, and Lady Angellon informed me that Skeleton Key had been arrested." Lumoz scanned the table. "But where is he?"

"Present." Skeleton Key thumped her hands, chains and all, onto the table top.

"A woman!" A huge smile broke out upon her face. "Just wait till I tell the others. We had bets down on what gift you might wield, but no one ever thought you'd be a woman," she said, bouncing on her toes. Her eyes sparkled at the revelation.

That never boded well when it came to her. "Lumoz," Baxley sighed, rubbing the bridge of his nose. His eyes clamped shut as he took a breath, pausing for a moment as annoyance threatened to build up within him. He loved his sister without question—truly. She just had a habit of inserting herself into delicate matters often. *Too* often. Their father was chasing her away from meetings where she shouldn't be every other day.

"Did you agree to help?" Lumoz's attention was still fixed on Skeleton Key.

"Were you planning on announcing our rescue mission as well as my arrest?" Skeleton Key drummed her fingers on the table.

"Of course not." Lumoz's eyebrows creased, her feet stilling.

"So, just going to give away our potential advantage to your enemy."

"I didn't—" She looked to Baxley, eyes wide.

"Gossip spreads. Your entire country knows Princess Adelaide is no longer in Aglar. Potentially, not even in Vesperis anymore. So far, rumors are leaning towards the engagement falling apart after spending too much time together...among other *things*." Her eyes flicked towards Baxley for a second before zeroing in on Lumoz again. "I suggest you keep any more information to yourself, Princess."

His sister's face fell, her bottom lip starting to quiver.

"You should go." Baxley stood, walking over to her. He placed one hand on her back, directing her to the still wide-open door. "I'll come see you before we leave."

"But I want to help," she pleaded, blinking up at him.

His heart swelled. "Not this time, my light." Baxley chucked her under the chin.

"But my gift—" she tried again.

"—is amazing," he cut her off, "but you're still too young." At sixteen, she'd only been wielding magic for a few years since she'd gone through puberty. Even if she wasn't his little sister, there was no way he'd allow someone with such little experience to come along—no matter how useful their gift might be. Lumoz opened her mouth to argue more. "No." He smiled down at her, his shoulders drooping. "Mother would have my ass if I let you come. Now off with you, and no listening at the door." He attempted to interject some sternness into his voice as he pushed her through the threshold.

She craned her neck back to look at him. "Fine, but I want to know *everything*."

"When I get back," he promised. He closed the door behind her.

"And I mean everything!" she shouted to still be heard.

"Where were we?" Baxley turned back to face the group.

Skeleton Key was leaning backwards in her chair with her feet propped on the table, staring up at the ceiling. "Well…there's where your court is spreading gossip around, or how you're trying to use brute force rather than finesse to break into a palace. Take your pick."

He stiffened. "My court will be handled."

"Really? Then how did the rumors about you and the princess get out in the first place?" The legs of her chair dropped to the floor with a sharp bang. "How long has she been missing, anyway?"

"Thirty-six days," he muttered. Guilt tore through him just admitting that. Worrying about what was being done to her consumed him in the beginning. He was lucky to get several hours of interrupted sleep since she'd been taken. Sometimes, when he first woke up, there'd be a brief moment where he didn't remember it happened. Then, all the doubts and worries would rush back in, to haunt and hound him throughout the day.

"And what have you learned in those thirty-six days?"

Edwin answered her, saying, "The royal family is all in attendance at their palace in Gleyra. The security along the wall surrounding the palace has increased. Everything going in and out is being searched. This leads us to believe that she is being held there. We've been unable to get anyone on the inside. But you," he stared hard at Skeleton Key, "have made it through that wall, haven't you?"

That wall gave the Voglarian's the advantage. When their capital city of Gleyra was designed, they built their siege wall around their palace rather than around the city like most countries chose to do. The royals could sequester themselves behind the wall for months without running out of supplies. In all the turbulent history between Vesperis and Volgar, Gleyra had never fallen.

Skeleton Key paused for a moment before replying, "I have."

Baxley's breath caught. It was the first time she'd admitted to it. That feeling of hope was creeping in again.

"The wall is a challenge, but not insurmountable for me. Which is why most of the people here will not be needed."

"They have been carefully selected and are among some of our best," Baxley argued, not appreciating her judgement of his decisions.

"Major Hillcrag is only useful for you to potentially control me—if you think I'm going to run. Major Farbough's gift might come in handy, especially if she can hold it for long periods of time, or wield it on another person..." Her eyebrow arched at the major.

"About ten minutes and only for myself," Arla answered the non-question.

Skeleton Key grimaced, continuing on. "And unless you were planning on levitating someone over the wall—which is a horrible choice—I hardly see why you'd bring Captain Dunn along. Same goes for Lieutenant Underwood. We won't be trying to collapse the wall or burrow through it. As for Sergeant Thorrig, well, I suppose he could send everything up in flames, just like your plan."

Embarrassment flooded his system. He had, indeed, thought of using Lieutenant Underwood for that exact purpose. "Well, I was planning on bringing Major Felix Yan as well, but you've taken him out of commission."

She waved him off. "If that's the man who can move quickly from last night, he'll be waking up in a few hours. Though if your healers haven't figured that out by now, then they aren't very good. It was a simple sleeping gas—wears off in twelve hours. But we won't be needing him as he can also be *seen* when he moves. Speaking of healers," she snapped her fingers, "we'll be needing one to come with us. We don't know what state we'll find your princess in and need to be prepared."

"Now just a minute." Roland bristled. "You can't just come in here and demand—"

Skeleton Key cut him off, saying, "That's exactly what I can do." She glared around at them all. "You clearly are ill-prepared and misguided. The best decision you made was getting a hold of me. So," she stood, her hands braced on the table, "let me do what I do best, and we'll get your princess back."

Everyone remained quiet.

"Agreed?"

There were murmurs from Roland and Edwin. Daimian outright declared his agreement.

"Then what *do* you suggest?" Baxley asked, resuming his seat next to her.

She also took her seat again. "Do you have anyone gifted in mind work? Erasing memories—changing or distorting them?"

"No," he said, shaking his head. "Is that even possible?"

"If you know the right people." She cocked her head, but elaborated no further.

"We have someone who can make a person see double," Roland offered.

"One person or a group?"

"Just one at a time."

"Not exactly what I'm looking for. Jumping from one place to the next?"

Again, Baxley shook his head.

"What's your sister's gift?"

He flinched. "She can walk through walls."

Her eyes lit up. "Now *that* could be useful."

"Out of the question," he replied, tensing.

"She'd be the safest out of all of us with that gift," she tried to argue.

"Not an option."

"Really. If she can walk through walls, then she can walk through a person. So, they couldn't even—"

"No!" he roared, slamming a hand onto the table. Anger flashed through his eyes as they locked onto hers.

Skeleton Key maintained eye contact for what felt like minutes before finally conceding. "Fine." She tipped her head towards him.

At least he'd won one round against her. Baxley never even considered that his sister could use her gift in that way. He didn't even know if it was possible, but now wasn't the time for experimenting. It made him cringe at the thought of how much more havoc she might wreak on her own. She was too curious for her own good. And even if she could do it, he would never take Lumoz into that kind of danger.

"And you yourself are giftless, correct?"

"Correct." His teeth clenched. It was a sore subject for him. His father often displayed his discontent over Baxley never having presented with one.

"So, really you're just an extra liability for us to drag along."

The muscle in his jaw twinged as he clenched down harder. "My presence is non-negotiable," he bit out the words.

"Are you at least decent with a weapon?"

"You won't have to worry about me," he assured her.

She sighed. "Just don't try anything stupid. We don't need a hero." She turned back to address the group. "How about illusions?"

"Yes," Edwin confirmed. "We do have an illusionist."

"Where are they now?"

His gaze slid to Baxley's before Edwin answered, "She's in Gleyra. Currently gathering information."

"She's one of your spies." She smirked at Edwin. His face remained blank of emotion, not giving anything else away. "How good is she?"

"Good enough to not be suspicious—but she won't be able to get the princess back. At least not on her own."

"I'm assuming you have means of contacting her."

Edwin dipped his head.

"Good. And what other gifts are you hiding amongst your spies?"

"None that could get here fast enough to join you." Edwin crossed his arms. "Other than that, you don't need to know. And what is your gift?" he asked, assessing her.

She tutted at him. "Did the prince not inform you how well that question went over last night? Now, let's get down to the real business." Her eyes flicked down to the map. "Major Farbough will come. We'll add your illusionist to our team once we get there. Pick a female healer that you trust. You can bring only two others to keep our numbers small. We want to remain as inconspicuous as possible. I would suggest asking the others, except for your advisors, to leave the room to keep this information as private as possible." Her eyes found Baxley's once more. "We wouldn't want any more court gossip getting out, would we?"

His anger reared its head again, his nostrils flaring. "You've made your point." He contemplated his options. Cain and Luther could help him subdue her, if need be, but so could Felix—if she was being truthful and he did wake up soon. The Lieutenant and Sergeant wouldn't be a huge help in that regard. Plus, she made it clear that she could get through the wall on her own without them. Decision made, he said, "Lieutenant Underwood, Sergeant Thorrig and Captain Dunn, if you'd please leave the room. Once Major Yan has awakened, send him to join us."

The three soldiers rose and exited the room without complaint, shutting the door behind them.

"Now then, let the fun begin." She grinned at the remaining group.

***

Fun was not the word he would have used. The next few hours were exhausting. Edwin and her butted heads at almost every decision. They both agreed that the fastest way to get there would be by ship, but that's where the unanimities stopped. Edwin wanted them to travel straight to the closest port to Gleyra—Ulgaris—before they began their full day of travel by horseback to the city. Skeleton Key insisted they swap ships at Parshindol, a city in Aswal close to their border with Voglar, before continuing on to Ulgaris. Having to concede that it was, indeed, a better idea to sail into Ulgaris on an Aswalian ship rather than a Vesperian one, Baxley agreed with their captive. His Master of Intelligence was likely never to forgive him for that slight. Daimian was to send an air message ahead of them to have a ship waiting in Parshindol.

Air messages were the fastest way to send letters, though one had to be careful they weren't intercepted. If a piece of zinc was broken in half, it would create a wind funnel through the sky between the two pieces, which could be used to send letters back and forth. The size of the zinc pieces determined how far the wind funnel could span. Most of the major cities had rooms dedicated just to these communications. Of course, natural weather also played a factor, so this wasn't always a reliable means of contact. Too much wind could force a letter out of its funnel and it would be lost. If it rained, the letter could become unreadable, or be so waterlogged that it would fall out of the funnel due to its weight. Unfortunately, waxed paper and pencils were too heavy to use.

They took a break around lunch time when Skeleton Key complained, in great detail, how she was about to wither away from hunger. He was already sensing a pattern with her and food. It was shortly after they all sat back down to continue hashing out their return route that they were interrupted for a second time. Felix, as it turns out, did wake up once the sleeping gas wore off and arrived to join them.

Baxley rubbed his temples, listening to Skeleton Key and Edwin arguing.

"They will be searching every single ship that sails. How long of a head start did they have when she was first taken? Your harbor is right here." Her finger hit the spot marked Aglar on the map, the chains on her rattling with the movement. "We have a day of travel to reach the ships again. They *will* find us."

"But it's the fastest way back!" Edwin threw his hands in the air. "If you get her at night, that could give you an eight-hour head start before they discover her missing."

"Which is less time than it will take us to travel back to the ship. An air message would beat us there."

"It makes no sense to try to travel by horse when they'll be searching those roads, too," he insisted. "It would take more than five days to get back to Aswal and over nine to reach Vesperis, and that's *if* you took a direct route."

"It all makes no difference if they find us. We can't fight our way out." She scowled at him. "Which is why we don't take a direct route." Her finger found Gleyra and traced in the opposite direction to the east instead of west towards the coast line. "We travel a longer way around the Cathburn Mountains, and then up the eastern coast back into Vesperis. Once there, we hire a ship to bring us the rest of the way back."

"You'd have to travel right through the Sutra Plains."

"That's what camels are for."

"It would take—"

"About sixteen days over land, plus five full days by ship. If we don't run into trouble, that is, and the weather favors us."

Edwin remained silent, studying the map.

"It could work." Roland tapped his finger on his chin.

"We'd be even more cut off going around the mountains," Felix noted.

"There will be no backup whichever way we choose." Baxley shook his head.

"I'd suggest taking the Mongol pass through the mountains, but assume your princess wouldn't be up for that type of travel." Skeleton Key looked to him for confirmation.

"No. I'm afraid that's out of the question," he replied. "She's..." he trailed off, thinking of the luxuries in which Adelaide surrounded herself. "Well, this journey alone will be tough enough for her." For the first time, doubt, not of his shortcomings but of Adelaide's, crossed his mind. He'd been so concerned with rescuing her from the palace that he hadn't considered how she'd do on the return trip.

It must have shown on his face, because Daimian chimed in with, "She'll make it." He gave Baxley a small smile. "We're decided, then?"

Baxley checked in with Edwin.

Edwin crossed his arms, leaning back in his chair. "I will admit that they should not expect you to take that route."

"Excellent," she said. "I'll make a list of all the items I require for our journey. I'm sure it won't be a problem for you to acquire them for me." She winked at Baxley.

He gritted his teeth. "Provide your list to your guards, and I'll make sure someone gathers everything for you. For now, you can be escorted back to your room to wait until we leave."

"You should leave during the night in case the palace is being watched," Edwin said, standing from his chair. "I'll go arrange a ship for you now." Baxley thanked him before he exited the room.

Skeleton Key stood next, moving for the door. "Make sure I get that contract before we depart," she called over her shoulder. Her guards were waiting outside to lead her back to her room.

Once the door closed, he turned to Arla. "I want her to be your priority during this. She doesn't do anything without you knowing."

"Understood," she replied, nodding.

"You think she'll try to run for it?" Roland asked.

"No, but—she's a thief. There's no telling what else she'll do either." Anxiety twisted his stomach. Right or wrong, there was no going back now.

Chapter 4

BAXLEY

AFTER THE MEETING, LUMOZ HADN'T WAITED FOR Baxley to come find her. She had burst into his rooms while he was packing, trying to needle him for more information about Skeleton Key. He simply told her that the thief seemed very fond of eating and left it at that, despite her pleading. Once he had finished packing, though, he did allow her to help carry his bags down to where they were all being gathered.

All of their belongings would be sent ahead of them to the ship. The group would be making their way separately from the palace to try and hide their movements. He'd chosen to have Skeleton Key accompany him in a carriage, stopping to transfer to a second one that Edwin had arranged for along the way, hoping to further confuse anyone who might be trying to keep tabs on him.

The list she provided the guards was quite extensive — some of it even outrageous. Why would she be needing several different sets of negligees for their journey? Baxley had gone to confront her about it, bringing along the contract his father had drafted. The contract she deemed acceptable and signed both copies, tucking hers into an inner pocket of her vest. As for the negligees, she claimed they were to prepare for all possible situations. He decided not to fight her on it after she said that if he wanted a preview, it could be arranged for an extra fee. There had been a feline twinge in her eyes that made him uneasy. Since his sister had insisted on being helpful, he delegated those particular items to her to secure.

After having a quiet dinner with only their immediate family—where his mother and sister wished him well and his father told him not to be a disappointment—he had settled in to wait for darkness to fall. It was shortly after one in the morning when Edwin gave him the go ahead.

At present, Baxley found himself in the first carriage with Skeleton Key. He peered out a crack in the curtain covering the window, examining the buildings he could see in the dark. If he had to guess, they had a few more minutes until they would arrive at the tavern where they would make the swap. A weird feeling that he couldn't identify twisted inside him. On one hand, he was relieved to finally be doing something after weeks of waiting. On the other, he still hoped it was the right thing...

The thief sat on the bench opposite him. He'd given her back the lightweight cloak she'd worn to the museum—light enough that even with their spring weather verging towards uncomfortable heat levels during the day, she wouldn't overheat at this hour. Her hood was up, hiding her face. Their ride, so far, had been mostly silent.

"You'll have to take these off of me before we get on the ship." She held her arms out to him, which still had the manacles and the cuff on. The keys to both were worn around his neck. "Unless you want the crew asking questions."

He let the curtain fall shut. "The cuff stays on. The manacles I'll remove once we arrive."

"You expect me to work miracles for you without my magic?"

"For now, it stays on — at least until we reach Gleyra."

They fell silent once more, until a problem occurred to him. "What should we call you, anyway?"

"Excuse me?"

"I hardly think you want us spreading around that you're Skeleton Key. What's your name?"

She scoffed at him. "You don't get my real name. Call me whatever you desire."

He studied her for a moment. "Okay, Coccyx," he said, smirking.

"What?" She snorted — actually snorted — at him.

"It's the —" he started to explain.

"I know what it is," she said, cutting off his words. Her hood fell back, revealing her face. Her very unamused face.

"It's part of the *skeleton*, and I thought it was fitting." Baxley shrugged, a full smile spreading across his face. Her expression remained unchanged. "No? What about Pubis? Femur? Clavicle? Patella?" She shook her head as he listed more bones. "I know," he said, snapping his fingers. "Phalanges." He was impressed the grooves between her eyebrows could get any deeper. "Fine, not bone related." He tilted his head this way and that, studying her. "How about Keys?"

"Keys is…acceptable."

Baxley sat back, listening to the sound of the wheels on the paved stones, until Keys asked a question of her own.

"What type of ship did Edwin manage to find us?"

"A merchant ship," he replied. "It was due to set sail in the morning, but with a little extra incentive they agreed to set sail early."

"What do they usually transport?"

"Why?" He eyed her with suspicion.

She shrugged. "Merely passing the time."

"It usually brings in fresh produce from Voglar and returns with shipments of magnetite and mica, among other things."

Her eyebrows raised. "Now that is surprising. Why wouldn't you withhold those shipments from the start of this?"

She did have a point. One his father threatened when they first received the demand letter; however, the King of Aswal urged him to hold off, so they could maintain the semblance of entering into negotiations with Voglar, while they bided time trying to pull off a rescue. It was those magnetite and mica shipments that were the driving demands in the new trade agreements that Voglar was after. Vesperis land contained the largest deposits of those minerals, and their merchants were responsible for the majority of its distribution to the entire continent. Geographically, both Vesperis and Aswal were cut off from the rest of the continent by Volgar. All their land trade routes had to run through their neighboring country, which Voglar often tried to take advantage of by raising taxes. Vesperis, in retaliation, would then withhold their supplies of mica and magnetite from Voglar. The two countries were known to fluctuate between periods of war and periods of tolerance. Their unstable history dated back centuries. Eventually, some monarch in charge would decide the agreements in place weren't advantageous enough for them and the fighting would begin anew.

"It's something that's been considered…" He didn't want to give her too much information.

"This would be the first royal marriage between any of the three countries, correct?"

"Between Vesperis and Aswal, yes. But there was a marriage alliance between Voglar and us in the past…It ended quite poorly." His lips pursed.

"What happened?" she pressed.

"The Voglarian bride was murdered on her wedding night. It resulted in the longest stretch of war between the two countries ever."

"Shame. Maybe if it had worked, your countries could have finally had some peace."

"My grandfather's reign was the only true period of peace between us. He fought hard to maintain that peace for our people, giving up a lot in doing so—sometimes conceding to less favorable trade terms. It made my father angry watching us be taken advantage of for that long." His fists clenched in his lap. "Tensions have been rising between us again since I was young."

"And Aswal can't help alleviate some of that tension?"

"No, they're not willing to risk potentially going to war. Besides, their deals with Volgar are more beneficial than ours. Always have been. They're better positioned than us geographically to trade with the southern countries through ships. Because of that, they've always maintained a more neutral stance on any disagreements."

"And you can't use your own ships and do the same thing?"

"We do to a certain extent, but it takes longer and they tend to try and sink our ships during times of unrest. If Echax were willing to trade with us, we'd be in a slightly better position." His thoughts drifted to the large island that sat off the northeastern shore of Vesperis.

"Echax has isolated themselves for thousands of years. There's no reason for them to break that."

"I suppose not," he replied, sighing. "My mother used to tell me bedtime stories about them to scare me into eating my vegetables. Even our libraries only contain rumors about them— nothing more. Any of our ships that sail too close have always been met with hostility, if they return at all. But were Echax ever to get involved, it would open up a whole new world of possibilities."

"If Voglar is such a problem, then I'm surprised the King of Aswal gave you permission to marry at all."

Baxley was saved from responding as the carriage rolled to a stop. "Hood back up." He lifted his own and stepped out into the night.

***

Their carriage exchange was seamless. They walked into a lesser-known tavern, only to exit out the back door straight into another carriage that was waiting for them.

Her words stuck with him all the way to the docks. Maybe he shouldn't have pushed for his own marriage so ardently to begin with. Adelaide's father, Aariz, had dragged his feet for years—not wanting to show more support one way or the other. He had only relented when Baxley had shown up to their court unannounced and begged him for his permission, saying he could never love another for as long as he lived. Maybe they were doomed from the start.

As promised, Baxley withdrew the key to the manacles and unlocked them for Keys when the carriage rolled to a stop at the port.

"Don't try anything," he muttered, unlocking the last one and tossing them on the seat next to him.

She rubbed her wrists where the skin was red and irritated. "Prince, you may find it hard to believe, but you've given me sufficient motivation to see this through. I'm *exactly* where I want to be."

He considered her words for a moment. Maybe getting that crown was enough for her to do all this for them. "Let's go." His hand closed around the handle, pushing the carriage door open.

They trailed through the docks side by side, his hand clasped around her upper arm. He spotted the schooner exactly where he was told it would be, directly off the third gangway. The Ocean Skimmer was on the larger side for a schooner—close to one hundred and fifty feet at least, if he were to guess. Its sails were furled and waiting. A few crew members moved around on deck.

He led Keys over to the plank that spanned from the dock to the deck of the ship. "You're up first." Her balance was impeccable, he noted, as she made her way up the plank. Following behind, he kept his arms outstretched. Taking an unexpected swim wasn't on his agenda for the night.

One of the crew met them, the cloudy night sky not revealing many of his features in the dark. "Name's Sapphiro." The man nodded at them. "The others are below. We set sail in a few." Sapphiro waved them toward an opening, which would take them below deck.

"A man of few words," Baxley muttered, making his way down the tight staircase, Keys ahead of him. The stairway took them to a small landing where there were several benches and a map pinned to the wall. Quartz light from below helped illuminate the space. A second staircase led them into the galley area. Arla, Cain, Felix, and the healer that was selected to join them, Sarja, were waiting at a table off to the other side. He knew Sarja in passing from seeing her in the palace infirmary, but he didn't know her well. She was shorter and slim with golden brown hair.

"No problems getting here?" Baxley addressed the group.

"None, Your Highness," replied Felix. He had been paired with Sarja to make sure she arrived safely. "They cleared out two of the cabins for our use. Three bunks in each. It'll be cramped quarters, but we'll fit."

"Good, and you might as well drop the title now. Better get used to it," Baxley said. "Go get some sleep. I'll wake you if anything arises." He moved to sit at one of the remaining chairs nailed to the floor.

"You're with Sarja and me." Arla stood, motioning Keys to follow.

The group trailed down the hallway towards the fore of the ship. Other bunks lined the one wall—every available space being utilized. There were curtains that could be drawn across the bunks to give the semblance of privacy.

Cain lingered behind, saying, "I can wait up, if you'd like to rest."

"No," he said, waving him off. "I couldn't sleep right now, anyway. I'll settle once we reach open waters and see no one behind us." The anxiety in him had been building all day. It felt like something with claws was trying to climb up and out of his throat. Swallowing had done nothing to help lessen the feeling. Hopefully, he didn't puke.

"We're the first door on the left, after the head. All of your belongings are already there." Cain turned, following after the others.

Baxley moved to sit on the padded bench along the wall side of the table instead of the chair. If he was going to wait, he could at least be a little more comfortable while he did it. He pulled out his watch, spinning it in his hands to help calm himself. Within about ten minutes, the ship began to move. The movement dampened his disquiet. Just a few days and they'd be at Parshindol on a second ship. Parshindol was even closer to Ulgaris than the current stretch of sea they sailed on. Ulgaris was only a stone's throw from Gleyra. They'd be in the city before he knew it. He could practically see it now—see Adelaide. In a little over a week, he could be holding her. Kissing her. Breathing her in again. Her blonde hair would glow in the sunlight, the blue of her eyes pulling him in.

His thoughts took him back to one of their last outings together. Her eyes had been sparkling, then. He'd taken her on a carriage ride to Brimere Park, where he'd had an elaborate luncheon set up at a stone gazebo overlooking the lake.

He had sat across from her on one of the large pillows brought for their comfort. Adelaide gleamed in the sunlight, her head tilting back to bask in its warmth. Her skin almost appeared to be luminescent, like the light emanated from her and not the sun in the sky.

"Do you know how much I love you?" he had blurted out when he couldn't keep his feelings in any longer.

She had turned her head towards him, a lazy smile spreading across her face. "You asked me just this morning."

"And I'll continue asking for the rest of our lives together. I still feel like I wake up in a dream every morning, having you here with me."

"I can hardly believe it myself." She let out a dainty yawn, stretching and repositioning herself on the pillows. "I could stay in this spot forever," she sighed. Her eyes fluttered closed, eyelashes resting on the top of her cheeks.

"Your wish is my command." Baxley beamed down at her as she curled up for a nap. He would be content to study her for the rest of the day.

His memories of them together carried him away along with the rocking of the ship—

A thud jolted him awake. Sapphiro sat in front of him, a wooden mug held in his grip—the cause of the thud that had woken him. The light illuminated Sapphiro's face, weathered from living on the sea. The sun had bleached highlights in his light brown hair that frizzed around his face. A bracelet of minerals was worn around his wrist.

The man started talking as Baxley rubbed sleep from his eyes. "We cleared the harbor about an hour ago. No one follows." Dark eyes pierced into him. "You want to tell me *why* I'm taking the crown prince to Parshindol?"

Baxley shifted in his seat. "You're the captain?" Sapphiro's only response was to raise his eyebrows. "Right—of course." He let out a breath. "It's best if you don't know." Their eyes held; he wouldn't back down on this.

Sapphiro leaned closer towards him. "Are you putting my crew in danger?"

"No harm will come to them. Nor to your ship."

"Then welcome, Prince." Sapphiro drained his mug. "Don't fall overboard." The mug thudded back onto the table.

Chapter 5

SKELETON KEY

THE BREEZE CARESSED HER FACE, SALTY AIR FILLING HER lungs as she took a deep breath. Home. The sea was her home. One she no longer indulged in despite the call she sometimes felt towards it, the yearning to be on the waves. Her face tilted up towards the early morning sun, eyes closed. She'd let herself take in this moment of peace for a few more seconds—

"Keys!" The abruptness of the call made her flinch. The panic that was laced through the voice had her groaning, not prepared to deal with him. Where did he expect her to disappear to on this ship? She was cuffed for fuck's sake.

"I have not run away, dear Prince," she called back. Turning away from the bow, she faced Baxley as his head emerged from the opening located at this end of the ship.

Last night, the three women had crowded into their cramped cabin. It was difficult to turn around and change in the room they had been given, let alone have all of them standing at the same time. Their belongings were stored in little cubbies lining the wall. The bunks were stacked on top of one another. If they weren't careful sitting up in the middle of the night, they would end up cracking their heads.

Arla had assigned Keys the top bunk, probably under the assumption that she would wake the other two women were she to try and leave the room without them. That was wrong, of course. Keys had no problem sneaking out unnoticed this morning, placing her pillow beneath the blankets, so if they didn't look closely, they may believe she was still asleep. One didn't get to her position without knowing how to move around a space without making a sound. It was worth it for this brief, uninterrupted moment. And maybe she enjoyed tormenting the prince—just a little bit.

"You weren't in your room." Baxley's panicked gaze darted over her, as if he were reassuring himself she was, indeed, still here and standing before him.

Her eyes rolled. "I told you this was where I wanted to be." Obviously not going to be permitted to remain there alone, she moved to pass him. "Now, let's go find out what's for breakfast."

His hand clamped around her arm as she drew level with him. "You will inform one of us of your movements."

Keys pivoted fast, her face inches from his. She had to tilt her head to look up at him with the few inches of difference between their heights. Anger had replaced the panic that was in his eyes. "We will not succeed if you cannot trust me."

Baxley still didn't release her. "I mean it," he growled, his hand squeezing her arm tighter.

Oh, he had a temper. She could play with that. "Relax, Prince," she purred. "If you wanted to spend more time with me, you only had to ask." A finger trailed down his chest. He grabbed that arm, too. She laughed in his face before she ripped her arms free and continued on her way.

The built-in ladder he had come up led her back to where the cabins were located on the ship. She felt his stormy presence stalking behind her all the way to the galley. A man, who she hadn't seen yet, was handing a plate of food to Sarja. Arla and Cain rushed down the narrow stairs and into the room, nearly upsetting Sarja, both gasping for breath. Their shoulders dropped in relief at the sight of Keys. Felix burst into the room a second later from a door that led to the aft of the ship.

Baxley had sent them all searching for her. "Really?" she muttered back at the prince.

Ignoring the others, she walked over to the man to retrieve her own food, her stomach rumbling at the smell.

"I'm Dom." The crew member introduced himself to her as he handed her a plate. "Self-appointed cook, because everyone else's cooking tastes like burnt dirt."

"It's much appreciated, then." She smiled at him. "Let me know if you'd like a hand with all the extra mouths you have to feed."

"If it's of no bother, I'd be glad for the help," Dom accepted with a grin.

The prince gaped at her like he couldn't believe she had manners. "You act like I'm uncivilized," she said to him as she passed.

Keys squeezed onto the bench next to Sarja, the healer already halfway through her eggs and oats. Eggs were a treat on the seas—a product of having just left port. They were too fragile when the waters were rough. A talc tattoo in the design of a tree mandala decorated the back of Sarja's right hand. The other minerals were worn in a bracelet, as was common practice. *At least they'd chosen a younger healer to accompany them*, Keys mused. She should have no problem keeping up with them.

The others gathered their own food and joined them around the table. They made small talk, not trying to include her. That suited her just fine; she wasn't here to make friends. It allowed her to focus on the comings and goings of the ship crew. Different members of the crew flitted in and out. Sapphiro came from the fore, grabbed a plate and mug, then headed back the way he'd come. A woman came down from above to retrieve two plates and retreated up the steps again, a bleary-eyed young man squeezing out of her way. Yawning wide, he took his plate from Dom. She reckoned he had been manning the helm overnight while the others slept. He gave them all a quiet "good morning" on his way to the fore, probably going to get some rest after eating.

Dom came to join them at the table with his own plate, indicating no one else was coming.

"You have a small crew for this size ship." Key's eyes flicked up to him.

"Captain picked each of us personally." His chest puffed out with pride. "Each of us is strong in air. We don't need as many crew. Plus, means less to share."

"Not water?"

"Air is more useful," he explained.

"Is it, now?" she replied, thinking of how many times she'd used water to get herself out of a tricky situation on the ocean. Standing, she took her empty wooden plate to the sink and washed it. On her way back, she crouched down by the prince, whispering in his ear, "I'm going to the head if you'd like to come watch me piss."

He stiffened, but remained quiet. She chuckled, continuing on towards the hallway.

"Come back when you're finished. We have things to discuss," Baxley called after her.

A raise of her hand was the only response that she'd heard him.

There were two heads on the ship. One contained only a toilet and sink. The other had a decent size shower along with a toilet and sink. Of course, all of it was salt water, but it was still better than nothing. Indoor plumbing had been around for ages.

All that needed to be done was mounting a piece of fluorite to a pipe. Once the fluorite was activated, the water would flow continuously and could be regulated by faucets. This allowed even non-magical families to still have running water. For hot water, a piece of pyrite was mounted to the pipe as well, heating any water that flowed past.

After grabbing her toothbrush and paste from her room, she entered the smaller head to brush her teeth and take care of her other needs. She decided against giving the prince a second heart attack this morning, returning to the galley once finished. Dom had vacated the space by the time she was back.

She slid into her seat on the bench, waiting to see what Baxley could possibly want to discuss so early into their journey.

Baxley looked her way, saying, "I'd like you to provide a general layout of the palace grounds and as much of the interior as you can. We should go over all possible contingencies so we can—"

"Why?" she asked, internally moaning while her fingers drummed the table top. "No one else will be coming in with me."

He bristled. "Be that as it may, we can still—"

"Worry over what-ifs that we can't even plan for?"

"We have to be ready!" He rose in his seat, his hands bracing on the table in front of him.

There was that quick temper of his. She rose to meet him, unwilling to be cowed by a self-righteous man, leaning across the space that separated them. "*You* need to do what I tell you to. Until we get there, find Edwin's contact, and learn what she knows, this is all pointless." She spoke faster, not giving him a chance to interrupt. "What you *can* do is some sparring up on the deck. I'd like to see how you are with hand-to-hand and close contact fighting. You'll be leaving those swords you brought behind. They'll draw too much attention. Concealed daggers only." If she was forced to drag him along, then she needed to know what she'd be dealing with.

"I told you; you won't need to worry about me." A muscle in his jaw fluttered with how hard he gritted his teeth.

"I'll be the judge of that."

Their eyes bored into each other, neither conceding.

"We're done here," she finally said. "Be on deck in ten; ready to fight." She slid out from behind the table, heading towards the staircase.

"You will sit back down!" Baxley thundered, trying to grab her arm as she passed.

Keys shifted before he could touch her. Her own hand latched onto his, twisting it back and down towards the table. At the same time, her other hand pulled a dagger she had stashed at her waist. Stabbing it through his sleeve, she pinned his arm to the table.

Sarja gasped, eyes wide. Cain, Arla, and Felix were on their feet in a heartbeat, swords drawn. The wrong type of weapons for such a cramped space.

"That's the last time you grab me like that," she hissed at Baxley, ignoring the others. Her own temper rose to make an appearance. It was just a matter of time with the way he was acting. The first time he'd touched her, she let it slide—she wouldn't make that mistake again. "Is that understood?" she asked, teeth bared. Cain tried to pull her away, but she threw off his arm. No one would move her from this spot. Tension permeated the room. Hands readjusted and clenched on swords.

Until—Baxley tipped his head down an inch. She released her grip on the dagger pinning him. Without a word, she turned and tried to leave once more.

"Where'd you get that dagger?" Felix asked, his voice soft and wary.

"Please," she condescended, not even bothering to face them, "I lifted that dagger back at the palace. I'm a criminal, remember?" They couldn't see the smug grin plastered across her face.

***

They arrived on deck in fifteen minutes, not ten. She decided not to comment on it, since they at least decided to show. They even dragged Sarja with them.

"You planning on making her spar as well?" Keys nodded at the healer.

"Thought she could use at least some self-defense practice considering where we're going," Cain said.

"Not a bad idea," she admitted. "Right, Prince. Let's see what you've got." She stepped into the middle of the deck. "No weapons to start. We'll work our way up to daggers. And no magic." She took up a fighting stance, feet spread apart, raising her fists.

"He won't be fighting you." Felix stepped forward, unbuckling the belt that held his sword. He let it fall to the deck.

"By all means." She stepped to the side, gesturing to the space she just occupied. "Although, it seems kind of silly for me to hurt him now when I could have already stabbed him."

"And yet, still not happening." Felix took her place.

Baxley moved to stand across from the soldier.

"Whenever you're ready, then." She waved them on, leaning against the railing.

Keys was loath to admit it, but it turned out the prince was a decent enough fighter. She let Felix put him through his paces for a while before having Arla swap with him. The woman impressed Keys with her fluid style. It kept Baxley on his toes, and he found himself on his back more often than with Felix.

She kept an eye on Cain's progress with Sarja as well. He showed the woman the best places to try and land an easy strike and where people were most vulnerable before moving on to how to make a fist without breaking her fingers. Sarja curled her fingers and punched Cain straight in the face.

Keys doubled over, howling with laughter.

"My sister's a soldier. She showed me how to throw a punch ages ago," Sarja sassed, while Cain clutched his bleeding nose. That's what he got for underestimating the woman.

"You could have just told me that." His voice was muffled and high-pitched.

"You didn't ask." The healer shrugged.

"I think you broke it," he lamented. He leaned his head back as the blood ran from his nose.

"Oh, stop being a baby and let me see." She batted his hands away from his face. Her hands replaced his for a minute before pulling away. "Better?"

"Is it still straight?" He tilted his head side to side.

"No, you're horribly disfigured now," she said in a monotone voice with a straight face.

Keys snorted. Sarja may be small and quiet so far, but at least she had some character. She turned her focus back to Arla and Baxley. Arla had Baxley flat on his back again.

"Enough," she called out to the pair. "Felix, swap back in and use daggers this time."

"We don't have practice blades." Baxley frowned.

"Then I suggest you don't get cut."

The blade Baxley pulled from his belt was the same one she'd used to pin him with earlier. The men paced in a circular pattern, not showing their backs to one another, neither making the first move.

"Any day now," Keys encouraged.

Felix lunged forward, his dagger aiming out wide, giving the prince plenty of time to react. Baxley blocked by grabbing onto Felix's wrist before he made his own swipe towards Felix's stomach with his dagger. Felix swung to the side, out of reach.

The next few attacks were just as half-hearted.

"Stop taking it easy on him," Keys yelled, her foot tapping on the deck.

Their efforts didn't show any improvement.

Annoyed after watching them for several more minutes, Keys prowled forward. "Give me the dagger." She held her palm out to Felix.

"Not happening." He wiped his light brown hair back off his forehead.

She turned her attention towards Baxley instead. "Are you *scared*, Prince?" she taunted. "Scared you can't handle me?" Her lips pulled up at the corners.

Cain and Sarja paused what they were doing to watch them.

Baxley's eyes locked onto hers, anger simmering beneath the surface. She winked at him, hoping it pushed him over the edge.

"Give her the dagger," he whispered.

"No." Felix took a step back.

"I said give her the dagger," he repeated louder.

"The queen commanded us to protect you. That includes keeping you out of…questionable situations if we can help it."

"Fine. I'll do it without one." Keys grinned, her eyes sharpening.

Felix hesitated for a moment, then nodded. He retreated, watching them from a short distance away. He still held his dagger down by his side. Cain abandoned Sarja, coming over to observe from a closer position as well.

Keys circled Baxley, tracking his movements. He rotated with her, his feet crossing over each other. "Does it make you feel strong holding that dagger?" she goaded him, trying to draw him into making a mistake.

His hand tightened on the grip. She took the opportunity to move—

Baxley tried to strike out with the dagger. She grabbed his wrist, ducking beneath his outstretched arm and twisting his arm with her. With her free hand, she jabbed him in the side with her fingers.

"That's one." She released his arm and darted away, resuming her circling.

Not waiting for another opportunity to arise, she feinted in towards the left, pivoting at the last second the opposite way. Baxley wasn't prepared, tripping on his own feet to try and follow her. She jabbed him in the back this time, sending him sprawling forward.

"Two," she stated.

The session continued in the same manner. She'd been too fast thinking he was a decent fighter. Put a dagger in his hand and he was atrocious.

The prince panted in front of her, sweat dripping off his face.

She realized something, remembering the way he pulled her dagger to him in the museum. "You rely on your magic while fighting with blades, don't you?"

"Why shouldn't I use my magic? It gives me an advantage."

"And what if you're too exhausted and have nothing left? What if someone puts a cuff on your arm, cutting you off from it?" She shook her own cuff at him. "What then?"

"Then I'd fight."

"And you'd lose." She moved again. This time, she grabbed his wrist and twisted it backwards. As he tried to move with her to put less pressure on his arm, she swept his feet out from under him. Baxley hit the deck, hard, eyes wide. He didn't react at first as she wrestled the blade from his grip. She straddled him, holding the dagger to his throat, blade scraping against his stubble.

Keys heard, rather than saw, the others lurch forward behind her, their steps heavy upon the deck. "Relax," she laughed, pulling the dagger away from him and holding it up. "Keep practicing." She patted Baxley's chest before pushing up and off him.

"Here." She tossed the dagger to Felix on her way to the opening leading below deck.

"How does a thief know how to fight so well?" Felix sized her up.

"Because I'm prepared."

"I'm better with a sword," Baxley called after her.

She looked back at him over her shoulder. "Prove it."

Chapter 6

BAXLEY

HE WATCHED KEYS FROM A DISTANCE THE REST OF THE day. It unnerved him how seamlessly she fit into the crew of The Ocean Skimmer. When she wasn't helping Dom cook lunch and dinner for everyone—she even gave the man some pointers—she was up on the deck helping them sail. The way she moved and walked, the way she understood what they were asking of her—she was *comfortable* here. She had done this before. Did she sail often? Did she live on a ship when she wasn't thieving?

Cain had asked him if he wanted her searched for other weapons she might have stolen. He didn't see the point if she'd probably steal them right back, anyway.

On the second morning, she was missing from her bed again. He gave up by the third morning when he found it, once more, empty. It was difficult for him to admit that she did make a good point. Where would she run off to? They were surrounded by water with no land in sight.

Baxley also loathed to admit that she was right about his fighting. If he was ever without his magic, he would be fucked. Each day, he spent time on deck having either Arla, Cain, or Felix put him through his paces. He was used to sparring with the palace guards, not these three. Roland had personally been overseeing his training since he was young enough to hold a weapon, and then incorporated his magic once he went through puberty. It took him longer than it should have to learn the three soldiers' fighting style. He'd grown rusty. Became relaxed with his training. Roland would have been disappointed—just like his father.

Most of the time, he would spot Keys spying on him from a distance, though she never came to join them again.

Typically, the crew sailed a little closer to the shore, keeping land in view; however, Baxley had insisted they avoid as many ships as possible, forcing the captain to adjust course to stay clear of the main sailing routes.

On that third day, the wind died on the sea, the water flat and calm. Sapphiro assured him it was nothing to worry about and to *watch*. Ali, one of the two women on the crew, took up position at the stern of the ship, raising her hands. Air filled the sails, propelling them forward across the still surface. The others—Dom, Kadir, and Valna—took turns rotating in until the winds picked up in the evening, and their magic was no longer required.

That night, Baxley woke up from the violent rocking of the ship. The constant motion sent Felix hurtling for the toilet. Baxley and Cain went searching for answers while Felix wretched in the head. None of the crew were in the other cabins or bunks lining the halls. He found Sarja and Arla in the galley area, drinking some ginger tea to try and help with nausea. Leaving Cain—who gratefully accepted his own mug—with the women, Baxley ventured up the stairs. The door leading to the deck was closed. He leaned into it, pushing it open.

All the crew, along with Keys, were on deck. Rain lashed him in the face, the wind whipping it around. Lightning flashed in the distance towards where he thought land might be. The sails had been lowered about halfway. Sapphiro spotted him first.

"Best to stay below, Prince," the captain warned, making his way over to him. "We're sailing into a storm. It's going to get rougher."

"Should we make for shore?" Baxley questioned.

Sapphiro shook his head, saying, "It appears worse that way. Usually, we'd try to dock or at least drop anchor. No—I'm afraid we'll have to ride this one out. Tell the others to prepare. You'd better hope that Death Adder doesn't have our names written down." He strode away without waiting for a reply.

Baxley shook off the common saying about the most well-known assassin on the continent and retreated back down the stairs, securing the door behind him. He was the reason they were out so far. If they didn't make it—guilt rolled his already unsettled stomach. Ginger tea sounded nice right about now.

Felix still hadn't joined the others around the table when Baxley accepted his own mug of tea, settling in to ride out the storm.

***

Sapphiro wasn't lying. It did, indeed, get rougher—much rougher. None of the crew appeared in the next hour.

Now he knew why all the cabinets locked; he could hear things shifting around inside them. This must be why all the plates and cups were wooden. Anything not bolted down or locked up was sent flying. Several times, he almost fell out of his chair. Sarja also retreated to the head. Felix never emerged from the other one.

Another hour passed.

A particularly large swell sent the ship almost sideways. He couldn't take much more of being down here without knowing what was going on topside. The ship rocked the opposite way, tipping almost as far. Water trickled down the stairs. How much more of this could the ship take?

Thunder vibrated the ship, making him flinch even though he was safe inside the hull. The ship pitched again. This time, he did lose his seat. He slid with the motion, skidding towards the galley. Baxley managed to catch himself with his feet braced on the lower cabinets.

That was enough. He was going upstairs to see what was going on up there.

"Baxley, where are you going?" Arla called after him.

Ignoring her, he clawed his way up the stairs, trying to work in tandem with the rocking of the ship. Water puddled on the floor and benches of the upper landing. At the top of the second small staircase, he forced the door open against the wind and found — chaos. This was chaos.

The sea raged around them. Waves broke over the hull, threatening to drag anyone not holding on tight along with them back into the unfathomable depths. The sails were completely lowered. Someone ran close to the railing, heading his way. They skidded to a halt when they saw him bracing in the doorway.

Eyes wide, Keys yelled, "What're you doing up here?" Not waiting for a reply, she started shoving him back down the stairs. "Get below!"

An even larger wave crashed over the deck. A loud crack rent the air, followed by a crash, and then a scream. She released him immediately, whipping towards the sound.

"Man overboard!" The yell tore through him, his face draining of color. Keys took off in the direction of the voice. He attempted to follow, making it to the railing and clinging onto it as he fought the rolling deck.

Dom leaned over the side, peering down into the waves. Baxley watched Keys join him in his search.

"He's gone," Sapphiro called from behind the helm. Dom stopped looking. Keys still searched the endless water.

Baxley's heart sank—this was his fault. "There must be something…" he pleaded.

Keys spun towards him, almost tripping over her feet. She closed the gap between them, fisting his soaked shirt. "I can save him." She shook him when he didn't respond. "Let me save him! Unlock the cuff." She shoved it into his face.

"You're insane!" His eyes bugged.

"I can do this. I've *done* this."

He took in her words. "You've done this." He was right. She had sailed before—and was quite experienced at it.

"Yes."

"Okay." Baxley pulled the chain holding the key over his head. His trembling hands fumbled the key, almost dropping it to the deck. He managed to snag the chain at the last second. As the key slid home, their eyes met. "Go," he whispered, turning the key and letting the cuff drop.

Keys nodded, then ran to where Kadir went over and jumped—

Chapter 7

SKELETON KEY

SHE DOVE. DOWN. AND DOWN. AND DOWN.

The current dragged her away. But she wasn't scared. Her magic flowed beneath her veins. She let the sea call to her—felt the water flow around her body. And then reached outwards, searching for a disturbance in the patterns.

There…

Kadir had drifted farther than she had hoped. Working with the water, she willed it to propel her to him.

Air. She needed air. Her lungs were out of practice but she was almost there—

Her arms wrapped around his lifeless body. Head tilting towards the surface, she rocketed them upward. Her head broke free from the water. She managed to gasp in a breath before a wave broke over them, forcing them back down.

It would be easier to remain under until she reached the ship again. She oriented herself, feeling for where the ship had traveled. Getting back required more effort, more force. Instead of riding with the currents, she willed them to bend and break. Forced them to do her bidding. Her lungs were on fire, but the clock was ticking for Kadir. She was at the stern...the middle...her head broke the surface for another breath by the bow.

"Here," she screamed as loud as she could over the storm. "We're here!" She shot a beam of light straight into the sky to get their attention.

Valna appeared at the railing, then yelled something behind her. Keys fought to hold them steady and in place, Kadir still unconscious in her arms. Ali came into view, holding a rope. Valna lifted her hands as Ali threw it, helping direct it using air. It landed a foot from Keys. She grabbed it, hastily tying it around Kadir's torso and under his arms. Dom joined the pair on deck as they started to pull the sailor up and back onto the ship.

Not feeling like waiting for the rope to return, Keys directed a wave to carry her high enough so she could reach the railing — her body slammed into the side of the ship as she misjudged the distance. Seconds after her hands grabbed ahold, a different set of hands latched onto her forearms, helping to secure her. Surprise flashed through her when her eyes met the prince's. She would have thought he'd have retreated below deck by now. Baxley helped hoist her back over the railing.

"You did it," he murmured. A look of shock stamped on his face.

"It's not over yet." She pushed him out of the way.

Kadir was flat on his back with Ali over him, pumping his chest.

"Move," Keys ordered, shoving her away. Ali fell backwards as Keys took her place kneeling beside the unconscious sailor. Keys held one hand over his mouth and placed another on his chest. Using her hands wasn't a necessity for her like it was for most others; nevertheless, she used them now to help give her more focus and control. She closed her eyes and reached once more — reached and searched for those water particles that were someplace they shouldn't be. And once she had them in her grasp, she pulled. A slow stream of water flowed out of Kadir's mouth. When the last of it escaped, she sent a puff of air straight into his lungs. His chest rose—and then he coughed. Relief flooded through her. Pure relief. That sweet sound of life.

Though Kadir's eyes remained closed, at least he was breathing. "Take him to Sarja," she said to no one in particular.

Standing, she assessed their situation. The ocean still roared. She felt its pulse, ebbing and flowing. And then she took hold. She became the waves and they became her. They rolled and moved together—caressing the ship rather than battering—parting instead of aiming to cleave. For hours, she remained planted in the storm, protecting the ship until it passed.

Afterwards, she barely remembered getting below. Couldn't recall what food someone had set before her, but knew that she ate. There was no way she would have made it climbing up to the top bunk in her room. Instead, she collapsed into the first available one down the hall, boots still on.

She didn't wake until dinner the next day.

Chapter 8

BAXLEY

BAXLEY HAD NEVER SEEN ANYTHING LIKE WHAT KEYS did last night. It was—well, he wasn't even sure what it was. She had maintained that level of power for *hours*. What she did was unheard of, even with the magic from the minerals not draining the wielder in the same manner as using one's gift. He'd never seen someone so strong with water in his life.

After he and Ali had gotten Kadir below deck and settled in a bunk, Baxley had returned to keep watch over Keys. He made sure she didn't also fall overboard—though the rocking of the ship had decreased significantly. Made sure she got below and ate something to replace the energy she had expended. Made sure she got to a bunk before she collapsed from exhaustion. And finally, closed the curtain to give her a little privacy.

She'd smelled like the sea, wild and otherworldly. The scent had stuck with him for hours.

Sapphiro confronted him after breakfast, which was really lunch for everyone. "You kept her powers locked down. I almost lost a man when she could have helped prevent that from the beginning. I want to know *why*." His slate gray eyes were hard as steel.

"I had no idea she could do that," Baxley placated.

"She said nothing to you before this?" There was skepticism in his voice.

"No. She's told me nothing of her magic."

"Then why keep it locked down to begin with?"

"I can't tell you that." Baxley straightened to his full height.

There was a pause on both sides.

Sapphiro lowered his voice, asking, "Who is she?"

Baxley took a moment to consider. "I'm starting to wonder that myself…"

Luckily, Sapphiro didn't press further.

Kadir made an appearance on deck around midday. Ali had gotten Sarja a bucket last night so the healer could leave the head and check on the sailor. Sarja said he should be extremely thankful he wasn't in the water for any longer. She was able to heal the minimal amount of damage to his lungs to ensure there wouldn't be any residual complications from his drowning, the man just needed some rest after that.

The crew had been inspecting the ship and fixing damages from the storm, but abandoned their tasks to gather around Kadir—slapping his back and expressing their joy that he was still with them. Valna joked that if he wanted a bath so bad, they could have filled a barrel for him instead. The first thing Kadir did was ask how he was alive. He remembered going over the side after a rope snapped, which caused a crate to slide and sent him tumbling, but the rest was hazy. He believed himself a dead man. Dom told him the miraculous story.

Kadir's eyes widened as he shook his head, asking, "Where is Keys now?"

Baxley stepped in, having watched the group's reunion. "She's still asleep." Kadir's face fell. "She's fine," he assured. "Simply used a lot of power and needs to rest."

Kadir relaxed. "I'd like to express my gratitude when she wakes."

Baxley nodded, then left the crew to themselves. He went and gathered together his own group, minus Sarja.

They all squeezed into the cabin the men were occupying. He hadn't gotten to know them very well in the short time frame they'd been working together, but he needed their help to navigate this.

"I want your opinions on whether to cuff Keys again or not," Baxley whispered. Keys was still asleep down the hallway from them, and he'd rather not have her know they were discussing her should she awaken. The original cuff she'd worn was lost in the storm, but they traveled with a spare for this exact reason.

Arla chewed on her lip. "She didn't need to save Kadir. It would have been easier to let him die."

"And she had that dagger for a while, but never used it against us." Felix flinched. "Well—didn't until she put you in your place," he corrected. Cain snorted. Felix's gaze flicked over to Cain and then back to Baxley. "Apologies, Your Highness. I meant no disrespect."

Baxley shrugged it off. "So, we leave it off?"

"The kind of power she wields..." Cain paused, scrubbing the back of his neck. "She could kill us all. I think we put it back on. If we hit another storm, we can take it off again."

"She could have let us all die last night, but she didn't. She helped us," Arla argued. "I say we leave it off."

"Felix?" Baxley pressed.

Felix looked around at them before sighing. "I think we trust her—unless she gives us a reason not to. Then we could put it back on."

"Alright." Baxley nodded. "We leave it off for now."

"We might not be able to get it back on her," Cain warned them.

Felix raised his chin. "You've known me for years. You think I can't manage it a second time?"

"I'm not doubting your abilities, but we had the element of surprise the first time," Cain pointed out.

"I can do it." Felix looked to Baxley.

They all paused, waiting for his final say.

"It stays off," Baxley reaffirmed.

***

They were just starting dinner when the curtain across the lowest bunk down the hallway slid back. Keys emerged, stretched, and then headed in the opposite direction, not even looking at them.

"Should we..." Arla trailed off, putting her fork down.

"Give her a minute," Sarja responded.

"I'll fix her a plate." Dom, who had regularly joined them for all their meals since that first day, stood up.

Those around the table went back to eating. Dom returned with a heaping plate of food and placed it at an empty seat.

Baxley's eyes kept flicking down the hallway as he ate, watching for her. His nerves squirmed, wanting to go check on her to see if she was alright. He didn't have to wait long. Keys reappeared within a few minutes, still in the same clothes she had fallen asleep in.

She sat down in front of the overflowing plate, yawning. And then dug straight in without even acknowledging the rest of them. His brows disappeared beneath his hairline. He wasn't even sure if she was breathing in between bites. It was impressive—or maybe he should feel disgusted? Using his powers normally left him tired and hungry, but never to this extent.

Before her plate was clean, Dom brought over a pan and piled on more food for her. He also retrieved a mug of ale and slid that in front of her.

She finally came up for breath. "Thanks." She grabbed the mug and drained it before going back to the food.

"You're going to make yourself sick," Baxley warned. She ignored him and kept eating.

Everyone else had long since finished their own food, yet stayed to watch her eat, transfixed.

"Where's it all going," Felix murmured.

Finally, she scraped the last bit off the plate and popped it in her mouth. She leaned back in her chair; her hands settled on her expanded stomach.

"Are you sure you don't want to lick it clean?" Cain laughed at her.

Her head swiveled towards him, eyes drifting down in the direction of where his crotch would be if the table weren't in the way. "I'm good." A lazy smirk stretched across her face. "Thanks for the offer, though."

"That's not—" he flustered.

Everyone else howled with laughter, Baxley chuckling along with them.

"I don't think I've ever seen a woman leave you this speechless before," Felix laughed.

Cain glared at his friend. "Reminds me of that time with Barion and you—"

Felix slapped his hand over Cain's mouth. "Go back to not talking."

"Oh, come on. Let him tell us." Arla said, her laughter subsiding.

"Don't you dare," Felix hissed. "Or I'll tell them about Eissa."

"You wouldn't," Cain gasped, clutching his chest.

"Try me."

"Fine," Cain whined. "Sorry, Arla. We take our secrets to the grave." He grinned, slinging an arm over Felix's shoulder.

Felix pushed him off, failing to keep his own smile off his face.

"Kadir would like to speak with you when you have a chance." Dom told Keys as they quieted down.

"Where is he?" She moved to stand.

"At the helm," he answered. Keys reached for her plate and mug, but Dom stopped her. "I'll take care of it. It's the least I can do after yesterday."

She thanked him again before heading for the stairs.

Baxley stood as well, trailing behind her. He waited for them to reach the small landing before he spoke. "A moment." Her foot had just hit the bottom step of the second set of stairs.

Keys turned to face him, removing that foot.

He really examined her face, taking in the curious creature before him. There were deep shadows beneath her eyes, suggesting she still needed more sleep. Her braided hair was in need of a wash and brush; salt crusted between the strands. *And yet*—he swallowed, deciding not to finish that thought. "What else are you hiding in there?" His eyes searched her dark brown ones.

"Nothing you need to worry about yet." Her tone wasn't sassy for once, just tired.

"But at some point, I should worry?" His brows furrowed.

"Only if you're not a good person."

"What does that mean?" Baxley took a step forward.

She leaned in close. "Hope you never find out."

A shiver rolled down his spine. He didn't stop her from walking away that time.

***

That night he found himself tossing and turning. Tomorrow would be their last full day on the ship. Sapphiro said the storm hadn't put them too far behind schedule, and they should arrive in Parshindol the following day around noon. He couldn't shake the feeling that he was missing something when it came to Keys, though.

Only if you're not a good person.

Why would a thief care if he was a good person? Most people wouldn't consider her a good person. Who was she to judge others?

He fluffed his pillow and rolled over. Maybe Cain was right and they should put the cuff back on her. But maybe trusting her would prompt her to trust them in return. *This was pointless*, he sighed. There was no way he was falling asleep right now. Maybe a hot shower would help him relax.

He shimmied out from his middle bunk as quietly as possible so as not to wake the others and fished around for a towel amongst his things. Towel secured and slung over his shoulder, he cracked the door, squeezing out and closing it behind him. The hallway was lit by quartz, the dim light allowing him to see while still not blinding him. There was no one else about at this time of night. The head with the shower was a short distance down the hall from his cabin. The door was silent as he opened it —

Baxley stopped dead — the door handle still clutched in his grasp, only opened about a foot. The shower was already occupied. He felt the blood rush to his cheeks from embarrassment.

Kadir and *Keys* were in the shower. Together. Holy fuck. He needed to leave — now. But he was rooted to the spot. The opaque panel of glass wasn't even helping to obscure the view because they weren't beneath the spray of the water. They were at the back, out of the spray and in his direct line of sight.

Kadir had her pressed against the wall, her left leg raised as he pounded into her. His legs were slightly bent so he could hit the right angle. Keys clutched his shoulders, her head thrown back. Baxley watched Kadir's cock take her over and over and over...

He swallowed hard—he needed to leave. *Pick up your foot and walk away*, he pleaded with himself. What was so hard about that—that wasn't the only thing that was hard. Blood was flowing to other places, his own cock growing erect and hard.

Was he imagining it, or could he see her arousal leaking out and spreading on that thick cock as it plunged into her core? His eyes trailed up her body. Water rivulets slowly ran down her skin, dripping off her peaked nipples. Nipples that Kadir took into mouth—first lavishing one breast and then the second. He flicked the tip with his tongue before he sucked it back in again.

Baxley's own cock pulsed with need, begging to be touched. His eyes continued upwards to take in her facial expression. Keys' head rolled to the side, mouth agape. Her eyes cracked open—and locked onto his.

Fuck—

But she didn't scream or cover herself. She smirked—and maintained that eye contact. Kadir released her breast and increased his pace. He pushed that raised leg wider, giving Baxley an even better view of her center. Her right hand trailed down, over her breasts, below her belly button, through that patch of hair and finally...finally to her clit. Not sure where to watch anymore, his gaze flitted between her eyes, still locked on him, and her fingers circling her own clit—seeking her own pleasure. Of course, she wouldn't wait for a man to bring her to completion. His hand clenched the door handle harder.

The pace of her fingers increased—faster and faster they swirled. Her breath hitched, and then she let out the most delicious keening sound. Her eyes finally broke contact with him and closed as if they were too heavy for her to keep open any longer. Kadir crashed his mouth to hers, swallowing the rest of that glorious noise she emitted. Baxley wanted to drown in that sound. Devour it. Bathe in all its glory. And he wasn't even the one to cause her to make it.

Reality crashed back into him. He was perving in the hallway, spying on an intimate moment. Even if it had been an accident at first, he still remained.

Hand finally releasing the handle, he fled down the hall and into the second head. His back pressed against the door, breaths sawing in and out of him. His own cock remained at attention, throbbing with need. He had never ached like this before now. Giving into his body's demands, his hand sank beneath his waistband and released his cock. Fingers wrapped around it; he stroked from base to tip. Over and over. He closed his eyes, picturing the scene he just witnessed. Imagined it was his own cock that disappeared within her soaking center. That he was the reason she made that glorious sound. The orgasm rocked through him, almost taking him to his knees. Baxley caught himself on the edge of the sink.

Glancing down, he took in the mess he'd made. Cum splattered the ground and still dripped from his tip. Guilt hit him faster than the orgasm he just experienced. He was trying to rescue his betrothed—the woman he loved. Yet, here he was, spying on a different woman—the thief who was supposed to help him rescue Adelaide—and taking pleasure in it. He felt dirty.

Baxley cleaned up as quickly as he could, flushing any evidence of his shame down the toilet, and then retreated back to his shared cabin.

He noticed the other head door remained cracked open, sounds still coming from within.

Chapter 9

SKELETON KEY

THE HOURS AFTER DINNER HAD DRIFTED BY AS KEYS chatted with Kadir up on deck while he minded the ship. Having slept all day, she wasn't tired in the slightest, even after the sun set over the water. At first, Kadir profusely expressed his gratitude for having saved his life, promising her anything she wanted to make up for it. After refusing for the sixth time and him still insisting she simply name her price, their conversation turned to flirtation when she asked, "Anything?"—and let her gaze trail down his body. He teased her that she would be in his debt instead, if they were to do that. The tension between them built for the next hour, though he didn't make the offer again. Valna came up to relieve him around midnight.

The pair wandered below, slowly making their way down the hallway before pausing outside her assigned cabin. They spoke of everything and nothing to keep from delaying their parting.

Finally, Kadir said, "I think you could use a shower." He tugged her salt-crusted braid. "Tell you what—I'll give you a few minutes head start. If you leave the door unlocked, I'll come join you and help you," —he leaned in close to her ear— "*wash.*"

Goosebumps pebbled across her skin from his breath. "Don't take too long," she countered, "or all the hot water might be gone." And then disappeared into her shared space to grab a pair of clean clothes. She needn't bother with a towel anymore, since they unlocked her magic. Neither of her roommates woke as she grabbed clothes and exited the cabin.

Leaving the head door unlocked at this time of night didn't concern her. Everyone except Valna should be sleeping. She turned the water on, letting it heat for a minute before stepping into the spray. Keys relished the feel of the water as it cascaded over her. She unwound the strip of leather that bound her braid and began working the twisted strands apart. It felt good to wash the other night from her skin, even if it was with more salt water.

Keys was just adding conditioner to her hair when the head door opened. Kadir closed the door behind him, asking, "Are you sure?"

"Get in here." She grabbed the bar of soap off the ledge, holding it out to him. "I need someone to wash my back."

He did, indeed, help her wash —at first. And then his touches started to linger. Then they stroked and caressed. Until finally — he kissed her. It was a full body kiss. They connected from their toes all the way up to their mouths. She felt his cock grow hard between them.

"Let's see how *grateful*," she grasped his cock, "you really are."

He spun them, pressing her up against the back wall, and hit his knees before her. The first stroke of his tongue was glorious. By the tenth, she knew he had used that wicked tongue of his before this. His hand lifted her leg to give himself better access to her heat. That clever tongue flicked and twisted over her clit. And then it dipped farther back —till he was thrusting into her with it.

She moaned and writhed beneath the torment. Her fingers fisted into his hair until he pulled out, giving her one more broad stroke with that tongue before standing again in front of her with his knees bent. His hand still supported her raised leg, then lifted it even higher, giving him better access to line up his cock with her opening. Their eyes met for a second as his cock pressed against her—and then he sank in. Kadir groaned. He pushed in an inch and then withdrew. Pushed back in a little farther with his cock soaked in her juices. Almost there. One more thrust and he was fully sheathed inside her. Damn—that felt fucking amazing. It had been too long since she had indulged.

They kissed slow and hard. His hips started to work up a rhythm. Head tilting back against the shower wall, her hands landed on his shoulders—holding on as he took her repeatedly. Her eyes drifted closed. Then his mouth was on her breasts, making sure each one got attention. They had become sensitive the more her arousal flared. His thrusts became inconsistent while he was playing with her nipples. Her head slowly rolled to the left, eyes drifting open—

To lock onto the prince. He had the head door cracked, standing just outside.

Holy fuck.

Baxley was watching them—watching *her*.

Her blood heated even further. She had been to plenty of brothels in her time, watched plenty of people be pleasured—but had never been on the other side of it. It was…hot.

She couldn't help the smirk that spread across her face. There was no looking away from the prince's stunned expression.

Kadir's mouth detached from her breast. He increased his thrusting and spread her wider. She needed more. Needed to touch herself. Her hand slowly carved a path down her body to her most sensitive part. When her fingers landed on that spot, she began stroking herself as Kadir continued to take her. The prince's eyes were darting between her fingers and her face. Who knew this feeling of being so exposed—so open—could feel so exquisite?

Her fingers moved faster...She was so extremely close, teetering right on the edge—a sound she had never made before rose from her throat. Then she was crashing—falling—plummeting over the other side. Her eyes closed and lost contact with the prince.

She was distantly aware that Kadir was kissing her again—stealing the rest of that sound that came from her.

When she came back to herself enough to open her eyes, the prince was gone. He had left the door still cracked.

"The prince saw us," she murmured on Kadir's lips, who still thrust into her.

His head whipped to the open door. "Well then," he thrust deep and held there, "let's give him a show in case he comes back."

She laughed, pulling his head back towards her. "Let's."

And put on a show they did. Until Kadir had her tipping over that edge for a second time.

The prince didn't return. Nor did anyone else.

***

The prince avoided her the entire next day. She only saw him at meal times. Every time she handed him a plate, his cheeks held just a hint of pink before he quickly looked away from her.

It was sometime after breakfast the following day that Keys managed to corner him up on deck. He had finally ventured away from the others to try and get a glimpse of Parshindol.

"I need to take Arla to get more supplies before we board the next ship," she said, coming up behind him.

Baxley started, spinning her way. The slight pink in his cheeks was back. "Fine." He nodded, turning back to watch for signs of land.

"Fine? No fighting and asking me why? No complaints that it's not necessary? No insisting you accompany us?" She stepped up to the railing next to him. Was he truly so embarrassed that he would let her do whatever she wanted now?

"I trust Arla to manage you. I'm sure you require whatever items you're acquiring." His eyes stayed locked on the horizon.

She let silence fall between them for a moment to study him. While it would make her job easier without him questioning her at every turn, something bothered her about his lack of response. Sure, it could be like he said and that he simply trusted Arla, but that didn't seem right based on his other reactions so far. Maybe a direct approach would help clear the air.

"You could have joined us, you know." His head snapped to her. He reached up to grab his neck after the rapid movement. "Unless you prefer to watch." A sultry smile stretched across her face. "I know the first time can be quite intimidating."

"I'm not a virgin." His response came out fast as lightning.

"Oh—" She chuckled. "I was referring to a threesome, but glad you felt the need to clarify that." Keys patted him on the chest.

She thought the pink on his cheeks spread farther, if that was even possible. "I'm engaged," he choked.

"And that matters to a prince?"

"It does to me." His shoulders pulled back.

"So, you've slept with the princess, then?" She cocked her head to the side.

"Of course not. I would never dishonor her like that."

"Ah, yes. Her country is more of a stickler with those particular customs." She paused for a breath before saying, "Tell me about her."

"What?"

"How long have you known her? When did you fall in love? When did you know you wanted to marry her?" She rattled off the questions. "What makes her worth it to have done all this to rescue her?"

She wasn't really expecting him to answer her, but he began talking. "I was sixteen when we first met. My father decided to take me along to negotiations that were held in Aswal. Adelaide didn't want to wait until the formal dinner that night to meet us and snuck out of her rooms. I spotted her leaning out from behind a statue while she spied on us. She was the prettiest girl I had ever seen. I think I fell in love right there. We became fast friends on that trip and would correspond on and off regularly over the years to come.

It wasn't until I was twenty-four that she fell for me, too. It was her twenty-first birthday, and I had been invited to the ball being held in her honor. That was the first night I kissed her. I asked for her hand in marriage only a month later. Her father denied my request, of course, afraid of the consequences that our union might bring when it came to Voglar. He finally relented six months ago. Maybe he was right to deny me in the first place..." Baxley trailed off, hands clenched on the railing. The pink had slowly receded from his face while he told their story.

"We'll get her back," she reassured him.

"How do you know?" Their gazes met. She saw the doubt lingering in his eyes.

"I haven't failed a job yet. Even if you don't trust me, trust that."

Keys left him standing at the railing.

The call of land came within the next hour. They would arrive at Parshindol soon.

Chapter 10

BAXLEY

SOMEONE MET THEM WHEN THEY DOCKED AT Parshindol. Daimian managed to secure them a ship that was only slightly smaller than their current one. The Deep Blue was moored within sight from the deck. The farewell with the current crew was short. Baxley's eyes tracked Kadir in particular; the way the man bent down to whisper something in Keys' ear. She murmured something back, grinning, then walked away.

Arla and Keys broke off from the group as soon as they disembarked, disappearing into the crowd, leaving the other four behind. Surprisingly, Baxley didn't find himself anxious in the slightest about Keys being out of his sight. The realization shocked him. She wasn't even wearing a cuff anymore. If she really wanted to, she could disappear and they might never find her again. It was only days ago that she had saved them, but somehow the dynamics within the group were already shifting.

Their remaining members filed onto The Deep Blue. He informed the captain that two of their members were securing more supplies and would be along shortly.

Conditions were a little more cramped on the smaller ship. They'd been given available bunks lining the halls rather than cabins. It seemed that Daimian hadn't informed this crew who they'd be transporting. Baxley wasn't surprised they didn't immediately recognize him—and wasn't about to correct them. Who would expect to find the Crown Prince of Vesperis this far from his own country without a full retinue in tow? This leg of their journey would take only a little more than a day. They'd make do with their accommodations in that short amount of time. Before tomorrow evening, they'd be docked in Ulgaris. His heart skipped a beat at the thought.

They decided to play cards to pass the time waiting for the women to return. Baxley found it hard to concentrate on their game as guilt kept plaguing him over how he'd reacted to watching Keys and Kadir having sex the other night. He'd been ignoring his body's response to the memory as best he could. What would Adelaide think of him if she ever found out about it? She would probably be horrified with how inexperienced she was.

He remembered her on the night of her twenty-first birthday. How shy she seemed as she spent most of the night in his arms, twirling around the dance floor.

During one of the slower songs, she'd looked up at him through her lashes, saying, "Tell me, Prince Baxley, have you ever kissed anyone before?"

He had glanced around at the other couples dancing near them to check if anyone was listening in before replying with, "I have." When she didn't say anything more, he said, "Is there a reason you were asking, Princess Adelaide?"

"Merely curious is all." She smiled up at him.

They made another turn on the dance floor before she posed another question. "What's it like? To kiss someone?"

"It's…hard to describe to someone who's never been kissed before," he replied, a crease forming between his brows as he searched for words. "I suppose it's different depending on who you're kissing as well."

She tucked her chin down. "And how do you think it would be if you were to kiss me?" Her voice was soft and quiet.

His eyes bugged, not sure he heard her right. Baxley's gaze darted to where he'd last seen her father. Not finding him, he turned back to Adelaide to see her staring up at him. He swallowed, licking his lips. "I think I'd quite like it." His heart pounded inside his chest.

Her hand trembled in his. "I think I'd like it as well."

The music came to a close as the current song ended. They stayed locked in place, gazing at one another.

Finally, Adelaide asked, "Would you like to take a stroll through the gardens?"

"If that's what you desire." He nodded.

She kept their hands clasped as she wound them through the other couples beginning to dance again as the musicians transitioned into the next song. A set of double doors stood wide-open, revealing the garden beyond it. Quartz lanterns dotted the pathways, providing dim lighting with which to see.

Adelaide pulled him down the path, picking up speed as they went.

"Slow down," he laughed.

She grinned back at him.

They came to a stop in front of a fountain, which was secluded from the rest of the garden by a row of hedges; no one would be able to see them here. Their breaths came in short pants as they faced each other.

"Adelaide," he murmured, taking a step closer to her.

She started at his movement, taking a half step back.

"Apologies," he said, pausing. "I shouldn't have presumed to be so informal."

"No." She shook her head from side to side. "You just surprised me." Stepping back into him, she tilted her head up towards him. Her tongue swept across her plump bottom lip.

Baxley tracked its movement. He wanted to taste her so badly.

She sucked her bottom lip in, biting down on it.

He reached up, pulling it free with his thumb. "Are you sure?" he whispered.

"Yes." Her eyes shuttered.

It was all the encouragement he needed. Leaning down, he pressed his lips to hers in a gentle kiss. He lingered there for a moment, letting her get used to the sensation, before he started to move them. Their lips melded like they were made for one another. He groaned when she responded.

"Adelaide," he murmured between kisses. His hand found her hair, pulling her —

"You okay over there?" A voice snapped him out of the memory.

"What?" Baxley jerked, dropping a card from his hand.

"You looked like you were miles from here," Felix said.

"Sorry," he said, placing a random card on the pile. "Just thinking."

"Did Edwin give you a location where we could find his contact?" Cain asked as he laid down a card next.

Baxley nodded. "There's an inn we'll head for."

Cain lowered his voice. "And have you considered what we'll do if she still hasn't found evidence of the princess being there?" He took a gulp of his drink.

"I—"

Cain spewed the liquid out his nose before Baxley could finish answering. He roared with laughter, bending over the table.

"What was that for?" Felix cried, attempting to mop up the drink soaking into the cards. Noticing what Cain was still laughing over, he abandoned the drenched cards. Hand over his mouth, Felix attempted to choke back his own laugh, failing miserably.

"What?" Baxley turned to see what had caught their attention. He found Arla and Keys behind him, holding several bags full of items. "I don't see—" He did a double take back towards them, eyes bulging. *Arla* was wearing an Aswalian style dress—her one shoulder and arm completely bare while the other was mostly hidden within the flowing fabric. He'd only ever seen her in pants. Even if all three of the soldiers had donned different clothing from their standard uniform when they set out from Aglar, she had still chosen pants.

"What happened to you?" Cain eventually choked out.

"Laugh all you want." Arla glared at him, throwing a bag at his face. "We bought clothes for you as well."

Cain caught the bag before it made impact. He peeked at the contents. "No," he immediately said, clamping the bag closed tight. "I'm not wearing that."

"Not up for negotiation." Keys handed out the other bags. "You all scream soldiers, even out of uniform. This was the best I could do for now." Baxley took the bag she offered him. "You think that's bad? Just wait till we arrive in Ulgaris and I dress you in their style."

Personally, Baxley didn't think the clothes were that terrible as he opened his own bag and found a pair of loose harem pants that flared and then cinched down at the ankles. There was a standard shirt and decorative vest to go along with it.

"But did they have to be so bright?" Cain grimaced, pulling out the yellow pants they'd chosen for him. "I thought we were supposed to be inconspicuous."

"Oh, we are." Keys patted him on the cheek, right where his mineral tattoo was. "But there's no hiding your tattoos so we'll have to maintain a certain level in society and hide in plain sight."

She turned towards Baxley. "If you could teach them a little swagger and arrogance by tomorrow, that would be helpful."

His eyes narrowed on her, chest puffing.

"Exactly! Just like that."

"I see you've skipped Sarja and yourself." He continued to glare, but deflated a little.

"Sarja will be fine in her current dresses. *I* planned ahead and included some dresses in my list. I guess you were too distracted by my underclothes to remember that, though." She tsked at him.

Baxley stuttered as Cain began howling again.

"And what were you doing with her underclothes?" Cain teased him.

"Nothing." Baxley's face heated.

"He was very interested in the negligees I requested. Even asked me to *model* some for him." Keys' eyes flashed as she smirked at him.

"That's a lie!" he sputtered.

"Would you like to see what we bought this time?" Arla joined in, reaching into her own bag.

"No!" Baxley slapped his hands across his eyes. "I'm quite alright."

"I'd like to see." Cain craned his neck, trying to get a look inside the bag.

"That's because you're a rake," Sarja declared.

"You wound me, madam. Besides, I only do what the ladies ask of me." He shot her a sly grin.

"She may have you there." Arla wagged a finger at him. "Even I've heard of your reputation in my unit."

"And every word is true," Cain said, throwing in a saucy wink.

"Only half," Felix corrected. "We try to keep him hidden away as much as possible. Can be a real embarrassment sometimes."

"Rude! My own best friend, betraying me. How can I ever go on?" He slumped dramatically across the table, scattering the still damp cards.

"I'm sure you'll recover," Felix deadpanned.

"Only for a kiss." Cain popped up, leaning towards Felix, lips puckered.

"No." Felix blocked him with his hand.

"Arla?" He turned to her instead.

"Try it and see what happens," she warned.

Baxley rolled his eyes at them; glad the conversation steered away from himself. Arla fit in with the pair nicely. Hell, he would have guessed they all knew each other before now if he didn't know otherwise. "I'm going to see how long before we depart," he said, pushing up from the table with his bag in hand. No one acknowledged him. They were too engrossed watching Cain try to force himself upon a valiantly struggling Felix.

***

They docked the next evening in Ulgaris without any issue. Keys did, in fact, have a dress similar to Arla's that she had apparently asked for in her long list. She led them to an out-of-the-way inn that she said would suit their needs for the night before she disappeared again. This time with both Arla and Sarja in tow.

True to her word, Keys bought more clothes for them. The men were just finishing dinner in the main room when they returned. He didn't even recognize the women until they slid into the remaining seats at their tables. All of them wore their hair pulled back in a low bun with some headpiece accenting their hair. Heavier embellished cloaks hung from their shoulders to combat the colder nights here.

"I purchased six horses for us. We'll buy another one or two, depending on what we need, once we reach Gleyra. I didn't want to be seen traveling with spares," Keys informed him. She waved at a server and asked for food and drinks for the three of them.

"We made sure to get you your favorite color, Cain," Sarja said, giving him a small smile. He ducked his head under the table, looking for the bags. "They're already upstairs. You'll have to wait to see." She wiggled her fingers at him.

Baxley leaned across the table towards Keys, tuning out Cain's reply. "When are you going to tell me *how* you plan to get her out of the palace?" he murmured to her, keeping his voice low.

"I won't be," she replied, leaning forward as well.

"How do you expect us to help you, then?"

"Bax." He jolted at her using his nickname. Only his sister called him that. Her eyes lit up at his discomfort. "Oh, come now, you said we could drop your title while we're here."

"Baxley will be fine," he corrected her.

"Bax," she ignored him, "while I might be willing to accept your help, since you're here, I don't *need* your help. Honestly, this might have been easier if you listened to me in the first place and stayed behind."

"I was hardly going to trust you to go alone," he hissed, his blood starting to heat.

"Then you should hardly expect me to trust you with all my secrets," she countered. "Listen," she said, when he opened his mouth to argue more, "I'll be giving you a location to wait at when I get her out so we can leave immediately. That's the most I'm willing to tell you." She leaned back as the server brought the food and drinks that she'd ordered.

Baxley stewed while they ate, polishing off two more ales. He might believe she had enough reason not to disappear on them, but not knowing her plans weighed heavily on him.

After downing the rest of her own ale, Keys pushed away from the table. "Let's go up so we can give you your clothes. I want to leave before sunrise." Her cloak fell away, exposing her full outfit underneath it.

His blood heated for an entirely different reason now. He felt it rush to his face. Her entire midriff was bare. She had chosen an embellished cropped top that matched the skirt that sat low on her hips. Sarja and Arla stood as well, revealing their own clothing. Sarja's dress had slits up both legs and both her arms were uncovered. Arla's was the most reserved, with a slit up the front of her dress, but she wore pants beneath it.

Baxley glanced away, not used to seeing so much exposed flesh. His country's nobility tended to favor a more reserved style, though their common citizens were more relaxed. Even Cain ducked his own head.

"Well?" Keys asked at the men's lack of movement.

His eyes slid back to her. "Coming," he choked out. He tried and failed to not let his eyes flick down to her toned stomach. That blood started to rush to a different area. This was stupid. He'd already seen more of her body than this. Why was he having this kind of reaction to seeing her bare midriff? Giving himself a shake, he rose from the table to follow the women upstairs to their rooms for the night. He reached down and adjusted his pants, hoping no one would notice.

Turns out, they did not get Cain yellow this time, of which he was very appreciative. Everyone had several different outfits for their coming stay in Gleyra. Even the men's clothing favored a more revealing style than they were used to. Voglar celebrated the human body, and flaunting it was common practice. Their views on marriage and sex were much more relaxed than either Vesperis or Aswal. Many didn't see the point in the practice and chose to live and make a life with their partner without ever marrying.

Cain traded his current shirt for one of the vests in his pile. "Belt?" he asked, holding it closed. "Or no belt?" He threw the vest open, tossing his head back.

Arla snorted. "Do a few more sit-ups first."

"You're just jealous," he teased, admiring himself in the mirror. "I think I could get used to this." He turned this way and that. "Voglarians might be onto something."

"Something that we can never erase from our minds," Baxley heard Keys mutter.

"What else did you get me?" Cain tossed his clothes all over Sarja's bed.

"Take it to your own room!" Sarja chided him.

"But then you don't get to see me wear it." He wiggled his eyebrows at her. "Ooo! What's this?" Cain pulled out a long strip of fabric.

"It's a sarong," Keys said, rolling her eyes. "And I'm regretting buying it for you now."

"Teach me," he pleaded, holding it out to her.

"No." She plopped down on her own bed.

"Come here," Felix sighed, beckoning him over.

"How do you know how to wrap a sarong?" Baxley asked, puzzled.

"My gram was from Voglar. Her parents moved away when she was young, but she still remembers enough about the culture that she taught us," he answered while he worked on wrapping the sarong and then rolling it tight. "Obviously, you wouldn't normally wear pants underneath, but you get the point."

"I like it," Cain said, moving his hips around. "Probably would feel nice in the summer. I imagine it would be quite *breezy*."

"And on that note…" Felix grabbed Cain's ear, tugging him towards the door.

"Hey! Take your clothes with you!" Sarja called after them.

That night, Baxley tossed and turned on his bed. His dreams were filled with never-ending corridors that twisted and turned. He kept getting a glimpse of skirts or a hand before it would disappear around a corner—only once he turned the corner, no one would be there. He began to run, calling out for Adelaide. Baxley careened around another corner—

There she was, standing halfway down the corridor, facing away from him.

"Adelaide," he whispered, moving towards her. His hand reached out to touch her shoulder—

The woman whirled around to face him, but it wasn't Adelaide standing there. It was Keys.

Baxley gasped awake, panting as if he had, indeed, been running through those halls.

He didn't sleep for the rest of the night.

Chapter 11

BAXLEY

IT WAS ALMOST SUNSET BY THE TIME THEY REACHED Gleyra the next day. The inn that Edwin had told him to find was quite a distance from the palace.

"Go find a table," Keys directed them as they entered the establishment. She returned a short while later with two keys, passing one to Baxley. "They'll move in extra cots for us. I only paid for one night so far."

"Why?" Baxley asked.

"If our contact has been here for too long, someone may notice and wonder why six people suddenly showed up to join her. We'll want to move." He hadn't even thought of that. "She might not even show tonight. We don't know her rotation for watching the palace. Personally, I'd be learning the guards' night schedule."

Her instincts proved correct. Their contact didn't make an appearance by the time they wandered up to their rooms for the night. Baxley's impatience started to show after breakfast when she still hadn't appeared. Keys banished him to their rooms after he kept looking at the door every time it opened.

When she finally allowed him back downstairs for lunch—after threatening to sew his eyes shut if he so much as looked at the door again—all the tables were full.

A woman approached them after their food arrived. "Mind if I join you?" She motioned to the empty chair left at their table. Her medium brown skin tone was a few shades darker than his. She wore the same style clothing as the women in their group, although in a slightly lower quality, and had her black hair slicked back into a low bun. There was a bracelet of minerals around her wrist.

Baxley stiffened in his seat.

Keys' hand landed on his thigh underneath the table, squeezing hard. "Not at all," she replied before anyone else could.

"It's busy in here today," the stranger said, lowering herself into the chair.

He opened his mouth to ask if she was who they'd been waiting for—

Keys' cut in again, her fingers clamping down even harder on his leg. "Come here often?"

"Only the last couple of weeks. My business involves travel. When did you arrive? I haven't seen you around before."

"Last night. It just so happens that our business also brought us here. We trade in unique *artifacts*." She paused for a breath. "Rumor is there's something worthwhile around here."

"I might be able to help you for the right prince...sorry, I mean price." The woman smiled, eyes twinkling.

He jolted at the word prince. His leg might never recover from the way Keys crushed it now.

Keys continued on like nothing was happening beneath the table. "Wonderful. We'd love to discuss it after we've finished eating."

Baxley wouldn't wait any longer. "No, now," he blurted out before Keys could stop him.

"After," she leaned in and hissed in his ear. She released his leg to grab his chin instead and cranked it to face her, their lips an inch apart. "Relax." Her eyes tunneled into him.

He glared back.

"Take a breath." Her own breath whispered across his mouth. His eyes crinkled at the corners further. "Take. A. Breath."

He relented, air rushing into his lungs, expanding his chest.

"One more."

The next one was deeper, more filling, his eyes easing up.

"Good." Her cheek pressed against his, bringing her mouth next to his ear again. From an outside perspective, one would probably think they were sharing an intimate moment. "Remember when I said not to do anything stupid?" She didn't wait for his answer. "We can't charge upstairs after just getting our food. Things will take time. We won't be getting her back tomorrow, maybe not even within the week. So, learn some patience. Fast." Keys pulled away to look back into his eyes. "Now, be a good boy and finish your food," she said, booping him on the nose.

Keys addressed the newcomer again. "Have you eaten yet?"

The woman nodded, saying, "I sat down for the company. There's a vendor up the street. Sells an amazing chicken kabob. You should try it."

"I'll have to swing by it. Any other recommendations for while we're here?" Keys returned to her food, shoveling it into her mouth.

The conversation veered towards sightseeing, Keys dragging the others into it as well. Baxley simmered in his seat while the others chatted, trying to choke down the remainder of his food. After weeks of waiting, he was finally here in Gleyra, and now she was telling him to be patient—when it was possible that Adelaide was across the city at this very moment. He wanted to plan. He wanted to move. He wanted to be doing *something* other than pretending to have a casual lunch and chat with a stranger.

It was irrational, but for some reason he foresaw them getting her back the day after they arrived here. And now Keys was telling him they might be here for a week. His hand clenched his fork, causing it to tremble. They'd get here, he'd have her back the next day, and then they'd leave. Nice and easy. How was he supposed to last a few more days without seeing her, let alone a week?

This was the same feeling he got every time he'd had to leave Adelaide behind in Aswal while he was courting her, never knowing when he'd next be able to make the trip and see her. The time between visits was agonizing for him, and his father was always unsympathetic to his plight.

His last visit before her father finally granted them his blessing was the worst. Adelaide had cried inconsolably in his arms the night before he was set to leave.

"I can't keep doing this," she had sobbed, gasping for breath.

"It's only for a little bit longer," Baxley had said, rubbing her back.

"You don't know that." Her head shook against where it rested on his chest. "What if my father never gives us permission to marry?"

He drew her away from himself, cupping her face. "He *will*." Smiling, he wiped away her tears that continued to flow.

"How can you be so sure? It's been years." She sniffled.

"Because I have faith in our love."

Adelaide's eyes closed. "If you weren't the crown prince, things would be different. He's too scared of Voglar. Too scared our marriage would lead us to war because of the implications."

"I'll convince him otherwise. Hang in there for a little longer. That's all I ask," he pleaded.

"I'll try," she whispered, still not meeting his eyes.

"Believe in this." He leaned down to kiss her. "Believe in us," he murmured against her lips.

She didn't respond, only kissed him harder.

His next trip hadn't been for five months.

Remembering that didn't help his current state. His brain spiraled down further. Maybe they got it completely wrong and Adelaide wouldn't even be here. What would they do, then? Randomly travel to the other palaces of the royal family and infiltrate them all? What if they never found her? What if she wasn't even alive anymore—

His fork crumpled in his hand. Baxley looked down at his fist, not even realizing he had wielded magic. The metal was like putty in his hands.

"For fuck's sake," Keys muttered, noticing what he'd done. "Give me that." She wrestled the fork from his grip, whipping it under the table. It was returned moments later, straightened out.

He folded his hands in his lap instead, giving up on finishing his food. The others' plates were all clean now, anyway.

Keys spoke up when there was a lull in the conversation. "Care to join us upstairs so we can discuss negotiations for your services in private?"

"I'd love to." The woman rose from her seat.

Baxley's feet felt like lead walking up the stairs. Minutes ago, this was what he wanted—to finally hear what the woman had learned. Now, dread bumbled in his throat that it might not be good news. He might no longer want to know it. His pulse thundered in his ears. He staggered to the side and thudded into the wall, leaning there for a second.

Keys glanced back at him, eyes widening. "Are you about to pass out?"

"I'm fine." He tried to brush it off, despite feeling a little lightheaded.

"You're pale as shit." She looked over his shoulder. "*Help him,*" she hissed quietly at the person behind him.

Felix stepped up next to him and put an arm around his waist, allowing Baxley to sling his arm over Felix's shoulder. He would never admit it, but he appreciated the extra stability as they followed Keys the rest of the way to the women's room.

She unlocked the door, muttering to herself. "I'm being punished. I know it. How did I get stuck with you? Fucking going to faint and we're not even doing anything yet."

Felix helped him over to a chair where he slumped. "I said I'm fine."

"Clearly." Her lips pursed together, closing the door after everyone had entered. She leaned against it; her legs crossed at her ankles.

Baxley felt slightly better now that he was sitting. He turned his attention to the woman who had taken up a perch on a chest of drawers in the crowded room. "Edwin didn't tell me your name."

The woman bowed her head to him. "Welcome to Gleyra, Your Highness. I've been going by Peri here."

"What have you found?" His stomach churned, fearing that she might give them bad news. He pulled his watch from his pocket, spinning it around.

"Wait." Keys stood straight. Her eyes trailed up and down the woman, examining her. "Your gift?"

The woman's head tilted.

"Edwin already told us. Now I'd like some confirmation — can't be too careful, after all."

The woman conducted her own examination of Keys. "You're the thief."

Keys remained silent, waiting.

The woman raised her palm. And then the princess was in front of them. She perched exactly where Peri had been, wearing the same clothes. Her eyes were exactly how he remembered them. Any remaining blood in his face drained out. "Proof enough?" The spy lowered her hand, dropping the illusion.

Keys nodded, leaning back against the door. "Proceed."

Peri turned back to him. "I haven't overheard any talk of the princess being here." He spun the watch faster, stomach sinking. His head swam with the weight of her words, but he still tried to listen as she continued. "All the guards I've…questioned have only suspected the countries are arguing over taxes. They think with Voglar trying to strong-arm both Vesperis and Aswal that the royal family simply wanted extra security. With that said…"

Baxley perked up, hanging onto every word.

"I still believe she's here."

"Why?" Cain asked.

"Their security measures are over the top. They have the wall already. A palace that's never fallen. Yet, they've more than doubled the guards. Shifts change every eight hours and they rotate positions on the hour. All supplies going in are being searched. Crates and barrels opened. Wagons looked under and ripped apart."

"Are the vendors themselves being allowed through the gates to make the deliveries?" Keys questioned her.

"No. The palace staff meet them and take over. The wagons are returned once they're offloaded. Everyone's name is checked on a list before they're allowed to enter. I've seen people turned away if their schedule changes haven't been communicated. Sometimes the guards even pull people to question them further."

"What kind of questions?"

"What they do. How long they've worked there. Who they report to." Peri listed off.

"I'll need you to make a list for me."

Peri nodded.

"Do they still have all the deliveries and staff entering through the side gate?"

"Yes. That hasn't changed."

"How about the schedule for the servants? When are they coming and going?"

"Servants mostly arrive in the early morning, but a much smaller shift arrives in the late evening."

Baxley's head was reeling trying to process everything. How could they possibly make this work?

"It's a good start." Keys stood from the door once more. "We need to find different accommodations. Have you stayed at Drunken Pumpkin yet?"

"No," Peri hopped down from the chest of drawers, "I haven't."

"Perfect. We'll head there. It has the right kind of crowd."

The others started to move around him. His head was stuck. What did Keys mean it's a good start? The watch stilled in his hand.

"If you've been there before, won't they recognize you?" He vaguely heard Felix point out.

If Keys heard Felix, she didn't respond. "Everyone, grab your things." She crouched down in front of him and patted his cheek. "You okay in there?"

Baxley's eyes focused a little more. "A good start for what?" He heard the door open and close—not sure who exited the room.

"All in due time, Bax. Now, up you get."

She made to stand, but he reached for her hand. "Please," his vision blurred around the edges, "I just—I just need to know." His head bobbed. He tried to force his eyes to remain open, clenching his hand tighter onto hers. "I can't—" His head dipped again.

For the second time today, he saw her eyes widen. "You're really going to pass out." She untangled their hands and reached for the back of his head. "Head between your legs," she commanded, shoving his head down. "And try to breathe this time." Her hand rubbed along his back.

Baxley finally let his eyes close. His breath came in short pants, never quite getting enough.

"Is he okay?" He could hear Sarja inquire.

"Panic attack." Keys kept up the motion on his back. "He'll be fine."

A minute passed with him still struggling for breath.

"Since you're only working yourself up more," she whispered in his ear, "I'll tell you some of it. I'll spend a few nights confirming her intel. I might approach some guards or servants on my own to see what I can get from them willingly." His chest eased slightly. "Eventually, we'll target one servant and abduct them the day I plan to go inside."

"Why?" He managed to croak out.

"I'm betting that's the only way we'll officially confirm her location. After all, servants hear and see everything, and they aren't trained like the guards. Even if we don't get confirmation, I'll still go in. I'll still do my best to make sure she's not inside."

"Okay." The overwhelming feeling eased a little more.

Neither of them said anything else. She continued rubbing his back until his breathing pattern returned to normal. His thoughts settled. He might not have the full picture, but he had enough now to understand. Keys was surprisingly reassuring — for a thief.

Baxley finally sat up when he no longer felt like he'd fall over. Sarja and Arla had found other things in the small room to occupy themselves with, not glancing his way.

"Thanks," he murmured to Keys, who was still crouched down by him.

"You're a mess, you know." She gave him a very small smile he'd never seen from her before. "Really should have stayed behind like I told you," she sassed.

That's the Keys he knew.

He grunted.

"Now, can you please get your shit so we can go?"

Chapter 12

SKELETON KEY

TWO NIGHTS LATER, KEYS FOUND HERSELF ON A rooftop within view of the side gate. The wall loomed high above her, stretching upward into the night sky. Guards patrolled the top of it. And some, though she couldn't see them, patrolled inside the wall. Arrowslits dotted the upper portion, where archers could shoot out at enemy forces. The prince was a fool for thinking he'd be able to break through the wall unnoticed. Hell, even she would struggle trying to use force to gain access, especially with the mortar being laced with copper to try and prevent such things. There was a reason it had never fallen. The side gate consisted of a large portcullis for carts and wagons and a smaller door for foot traffic. The former remained closed at this time of night.

Keys wore a darker outfit with pants and a stomach-baring top instead of the more favored skirts. The dark cloak she chose was heavier than her one from Vesperis to help keep the chill off. A few knives were stashed in easy to reach locations around her person—two supplied by Cain, and several that they still didn't know she had acquired.

Servants started trickling in around eight, and she marked each one in the light from the quartz hung along the wall. The lights were evenly spaced in a way that left no area in shadow, making it impossible to approach without being seen unless a guard wasn't paying attention. She had tailed a promising woman this morning who had turned out to have a young daughter and husband waiting at home. Ideally, they'd be able to find a woman who was unattached. They didn't need anyone alerting the guards of a missing person while in the middle of her plan. The person she sent Peri after had been a wash as well.

Baxley tried to insist on accompanying them yesterday, but she nixed that idea immediately, reminding him of his near fainting spell.

"You'll be no good to us lying on the roof," she had said to him.

The comment seemed to have gotten under his skin, because he kept quiet after that. His silence caused an uncomfortable twinge in her—that she refused to acknowledge was guilt—for the rest of the evening. It ate at her enough that she instructed them to spend the night drinking below and see if they happened to overhear anything useful—but to not outright question anyone. They didn't need anyone getting suspicious from their lack of tact.

Drunken Pumpkin was in a seedier part of the city; however, she knew the establishment was discreet and the staff would keep their mouths shut about who came and went. The tavern could get rambunctious at night, providing perfect cover so no one would watch her comings and goings. Granted, the rooms above it weren't especially clean, but they were good enough. No one was trying to eat off the floor, anyway. Keys had heard Felix ask about them recognizing her and chose not to answer him—hoping the soldier would forget about it. She didn't have to worry about being recognized due to her gift. A gift she still planned on keeping a secret from everyone.

Tonight, she'd sent Baxley, Cain, Arla, and Sarja out to one of the more popular taverns—still under orders not to question anyone. Felix came along with Peri and herself in order for them to be able to follow a third person. Peri's intel, so far, had proven correct. The guards rotated like clockwork. Every inch of the wall was being monitored. Luckily for her, that wouldn't matter. She clicked her tongue, watching the guards begin their rotation of positions. They could watch the wall all they wanted. What did she care? The plan wasn't for her to go over or through the wall; she'd be walking right through the gate.

"That one." She pointed out a woman to Felix. He nodded.

The woman appeared on the younger side, her blonde hair braided tight against her head. All the women she'd been selecting were blonde. While blonde hair wasn't as common as it was down south in countries like Amarands and Fratrana, it was still found enough around here that she'd seen multiple women who might fit her requirements.

Over the next hour, she selected two more women for Peri and herself, then settled in to wait. Some servants with earlier shifts left to make their journey home. Only a select few had rooms in which to stay at the palace. Most of the living quarters were reserved for those who held higher positions, and whose presence might be required at all hours. The flow of servants ceased after eleven, only for new guards to begin arriving for their shift change. It was relatively silent after midnight.

The moon drifted above their heads to mark the passing hours. Shortly before five in the morning, more servants began arriving. Their numbers greatly exceeded those who arrived the previous evening for the overnight shift.

Felix was the first to leave when his mark appeared, weaving through those still arriving. The next servant she'd selected left a few minutes later, Peri slipping away to follow her.

Twenty minutes later, Keys dropped down from the rooftop, having spotted her own target. She tracked the woman's progress through the flow of people while remaining a fair distance back. The farther from the palace they travelled, the less crowded the roads became. Only a few other people milled about, most of them merchants getting ready to start their day.

The woman led her to a building that had a shop on the first level and living quarters above. Keys selected an adjacent building to climb while the woman walked up a set of stairs at the back of the building. From her vantage point, Keys could see into what looked like a kitchen and small living area. A second woman was there eating breakfast. The two women greeted each other as the woman from the palace sat down at the table. They ate and chatted together. When they finished breakfast, the second woman left the building and made her way into the shop below. The woman from the palace washed the dishes, then disappeared from view. Keys watched for another hour before making her way back to Drunken Pumpkin.

It was a little before eight, the sun lighting up the city, when she walked through the door. Felix was already seated with the others eating breakfast. She flagged down a server on her way to the table, requesting food and tea for herself. Her stomach grumbled in anticipation.

"Well?" she asked, sliding into a seat.

Felix shook his head, mouth full, having just taken a bite.

"Mine's possible, though not the best. I'd like to monitor for another day or two."

Her food and drink arrived. "Thanks," she said to the server. "How about you?" She looked to Baxley and the other three.

"We kept to ourselves like you *suggested*." Baxley drew the word out. She could hear the discontent in his tone. "And learned nothing."

She let out a deep exhale, begging for more patience. "If you want to help more, I'll set you up watching someone during the day."

"I don't know if that's a good idea." Cain wrung his hands. "Him all on his own here..." His eyes darted over to Baxley.

"Fine." Keys poked her fork at Arla. "Arla can go with him."

Peri joined them at that moment, sitting in the last available chair. "Mine should work," she said. "Lives in a building that rents out small apartments from the looks of it. There wasn't anyone up when she returned and no one else appeared in hers by the time I left."

"Perfect," Keys mumbled around a slice of bacon, her stomach purring. "You'll take Cain back after breakfast. Baxley and Arla will watch mine." She turned to Sarja, saying, "I think I can trust you not to get yourself into trouble during the day?"

"I'll hang around the tavern," Sarja replied, nodding.

They all quieted as a server brought over Peri's breakfast.

"Peri and Felix, I want you on watch tonight," Keys instructed after the server walked away. "I'll follow my mark back to the palace, but then I'm going to hit some of the taverns. See if I can *extract* any information that way."

"What does that mean?" Baxley stiffened in his chair.

She tossed him a sly grin. "It means those negligees I requested might come in handy."

He blanched. "You're going to sleep with a guard?"

She shrugged her shoulders. "Wouldn't be the worst thing I've done to get information." Plenty of other things came to mind.

"What about Kadir?"

"What about him?" she asked, laughing.

"I thought..." He trailed off, no longer meeting her gaze.

"What? That we were together after one night of fucking? That I'd go rushing back to him after this because I saved his life?"

The others around the table all found their plates extremely interesting, even though most of them were empty at this point.

"I'm not comfortable with you having to do that," he eventually said, lowering his voice.

"Who knew you would have lines you weren't willing to cross?" She leaned back in her chair, crossing her arms. She wasn't joking. There'd been a lot worse things she'd done on other jobs. Keys wondered what the prince would think of her if he knew every black mark upon her soul. "Fine. I'll agree to not have sex with anyone—unless I want to, that is—if you give me back my tactical belt that I know you brought along."

"You went through my bags?" he whisper-shouted at her.

"Naturally." She waved him off, snatching the last couple slices of bacon off her plate. "Now, if you're both finished eating, I'd like to get at least some sleep today. I can hear my bed calling my name."

"Not sure that's possible over the rumbling of your stomach," Cain laughed. She threw a piece of bacon at him which he caught, stuffing it into his own mouth.

***

She found herself back on a different rooftop later that night with Felix and Peri. Both women they'd been watching were working at the palace again tonight.

"Baxley said the woman's roommate came back around lunch time before heading back down to the shop. The woman left around three for the market and met someone for tea on her way home. After I relieved them, the roommate closed up the shop and the two had dinner together," Keys reported to the pair.

"Looks like mine is a little more promising, then. Cain didn't see anyone else in her rooms. She did stop for dinner on her way here tonight, but wasn't meeting with anyone," Peri said.

"We'll focus on yours. Keep an eye out for mine as a backup, though, just in case." Peri nodded. "I'll be back before they finish their shift."

"See you then."

Keys left Peri and Felix on the roof and headed for Drunken Pumpkin. She hadn't dressed for a night out in case her plans changed. Her walk back was pleasant. The night was warmer than it had been since they arrived. There weren't too many people out and about yet. Plenty of time for her to get ready and make it to a tavern before they became too crowded.

The noise from Drunken Pumpkin flooded out into the road when she pushed open the door. A bard was in one corner, tuning his instrument. Tonight would get rowdy with a bard here. Eyes scanning the room, she spotted her crew seated at the bar. Weird—when did she start thinking of them as her own crew? At the sound of the door closing behind her, Baxley's head swiveled her way. Annoyance flooded her system. Their eyes locked, and she jerked her head towards the stairs.

"What did I say about looking at the door?" She lectured him when he met her there.

"I haven't been," he argued.

"I'm sure." Her lips thinned. She turned away from him and headed up to the bedchambers.

His footsteps sounded behind her. "I thought you were going out tonight?"

"I can hardly go dressed like this. Besides, I needed to get my belt from you. There's something in there I can use."

"What is it?"

She unlocked her door. "So many questions." She tsked. He tried to follow her inside, but she blocked him, putting her hand on his chest. "Belt first."

He grumbled before conceding, heading down to the next door. Keys left the door unlocked for when he returned. She took a seat at the small desk where she had propped up a mirror. The door opened and closed as she was letting her hair out of the low bun she'd been keeping it in.

"You can leave it there," she said, gesturing to the small bed in the corner. Arla had claimed the bed closer to the door. Since adding Peri to their group, the women were no longer sharing one room between them. The sound of the mattress compressing made her look to see the prince sitting upon her bed. "That wasn't an invitation for you to stay."

"What happened after Arla and I left today?" He settled farther onto the bed, making himself comfortable, clearly not intending to leave.

She turned back to the mirror, picking up a brush to comb through her hair. "Nothing exciting. She ate dinner and then headed to the palace."

"What about Peri's?"

She finished brushing out her hair before answering. "Hers seems a little more recluse." Her fingers separated strands of hair, twirling it around while wielding heated air to help create waves. It was a trick most couldn't perform. The corner of her mouth pulled up as she remembered the time she almost set her sister's hair on fire when she had still been learning.

"That's a good thing, right?" His voice pulled her back from the memory.

"Yes." She didn't elaborate further, focusing on her hair. It tumbled down over her shoulders. Satisfied with her work, she picked up a gold powder to dust her eyelids and then added kohl, outlining her eyes.

"What did you want out of here?" The prince rifled through the pouch on her tactical belt, causing the vials to clink together.

"Can you try not to break anything?" she huffed, moving on to rouge for her cheeks.

"That's not an answer."

"Maybe you should stop asking, then." She used a slightly darker shade on her lips, rubbing them together.

"Or, you could finally answer something."

"Where's the fun in that?" She stood and moved to the small chest of drawers. Her cloak hit the ground first, shoes and pants following.

"What're you doing?" Baxley squeaked.

"Changing." She turned to face him. In just a pair of panties and cropped top, she was mostly exposed. There was a dagger holstered to a thin belt around her waist that had been hidden by her pants. Another was strapped to her ankle.

His mouth dropped open, taking her in, before he slapped his hands across his eyes. "But I'm *in* here."

"And? You've already seen me naked. And getting fucked, I might add."

"*And*," he yelled in a higher pitch, "maybe you should wait till I leave!"

"Feel free to leave, then." She returned to the drawers, pulling out a long teal high-waisted skirt that had a slit up the thighs on either side. "I thought you were leaving?" she asked when she still hadn't heard him get off the bed.

"I'll keep my eyes closed."

She snorted, pulling out a matching embellished top. It was a sleeveless shortened-style corset that laced up the front. Removing her current top and bra, she wrapped it around herself and started on the laces. Keeping the front tight enough while tying it proved to be a struggle. Keys walked over to Baxley who was still reclined on the bed, hands clamped over his eyes.

"I need help." She nudged his legs, then turned her back to him.

"With what?"

"Can you hold the sides in while I tie this?"

"Is it safe to look?"

"I'm decent," she chuckled.

His hands wrapped around her rib cage, pressing the top together more in the front. She pulled the laces tight, tying them.

"All done." She spun around to show him.

His hands stayed where they were; she had moved so fast. They settled back on either side of her once she was facing him. His head was almost in line with her breasts with him sitting on the bed. His eyes widened when he saw the front. The laces didn't connect the fabric at the top of her breasts, which had been pushed upwards—leaving a V of exposed flesh.

"You can't wear that," he choked, quickly removing his hands like he'd been burned.

"Why not?"

"Everyone will be staring at you." The hint of pink she sometimes saw on his cheeks was back.

"Everyone including *you*?" She stepped closer to him, standing in between his thighs.

He ignored her question, ducking his head. "I thought we were trying to avoid being noticed."

Keys took pity on him and stepped out from between his legs. "Not tonight. Tonight, I *want* to be noticed." She propped her foot on the bed next to him to unstrap the dagger from her ankle. His eyes flashed to her exposed thigh for a second before he looked away. "You know," she tossed the dagger towards her pillow and lowered her leg, "for a non-virgin, you're pretty awkward around a female body."

"I said I wasn't a virgin. Not that I was a rake," he replied, as she searched for the vial she wanted.

Nothing seemed to be missing. Only the vial she'd used on Felix was gone from the ones she kept lining the belt; all the non-emergency ones were kept in the small pouch. "Surprising for a prince," she mused, finally spotting the two she needed. Clear liquid sloshed around inside of one, while the other had a slight shimmer to it. She tucked the small vials in her top to the side of one breast.

"Are you going to tell me what those do?"

"No, so stop asking." She pulled out a pair of strappy sandals that wove up to her mid-calf. "But I will let you come along if you promise to behave." To finish the look, she grabbed a nearly see-through cloak that would provide almost zero warmth. "Shall we see what I can catch?" she asked, whipping the cloak over her shoulders. Her eyes twinkled.

Chapter 13

BAXLEY

HOW HAD HE EVER THOUGHT HER PLAIN? BAXLEY stalked her movements from the moment they entered the Moonshine Tavern. She had pulled Sarja and Arla onto the dance floor with her as soon as they walked through the door, tossing her cloak back at him. Her body undulated in a hypnotic movement. He was transfixed as she whirled around the other people crowding the floor.

Somehow, Cain had convinced her to let them all come along. There might have been a promise of caramelized nuts that had something to do with it. The men had found a small table to occupy while the women danced. By Baxley's second drink, a man had joined the women—gravitating towards Keys.

Now, Baxley was on his fourth. The whiskey burned a path straight to his stomach. The more he drank, the more he found himself watching her. His eyes lingered on the exposed skin between her skirt and that damned bra she called a corset. The man that danced with her was growing bolder—hands grazing her flesh every so often. Keys didn't seem to mind.

Several other men throughout the tavern watched her, her hips swiveling to the sound of the music. Something twisted inside of him, urging him to do something—but what, he wasn't sure. His fist clenched on his glass.

"You good?" Cain asked.

Baxley shot back the rest of his drink. "Perfect." He motioned to a server for another one.

"You're staring..."

"So are you." He'd noticed how distracted Cain had also become.

"Not at who you think."

That caught Baxley's attention, his eyes finally leaving Keys to swing towards Cain. "Then who?"

"Sarja. I know what *I'm* doing—but what are *you* doing?"

The question hung there between them.

"It's not that—I'm not—" He struggled to find the words to explain. "I don't like the thought of her doing—that—to get information."

"Why?"

"It feels," he paused, "dirty."

The server returned with his drink.

"Even if the end outweighs the means?" Cain asked.

"I don't know." Baxley dragged his hand through his hair, messing it up. "I just don't like it. Anyways, why haven't you made a move on Sarja yet if you're interested? Seems like you wouldn't normally be one to hold back."

Cain's eyes locked onto the woman in question before he answered. "She's different."

"How so?"

"I'm not looking for a quick fuck. I think there might be something more there. Something worth waiting for. She comes off as shy, but really, she's been learning all about us. Our likes. Our dislikes. You know she noticed that Arla sometimes tends to get migraines and has been leaving herbs for her each morning without being asked? And her wit—she's kept even me on my toes when she does actually speak. No, I'm perfectly fine waiting."

"I could request you be stationed at the palace for a while when we return. If you'd like, that is."

"That'd be much appreciated." Cain smiled at him.

They both returned to watching the women dance.

While Baxley nursed his fifth drink, Sarja came and pulled Cain out to dance with her—claiming she needed help keeping away the advances of the men really interested in Keys. Baxley suspected that was just an excuse. Perhaps Cain wouldn't be waiting for as long as he thought. Keys, on the other hand, was on her third partner. He wasn't sure how she was even still standing at this point. They'd been dancing for hours.

By his sixth drink, guards still in their uniforms entered the tavern. The mixed group of men and women joined someone seated at a larger table. Within a minute, they all had drinks in front of them, the server appearing to know them, which meant they came here often.

Keys must have noticed them, too, because she disengaged from her current partner—number seven, if he was counting correctly. She weaved through the other dancers as she spun around, arms lifted overhead, laughing while she twirled. And then she stumbled—he jerked in his seat as if he could catch her from across the room.

She caught herself from falling by planting her hands on the guards' table—her breasts right in the face of one of the men. Baxley settled back in his seat. Undoubtedly, she planned that stumble. He had to admit; she was good.

Keys straightened herself and smiled, saying something to the man. Baxley had no hope of hearing their conversation. The man must have replied because Keys laughed before walking away towards the bar. She leaned over it, waving to get the bartender's attention. The guard's eyes never left her. He rose to follow—caught in that magnetic pull she seemed to exude. Keys jolted when the man cozied up next to her, ducking her head. *Nice touch*, Baxley thought. The guard whispered something in her ear that caused her to smile up through her lashes. The man extended his hand, which Keys took, leading her back to the dance floor, drink forgotten.

He couldn't stand watching much more of this. A pressure was building inside him as he watched the man wrap his arms around her—or maybe that was his bladder from all the alcohol. He didn't want to be here anymore. Getting off his stool, he staggered into the table. His legs wobbled beneath him. Nope— definitely his bladder he realized, making his way towards the bathing rooms.

The men's room wasn't crowded. He walked right into a stall to relieve himself.

"Did you see her?" His ears perked up at the words.

"She's divine." A second man groaned.

"Doesn't matter now that the major spotted her." A third remarked.

Baxley remained in his stall, listening.

"I give it fifteen minutes before he manages to take her home. They all end up leaving with him," the third continued.

"Fifteen? My money's on less than ten," the first responded.

"I'll take those odds." The sinks turned on, then off, followed by the creak of the door closing behind them.

He waited another minute to head out himself. The reflection in the mirror above the sinks showed him bloodshot eyes. Too much whiskey. Grimacing, he washed his own hands. So, she had found a major. Coincidence, or was it planned? He wouldn't put it past her to somehow set this all up without them knowing. And if the men were right, she might be leaving with him. Could he stomach watching her leave?

The full noise of the tavern crashed into him when he exited the bathing room. That many drinks was definitely a bad idea. On legs that threatened to buckle, he made his way back to the table. Water. He could really use some water. And maybe some food to help soak up all the alcohol. Groaning, he slid onto the stool and let his head hit the table top. The regret he expected to feel by the morning was already making an appearance.

"That's what you get for drinking too much," Arla said, sliding onto the stool next to him. Sweat dotted her brow from all the dancing, her black hair frizzing around her temples.

"I'm fine." He attempted to smile at her, only managing a grimace instead. "Actually, I could use some food."

"Come on," she chuckled. "Let's see what street vendors we can find at this time of night."

"What about the others?"

"They can handle themselves."

Baxley looked to the dance floor for them. Cain and Sarja were dancing close to one another, but still kept a respectful distance between themselves. He couldn't spot Keys at first, until the crowd parted and there they were.

The major was wrapped around her from behind, her backside grinding into him. His one hand trailed up the slit in her skirt, disappearing underneath. Keys arched into the man further, her head falling back onto his shoulder. He leaned in and kissed her neck. His other hand curled possessively around her stomach, holding her tighter to him. Keys tilted her head towards him. Their lips locked together, tongues clashing.

Heat roared through Baxley's veins. It was a different feeling than when he'd seen her with Kadir. While that had left him hot and bothered, this made him angry and—he cut the thought off before he could finish it. He knew what the difference was. That had been her choice. This she thought was her job. Her duty to him. He couldn't let her do this. It didn't matter to him that she might have done this before for her own goals. There was no way he could condone it for his own needs, no matter the cost. He needed to stop them—his mind blanked and he moved.

"Where are you going?" Arla called after him.

Pushing through the crowd, he made a beeline straight for the pair like he was being pulled by an invisible thread. Keys broke the kiss and spun to face the major instead, smiling up at him. In seconds he was there, ripping the man away from her. His body was three steps ahead of his brain.

"Get your hands off her," he heard himself say.

The major stumbled back a step, caught off guard. "Who the hell—"

And then Keys was between them, shoving Baxley back. Wait. Why was she shoving him away? He was just helping. She said something to him, but he couldn't make out what it was—the fog in his head growing worse. Her hand struck him across the face. It helped a little. Different hands wrapped around his upper arms.

"Get him—" The rest was lost to him.

Those hands pulled him away from Keys, who was still with the major, her palms pressing into the man's chest.

That was the last he saw of her as he was shoved towards the back exit. He tumbled out the door, catching himself on the building across the alleyway. The cool air of the spring night cleared his head further, his forehead resting on the building.

"I thought you said you were good." Cain. Those hands had belonged to Cain.

"Give him a minute." Arla was there, too.

Baxley breathed deep.

"Go back and make sure his tab is paid. Stay and watch Keys in case she can't smooth it over. Sarja and I will get him back."

The back door opened once more, the noise and music spilling out before the door closed. No one spoke.

What felt like hours later, but was probably only minutes, a hand touched Baxley's back.

"Are you okay?" Sarja asked.

He nodded, which was a mistake. It caused his head to swim, nausea rising. "Fine, but a little nauseous," he admitted.

"We'll try to find you some food on the way if you can walk."

"Okay."

She took his arm, allowing him to lean into her for support.

They passed one vendor who was selling food to all the people milling about outside of the taverns. Baxley turned his nose up at the smell. It only made his nausea worse. When they got him to his room, he sprawled out on his bed, but it didn't help. His head spun. He jolted up, lurching for the bathing room. The rest of the night he spent spewing his guts up into the toilet.

Chapter 14

SKELETON KEY

"WHO THE HELL—"

Keys was there before the major could finish. She shoved Baxley away, trying to get space between them.

"Are you insane?" she hissed. "What're you doing?" Her eyes searched his own. They were red-rimmed and glossed over. The smell of alcohol was heavy on his breath. Drunk. The prince went and got himself drunk and then did something stupid. Why was she not surprised? Her palm struck out, slapping him across the face.

Cain mercifully appeared behind Baxley, taking a hold of his upper arms.

"Get him out of here," she commanded. She didn't wait to see if he complied, turning back to the major.

Her hands splayed across the major's chest, slipping beneath the slit of his uniform. She had to hand it to the Volgarians, their style of clothing was by far her favorite. Everything was easier to access. Hell, even the prince looked more roguish in their open belted vests. She could finally see what all the women of his court raved about—though only a little.

"Apologies," she said, gazing up at the major.

"Who was that?" He craned his neck, trying to see as people filled back into the path Cain created in their rushed exit. Everyone around them stared.

"He's just a friend—a friend who wishes he was more."

"How could he not?" The major leaned away to ogle her, taking in her body.

She ducked her head, pretending to be shy. "Can we take a break for a second?" she asked, glancing around at the people who hadn't resumed dancing yet. "It's feeling a little crowded."

"Of course." He took her by the hand, leading her towards the bar. "You never got that drink." He waved a bartender over.

"How could I, with someone distracting me?"

The major smiled down at her. "Guilty." He ordered himself an ale when the bartender came over. "And for the lady?"

"I'll take wine. Anything sweet."

Their drinks were placed before them.

"So, are you going to tell me your name?" He looked at her over the rim of his glass.

"Elora." She held out her hand for him.

"Duka." He took the offered hand, kissing the back of it. "A bit formal, don't you think, after where your breasts have been?"

"I seem to recall you not minding that one bit." Their earlier exchange flashed back to her.

"*I apologize. I usually try to get to know a man better before shoving my breasts in his face.*"

"*Not a problem. I enjoyed the view.*"

"I wouldn't mind it happening again." Duka winked, tucking a strand of hair behind her ear.

"Be careful what you wish for." She took a step closer.

"Or what?" He placed his drink down.

"Or you might end up with more than you can handle."

"I think I can *handle*," his arms slid around her, "you just fine." And then he was kissing her again. She let him lead — let him devour her, his tongue swiping along her bottom lip. She opened completely for him. His tongue swept in, caressing hers. Fuck. She could kiss him all night.

When he eventually pulled away, she took a drink.

"I haven't seen you here before," he said, picking up his own drink.

"Are you so sure?" Her eyes flicked to his, her smile teasing.

"I'd remember seeing you."

"We're just passing through."

"When do you leave?"

"Potentially tomorrow. Unless my friend is too hungover after his…" She didn't finish the sentence. "What about you? Are you usually stationed here?"

"No, my unit was called in for extra support."

"So, you're a soldier. But the guard uniform looks delicious on you." She took another sip, licking a drop that ran down the side.

His eyes followed her tongue. "I'm more than happy to put my other one on for you to compare."

"Tempting. Do you have your own place or…" Her fingers trailed over the four gold bars on his shoulder which denoted his rank.

"I'm renting a townhome."

"By all means, then." She left the rest of her drink on the counter.

Duka clasped her hand, pulling her back towards his original table. After collecting his cloak and saying farewell to his group, they made their way towards the door. Keys spotted Arla at the small table Baxley had occupied most of the night. She gave the woman a tiny nod to let her know everything was still alright. Baxley's stunt hadn't screwed up the rest of her night, after all.

***

They toppled through his door, laughing and tripping over one another.

"Not bad for a major." She disentangled herself from Duka to look around the first floor.

The door opened into the living area, which was moderately furnished. A staircase led up to the second floor, and she could spot the kitchen through an opening towards the back of the room. Her attention caught on the drink cart to the left of that opening.

"Make yourself at home," Duka said as she made her way towards the cart.

"Oh, I plan to." She simpered back at him. He placed his cloak on the back of a chair. "What would you like to drink?"

"Surprise me."

She started pulling the tops off of the many decanters he had, smelling each. Whiskey. Brandy. Vodka. Gin. "A man of many tastes," she commented. The couch made a sound as he sat down upon it. Keys bent to pull two glasses from the lower shelves. She quickly slid the clear liquid vial from her top while doing so.

"I think you'll find I enjoy quite a range of flavors," he chuckled.

The glasses clicked as she set them down. "Lucky me." She poured a small amount of the liquid into one glass and tucked the vial away. Settling on one of the brandies, she added that to both.

Keys walked to Duka with both glasses in hand. His arms were draped over the back of the couch. Instead of sitting next to him, she straddled his lap. "Cheers," she said, raising his glass to his lips.

He grinned at her before taking a sip. "Good choice." His tongue swept out along his bottom lip.

"Hmm, I'll be the judge of that." She moved the glass out of the way, leaning down to kiss him. Her tongue delved inside his mouth, hunting down the brandy. His one hand came around to cradle her head, but she pulled away, tutting.

"I don't know. I think I need to try again." She raised his glass back to his lips.

Duka took it from her this time, downing it in one go. Their mouths met for a second time in a mix of tongues and teeth. She allowed him to thread his fingers through her hair now. He tilted her head just right, their tongues swirling together. Her teeth tugged on his lower lip as she pulled away.

"You're right." She leaned to the side, setting her untouched glass on the end table. "That is a good choice."

He let his empty glass fall to the couch. Their eyes burned into each other—and then they collided, detonated together. He kissed her with a punishing force. Her hands landed on the back of his neck, clinging to him. She gasped when he drove her down onto his hips harder, pushing his erection right where she needed it. Taking full advantage, Duka plundered her mouth. Keys chased his tongue when it retreated, returning the favor.

"That tongue," she groaned, grinding down even harder.

"Let's see what else it can do," he chuckled, the vibration rumbling through her with their chests pressed so close. He abandoned her lips and moved down her neck, sucking and licking as he went.

Her head fell back, giving him better access, fingers threading through his dark brown hair. Duka shifted her farther away, moving down her chest now.

"Right back to where we started." His hands cupped her breasts through her corset.

"Take it off," she encouraged. The fingers of her right hand slipped underneath the bottom of her top, clamping the vials in place.

Duka's fingers made quick work of the laces holding the corset together. She pulled it away, exposing herself. She kept it and the vials clasped in that one hand.

It was Duka's turn to groan. "I've been imagining these all night." His fingers circled her nipples, causing them to harden. He pinched one between his fingers harder than she liked.

She hissed. "Not nice." Her free hand pulled on his hair, so she could glare down at him.

"Apologies." His fingers went back to circling. "Let me make it up to you." She allowed him to dip his head back down. And then he feasted —

Forgiven. He was already forgiven. Her eyes closed as she arched into him more. She almost forgot about the vials and corset she was still holding. Right — because she was supposed to be questioning him, not just fucking him. Forcing her eyes open, she checked to make sure he was fully distracted before shoving the top and vials down in between the cushions. The potion should be taking effect any minute now, lowering his inhibitions even more than alcohol would. She could enjoy herself for a little longer...

He swapped to her other breast. His tongue circled the hardened peak before he sucked it into his mouth. She clung to him, grinding against his thigh for some sort of friction. Maybe she wouldn't question him at all. There were plenty of days left. She could always find someone else...Someone who wasn't as attractive...Someone who's mouth didn't make her feel like she was being worshipped.

Baxley would be disappointed, but he would survive. Although, maybe that would lead to another one of his panic attacks. She could just say she didn't learn anything new. It wouldn't be lying per se. And, what was up with him tonight, anyway? Why was a hoity-toity prince so concerned with what she did? Her nose crinkled. Why were her thoughts stuck on Baxley when a perfect specimen of a man was between her legs?

She squeezed her eyes shut tight, trying to focus on the feel of his mouth.

One...

Two...

Three...

Seriously, what was Baxley's problem? How dare he make her feel bad about doing this? It's not like she was whoring herself out to every man and woman that glanced her way. And even if she was, that still wouldn't be any of his damn business.

Keys sighed internally, her lust officially drying up. She pulled Duka's head away, staring into his eyes.

"How're you feeling?" she asked, studying him.

He gave her a lazy smile. "Like I'm," he paused, searching for the word, "free."

"Good." Her hands caressed down his chest, moving to the belt of the vest. "Why don't you just relax a bit and let me take care of you? Hmm," she hummed. With the belt untied, the vest fell open, revealing his toned chest and stomach.

Keys groaned.

So. Not. Fair.

Her mind cursed Baxley and his stupid face for popping into her head at the worst possible time.

She eased farther off Duka, her hands kneading his shoulders. "Have you noticed anything interesting while guarding the palace?"

"Like what?" His head fell back against the cushion, face tilting towards the ceiling.

"Seen anyone well known coming and going?"

His head rolled side to side.

"How about the dungeons? What're those like?"

"I don't guard the dungeons. Only the wall."

"So, they haven't posted extra guards there?" Keys pressed.

"No." His brows furrowed. "Why would they?"

She moved in and kissed down his neck to help distract him more. "No reason." Her hands trailed to his biceps. "You must train every day." She squeezed them.

"I could show you some of my *training*." His hips thrust upward.

"Down boy," she laughed. "What about the rumors?"

"What rumors?"

She moved her lips down his chest, sliding her knees onto the floor. "About the woman."

"There's no woman." Her hands played with his waistband. "Except for you." His eyes stayed glued to what she was doing.

She smirked, hands moving to his thighs. "How about a hostage?" Her fingers drifted dangerously close to the bulge in his pants.

"A hostage?"

She stroked even closer. "Yes. Do you know of one?"

"No...maybe I shouldn't be telling you these—" She took a hold of him through his pants. He groaned, closing his eyes. "That's what I want."

Keys felt him pulse in her fist. It was almost enough to revive her heat from a few minutes ago. Almost—until Baxley popped into her head again. She cringed.

"Why don't you go upstairs and I'll come join you after I freshen up?" She released him and stood to move away.

He followed after her, claiming her lips once more. "Hurry," he whispered against her mouth.

Life was so cruel.

She watched him walk up the stairs, then turned to retrieve her corset and vials. Taking the second vial with the shimmer to it, she added some to her untouched drink. This one was a simple sleeping potion. Unlike the vial she used on Felix, it didn't turn into a gas and had to be ingested.

Keys made her way up the stairs. One of the three doors off the hallway were open. Duka was waiting for her, sprawled across the large bed. His erection jutted proudly into the air, his discarded pants on the floor. Fuck, he was gorgeous. She cursed Baxley over and over in her head, promising to make him pay for this tomorrow.

"I brought you a drink." She smiled, walking alongside the bed.

Duka took it without question, gulping it down before placing it on the nightstand. "Come here."

She moved her skirt between her legs, so she could kneel on the bed next to him. "I've enjoyed our time together immensely." She pushed him till he was laying down flat. "This mouth has been amazing," she said, tracing a finger along his lips. Lips that pulled apart in a yawn.

"Sorry," he slurred a little.

"It's okay," she soothed, rubbing his chest. "You must be so tired after that performance."

He yawned again, eyes fluttering. "But we haven't—"

"Of course we did," she cut him off, putting a finger over his lips. "You were amazing. Made me finish twice and everything."

His eyes struggled to stay open. "I don't remember—"

"Well, you did have a lot to drink."

His eyes lost the battle, closing. "Right."

"Just take a nap and then we can go for another round."

Duka didn't respond, his breaths quickly evening out.

She sighed. "I really did enjoy this." She kissed his mouth one last time before starting to stage the room.

Keys tossed a blanket onto the floor and rumpled the sheet before haphazardly throwing it over him. She pulled her panties off and dropped them by his pants. In the bathing room attached to the bedchamber, she found a washcloth that she wet and laid next to Duka, so he'd think he'd cleaned himself up after they were together.

Satisfied with her work, she headed back downstairs. Her corset and vials were on the couch where she left them. It was difficult to retie the laces without Baxley's assistance, but she managed. She tucked the vials back into her top, snagged Duka's cloak off the back of the chair, and headed out into the night.

Chapter 15

SKELETON KEY

SHE POUNDED ON THE MEN'S DOOR, ANNOYED.

Last night, Keys had returned to Drunken Pumpkin for a second time to change before returning to Peri and Felix. She informed them of how her night had gone so far while they waited for five o'clock to roll around. Once they spotted the woman they were targeting exit, Peri led the way towards the woman's apartment building. Keys stayed behind to monitor things herself, while the two others returned to the tavern. They were to send Cain to replace her.

From what she could see, Peri had been right and the woman didn't seem to interact with anyone when she first returned home, nor did she have a roommate. Cain showed up about an hour later.

When Keys made it back to Drunken Pumpkin, she found Arla, Sarja, Peri, and Felix finishing up breakfast. Baxley was nowhere in sight. She'd sent Felix to retrieve him while she dug into her own food.

That had been twenty minutes ago, which is why she was now at their door, hammering on it.

The door cracked open, Felix appearing in the gap.

"Where is he?" The words came out clipped, revealing her exasperation.

"In the bathing room..." He grimaced, opening the door wider for her to enter.

The door to their small bathing room was wide open. Keys walked over, cringing at what she found. Baxley was curled up on the floor, still sleeping next to the toilet. She kicked his shoe. And then kicked it again when he didn't stir the first time. A groan came out of him, or at least that's what she thought the strangled sound was.

Turning on the faucet, Keys directed the water to form a sphere floating in front of her, shutting the faucet off once she was satisfied with the size. The ball of water floated over Baxley's head—and then she released it, letting it crash over him.

Baxley gasped awake, bolting upright. "What's going on?" he moaned, wiping the water from his eyes.

"You should shower. Who knows what you caught lying on that floor all night." Keys scrunched her nose, looking around at the grimy bathing room floor. She closed the door behind her and sprawled out on one of the beds. "If I don't hear water running in a minute, I'm coming back in," she called out in warning.

The shower kicked on.

"I'll go get him some food," Felix said.

"Bring the others up when you come back."

Felix left the room, leaving her alone with Baxley. She pulled out a dagger, flipping it into the air and catching it to pass the time.

A few minutes later, she heard the shower turn off. Keys sheathed the dagger as Baxley shuffled out of the bathing room with a towel slung around his hips. His gaze hadn't moved her way, but she noted the dark circles beneath his eyes. He stopped in front of the small dresser, letting his towel drop as he ruffled through a drawer.

She whistled at the unobstructed view of his ass. "And you complained about me undressing in front of you."

He spun around to face her, lurching a little to the side. "What're you doing here?" he yelped, regaining his balance, while also now giving her a full-frontal view.

Keys raised her eyebrows at him. "Did you already forget that I'm the one who woke you up a few minutes ago?"

"I thought you left..."

"Clearly still here. And while I don't mind the view," her eyes trailed down his body, taking it all in, "I feel like you'll mind in a few seconds when your brain catches up."

He glanced down at himself and then slapped his hands over his penis. "Close your eyes."

"A little late for modesty, though I suppose it's only fair since you have seen me naked, after all," she chuckled.

"Please," he whined.

"Fine." She closed her eyes.

Seeing a prince naked hadn't been in her cards for the day. She had to admit he did have an appealing physique, but not enough to tempt her—he was still a prince. An *engaged* prince. His body wasn't quite as built as Duka had been; however, with a bit more training, he could probably get there. His ass was firm and toned. She could see the hint of abs on his stomach. His cock—

"Tell me, Bax. Are you a grower or a shower?" Based on what she saw, she guessed the former. Although, she'd been with a man who was more skilled with his smaller cock than some of the larger ones she'd encountered. She chuckled when she heard Baxley choke.

"That's hardly—I'm not—you—" he floundered.

"Relax. I won't tell anyone. But I should after the stunt you pulled last night."

There was a pause.

"Did you learn anything?" he finally asked.

"Are you dressed yet? I'm not having this conversation with my eyes closed. Besides, the others should be here any minute now."

"Did you sleep with him?"

"Does it matter?"

"It does to me."

She sat up, opening her eyes. He was finally wearing pants, but still held his shirt in his hand as he stared at her with his green eyes—eyes that were another reminder of who he was.

"Why does the Prince of Vesperis care who I fuck?"

He twisted the shirt. "Because it doesn't feel right."

"Oh, trust me, when I fuck, it feels very *right*."

"That's not what I meant and you know it."

They continued to stare at each other, neither speaking. She couldn't figure him out.

The door opened just then. Felix, Arla, Peri, and Sarja walked through it as Baxley pulled his shirt over his head.

"Breakfast." Felix passed Baxley a plate piled high with eggs, bacon, and chopped potatoes.

"And something for your head." Sarja handed him a small glass that he shot back with a grimace.

Baxley thanked them both and then moved to sit next to her. "You're on my bed," he groused.

She stole a slice of bacon instead of responding. The scent of his soap wafted over her; at least he no longer smelled like something that died in a gutter last night. When the others found places to settle around the room, she said, "According to the guard, they haven't stationed extra security around the dungeons. He hasn't heard any word of a hostage or a woman. Nor has he seen anyone of importance entering or leaving."

"How'd you ask all that without him becoming suspicious?" Arla asked.

"I have my ways..." She left it at that.

"It's those potions you have, right?" Peri guessed. "Arla showed them to me this morning. I recognized a few, but...not all of them are the normal ones our healers can make, are they?"

Keys' eyes snapped to Arla, who glanced away as their eyes met. Guilt plastered all over the soldier's face, clear for everyone to see. She shouldn't be surprised that Arla would look through her things. She just didn't know the woman had the balls to do it. Turning back to Peri, her eyes narrowed. Peri was astute, Keys would give her that. Maybe *too* astute. Indeed, Peri was correct. Some of those vials contained things that weren't known on this continent. "Wouldn't you like to know?"

"We're still proceeding with the plan, though, right? Even with the information not being promising?" Baxley questioned, his fork hovering over his food.

"Yes." She swiped another piece of bacon.

"How long do you think before..."

"It depends. I want to confirm the woman's days off before we move." She chewed her pilfered bacon.

"Why?"

"Because I need her to work the next night after I take her."

"Won't the servant's absence be noted?" His brows scrunched.

"That's for me to worry about."

"She's going to disguise the princess as the servant," Peri stated.

Keys pressed her lips together. Yes, Peri might very well become a problem. Everyone looked between her and the spy, their eyes wide.

"The blonde hair gave it away," Peri explained. Her gaze swung to Felix. "You really didn't figure that out?"

"I—" he began.

"Enough," Keys snapped, snatching another slice of bacon and chomping into it. "No more questions or guess work." Peri crossed her arms, but remained silent. "I'm going to get some sleep." She rose, walking to the door without looking back.

The rest of the bacon was in her mouth before she was at her own door. The men's door opened again as she fit the key into the lock. Keys tensed at the sound, already anticipating it being Baxley that followed her.

Her hunch was confirmed as Baxley's voice rang down the hallway. "She's right, isn't she?" He jogged to catch up with her. "That's part of how you're going to get her out."

"Just shout it for everyone to hear, why don't you?" She glanced up and down the hall, making sure they were alone. Thankfully, no one else was in sight. Grabbing a hold of him, she shoved him through the door she swung open.

Keys side-eyed him as she shut the door behind her. "It might be a small part of it. I'm not relying on it, though."

"What else?" he pressed.

"You ask an annoying amount of questions for someone who's been told they won't get any more answers."

"I just need—"

"Control." She took a step towards him. "You're used to control. And you can't accept not having it."

"That's not true." He squared up against her.

"No? So, your little panic attack over being kept in the dark was what?"

He just stared at her.

"That's never happened before," Baxley finally murmured.

"Because you've never been told no." She jabbed her finger into his chest.

"I—" he started to argue.

"Your own mother convinced your father to give me a thousand-year-old crown for you." She raised her brows in challenge.

"Why's me knowing the plan such a problem?"

"Because if you learn much more about me, your father may not let me go. *You* may not let me go. And if that happens, it will not end well. For you." Her eyes seared into his.

"I don't understand." His forehead wrinkled.

"You're not meant to," she hissed at him, pressing her fingertips into her temples.

"This has to do with what else you're hiding. What you warned me about."

"Stop pushing," she snarled in his face, their noses inches from each other.

"Why?" His eyes flicked back and forth between her own.

"You will not like what you find. I am *not* your friend. I am *not* your soldier. I am a *criminal*. You'd do well to remember that." Her heartbeat pulsed in her ears.

Baxley remained silent.

"Get out." She pushed past him, bumping into his shoulder. "Unless you want to join me for a second shower and help me *take care of things*, since I didn't even have sex last night because of you," she grumbled.

His shoulders stiffened as he still faced the door. "I'm going to ignore the first part of that, but thank you."

"For what?"

"For not sleeping with him."

"I didn't do it for you." she snipped, ready for this conversation to be over.

"Still."

The word hung between them in the air.

"I'm about to take my clothes off," Keys warned when Baxley still hadn't moved or said anything else.

He jumped. "Right, I'll see you later." When he closed the door behind himself, she returned to lock it.

Her clothes hit the floor on her way to the bathing room, leaving a trail behind her. The water quickly heated after she turned it to an almost scalding temperature. Once she deemed it warm enough, she stepped into the spray, letting it drench her hair. As she scrubbed herself down, her mind wandered.

The prince was proving to be more of a hassle than she had anticipated. His constant pestering grated on her nerves. Teasing him only helped calm her so much. Hopefully he'd relax once they had the princess. Unless he hovered over her and fussed—she groaned internally. She bet he was a fusser. Maybe she could knock him out for their return journey. After all, the king said nothing about how his son was returned to him, only that once the princess was returned would she be given the crown and freed.

She rinsed her hair. A few more days. Only a few more days in Gleyra and then she'd deal with anything else that followed. One step at a time. The tightness eased from her shoulders.

Thoroughly washed, she turned the water off, using her magic to dry herself. Sans towel, she walked out into the room and grabbed a comfy set of sleep clothes. Her worries drifted away once her head hit the pillow.

Chapter 16

BAXLEY

KEYS WAS ALOOF WHEN SHE REAPPEARED LATER THAT day, and her distant mood continued into the next one.

She asked Arla to join them that first night and then only allowed Peri to accompany her for the overnight watch after that. She also forbade the entire party from going out to any of the other taverns around the city anymore. Apparently, his actions from the other night proved he couldn't be trusted, and he was deemed a threat to the mission. He had scoffed at that. Sure, he might not have made the best decision, but he would never intentionally do anything to sabotage them.

In the evening of the second night, Keys returned early to Drunken Pumpkin without Peri, which was strange as it was only around eight o'clock.

Arla spotted her first from their corner table, pointing her out to the others.

Baxley's head whipped in her direction. He started to rise from his seat, until Felix's hand clasped his arm.

"Sit down," Felix cautioned. "She'll be over."

"Yeah," Cain chimed in. "She'd probably yell at you again. Who knew a thief could be such a hard-ass." The last sentence was muttered.

They watched her retrieve a drink from the bar, chatting with the bartender, before heading their way.

Keys sat down in between Sarja and Arla. "She's off tonight," she informed them, taking a sip of her drink.

"So, we take her tomorrow?" Baxley leaned forward, eager.

"No. She seems to be more of a loner, but she could have made plans on her days off. *I'll* take her after her first shift back. *You* will be far away from it, so you don't ruin anything."

"I didn't ruin anything," he grouched, crossing his arms.

"Not from your lack of trying."

"Mommy and daddy are fighting again," Cain moaned to the others.

Both Keys and Baxley glared at him.

"Never say that again," Keys threatened in a low voice. Baxley saw a shiver work its way through her body.

Felix smacked the back of Cain's head.

"Ouch." Cain rubbed where he'd been hit.

"And on that note, I'll be turning in early." Keys took a large gulp of drink. "Felix, if you don't mind taking over for Peri around four, and then I'll come relieve you around breakfast. I'll be following her during the day."

"Can I—" Baxley started.

"Alone," Keys declared, pushing back from the table. She walked off before he could protest further, her drink left behind.

Felix rose next. "I'm going to turn in as well, since I need to get up that early." He waved goodnight to everyone.

Three more days. Baxley would get to see Adelaide in just three more days. It seemed like a lifetime away. His hands shook on the table in front of him. He tucked them into his lap. The waiting around was the worst. Even if they hadn't learned anything from it, going out to the taverns at night at least had given him a sense of purpose. Now, Keys wasn't even letting him do that. She was treating him like a child.

His hands clenched, frustration quickly replacing his anxiety. He was a prince. He didn't need to answer to a thief. Who did she even think she was to treat him this way?

Alone.

The word taunted him. He wasn't going to stand for this any longer. Damn her and her thoughts on him needing to be the one that was in control. Maybe she should look in the mirror. She was the one who needed to be in control. And he was done with it.

Baxley's hands landed on the table as he made to rise for the second time in a few minutes—

Sarja slid into the seat next to him, halting his movements.

"I hope you don't think I'm overstepping by asking this," her eyes full of concern when she looked at him, "but—are you okay?"

He deflated instantly, his breath whooshing out of him. Tears welled in his eyes. Tilting his head up, he fought to not let them fall. His emotions were all over the place. What was wrong with him? It felt like he was going through puberty all over again, minus the uncontrollable magic.

"No," he choked out, clearing his throat. "I'm not."

She took his hand. "It's okay to not be okay." She gave it a squeeze. "I know you brought me along to be there for her should she need it, but that doesn't mean I can't be here for you as well along the way. Healing isn't just for the body."

He just breathed for a moment.

"I feel like I'm crawling out of my skin. She's right there," he gestured with his other hand, "and I can't get to her. I don't even know if she's hurt. If she's in pain. My own home wasn't safe. I couldn't protect her." That fist slammed down onto the table. "And now I'm useless. I've done *nothing*, except be here. And what good has that been?" Baxley swiped at a tear that managed to escape.

"You found the one person who has any hope of getting her back. *You're* the reason we're all here and ready to support in any way we need to. Perhaps you haven't played a huge role yet, but that doesn't mean you won't end up being needed."

He finally looked over at her. "And if it turns out I wasn't needed at all?"

"I'm sure the prin—Adelaide won't see it that way." She gave him a small smile.

They hadn't known each other long on this journey, and yet he found her presence soothing and was grateful for her words. He was starting to understand what Cain meant about her. She truly cared about people and wanted to help them.

"Thank you." He squeezed her hand back.

"I can give you some herbs to help you relax and sleep at night if you'd like."

"I'd appreciate that."

She withdrew her hand, rising. "I'll go get them." He watched her retreat up the stairs.

"We can sneak out tonight," Cain leaned in, whispering to him. Evidently, he had been eavesdropping on their conversation. "Go to some more taverns," he suggested. "It might make you feel better."

"And if Keys catches us then he'll be in even worse shit," Arla pointed out.

"Please," he shrugged it off, "how would she ever know?"

"Really?"

"She's already gone to bed. Nobody is going to know."

She stared at him, lips pursed.

"How would she know?" Cain threw his hands into the air.

"She knew it was you when you slipped that fish into her pillow on the ship."

"You did what?" Baxley gasped.

They both didn't respond to him.

"I still think you sold me out on that one." Cain wagged his finger at her.

"She knew you added syrup to her fancy soap."

"That could have been any of us."

"And," she drew out the word, "she thinks you stole the last of her caramelized nuts."

"I didn't touch those! I gave them to her!" he exclaimed.

"But she thinks you did," Arla taunted. "She's just biding her time to get revenge."

His eyes narrowed on her. "You set me up, didn't you?"

"Maybe." She made a popping sound with her mouth.

"You guys are pranking her? Are you insane?" Baxley's eyes flicked between them.

They spoke at the same time.

"Only a little."

"He started it!"

Baxley hung his head. Is this how Keys felt when dealing with him? If so, maybe he should pity her.

"How else were we supposed to pass the time?" Cain entreated.

"Not piss off a thief who's likely to stab you if you make her mad enough," he hissed.

"Well then, I feel pretty safe, because you've pissed her off plenty for the rest of us, and she hasn't stabbed *you* yet."

"He does have a point there," Arla agreed, nodding.

"I should give your parents a reward for putting up with you both through childhood. If this is the kind of trouble you start now, it's a wonder what you did back then." Baxley glared at them.

"I was a perfect child." Cain stuck his nose in the air. "My parents adored me."

"Maybe that was the problem," Baxley muttered under his breath.

"My father wasn't around much," Arla shrugged, "what with being a soldier and all. My mother spent most of the time chasing me around with a broom trying to keep me away from the children who played at sword fighting." She scratched the back of her neck. "I think it had the opposite effect of what she was going for, though. Made me faster and better at dodging."

Baxley let out a deep sigh.

"So...not sneaking out tonight I take it?"

"No." He forced the word through his lips, hoping Sarja would return soon. "And for fuck's sake, stop pranking her!"

"No promises," Baxley heard Cain mutter. He chose not to reply.

***

Sleep found him quickly that night with the help of Sarja's herbs. He didn't even stir when Felix rose early to leave. It was late morning by the time he finally got out of bed. Keys was long gone. He felt more settled than he had yesterday, though the whole situation still irked him.

Peri joined them downstairs in time to have lunch, making Keys the only member of their party not present. It occurred to him how lax he'd become since arriving in Gleyra when it came to her. How many times had she been out in the city alone doing who knows what? That wasn't what he originally planned. He wanted Arla watching her at all times. Hopefully he wasn't making a mistake in not sticking to that.

His spoon paused halfway to his mouth, another thought suddenly striking him. "Peri," he looked her way, "Edwin told us you wouldn't be able to retrieve Adelaide yourself, but from what you displayed when we first met..."

Peri lowered her own spoon back into her bowl of stew. "I could potentially get through the gate as long as nothing touches me. Touch disrupts the image," she explained. "I could even illusion her as well if I managed to find her in time before I became too exhausted. But if I ran out of time, I might not only get myself caught, I could make her situation worse."

"What if you work in tandem with Arla?" He was shooting arrows in the dark.

Arla shook her head. "I can only make myself invisible, remember?"

He hadn't. He was hopeless at this. His education was based on politics and battle strategies, not spy work.

"Why are you asking about all this now?" Peri shifted forward. "We're days away from making a move."

"I—" How could he explain to her his unease? "You truly believe Keys will be able to do it?"

"I believe she wouldn't put herself in this situation if she couldn't. I believe her gift is what sets her apart. The reason why she's never been caught...until now."

"What do you think it is?"

The spy shook her head. "No idea, but I wish I knew. I'm not surprised she's keeping it a secret."

"I feel like I'm going mad with all the things she's hiding." He dropped his spoon back into the bowl.

"I suggest you exercise some patience," she chuckled.

"What are your plans for after we have her?" Felix asked Peri. "Your gift could come in handy if we need to disguise her."

"Keys and I already discussed it. I'll be heading towards the border and letting certain people see me illusioned as Adelaide to help lay a false trail. The hope is that it distracts them enough that they won't be looking the way you actually travel."

While it was a sound idea, Baxley would have felt more comfortable if Peri traveled with them—not only to help out with her gift, but to also monitor Keys.

"So that's it, then; we just trust her completely," he said, defeated.

"I never said to trust her. She could still have her own second agenda in all this."

"You think that it's wise to leave us alone with her, then?"

"I think it gives you the best chance to make it out of the country. Just watch her as close as you can. Not much else you can do in this situation." She shrugged. "I could be wrong, anyway."

"But you're normally not, are you?" Arla asked.

"No," her mouth thinned, "I'm usually not. And it's very strange how you even managed to catch her in the first place."

"Why?" Felix asked.

"The trap was solid," Cain added.

"You've seen her work. You truly believe you were able to capture her against her will?"

"We had her outnumbered. Used all our gifts against her to subdue her," Cain tried to explain.

"It's not just that." She waved his words away. "She's meticulous. The way she watches her surroundings—" Peri paused for a second. "I think she went into that museum knowing it was a trap."

"Why would she ever allow herself to be captured?" Baxley frowned, thinking back on all his interactions with her, trying to pinpoint a moment that would suggest she let them take her on purpose.

"Why indeed?"

They all stayed silent, thinking. Baxley returned to eating his soup. If Peri was right and Keys let them capture her, what the hell did that mean for them? He almost wished she'd kept her suspicions to herself as his imagination tumbled down into a dark abyss.

Chapter 17

SKELETON KEY

NIGHT HAD SETTLED BY THE TIME KEYS RETURNED TO the tavern. She found Peri upstairs in her and Sarja's room, and asked her to go watch Laria—the woman they'd been targeting—for the night. The night Keys asked Arla to join them, they'd learned the woman's name. Arla tailed invisibly behind the servant as she neared the gate. When the guard had asked for the woman's name to check it was on his list, she had answered with Laria Bellon.

Laria went to the market after lunch time today. Keys picked up a few items she might be needing in the coming days, while she shadowed along at a distance. A group of children almost bumped into her at one stall. They ran among the crowds, playing a game of guards and criminals.

"I want to be Night Phantom!" a young girl with long, dark hair yelled.

"Fine. Then I'm Death Adder," a taller boy replied.

"Ghost Reaper," another boy claimed.

"I call Rogue Menace!" a boy, who had light brown hair and freckles dotted across his nose, piped up.

A younger girl, who Keys guessed was the boy's sister based on the similar smattering of freckles across her face, stomped her foot. "I wanted to be Rogue Menace," she whined, crossing her arms with her bottom lip jutting out.

"You can be Skeleton Key!" her brother called back to her as he raced after the others, heading towards the group of children who were the guards.

The girl dug the toe of her shoe into the dirt street. "Skeleton Key is boring," she pouted.

A soft smile pulled at Keys' lips. "Skeleton Key isn't boring." She squatted down to the girl's height. "They're the sneakiest of the lot. You get to steal anything you want from the others."

The girl didn't look up at Keys. "Anything?" she whispered, still kicking at the dirt.

"*Anything.*"

"Okay." The girl finally looked at Keys before tearing off after her friends. "I'm going to steal all your things!"

Keys' eyes sparkled as she watched them play for a moment.

After the woman finished shopping, she returned to her apartment, dropping off all her purchases, before departing again. This time, she led Keys to a park where she sat on a bench for hours reading. No one came to meet her. It wasn't until the sun was sinking in the sky that the woman rose to make her way home, stopping at a street vendor along the way for a bite to eat. Based on her previous movements, Keys was sure the woman would be staying in for the rest of the night.

After leaving Peri, Keys made a stop in her own room to drop her small purchases off and change. She traded out her current casual day ensemble for a tight fitted top that landed just above her belly button and a pair of dark leather pants. Her leather harness went over top and she filled all the empty sheaths with daggers. None of the others knew how many she'd been collecting over time. Why pay for a weapon when she can steal it? Her tactical belt fit snug around her hips. The boots she chose laced all the way up her calves, stopping before they reached her knees. To round off her outfit, she put on a long-sleeved cloak and grabbed a strip of fabric that could be tied across her face later. For the final touch, she let her hair out of the tight, low bun, letting it flow around her face.

Arla emerged from the bathing room, almost ready for bed, right when Keys was heading back out the door. She gave her a nod before closing the door behind herself and walking towards the men's room. Hopefully this interaction would go quickly, and she could be on her way sooner rather than later. The less time she spent around the prince the better at this point.

Her knuckles rapped on the door. It swung open, revealing Baxley. She cursed her misfortune.

"Why are you dressed like that?"

"Starting off with a question, great," she muttered as she shoved past him, annoyance immediately spiking. "Felix," her eyes tracked to where he was sitting on the extra cot set up in their room, "will you take the early morning shift again?"

"Sure." He gave her a thumbs-up.

"Nice outfit," Cain called from his own bed. "Looks like you're going to *stab* someone." She noticed how his eyes went to Baxley, his lips quirking up at the corners.

Her brows scrunched, wondering what was up with that. "Right, well, good night." She pivoted —

"I want to help." Baxley blocked her path.

Her right eye twitched. If she punched him once, it wouldn't hurt anything. "With?" she responsibly asked instead.

"Something — anything."

She could give him *something*. "We need two more horses. You can buy them tomorrow before we move locations."

"Fine," he agreed.

She was shocked he didn't argue about the menial task.

"Where are we going?" Her head turned back to Felix.

"I'll find another tavern tonight."

"You're not dressed like that just to find a tavern." Cain observed.

"I need to make other arrangements as well."

Felix shifted on the cot. "For where you'll be taking the woman?"

She chewed on her tongue before deciding to answer. "Perhaps."

"You're not going to hurt her, are you?" Concern flitted across Baxley's face.

"It's a little late for you to be asking that kind of question, isn't it?" She hoped he wasn't about to make this a problem, too. Since his stunt at the tavern, she hadn't gone back out trying to get information that way. It wasn't that she was avoiding it—no—she just didn't believe most of the guards knew anything after talking with Duka. And servants were harder to locate at taverns. They, unlike guards and soldiers, usually changed out their uniforms before frequenting those types of establishments. Or, at least that's what she'd been telling herself. No, it didn't have anything to do with the prince at all.

"I—I'd rather she not be harmed if she doesn't have to be." He shifted under her gaze, pulling his watch out to play with it.

"That'll be up to her."

"I want to be there." He stood tall, his spine straightening.

Here we go again.

"Absolutely not."

"Then take Felix or Cain." It was the second time his response stunned her. She was expecting him to push back more on it.

"I'll," she paused, looking them over, "consider it." It was the most she was willing to give at present. "Now, if you'll excuse me." Keys darted around him before he could stop her for a second time.

***

A rightness settled in her as she stalked through the city. She moved through the shadows like a wraith come to claim the lives of those who had wronged them. Other than the sea, this was where she felt at home. Where she felt free.

The place she was heading—a branch of The Underground—was hidden in the middle of the city. The entrance was in a tavern about twenty minutes away from where the servant lived, which was unfortunate but unavoidable. It was why bringing Cain or Felix along might actually be useful. She didn't want Peri for this, because the woman was already perceiving more than Keys would like. It wouldn't help giving the spy information about the secret criminal organization that had locations spaced all throughout the northern part of the continent and was slowly spreading south.

Most of the upper class looked down upon those beneath them. They underestimated them. And people like her were more than happy to continue to let them do so. They didn't need to know how organized they actually were. How they were building their own communities amongst them, and even *below* them.

Keys entered Dancing Prawns and wove through the crowd, heading for the hallway in the back of the tavern. She bypassed the bathing rooms, turning a corner, and went straight towards the storage cellar door. A set of stairs took her down into the dank space. All the shelves and boxes closest to the door were dust free, regularly used in the above establishment. Dust and spiderwebs collected on everything towards the back of the room, where she found the door that blended into the wall. There was a small scorpion painted at the top of it, marking its location. Pushing on a wooden panel, it popped out, allowing her to pull the door open.

Another staircase led deeper into the earth. The space was illuminated by the soft glow of quartz hanging on the wall. Keys took out the strip of fabric she'd brought along, carefully tying it to cover the bottom half of her face. Once it was secured, she proceeded down the stairs, making sure the door closed fully behind her. Another door with a peephole slot waited at the bottom.

She tapped her knuckles on the door. The little piece of wood covering the peephole slid back, revealing dark eyes that peered out at her. Raising her one hand, she held up her rings for the person to see. One of them had a scorpion stamped into it. Just like the scorpion that marked the upper door.

Satisfied, the wood slammed back into place. Multiple locks clicked and the door swung open. She nodded at the large man who guarded the door. He didn't react as she walked past him and down the hallway. It turned to the right and then continued on for several more paces to yet another door. Almost at the door, she walked through two walls of air that created a vacuum in between them. Zinc lined the walls to create it. Sound hit her on the other side, still slightly muffled from the door. She pushed it open, revealing the large cavern The Underground had created here to house all their illegal activities.

The cavern was full to bursting at this time of night. A band played off in one corner, drowning out any sound—pleasure or pain—coming from the tunnels leading off the main room. Half-naked women and men danced on platforms throughout the area. Sometimes a patron pulled them off, leading them down one of those tunnels. Other people were content to dance with each other on the floor. On the opposite side of the room, vendors were selling all manner of illegal items—potions, weapons, and stolen historical artifacts, among other things—they wouldn't dare sell at the regular market. If they didn't have it, someone would surely be able to acquire it for the right price. In another corner were the gaming tables. If a fight broke out, it would come from over there. It wasn't possible to have a group of criminals together without someone trying to cheat. The circular bar in the center was her destination. Tables and chairs were spaced around it where people drank, ate, and relaxed. Some chose to mill around the bar. Half the people here wore some kind of face covering just like her. Others weren't as concerned about their identities, smiling and chatting with those around them.

Keys breathed in the atmosphere. It had been a while since she'd frequented this particular location. There hadn't been a reason for her to visit Gleyra in quite a few years.

She cut a path through the throng of people straight to the bar, letting her cloak fall open to show off the weapons beneath. They moved out of her way, some even stopping and staring. She didn't give them a second glance.

A smirk pulled at her lips under the mask when she noticed who was behind the bar—Harben, the owner of this branch of The Underground. He just so happened to despise her. It couldn't have anything to do with all the times her sister and her had broken into his office to steal back everything he tried to cheat them out of. Or how they try to terrorize him in general whenever they see him. Or that time she held him suspended in a bubble of water because he had made her particularly angry that day…No, it couldn't have been those things. Her smirk widened.

"Harben," she called out, reaching the bar. Her voice, even muffled, still pulled his focus. To most people here, he went by Under Taker—a stupid nickname if anyone asked her. That's why she learned his real name within the first week of meeting him and refused to call him anything else. Add another notch in his list of reasons to hate her.

Harben set down the bottle he was holding and walked her way, a crease between his brows. "Do I know you?" His eyes scanned over as much of her exposed face as they could with her hood and mask.

"I'm hurt, Harben." She clutched her chest. "It's been a few years, but how could you forget after the way we parted?" She reached out with her senses, pulling the water particles in the air together to form a sphere floating next to her head. "I can always give you a repeat performance...if we need to jog your memory."

His eyes bulged out of his head. "It's you," he rasped, lips quivering. "You're not welcome here." He pointed a finger towards the door. "Leave." That finger started to shake.

He knew better than to try and throw her out based on her status alone within the organization—there would be ramifications that he wouldn't enjoy. "Now, now. Is that anyway to treat a paying customer?" She made the sphere grow larger until it broke into strands, weaving around his body. The man trembled. "You don't even know what I want yet."

"W—what?" He barely got the word out.

"One room, starting tomorrow at midnight. I'll just need it for twenty-four hours and then I promise to be out of your hair." She let some of the water hit him in the face.

"Just one day?" he squeaked, holding his breath when the water swept close by again.

"Just one."

"And that's all?"

"And then I'm gone."

He bit his lip, eyes darting around, watching her water swirl. "Alright," he finally gasped. "But I want triple."

"Harben," she warned. The water spiraled faster.

"Fine—fine," he relented, sweat dripping down his forehead.

"Excellent." She withdrew a pouch of coins from inside her cloak, tossing it to him. "Make sure it's my usual room." She winked at him, sauntering away. The water shot straight towards his crotch, making it look like he peed his pants.

***

Keys stood on the rooftop with Felix, waiting to spot Laria in the flow of people leaving the palace. Her fingers drummed against her tactical belt.

After breakfast this morning, she'd asked Arla to go replace Felix. Cain would swap out partway through the day, and she'd take over with Felix in the evening. She'd decided he would be less likely to cause a scene in The Underground than Cain—and more likely to keep his mouth shut about it. Peri was still sleeping, but she had all the others come upstairs to go over the plan.

The tavern she'd chosen to move them to was on the east side of the city, closer to the direction they'd be heading. They'd be taking the servant when she was on her way back to her apartment the next morning. Once the sun began its descent, she'd help Felix get the woman back out of The Underground—not that she told them that's where they'd be—where Peri would be waiting to meet Felix and illusion them on their journey back to the apartment. They would tie her hands together—to help ensure she didn't get accused of helping them, per the prince—and give her a second dose of sleeping potion. Peri would stay until after midnight to make sure no one happened to come by and ruin everything. After leaving the apartment, Felix would go to meet the others at the tavern, and from there head to a designated spot outside the city to wait for her and the princess to meet them.

Meanwhile, Keys would be entering the palace. Waiting to leave The Underground at sunset should give her enough time to make it there for the woman's shift. What Keys left out was that she'd be breaking into the woman's apartment during the day to steal two sets of uniforms—one for herself and one for the princess.

Leaving Baxley behind to wait until Peri woke up and for Felix to arrive back at Drunken Pumpkin, she had taken Cain and Sarja to show them the meeting location. It was a short ten-minute horse ride outside the city in a wooded area nearby the bank of a large river.

They had arrived at the tavern she'd selected before the others, which wasn't a surprise—Baxley also still needed to buy the two horses. After securing rooms, she had napped as much as she could to prepare for the long hours to come.

Now she patiently waited, examining everyone exiting the palace gates. There—she spotted Laria, nodding to Felix. The pair made their way down from the roof, weaving into the crowd as if they belonged. The people thinned out as they walked, some breaking off in other directions, until the woman and them were the only ones on the road. The streets grew narrower.

Having learned the woman's route, Keys split off from Felix, motioning for him to continue on without her. She cut down an alleyway, increasing her speed so she could overtake the woman. As she hurried, she pulled a new vial from a slot on her belt, dumping part of the contents onto a cloth. It was something she picked up from the vendors in The Underground. The vial slid back into place when she rounded a corner into another alley. Dashing to the end, she glanced around the corner of the building. The woman was almost there, Felix some distance behind her. No one else was in sight.

Only a few more steps…

Keys moved—

The woman didn't have time to scream as she clamped the cloth across her face. Keys wrapped her other arm around her chest, starting to drag her towards the alley while the woman fought. Felix was at their side in a blur, having used his gift. He helped force Laria into the alley. They had her out of sight in ten seconds, the potion kicking in shortly after that. The woman slumped in their arms, knocked out. Anyone looking out their window shouldn't have been able to see much with the sun not having risen yet.

"Now what?" Felix looked at Keys, lost.

"How good are you at carrying a tune?"

Chapter 18

SKELETON KEY

TURNS OUT, FELIX WAS A HORRIBLE SINGER. WITH AN arm draped over each of their shoulders, Felix and Keys carried the woman between them, singing and swaying as they went. Anyone looking at them would see some friends heading home after a long night out drinking.

Dancing Prawns still had a few patrons drinking and dancing when they entered. She headed straight to the door leading into the cellar.

"Put her down for a second," Keys said once they were down the stairs.

The two lowered her to the ground.

"Put this on." She handed him a matching strip of fabric before taking out her own and securing it. "If you tell anyone about what you see down here, you'll answer to me. Keep your head down and mouth shut. Got it?" Her eyes bored into his.

"Understood." He nodded.

"Good."

They supported the woman between them again as she led him to the hidden door and down the next flight of stairs.

"Take her and turn away," she commanded. He did so without complaint. Knocking on the door, she held her hand up for the ring to be viewed when the wood pulled back. The door opened to admit them.

The guard spoke up as they stepped through the threshold, saying, "Word is Death Adder is around. Watch your step."

"Appreciated," Keys replied.

The two followed the same path she took last night.

Once the guard was out of ear shot, Felix hissed, "Death Adder as in *the Death Adder*? The deadliest assassin on the continent, *Death Adder*? More renown than you?"

"Not here," she scolded.

They'd made it to the next door by then. When it swung open, it was to a much quieter cavern. Everything was winding down for the day. They took the first tunnel on the right side, the path twisting and turning as they walked. Other tunnels branched off from it, leading to more private rooms. Still, they continued on until it dead-ended at a single door.

Keys pushed the door open, her hand reaching for the quartz mounted on the wall. The light overhead flicked on, illuminating the space. A large bed was set off to one side of the room with a table next to it. An open door on the opposite side showed a small bathing room. And right in the center sat a chair with shackles. Copper shackles. Keys hadn't bothered removing the bracelet the woman was wearing that contained all the minerals; any magic she wielded wasn't a threat with her unconscious. With her being a servant, it wasn't a surprise that her magic wasn't deemed important enough to receive a tattoo.

"Let's get her in the chair." After they lowered her, Keys turned to close and lock the door, sliding multiple locks into place. There were no keys for the doors down here. They could only be locked from the inside, and someone would need to break down the door if they wanted access to the room while it was in use.

"Should we be here with Death Adder around?" From his tone, Felix was clearly nervous—as one should be when it came to Death Adder.

"They won't bother us. If they're even here, that is. Chances are someone got spooked and made up a story."

"Have you ever met them?"

"Once."

Felix's eyes bulged. "What're they like?"

"Don't know." She shrugged. "The person next to me dropped dead from one look, and I didn't stick around to learn what happened."

"Seriously?" he croaked.

"No," she deadpanned. "Now let's get back to it."

"This place is *insane*," Felix muttered.

"Remember what I told you. Not a word—to anyone." She returned to the woman, clamping the shackles around each wrist and ankle. The chains would allow her minimal movement, but not enough for her to stand.

"Are you going to try to stop me at all during this?" she asked.

"He told me to not let you take it too far."

"And what's too far?"

His weight shifted from foot to foot. "I don't know. I'm hoping I don't find out."

"Well, let's get started. I suggest you have a seat." Her head jerked to the table and chairs. Keys opened the pouch on her belt and removed another vial containing smelling salts. Uncorking it, she wafted it beneath the woman's nose.

Laria jolted awake with a gasp. Her eyes rounded, scanning her surroundings. "Wha—"

"This can go one of two ways for you. You cooperate and no harm comes to you. Or you don't, and I still get the answers I need."

Tears instantly tracked down the woman's face. "Wh—what do you want? I haven't done anything…" Her lips wobbled.

Keys put the salts back and withdrew the same clear potion she gave Duka; the one that lowered his inhibitions. "First, you're going to take some of this."

"What'll it do to me?" the woman asked as Keys held the vial right below her lips.

"It won't poison you, just help me believe your answers." She didn't give the woman more time, tipping the vial forward. Laria coughed, but drank what Keys poured into her mouth.

"We'll start easy." She slipped the vial back into the pouch. "What's your name?" A test. To see if she'd be truthful from the start.

"I still don't understand." Her eyes darted left and right as she pulled at the chains holding her in place.

"You"—Keys pulled out a dagger that was sheathed in her belt—"have information"—she trailed the dagger over the woman's arm without cutting her—"I need. Simple as that."

The woman tried to move as far away from the dagger as possible.

"Your name," Keys growled.

"Deva," the woman gasped out.

"You're lying to me." The potion would need a little longer to take effect. She stalked around the back of the chair, dragging the dagger along the woman's shoulder now, coming to rest along her neck. It pressed into the woman's skin, but still didn't cut her.

"N-no."

Keys felt for the air moving around the room. She felt the woman breathing in, then breathing out. And then she took hold of that air and *pulled*, ripping it from her lungs. The woman's mouth gaped, opening and closing like a fish, making no sound. Keys withheld the precious oxygen for several more seconds before releasing.

Immediately, the woman sucked down the much-needed air, panting. "Help me!" she screamed when her breath came back to her.

"Someone might hear you...if you're loud enough. But they won't come. Here, let me help you." Keys let out a loud scream that echoed around the chamber. The sound faded away. "See?" she said a minute later. "No one is coming. Now, try again," she crouched down, whispering in her ear.

"Laria." Her throat bobbed against the dagger still at her neck.

"Good. Last name?"

"Bellon."

"Laria Bellon." She pulled the dagger away, circling to the front. "What's your job in the palace?"

"I'm one of the servants."

"And what exactly do you do there?"

"That's what this is about?" She tried pulling on the chains again, letting her arms fall to the armrests when they didn't budge.

Keys tsked. "I ask the questions. What do you do?"

"I clean some of the rooms used during the day. Prep for the morning shift. Sometimes take care of other tasks that come up and need to be done. It just depends on the night. I'm a nobody. I'm not worth anything." Another tug on those chains.

Everyone was worth something to someone—it just depended on what they *needed*. Right now, Laria was worth a great deal to Keys. "How long have you worked there?"

"Almost five years."

"Who do you report to?"

"Rakia Durameur."

The questions continued, until Keys ran through everything that Peri said the guards might ask at the gate, and anything else she thought she might need to know. And then she started again, changing up the order and asking them faster, trying to trip up the woman. The potion should be working by now—evident by Laria's more relaxed posture—but she wanted to make sure Laria was telling the truth. Once she was satisfied, Keys moved on to other questions.

"Do you know why there's been an increase in guards along the wall?" She studied Laria's face, looking for any tell that might indicate she was trying to hide something.

"The guards keep saying it's because of trade negotiations and because they went after both Aswal and Vesperis, but…"

"But?" Keys prompted.

"There was a huge fight a few weeks ago between Prince Calbex and the king. I didn't see it, but it was all anyone could talk about. Shortly after that was when soldiers were called in to help man the wall."

"You don't know what they fought about?"

"No."

"Was anyone new taken to the dungeon around that time?"

"There's been more people taken down there than usual lately." Laria's brows creased.

"Anyone well known and important?"

"No."

"Nothing unusual you've heard about down there?" Keys pressed.

"I've heard there's been weird sounds coming from down there."

"Weird how?" She heard the chair Felix was sitting on creak.

"Lots of moaning and screams, but it almost sounds…like animals." Laria gave her head a sharp shake. "But that doesn't make any sense."

Strange—but Keys didn't think that would be the princess. "Anyone well known that wasn't taken to the dungeon, but you've heard of being around the palace?"

"No."

Her stomach tightened. Maybe the princess really wasn't there. She'd keep her promise to the prince and investigate as much as she could, but she really thought—something else occurred to her.

"Prince Calbex...has he been seen with anyone new?"

"Actually," Laria's eyes widened, "he has. No one knows who she is, though."

Keys rolled her eyes, her own wording of the previous question working against her.

"Apparently, he's kept her pretty secluded from everyone, but some servants have seen her around the palace with bodyguards."

That must be Adelaide. Her pulse picked up, itching for confirmation. She was so close. "Where's she staying?"

"The guest wing."

"What floor?"

"I'm not sure. I don't usually go there unless someone rings for something, but it's one of the higher floors. I overheard one of the women complaining about all the flights of stairs."

"Do you know how I can find out which room is hers?"

"I think the guards are stationed outside her room."

A smile spread across her masked face. "You've been most helpful."

"That's it?" Relief filled the woman's voice. "You'll let me go?" Her eyes shined with hope.

Keys pulled the second vial that she used on Duka from her pouch. It shimmered in the light. "This will help you sleep," she said, holding it out to Laria.

"But you're letting me go, right?" The woman tilted her head back as far as the chair allowed, pulling away from the vial.

"Tomorrow. You'll wake up in your apartment tomorrow." Keys forced the vial past her lips again, dumping some of the potion down her throat.

"You're not worried about me telling anyone about this?" Her eyes were already drooping.

"It might be in your best interest if you don't. But I'll leave that up to you."

"What does that mean?" Her eyes closed.

"It means that if they know you gave me information, forced or not, it might cause more problems for you."

Laria's head dropped to her chest. She didn't respond.

"What was in that first vial you gave her?" Felix spoke for the first time since the interrogation began.

"*That* is a secret worth killing you over." She didn't look at him, retrieving a key that was hanging on the wall behind the chair. "If you value your life, then I suggest not trying to figure it out." Fitting the key into the shackles, she first unlocked one wrist and then the other.

"I thought we weren't moving her until tonight?"

"We aren't, but that doesn't mean she needs to be strapped in an uncomfortable position the entire time." She next unlocked one ankle. The chain on the last ankle allowed for just enough room to lay the woman down on the ground, while still remaining attached to the chair. "Bring me a pillow."

Felix tossed her one from the bed. She slid it under the woman's head, trying to make her somewhat comfortable. The cloak she was wearing should keep her warm enough. Keys checked her pockets, finding a key which she assumed was for the woman's apartment.

"Try to get some sleep." She tucked both keys into her own pocket. "I'll be back in a few hours. Make sure to lock the door behind me. I'll give three quick knocks, pause for a second, then give one more. Don't open this door for anyone else. Not everyone down here is a friend."

"I would never dare to assume you have friends," she heard him mutter.

***

A few hours later, Keys returned to the room, rapping on the door.

Knock, knock, knock. Pause. *Knock.*

It took Felix a minute to open the door for her. His light brown hair was standing up in all directions; the quartz dimmed to a low level.

"Breakfast," she said, thrusting a paper bag into his chest. It contained an assortment of different pastries. Felix opened the bag, investigating, while she secured the door.

The covers on one side of the bed were thrown back. She walked around to the other side, untying her mask as she went. Dumping the canvas bag that was draped over her shoulder, she sat on the bed. There had been no problems getting into the woman's apartment and acquiring two sets of uniforms. The people she passed in the hallway of the building hadn't even glanced her way.

Yawning, she unlaced her boots, pulling them and her socks off before moving onto the daggers she had stashed around her person. Felix was at the table, munching on a chocolate filled pastry. "You should try to get more sleep if you can," she said to him, climbing under the covers.

"In the same bed?"

"I don't bite, unless you're into that kind of thing." She winked at him.

"You're not my," he paused, considering, "preference."

She noted his word choice. "You prefer men?"

His lips thinned, but he inclined his head.

"Stop being squeamish, then."

"It doesn't bother you?"

"Why would it?"

"Some people have a problem with it."

"And those people are dullards." Her head hit the pillow. She closed her eyes, rolling onto her side and facing away from the table. She'd like to get at least six hours of sleep. The woman would need another small dose of sleeping potion before too long.

A few minutes later, she felt the other side of the bed dip. "Thank you," Felix whispered, climbing in next to her.

Keys rolled over, their eyes connecting across the space between the pillows. "You don't need to thank me for human decency."

"Still—thank you." His eyes closed.

She studied him. Without it shimmering, the brown tattoo on his cheek almost blended in perfectly with the color of his skin in the dim light. Besides Sarja, she liked Felix most out of the group. He was quiet, calm, loyal—even if that loyalty pitted him against her sometimes. Most importantly, he used his brain before acting, unlike someone else.

"My sister has been discriminated against due to how she chooses to live life as well." He opened his eyes to look at her again. "Not everyone in our family was accepting of it. It's not something I'd wish for anyone to have to endure."

"I'm sorry she's had to go through that," he murmured.

"I'm sorry you've had too as well."

"My family has been accepting of it. They figured it out on their own when I was younger, so it didn't come as a shock to them when I finally admitted it. But not every soldier is as welcoming."

"But Cain is. And Arla seems like she would be, if you haven't told her yet."

"Cain has been my rock, even if he doesn't know it. I don't know how I would have gotten through my first years of service without him." A tear leaked out of his eye, rolling down his temple to soak into the pillow.

"I'm glad you have someone like him." Her lips quirked up at the corners.

"I'm glad your sister has you."

Keys left it at that, rolling back over to face away from him.

Chapter 19

SKELETON KEY

THERE WAS A REASON THAT SHE AND HER SISTER ALWAYS requested this particular room, and Felix was about to find out why. She'd debated on if she should blindfold him or not, but couldn't find the harm in him knowing about this on top of everything else he had already observed down here.

Just after seven, they gathered their things, preparing to leave. She left the door to the hallway unlocked. "I need you to take my belt and daggers back for me. I can't go in wearing them." She handed them off to him. "Don't let Baxley deviate from the plan. Unless an alarm sounds, there's no need to worry if I'm not at the rendezvous point right away."

"Got it." Felix buckled the belt around his own waist.

"Here's the sleeping potion and key for her apartment." She handed him those next. "Tell Peri that about half of what's left should do it."

He pocketed them.

"Right." She slung the canvas bag over her shoulder. "It's time."

Supporting the woman between them, Keys directed him over towards the wall with the bathing chamber.

"This is a wall..." Felix said, his face scrunching up as he examined it.

"Patience." She reached out with her senses, feeling for the edges she knew would be in the rocks. When she found them, she willed it to *push*. A doorway slid back a few feet. With one more thought, it then slid into a pocket off to the left side, revealing a narrow passageway. She and her sister had carved out the passage years ago without Harben's knowledge. It was how no one was ever able to track their movements. Felix and her would have to move sideways through it, since they were carrying Laria. Ten feet into the passage were stairs leading up to the surface.

Felix's mouth dropped open. "How?"

"Time. Lots of time." They had worked methodically over the course of a month, making sure no one was aware of how much rock and dirt they were secretly hauling away.

"Impressive."

"I'll go first."

"By all means." He waved her ahead.

Keys sent up a ball of light, and once they were inside the passage, she sealed the doorway behind them. The stairs led them straight to the surface, where Keys needed to shift another stone above their heads. Dimming the light, she willed the stone to lift up and slide sideways. She popped her head up through the gap, making sure the alleyway it opened up into was clear.

"All good," she said, shifting the rock farther to widen the hole, extinguishing the light completely. They made their way out of the passage. When the stone slid back into place, it blended in perfectly with the ground. "Peri should be right across the street. Wait here."

Oranges and yellows still tinted the sky as the sun went down. With Peri's help, they should be able to get Laria back to her apartment unnoticed. The entrance to the alley let out into a smaller side street. Peri was propped up against a storefront, right where Keys expected her to be. She watched the woman survey the street. Peri noticed her as she revealed herself, stepping out from the alleyway. Satisfied that she was on the way, Keys returned to Felix.

Peri joined them not even a minute later, taking Keys' place carrying Laria.

"If you run into trouble, I trust you to handle it however you need to," Keys said to the spy.

"You don't have to worry about me." Peri grinned back. If only she didn't need to worry about other members of their party.

"Good luck." Felix nodded to her as they moved to leave.

"I don't need luck. I make my own." She watched Peri wield an illusion over them, making it look like three people walked along arm in arm.

Once they were around the corner, Keys pulled the uniforms out of the canvas bag. They would need to be worn double layered so the guards wouldn't question why she was carrying an extra one into the palace. The flowing pants weren't a problem except for being short on her. Putting on both tops, however, was more of a challenge. The servant uniform revealed a small strip of midriff, not quite as revealing as what was considered the normal style—after all, even noble eyes tended to wander. The top still had a lower cut, though, where she was able to stash the vials she might be needing. She had picked up a bracelet containing all the minerals from the market the other day, which she put on now. After making sure the second uniform wasn't poking out anywhere, she donned her cloak and slicked her hair back into a low bun.

There was one more thing she needed to change—*herself*. Picturing Laria's essence clearly in her mind, she willed herself to *become* her. Her lips filled in more. Her eyes turned from a deep brown to a bright blue. Her eyebrows and hair lightened to blonde. Her nose lengthened and thinned. And then, she shrank down by several inches, the too-short pants fitting perfectly. The whole process took seconds. Laria now stood in the alleyway exactly where Keys had been.

Keys was a *morph*—able to change her appearance at will, whether it was changing into someone else by reading their essence or only changing certain features on herself. The first time she'd ever done it, she got stuck as the other person for a week before she managed to change herself back. The reason why no one ever learned her face was because the same woman never showed up again after a job was executed. She was going to walk right through the gate and the guards would be none the wiser.

Her walk to the palace took no time at all. She ditched her old clothes and bag along the way, not needing them anymore. Multiple guards lined the gate, scrutinizing everyone. Other servants flowed around her. Her heart pounded. The risk didn't make her anxious, though. *It excited her.* She lived for this— thrived in this feeling. There was a short queue at the door where the staff were giving their names to a guard comparing them to a list. Joining at the end, she waited. When the man in front of her was pulled out of line, no one batted an eye.

Keys stepped forward into his place, saying, "Laria Bellon." Laria's own voice reached her ears.

The guard flipped a page, scanning the names. "Cleared," he grunted.

None of the remaining guards moved to stop her as she continued to the doorway.

And just like that, she was through. The large palace grounds spread before her. From her time here previously, she knew there was a large field around the other side where festivals were held. There were extensive gardens and even a small wooded area where game was sometimes brought in for the nobles to hunt. Not very sporting of them, in her opinion.

The current path took her straight to a side entrance where the other servants headed. She'd find Rakia Durameur in the laundry area to receive her assignment for the night. Some of the servants in front of her broke off down other corridors. Keys pulled a vial from between her breasts and took a swig of it. Her stomach rolled almost instantly. She had only a few minutes at most.

A few more turns and she entered the laundry area. There were several servants washing clothes and sheets; laundry in the palace never ended. A woman stood off to one side where other cleaning supplies were kept. She was just finishing up talking with another servant, who turned to grab some of the supplies.

"Laria," she said, noticing Keys walk in, "I'll have you start on the second-floor drawing rooms tonight."

That must be Rakia then, she assumed. Keys' stomach gave a huge lurch. She gagged.

"Are you okay?" Concerned flitted across the woman's face.

"I'm fi—" Keys didn't get the rest out. Clamping a hand across her mouth, she rushed to what was hopefully an empty bucket before spewing her last meal into it. Bile burned the back of her throat. Throwing up was the worst, but it couldn't be avoided in this instance.

"Oh, dear," Rakia said. "Did you eat something bad?"

Keys managed to shake her head in between heaves.

"Well, either way, you won't be able to stay. We can't risk others getting sick if that's what it is. Get to the bathing room and then head home when you can. We'll make sure your work is covered for the night. Send a note tomorrow if you still aren't better by then."

"Thanks," she choked out, picking up her bucket to shuffle out of the room. Another servant waiting behind her gave her a wide berth as she passed. There was a bathing room a few doors down the hall if she remembered correctly. She pushed the door open, retreating inside. In about thirty minutes, the potion should wear off completely. It was a common tincture that healers used if someone had ingested poison and they caught it in time. While she waited, she took up position in front of the toilet instead of the bucket, moaning her displeasure.

Once the effects wore off and she hadn't puked in the last five minutes, she rinsed out the bucket and left it and her cloak in the room. As long as she didn't bump into Rakia or that other servant, no one should question why she was still here, leaving her to move around freely. A stop in the kitchen provided her with a tea tray and biscuits. The servants prepping food for tomorrow didn't question her when she said someone requested it.

She stuck to the servant passageways as much as she could on her long walk to the guest wing. Those she passed nodded in greeting. There were no guards about. It appeared they still stuck to their old ways, probably only guarding the grounds and the royal wing. The royals were arrogant in believing no one would be able to infiltrate the palace. How wrong they were. They thought the wall was their biggest asset when she made it their biggest weakness.

The guest wing consisted of thirteen floors. The first floor was strictly lounging areas. Drawing rooms and some private dining areas were on the second floor, while guest suites started on the third. She made her way directly there via the servants' staircase on the far side. There shouldn't be too many guests in residence with the palace as locked down as it was. During festivals, the rooms would be full to bursting—it was during one of those times that she had last visited the palace.

Upon reaching the third floor, she poked her head around the corner. No guards were in sight. She continued on to the next floor, and then the next and the next after that. A few guests were returning to their quarters on the lower floors, but she found no guards. Her legs were burning around the seventh floor. She'd been too inactive the last few weeks. By the tenth floor, they screamed. How did the servants manage to do this all the time?

The princess wasn't on that level either. Nor was she on the eleventh or twelfth floor. Only one floor left. She pushed onward. No sound came from the hallway once she reached the landing. She peeked the smallest part of her head around the corner, and then whipped back out of sight. Two guards stood about halfway down the hall, stationed outside one of the suites. Of course they wouldn't put the princess by anyone else, but did they really need to assign her a room on the highest floor?

Keys backtracked to the floor below. The look she managed down the hallway didn't give her the exact location of the suite, but she'd worry about that in a minute. The floor was still deserted when she rounded the corner, which wasn't a surprise. Choosing a random door at the halfway point on the same side as where the princess was being kept, she knocked and waited. A minute passed without a sound. Confirmation that no one was occupying the space, she turned the knob and stepped inside the dark room.

She left the light off, not wanting to alert anyone watching from the wall or the grounds. The room she entered was the sitting room. There was a bedchamber through an open door to the left. She set the tea tray down on a low table by the couches and walked to the balcony double doors. She opened one, stepping outside. The bedchamber also had its own separate balcony, which she could step over to if she wanted.

A glance up showed her how close she had gotten to the princess' suite. It was only one over based on the glow of the lights within. She returned inside, picked up her tea tray, and moved to the next suite over, repeating the knocking process. Just in case.

The balconies off of this suite were identical to the ones next door. Keys examined the outer wall of the palace, finding plenty of handholds between the stones. Even if she fell—which she wouldn't—she could always use her air magic to catch herself. After checking the grounds below to see if anyone on patrol was looking upward, she started her climb. Really, this was child's play for someone like her. She snorted, remembering how frantic Baxley had been, especially since arriving in Gleyra. Hopefully he wasn't causing too many problems for Felix and the others. The group should be heading out of the city by now.

She eased herself over the balcony railing, trying to see if anyone was in the sitting room. She couldn't spot anyone through the gaps in the curtains. The light in the bedchamber was on as well so she hopped up onto the railing of the balcony before stepping over to that one instead.

Keys jumped down, creeping up to the double doors to look through. Her eyes widened at the sight that greeted her, shock freezing her in place. Now *this* was an unexpected development.

Chapter 20

SKELETON KEY

THERE WAS A MAN IN THERE WITH THE PRINCESS. THERE was a man in *bed* with the princess. A naked man. A naked man having *sex* with the princess.

Oh fuck.

Oh fuck, fuck, fuck.

Keys paced across the balcony, tugging at her fingers. What was she going to do? Her mind raced. Maybe the princess didn't even want to return home. Maybe she *had* left on her own. What the hell was she going to do, then? And who was the man with her? Was it Prince Calbex? Laria had said the heir was seen spending time with the princess. Was he forcing himself onto her? Should she go in and stop it?

She raced back to the doors, pressing her face up against the glass. The man had the princess propped up on all fours, pounding into her from behind. From what Keys could see, the princess appeared to be enjoying herself. Just then, the man slapped her across the ass. The princess' cry of "harder" reached Keys through the balcony doors. Another slap followed. Really enjoying herself—unless she was pretending. Keys wouldn't hold it against the woman for doing whatever she needed to do in this kind of situation. She would never be one to cast that kind of judgement on people, seeing how her hands weren't clean either.

A third slap had the princess falling forward, dislodging the man's cock from her entrance. He took advantage of being released and leaned down to bite her ass instead, his head tilting the wrong way, preventing Keys from making out his face. The cry the princess let out this time as she flopped down flat on the bed had Keys questioning how much of this was really consensual. Indents were left in her ass cheek when the man pulled away.

He seemed to abandon his earlier position, instead moving up to kneel next to her head. His hand tangled in the princess' hair, lifting her up to take his cock in her mouth. Head thrown back, the man started thrusting forward. This new angle gave her a full view of his face. The face of Prince Calbex. Both of his cheeks were tattooed, the pattern flowing down his neck to connect together. She couldn't make out the design from here, but knew it would have a horned viper woven into the mandala for his family crest. Dammit all to hell.

Her head leaned to the side, involuntarily passing judgement—at least he had good form. Nope. Not getting distracted. Or going there with a prince.

Wait till he leaves—if he leaves—get her out, and return her to Baxley. Fuck, *Baxley*. What was she going to tell him? Her thoughts raced: *Just caught your fiancée fucking a different prince. No big deal, though. Got her back all safe and...fucked?* No, best not to say anything at all.

The prince's pace picked up, his hips driving forward.

Oh, please let him be finished soon.

The princess' hands tightened on his thighs as he fucked her mouth. His movements turned jerky. One final big push, and he stilled inside her.

Keys ducked back as the prince pulled out, clambering off the bed to collect his clothes. The prince cleaned himself on something that he dropped to the ground before pulling on his pants. He moved to the princess, who was still lying prone on the bed where he discarded her. Patting her cheek, he bent down to whisper something in her ear. He straightened, laughing, snagged his vest off the ground and walked out of the room while putting his arms through the holes.

Keys followed him, stepping back to the other balcony just in time to see the prince exit out into the hallway. By the time she made it back to the balcony outside of the bedchamber, the princess had disappeared. The bathing room door was now closed. Picturing the body she previously occupied, she willed the change. The Keys the others knew stood on the balcony, her pants becoming too short once more.

She opened the one door, entering the bedchamber. Next to the bed, she found what the prince used to clean himself. It was a pair of panties. She cringed away from them. Very classy for a prince. Keys stripped off the extra uniform and folded it on the bed while she waited for the princess to emerge.

A few minutes later, the bathing room door opened, revealing the princess in a robe.

The princess gasped when she saw Keys, clutching her chest. "You frightened me." Her brows furrowed. "Why are you here so late? I didn't request anything."

"Your prince sent me for you," Keys explained.

"Calbex sent you? But he was just here," she said, pointing to the door. "Why—"

"Not that prince." Keys cocked her head to the side. "*Your* prince." Understanding still didn't show on the princess' face. "The one you're betrothed to..." She raised an eyebrow.

The princess' face drained of color. "Baxley," she murmured. "I don't understand." Her body swayed. "Why would he—"

"For the love of..." Keys rushed to her side and forced her to sit on the bed. "What is it with you nobility and lightheadedness?"

"What's going on?" The princess grasped her arms. Her grip bruising, eyes pleading.

"The prince sent me to bring you home." Both her brows raised this time. "That is what you want, yes? To return to Aglar?" The possibility that the princess left willingly was still there.

"What—yes, yes of course." She released Keys' arms and combed her fingers through her hair, catching on snags. "I just..." Her eyes zipped around the room, roaming over her panties and other articles of clothing spread around, until finally landing back on Keys. "How much did you see?" she whispered, cheeks flushing.

"Of you and the spare?"

She flinched. "Yes."

"Enough."

Tears welled up in the princess' eyes. "You can't tell him," she begged, her tone frantic. "Please, he can't know. He won't—"

"Relax." Keys grabbed her shoulders to ground her. "It is not for me to judge what you had to...*endure* to survive here. I will keep your secret if you keep mine. Deal?" They stared into each other's eyes.

"What secret?"

"How I'm going to get you out of here."

The princess' breathing evened out as she wiped away the few tears. "Deal."

"The guards in the hall, will they allow you to walk around unescorted?"

She shook her head. "No. I've been allowed to roam in the evenings, but they'll follow."

"Then we go back the way I came in." Keys picked up the extra uniform she brought. "Put this on and pull your hair into a low bun."

The princess accepted it, retreating to the bathing room.

"And wash off your makeup," she called through the door.

When the princess returned, she looked closer to a commoner, though it would be hard to correct her posture in the next few minutes. The mineral tattoo on her forearm would be a dead giveaway.

"Do you have makeup that will cover that some?" Keys nodded down at it.

"It won't be perfect." The princess bit her lip.

"Anything will help."

As the princess moved to the vanity, Keys entered the walk-in closet, looking for a sturdy pair of shoes. What she found was woefully lacking—at least in her requirements. Heels and strappy sandals lined the shelves. Didn't this woman even own anything for travel? She settled on a simpler, flat-heeled shoe. It wouldn't be the best, and she made a mental note to buy her a different pair in the first town they stopped.

"Put these on." She passed the shoes over when she returned. The princess slipped her feet into them. Keys took her hand, turning her arm back and forth. The shade of brown was slightly too light for her tanner arms. "It'll do," she said, examining the princess' handiwork. She unclasped the mineral bracelet and slipped it onto the princess' wrist instead. "If anyone stops us or questions us on the way out, your name is Laria."

"Won't they recognize me?"

"No. Are you ready?"

"Yes," she said, even though her lips wobbled.

"Adelaide." Keys grabbed both her hands. "You need to be strong for a little longer, and then I'll have you out of here. Can you do that?"

"Yes." Her voice held a little more conviction.

"Good. We're going to turn out the lights and then head out." Keys found the quartz mounted on the wall, switching it off and plunging them into darkness. She led the princess out to the balcony connected to the sitting room.

"Can you climb down the rockwork to the balcony below?" Keys asked, fully anticipating that not to happen.

"You want me to climb down that?" Adelaide squeaked, peering over the edge.

"I'll take that as a no. That's okay," she placated. "Watch me and I'll catch you." Keys jumped onto the railing, spinning to face the princess. "All you have to do is step." She held her arm out wide, and then took a step back into open air, letting herself fall.

She beamed, unable to help herself as the thrill buzzed through her. Wielding the air around her, she slowed her descent, pushing herself sideways onto the below balcony. It was something she'd done a hundred times. And from much greater distances. Her pulsed thrummed, seeking a longer rush, a farther fall, craving that feeling of teetering on the edge of life.

Adelaide's head popped over the railing, looking for her. "See? Easy. Whatever you do, don't scream."

"I can't do that," Adelaide whimpered.

"You have to. Sit on the railing if you can't stand." The princess at least moved to do that much, her legs dangling.

"There you go," she encouraged. "Now, push off."

"I can't!"

Keys scanned the ground and wall, checking to make sure no one was watching them. "You can," she reassured when she spotted no one. She firmed the air beneath the princess' feet, pushing up on them. "Do you feel that?" She pushed again. "I have you."

"Okay—okay," Adelaide said. "I'm coming down." She slowly rotated so her stomach was against the railing, easing off with Keys supporting her weight.

Working against the air currents was harder than working in tandem with them, just like with water. Sweat dotted Keys' forehead. "Let go," she said when the princess still held on with her hands.

Finally, Adelaide released her grip, a small sound escaping her mouth. Hopefully the sound wouldn't travel far. Keys directed her fall the same way she'd done her own. Her arms clamped around Adelaide once she was within reach. "You're okay. I got you." The woman buried her face into Keys' chest. "That's the worst of it. I promise. All walking from here on out."

It took a few minutes for the princess to compose herself.

When she began to pull away, Keys reached out and held her face. "One last thing." Keys felt for the princess' essence, memorizing it for later. And then she pushed her powers *inside* the princess, willing her to change and transform into Laria—but only her face. They were close enough in height and doing a full transformation on another person would exhaust her. Even this would be tough enough. She still needed to get them out of the palace and transform Adelaide back into herself. And if they ran into trouble, she'd need her magic to fight. She removed her hands when the transformation was finished, breathing heavy.

"What did you do to me?" The princess touched her face.

"If we run into anyone, they won't recognize you. *That* is my secret, which I expect you to keep. Just follow my lead if we run into trouble."

Keys picked up the tea tray on the way out of the room. They didn't encounter anyone else on the servants' staircase. The princess followed along dutifully behind her as they backtracked through the palace. A few servants were moving around the ground floor, on their way to perform different tasks. No one stopped them. Halfway back to the kitchen, Keys veered in the opposite direction, taking them deeper towards the center of the palace.

"Where are we going?" the princess asked.

"To the king's study," Keys whispered.

"Are you mad?" The princess grabbed her elbow, making the tea rattle on the tray.

"Not at all." She smirked.

She took them around the long way to bypass the grand staircase leading to the royal wing that was guaranteed to have guards posted there. They ran into more servants going this way, but it was worth it. No one realized they had a criminal, or a princess, walking among them.

The hallway leading to the king's study was empty, exactly like she was expecting. No reason to guard it at night with the king safe in his bed. Fools, all of them. When would they ever learn they were only making things easier for her.

"Inside, quickly," Keys urged when they reached the door, balancing the tray with one hand and pushing the door open. She sent up a light to illuminate the room.

The room was quainter than one might expect for a king. It had a homey air to it with the large overstuffed furniture in the middle of the room. A large oak desk overflowing with paperwork was off to one side. One wall was all bookshelves; every available space was being utilized to display an impressive collection of history and politics—though she had found a romance or two shoved behind the other books before. Instead of portraits decorating the walls, there were nature scenes depicting the landscapes found throughout the country: from the white sandy coast to the rolling plains of the Sutra.

"Now what?" The princess whirled on Keys once the door closed. "The other door just leads to the throne room," she said, panic edging her voice.

"That door does," Keys walked to the right side of the bookshelves, "but the other door doesn't."

"There's no other door," the princess cried.

"There is, if you know where to look." She balanced the tray again, reaching her right hand into the gap between the bookcase and the wall. A few inches in, she felt the release, pushing it down with her hand. There was a click, and the bookshelf swung open before them, exposing a dark passage that led downwards into the earth.

A gasp sounded from the princess. "How did you know that was there?" She stepped up beside Keys.

"Like I said, you just need to know where to look. After you, Princess." She nodded towards the passage, holding the tea tray with both hands again. She'd have to take it with her to not leave behind any evidence they were in this room. "I believe you have a prince waiting for you."

Chapter 21

SKELETON KEY

THE EXIT OF THE PASSAGEWAY WAS HIDDEN IN THE rocks lining the bank of the river that wound around the outside of the city. It had taken them longer to reach it than Keys had anticipated, not accounting for how slow the princess would walk. Even still carrying the tea tray, she constantly had to stop and wait for her to catch up. If this short stretch was a good indicator, the return journey was going to be a nightmare. Who knew she'd find something more to dread than spending time with Baxley?

"It's just up ahead," Keys encouraged.

"You said that twenty minutes ago." The princess bent over, breathing heavily, bracing her hands on her thighs.

"Maybe if you picked up your feet more," she muttered to herself.

Sure enough, the doorway came into view in the next minute. It was designed to only open from the inside and was lined with copper to prevent anyone from the outside trying to get in using their magic, if they knew of its existence. She would have had to tear a hole in the side of the bank to get through it. Even with how clueless they were guarding the actual palace compared to the wall, they might have noticed that.

"Hold this," she said, handing the tea tray to the princess when they reached the door. Keys cupped the princess' face, willing her to return to her original essence. The strain was heavier this time, her hands trembling as they pulled away. She examined Adelaide's face, making sure every feature returned to normal. Satisfied, she turned to the doorway, pressing down on the lever and pushing with her shoulder, digging her feet into the ground for traction. It took all of her weight to move the door. It creaked on unused hinges, slowly moving inch by inch.

When she had it open wide enough, she motioned the princess through before stepping away, letting it snap shut behind her. The boom it caused was drowned out by the rushing water. The door blended in perfectly with the rocks, even to her eyes. She extinguished the light that hovered above them, the moon providing enough light for them to see. Keys took the tea tray back and chucked it into the current, watching as it drifted a short way downstream, where it sank beneath the surface.

"The prince is waiting on the other side," she said, gesturing to the river.

"What? He's here? You didn't say he was *here*. Why would you bring him along?" the princess spewed, tugging at her fingers. "I can't see him like this. How am I supposed to face—"

Keys grabbed her hands, stilling them. "You don't have to tell him anything you don't want to, okay? And trust me, *I* tried to get him to stay behind. He's been a pain in my ass," she grumbled.

"You really won't tell him?" The princess' blue eyes flicked back and forth between her own.

"I told you I wouldn't." If the princess wasn't comfortable sharing what happened to her, it wasn't her place to say anything.

"Okay." Adelaide let out a big sigh. "How are we getting across that, though?"

"Walking. It's not too deep."

As the two women waded across the river, Keys used the last of her energy to part the current around them, slowing it so it didn't sweep them away. The water only rose to their waists at the halfway point. Once on the other side, Keys pulled all the water from their clothes, drying them. Getting the princess up the steep bank showed what little athletic ability the woman possessed. She might as well have been a corpse from the amount of pulling and shoving Keys had to do.

Sweat dripped down Keys' spine when they finally crested the top, her breathing even heavier. "Not much farther," she panted, bending over for a moment to rest.

She led the way into the forest, hearing voices after walking only a short distance—arguing voices. Of course they wouldn't be able to keep quiet. Keys fought the urge to say screw them all and return with the princess *alone*. She could make out the words as they grew closer.

"—something could have happened."

"There's been no alarms."

"That doesn't mean anything." The voice rose in volume. Baxley, that was Baxley.

"She said to stay *here*," Felix responded.

"I just want to go look." Baxley had one foot in the stirrup when the group came into view between the trees.

"By all means," she called out, "go gallivanting off by yourself. It'll save me loads of trouble."

Baxley almost toppled over, twisting around to face her, his foot snagging in the stirrup. He barely managed to grab onto the saddle and free himself. "Where is she?" he cried, hurrying towards her.

Keys rolled her eyes. "Right here." She stepped to the side, revealing the princess who trailed behind her.

"Adelaide," he whispered, freezing in place, staring at her for a second. In the next breath, he was moving again, colliding into the princess and crushing her against him. He rocked her side to side, one hand cradling the back of her head. "You're here," he repeated over and over.

The princess didn't say anything. Her eyes flicked to Keys for a moment before she closed them, tucking her head into his neck.

Weird. Maybe she was simply overwhelmed by the whole ordeal.

"Are you okay? Do you need a healer? We brought one. Sarja," he called, releasing the princess somewhat, turning his head to find Sarja.

"She's uninjured. Stop smothering her," Keys ordered him, waving Sarja off.

"Truly?" He turned back to the princess, cradling her face. "You're not hurt?"

"No," Adelaide whispered despite a tear running down her cheek. "They didn't harm me."

He wrapped her in his arms once more. "I thought I'd never see you again. What happened?"

The princess' eyes found Keys for a second time, the pleading in them clear for anyone to see.

"There'll be enough time for questions later," Keys said, taking the hint. "Time to move out. Now. In the next day, we need to put as much distance between us and here as we can." She walked to her own horse, climbing into the saddle. Everyone except Baxley and the princess moved. "Let's go," she called, her tone a touch irritable.

Baxley ignored her, his eyes only for Adelaide. "You're sure you're okay?"

"Yes." The princess nodded, wiping away her tears. "You know I'm not good on horseback, though." She side-eyed the horses.

"You'll have plenty of time to practice, then. A carriage would slow us down and draw attention," Keys said, nudging her horse closer to them. "Now, mount up."

Baxley glared at her, but finally did as he was told, leading the princess to the extra horse and helping her into the saddle. Peri had taken the second horse they purchased.

Keys dug into her saddle bag, while she waited for him to mount his own horse, pulling out several slices of jerky to munch on to recover some of the energy she expended tonight. At this point, if they ran into trouble along the way, she'd need to count on her skills with a blade—precisely why she had told Baxley not to rely on his magic in a fight.

Once Baxley was on his own horse, she said, "We'll ride until daylight. No breaks unless absolutely necessary." She urged her horse forward, leading the way through the trees and away from Gleyra.

***

She pushed them as hard as she dared overnight. They had to stick to the main road or else risk a horse tripping over a root and breaking a leg. The princess complained within an hour, saying her thighs were sore. The hour after that, it was that her butt hurt. An hour more and she wanted to stop and sleep. Keys told her that they might as well deliver her back to the palace themselves if they stopped now. That shut her up for almost two hours, until she informed them she needed to relieve herself. Reluctantly, Keys allowed them a short rest, but the princess refused to pee in the forest.

"Fine, piss yourself for all I care," she had said to the woman, running out of patience. Keys may feel bad for what happened to her, but that didn't mean she'd treat her as if she was made of glass.

With some persuasion from Baxley and help from Sarja, the princess finally had marched off the path and behind some trees. Keys took the opportunity to inform Baxley that she was his responsibility and he needed to keep her moving—*no matter what.* The prince offered up excuses for his betrothed, but she was pretty sure even his patience was wearing thin dealing with all the complaints by the time the sun rose.

They started seeing other travelers on the road when the sun was shining through the trees. Everyone moved in the opposite direction, heading towards the city.

"When are we going to stop? We've been riding all night," the princess whined right as another group was passing them.

"Keep your voice down," Keys hissed at her. She glanced back at the other travelers, trying to see if they had overheard. If they did, they didn't react to it. She breathed a sigh of relief.

Baxley and the princess bickered in hushed voices. Keys tried to tune them out, focusing on the road ahead. This was going to be a long journey. A long, miserable journey.

"No. I refuse to go any farther." The princess' voice grew louder and she pulled her horse to a stop. "We've passed plenty of villages along the way. One of them must have an inn we can stop at," she moaned.

Keys whipped her head back to see where the group was. They were just rounding a bend in the road, almost out of view. Lucky. They got lucky. She checked to make sure no one else was coming their way while Baxley pleaded with the princess to continue.

"I won't." The princess crossed her arms. "I've been dragged away in the middle of the night and forced to ride nonstop. I'm *tired*," she fussed, drawing out the word.

"What? Did the Voglarians have a golden ship and carriage for you when they stole you in the middle of the night?" Baxley snapped back. "Sorry your rescue isn't living up to your standards."

Oh, yes. He was getting annoyed with her as well. Keys snorted. This was payback for all the trouble he'd caused her along the way.

"I—they—" the princess choked, trying to find the words.

"That's enough of that, love birds." Keys interjected before things could get too out of hand. "A few hours' rest. That's all we can afford at present. There's a small city a little more than an hour's ride away. Some of us will ride ahead to gather supplies and then double back to meet up before continuing on together."

"I'll come," Cain said, quickly volunteering.

She nodded at him. "Sarja, if you wouldn't mind as well." She wanted two of the soldiers to stay with Baxley and the princess in case there was trouble.

The healer nodded her consent.

"Right, off the road before anyone else comes along." She pointed the others into trees. "Go far enough that no one can see or hear," her eyes flicked to the princess, "you."

"That's not what I meant when I said I wanted to stop," the princess grumbled, her horse trailing behind Arla who led the way.

"That's all I'm willing to offer," Keys called after her. She nudged her horse forward, cutting Baxley off before he could enter the woods. "If someone discovers you, you fight and then make a run for the city. Otherwise, you *do not leave*."

His hands tightened on the reins. "Understood," he replied.

"See you in a few hours." She moved out of his way, watching him join the others. Keys waited till they were out of sight to erase any trace of them leaving the road. Next, she uprooted a small tree to mark the spot, so they'd be able to find them on the way back.

"I don't envy them," Cain muttered when they started on their way again.

"Why do you think I agreed to come along?" Sarja laughed.

Keys chuckled to herself. Yes, the prince was going to have his hands full for the next couple of weeks. She couldn't wait till they got to the camels.

Chapter 22

BAXLEY

THE WOODS STRETCHED OUT BEFORE THEM, LIGHT filtering down between the canopy. The trees were spaced far enough apart to allow them to ride easily between them. After riding a short distance away from the road, Arla called a halt, deeming them far enough to not be discovered. She'd stopped them in a small clearing where everyone could be within sight while resting.

Baxley had felt his heart skip when he'd finally laid eyes on Adelaide back in the forest. She was exactly as he remembered her. Even dressed in servants' clothing, she was breathtaking. Her floral scent flooded his senses, overpowering everything else. He wanted to hold her in his arms and never let her go again.

His euphoria was short-lived as they rode through the night, though. Yes, he expected this not to be easy for Adelaide, but he didn't foresee her being so averse to travel on the first day. He thought she'd be more appreciative—more enthusiastic about being rescued. His nerves were frayed after weeks of worrying and a sleepless night. They could all benefit from a little rest.

Now, he dismounted and moved to help Adelaide down. She collapsed into his arms, dead weight. He stumbled trying to hold her upright.

"Are you alright?" he asked.

"How could I be alright?" she replied, teary-eyed. "I'm tired. I'm sore." She stepped out of his arms. "I don't understand anything that's happened. Why are you even here?"

A frown creased his forehead. "How could I not come for you?"

"What happened? After I..." Biting her bottom lip, her gaze slid to the ground.

His heart hurt for her despite his frustration. He couldn't imagine what she must be feeling after everything she'd been through. "After you were taken," he finished for her. "We received demands a week later. Voglar wants new trade agreements with both Aswal and Vesperis. They were going to keep you to ensure it was upheld."

"What?" Her eyes snapped back to his.

Baxley saw the panic within them. "Of course I came for you. *Of course*," he assured her, trying to soothe that anxiety. He stepped towards her, taking her hands in his. "I would never leave you with them."

"That's not—I didn't—" She took a deep breath. "I didn't know," she finally got out, her tears spilling over. "He didn't tell me," she whispered, turning away from him.

"Who?"

Adelaide shook her head. "It doesn't matter now. I just want to sleep," she sniveled.

"Okay." Baxley looked around to see where the others were.

Felix and Arla were tending to the horses, trying to give them as much privacy as possible in the small space. They tied them all to low tree limbs and were relieving them of their saddles. He led Adelaide in the opposite direction. There wasn't too much he could do to make the ground comfortable, but he at least used his meager air magic to clear a spot of sticks and leaves. Putting his cloak down first, he helped her lay down, tucking her own cloak around her tightly. The early morning air still held a slight bite from the colder spring night.

"Try to get as much rest as you can before they return." He knelt down to kiss her on the forehead.

"Who is that woman, anyway?" she asked, nestling into the cloak.

"Skeleton Key."

Her eyes popped open, widening. "No, truly?" she exclaimed.

"Yes, but I can tell you about that later." Baxley smiled down at her. "Sleep."

She closed her eyes again when he stood. He walked over to where the others still waited by the horses.

"How is she?" Felix asked him.

"As well as she can be considering the circumstances."

"Did she say anything about...what happened to her while she was in there?" Arla's face was etched with concern.

"She didn't say." Baxley shook his head. "And I didn't ask yet. I don't want to push her if she's not ready. Though she did mention a he. I don't know who she was referring to. She mumbled something about a man not telling her..." He frowned, pausing for a second. Did someone visit with her while she was held captive? "I don't think they told her anything after they abducted her."

"Why don't you try and get some rest as well? I can take first watch," said Felix.

"No, I don't think I'll be able to sleep until we're farther away. You both go get as much rest as you can now."

A small, knowing smile graced Arla's face. "Wake us if you change your mind." She reached out to clasp his arm gently before they both walked off to find a spot to settle.

Baxley propped himself against a nearby tree where he could watch over everyone.

***

It turns out he must have been more tired than he thought he was. Baxley awoke to his chin resting on his chest, drool pooling slightly at the corner of his mouth. His neck complained from being in that position for too long. He lifted his head to stretch — and then jerked as his eyes connected with someone crouching in front of him.

"What the hell?" he yelled, toppling over.

"Rise and shine, Bax." Keys smirked down at him.

"Don't do that," he complained, pushing himself upright.

"Don't fall asleep while on watch, then." She rose, turning away from him. "Come on. We're cooking lunch now and then we'll head out."

"You got all the supplies we needed?" he asked, brushing himself off as he made to follow her towards the small fire they had going.

"Camping gear, bow and arrows, food supplies, extra water skins," she listed. "The works. We'll be set for a little while. I want to take us on a more direct path. It'll take us away from the major cities and villages, but we'll get there faster."

Everyone except Adelaide was gathered around the fire. Someone had already hung a pot over it, heating the contents inside. Based on the smell, it was a stew. His stomach gave a loud rumble when he breathed in the scent.

"I'll go get Adelaide," he said, glancing over to where she was still sleeping.

"Let her sleep longer. Food will be a few minutes still. It's been nice having a break from the constant complaining," she grumbled.

"Give her a break. She's just not used to this," he defended her.

"We haven't even been traveling for a *day*, and she's acting like she'd rather have stayed at the palace. Don't pretend that you haven't gotten annoyed with it as well." Keys waved a large wooden spoon at him that she used to stir the stew.

"She'll get better."

Cain snorted.

"Something to say?" Baxley turned to the soldier.

Cain ducked his chin. "Apologies."

He clenched his jaw, teeth grinding together. "If you have something to say, then say it."

"We're talking about the princess who complains about walking through the gardens because her shoes get too dusty. She's going to give us hell the entire way," Cain said, shrugging.

"Wonderful," Keys muttered. "You said she wouldn't be able to cross the mountain path, not that she'd be *that* bad." She frowned at Baxley.

"Would it have changed anything?" He shot back at her.

"I might have brought a gag for her mouth." She tossed back.

Heat surged through him. "If you touch her..."

"Oh, relax," she tutted, ladling a portion of the stew to sniff it. "Go ahead and wake her. This is ready."

He left the others while they moved forward to collect their bowls. Adelaide had covered her head while she slept, blocking out the light.

"Adelaide," he said, pulling back the cloak. "It's time to get moving again."

She moaned, her eyes slowly blinking open. "What time is it?"

"Around midday. We have food ready." He rubbed her shoulder, trying to rouse her further.

"It's barely been a few hours," she whined, rolling over to face away from him.

"Please, Adelaide. The faster we move, the faster we get home. The faster we get you *safe*. I couldn't—" His voice cracked. Clearing his throat, he tried again. "I couldn't live with myself if they took you again."

She rolled back over to face him, eyes more awake now. "They let me send you a letter when I arrived at the palace," she whispered. "You didn't receive it?"

"No." His brow creased. "I received nothing. What did it say?"

"I—just that I wasn't being mistreated. That they were treating me with respect." She played with the edge of the cloak.

"They must have lied to you," he reasoned. "Wanted to keep you compliant thinking they allowed you to contact us."

Her eyes brimmed with tears.

"It's okay. You're here now," he said in a rush, not wanting to upset her more. "We got you back and now we just need to get home. So, please. I know it won't be a comfortable journey back, but we really need to get moving again. Okay?" He took one of her hands in his.

Adelaide gave him a slight nod and he helped her to her feet, collecting his cloak and shaking off the dirt. He took her hand again to lead her over to the others. Baxley spread his cloak out for her to sit on before going to get a bowl for each of them. Handing one bowl to Adelaide, he sat down beside her. He groaned as flavor burst over his tongue with his first spoonful, savoring the rich taste.

"This is delicious," he said to Keys.

"Just because we're roughing it, doesn't mean we need to eat like shit," she replied. "Here." She tossed a pair of sturdy boots in Adelaide's direction. "These should fit you."

Adelaide gave her a nod, but didn't say anything.

"Thank you," Baxley responded for her.

"Anything to keep the princess in better spirits," she said, going to fill her bowl for a second helping.

When everyone had their fill and took care of their own needs, they redistributed the supplies amongst the horses and were on their way. The road was busier than it had been in the morning. None of the groups they passed wore the uniforms of soldiers. Nor did they overhear any gossip about a prisoner breaking out of the palace.

After riding for about twenty minutes, Keys had them veer off into the woods again, heading in a northeast direction. She slowed their pace down now that they were off the main road, not as concerned with someone catching up to them. Adelaide, to her credit, lasted a few hours this time before starting to complain. The second her mouth opened to state that her thighs were chafing and would never be the same after this, he noticed Keys increasing the distance between herself and the group. Once the complaining did start, though, it was constant. Baxley did his best to placate her, but as the day wore on, he was running out of encouragements. During one break Keys allowed them to take, Sarja offered to see if there was anything she could do for Adelaide to help soothe her aches.

While they were off behind some trees to provide some privacy, Keys walked by him, patting him on the chest. "You're a lucky man." The smirk that accompanied it told him what she really thought—that he was stupid for being with Adelaide.

Baxley let the comment go, not wanting to start anything with Adelaide within hearing distance. Everyone else looked away from him when she said it. Maybe after this, they agreed with her, too. Adelaide was really a lovely person—truly. She was simply out of her element here. Which he continued telling himself every time a new woe slipped from her mouth. Her gorgeous bow shaped mouth. The mouth that he worshiped with his own. The mouth that usually whispered about how their love could last through anything before kissing him. He tried to focus on that thought when they mounted up again. They had several more hours of daylight and Keys intended to use all of them.

By the time the sun started to sink in the sky, he had grown envious of Keys being able to ride ahead of them—but only slightly. Unfortunately, there was only so much that healing could do for sore muscles, so Adelaide had kept up a steady stream of discontent until Keys called a halt for the evening.

Keys selected a small meadow with a pond for them to spend the night. She slipped away with the bow as the others began setting up camp. He found a spot for Adelaide to rest while he and the others unpacked. They had the tents pitched and a fire going by the time Keys reappeared, carrying two small animals already skinned and dressed.

"I'm not eating that." Adelaide gagged as she watched Keys cutting the meat from the bones and adding it to a large cast iron skillet.

"Where do you think all the meat you eat comes from?" Keys didn't look up from what she was doing.

"That's different," she huffed.

"Why? Because you don't have to watch it being prepared for you? You didn't seem to have a problem with it earlier."

"What do you mean?" Adelaide frowned at her.

"What do you think was in the stew?" Keys finally looked up, cocking her head.

Adelaide gagged again. "I think I'm going to be sick." She lurched up from her spot beside him, heaving as she rushed towards the trees.

"Was that really necessary?" he snapped, pushing himself up to follow her.

"Better she gets used to it now," Keys called after him.

Adelaide hadn't gone far. She leaned against a tree, facing away from everyone, her shoulders shaking slightly.

Baxley sighed, bracing himself. "Are you okay?"

"How could I be okay?" Her voice wavered. "None of this is okay."

His heart dropped, assuming the worst. "Adelaide, what did they do to you in there?"

She turned to face him, tears streaking down her cheeks. "Nothing. They did *nothing*. I was treated with the respect due my station."

"Except for the whole kidnapping thing," he growled.

Adelaide didn't respond to his outburst. "Where are we even going? Why are we not on a ship yet?"

"It was too dangerous to head straight for the coast. We're heading east first."

"East?" Her voice rose higher. "You can't be serious, Baxley. That will take *weeks*. How do you expect me to live like this?" She waved her hand at the tents and fire.

"What do you want me to do, Adelaide? Your safety is a higher priority than your comfort right now."

She swiped at the tears on her face, but stayed silent for a moment. "An inn. I want to stay at an inn."

"I'll talk with Keys and see if that's possible. For tonight, you'll have to make do. Please, can you do that?" He cupped her face, smiling softly down at her. All his efforts had been focused on getting her back, he hadn't spent more than a moment thinking about how hard this journey would be for her. While he had been put through rigorous training both with sword and magic since he was young, she hadn't gone through the same as a princess.

This whole ordeal was probably the hardest thing she'd ever had to live through.

"I'll try." She gave him a tight-lipped smile.

"That's all I ask." He dropped one hand, curling it around her waist, pulling her tight against him. "I think I can convince your father to move the wedding forward when we get back." His thumb stroked across her jaw. "No more waiting. Just you and me. *Finally.*"

Her breath hitched at his words. "Are you sure that's a good idea?"

His eyes flicked down to her mouth. "I need to make you mine."

"Baxley," she murmured.

He dipped his head and claimed her before she could say more. It took a second for her to respond to him, their lips perfectly fusing together. Fuck, how he had missed this mouth of hers. His hand wound into her hair, tilting her head back. His tongue swiped along the seam of her lips until she opened for him. He tasted her. Devoured her. Breathed her in until he felt like she was imprinted on his soul. This was where she belonged — in his arms.

Eventually, she pulled away. "Baxley," she muttered in between his kisses.

He moved down her jaw instead, trailing kisses along her skin.

"Baxley." Her hands landed on his shoulders.

Her neck was one of his favorite things about her. He licked and nipped his way down it.

"Baxley." She gave him a little push.

He sucked her skin into his mouth, causing her to squeak. If he wasn't careful, he would leave a mark. The thought pleased the certain part of him that needed to claim her for his own.

"Baxley." She shoved him harder, forcing him to detach from her neck. Her eyes were fixed over his shoulder at the camp behind him. "The others are watching."

He glanced towards them. They were far enough away that in the dark and with the light from the fire it would be hard to tell what the two of them were doing over here.

"It's fine." He ducked his head to continue where he left off—

"We aren't married yet," she said, bracing her arms to keep space between them. "I don't want to give them the wrong impression."

"Of course," he sighed, disappointed. He let his forehead rest on hers. "I'm sorry. I wasn't thinking. I feel like I'm in a dream and at any moment I'll wake up and you'll be taken away from me again."

"I'm right here," she breathed.

They were both silent for several minutes, simply basking in each other's presence.

"Are you ready to go back?" he finally asked.

"As ready as I can be. I don't want to eat that," she moaned.

"I'll try it first, okay?" He took her hand, tugging her along. "Keys is an excellent cook."

"How well do you know her?"

"Enough to trust her cooking." He still had reservations about her true intentions, even after successfully rescuing Adelaide as promised.

Baxley was able to cajole Adelaide into trying the meat that Keys served them over rice after everyone had gone back for seconds. If she wasn't one of the most notorious thieves of several countries, he might have convinced his father to hire her as a cook at the palace. His taste buds would never be the same after this.

After they were finished, Keys pulled a small tin from her saddle bag and handed it to Adelaide. "Here. Rub that on your thighs. It'll help."

"What is it?" Adelaide asked.

"Just a muscle rub I know how to make. You'll be in that tent with me." Keys pointed to one of the four tents, each one large enough to fit two people. He lucked out on having his own.

"But—" Adelaide looked to Baxley for help, her eyes wide.

"You'll be safest with her." He reached out, squeezing her hand. Baxley might not fully trust her motives, but he did trust her with this. "Do we need to set up a watch?" he turned to ask Keys.

"No," she replied. "We only need to worry about soldiers spotting her during the day. And anyone else who tries to bother us during the night…well, I can handle them. Now, come along, Princess. You've been complaining all day about how tired you are. We'll be up with the sun again come morning."

Chapter 23

BAXLEY

DESPITE HIM ASKING KEYS IF THEY COULD FIND lodgings somewhere for the next night, they passed no taverns or inns the next day or even the following after that. The landscape changed around them as they traveled, the woods thinning, opening up into rolling plains that stretched before them. He had no idea how Keys wasn't completely lost when all she used to navigate with was a compass.

They all fell easily into a pattern at night as if they'd known each other longer than weeks. Keys would go off hunting for dinner. Felix prepped the fire, making sure it was hot and ready for when she returned, while Cain and Arla would start on the tents. And he and Sarja would try to see to anything that would make Adelaide happy—or happier than she was. That was perhaps the hardest task.

On that third night, Baxley caught Arla, Cain, Felix, and Keys whispering amongst themselves after seeing Adelaide to her tent.

"That doesn't count," Cain hissed. "You baited her into that one."

"Oh, just like you did, asking about her nails at lunch?" Keys argued.

"That was different."

"Or, how about when you said you couldn't wait for a proper bath because you still didn't feel clean after bathing in the pond?" Arla chimed in, pointing a finger at him.

"Fine." Cain gritted his teeth. "It counts."

"What're you talking about?" Baxley asked, making his presence known.

The three soldiers were startled by his voice, looking guilty. None of them would meet his eye.

"Just a game." Keys said, an impish grin spreading across her face.

His eyes narrowed on her. "About?" He drew out the word.

"Looks like a good time to turn in." Sarja yawned from her position on the other side of the fire. "Good night, everyone." She rose, hastening to her and Arla's tent.

"Excellent idea. I think I'll turn in, too—" Cain said, pushing up from the ground.

"Sit," snapped Baxley.

Cain immediately plopped back down.

"What game?" He scanned the group. Keys leaned back on her hands, her smile growing wider, clearly not intending to answer him. "Don't make me ask again." He waited to see which of the others would crack first.

Felix proved to be the weak link. "We're just keeping track of how often the princess complains about certain things." He grimaced, still not looking at Baxley.

"Oh, is that all?" His voice dropped. "How do you win, then?"

"By guessing the most voiced complaint," Keys snorted. "Her thighs and ass are obviously off limits, because she never stops complaining about those."

He felt the blood pulsing through his veins, fury rising. "You're betting on her discomfort?" Here she was trying her best, and they were making fun of her behind her back. Sure, the last two days hadn't gone any better than the first, but she was making progress. Very small progress, but progress nonetheless. She'd only claimed she could go no farther at least a handful of times today.

"You *dare* treat your future queen like that? You—who are supposed to be protecting her and putting her above your own lives? I should have all of you stripped of your ranks when we return!" He raged at them, trying to keep his voice low enough that Adelaide wouldn't hear. The three cowed before him.

"Lay off them." Keys broke into his tirade. "Listening to her has been like going through torture. We had to stay sane somehow. Besides, you're the one who's going to marry her. Why should the rest of us suffer?"

His nostrils flared. "You still owe her respect."

Keys straightened up, her expression growing hard. "Respect is earned. She's been nothing but a pain in the ass since leaving the palace. She's slowed us down at every opportunity. Hell, it doesn't even seem like she wants to go back. Why is that, Bax?" She glared at him.

He met her glare with one of his own. "I told you; she's not used to traveling like this."

"You sure that's all it is?"

"Of course," he said, frustrated. "What else would it be?"

She looked down her nose at him, despite her sitting below him. "We'll find out soon enough. Tomorrow, if we push hard, we can stop in a small village—see how amiable she is after that. I still don't advise it, but if we keep our heads down—and her quiet—well, we should be fine." Keys stood, dusting herself off. "If there's nothing else..." She made to walk the way from which he came.

"Almost forgot," she said, snapping her fingers. "Here." Keys tossed a coin to Arla. "You won."

Baxley's curiosity won out and he asked, "What you'd guess?"

"Her hair," Arla murmured.

***

It was sometime after lunch the next day that they came across a smaller road than the main one they had traveled on leaving Gleyra.

"There's a farming village we can stay in tonight if we don't stop every hour," Keys said, her eyes finding Adelaide. "The tavern even has a bath if you pay extra."

Baxley saw Adelaide perk up at that.

They rode hard the next few hours. It was decided they'd forgo a hot dinner and snack on the other foods they had in their packs in favor of making it to the village. He was proud of Adelaide. She only asked them to stop once to relieve herself. Even when the sun dipped behind the horizon, she didn't ask them to stop. Maybe the promise of a bed and bath was really all she needed from the beginning.

They rode by the glow of the light Keys wielded when the sunlight faded. Within an hour, they arrived at the village, which had only one road. Keys led them straight to the single tavern and the stable attached to it. There were no stable hands to be found.

"I don't think my legs work anymore," Adelaide bemoaned as Baxley helped her dismount.

"We're almost there," he assured her.

"Why don't you go on ahead," Felix said. "We can take care of the horses."

"Not without me, you're not," Keys called out. She pulled her saddle bags off her own horse, slinging them over her shoulder. "Remember, keep your head down and mouth shut as much as possible while we're in there. Don't draw unnecessary attention to yourself," she whispered to the both of them. "See the rest of you inside," she said over her shoulder.

The tavern was decently packed with people, several heads turning to regard them as they entered before going back to their own conversations. It probably wasn't every day they had travelers come through being this remote.

"Go grab a table over there." Keys nodded to several that were unoccupied.

They'd have to split up, since none of the tables were large enough for their entire party. Baxley led Adelaide to a table in the far corner. He pulled back a chair for her that would put her facing away from the rest of the room and took the one next to it for himself.

Keys joined them shortly, sliding a key across the table to him. "They only had two rooms available. We'll have to make do."

"And a bath?" Adelaide asked, her eyes gleaming.

She nodded. "There's a bathing room being prepared for you."

He saw Adelaide's shoulders visibly relax at the news.

The others arrived before the food and drinks, taking up a seat at the table next to them. Two servers came, carrying large trays loaded down with the meal Keys had ordered.

The server who placed the food in front of Keys addressed her, saying, "The bathing chamber is the first door on the right upstairs. It'll be ready for you once you finish your meal."

"Thank you," she replied.

Baxley picked up his silverware to dig into his chicken and potatoes.

"I wonder if she has any scented soaps..." Adelaide's gaze followed the server as she walked away. She was up and out of her seat in a flash.

"Don't—" Keys tried to stop her—but it was too late. Adelaide was already several tables away, following the server.

"Fucking hell," muttered Keys, her fists clenching on her fork and knife.

His eyes widened, neck twisting back to watch her. "What do we do?" His heart rate picked up, pounding through him.

Adelaide caught up to the server and was talking to her. He grabbed the watch in his pocket as he scanned the room, looking for anyone who might be paying too much attention to Adelaide.

"Strangle her when she gets back to the table," Keys growled.

The server nodded and said something to Adelaide, who promptly turned around and walked back to them, resuming her seat as if nothing had happened. He released his grip on the watch, heart still racing.

"Are you *out of your mind*?" Keys hissed at her.

He watched Adelaide's eyes round at the venom in her voice.

"What?" Adelaide questioned.

"How is darting across the room by yourself keeping your head down?"

"I—I just wanted scented soaps," she replied, her eyes shifting to him for help.

For once, though, he agreed with Keys and kept his mouth shut.

"And are those scented soaps worth your freedom? Worth your life?"

"I—" she started, but stopped, pausing. "No," she finally admitted.

"You stick with one of us from now on. You need something, we'll get it for you. Understood?"

"Alright."

The silence as they ate was awkward. Baxley didn't work hard at alleviating it. He flinched at any loud noises around the tavern, thinking the worst—that someone had recognized her and was coming to take her away again.

At one point, a louder crash had him whipping around, half rising from his chair, only to find a drunken pair of men had collided with a chair and sprawled on the floor together, laughing. Keys snapped at him for that one and threatened to banish him upstairs whether he was finished eating or not. He worked at hiding his reactions better after that, but remained on high alert until Keys took Adelaide upstairs for her long-awaited bath. He was finally able to breathe a little easier.

Chapter 24

SKELETON KEY

AS SOON AS THE PRINCESS WAS FINISHED EATING, KEYS took her upstairs to the bathing room. The others had brought Adelaide's saddlebags inside with them, and Keys carried them upstairs for her. They were filled with plenty of different outfit options for the princess to choose, though none lived up to her standards. Perish the thought that she might have to dress like a commoner for a few weeks.

Pushing open the bathing room door, Keys surveyed the room, making sure it was secure. A large tub sat along the back wall, already filled with soapy water. Satisfied, she set the bags down to the side, saying, "Lock the door. I'll be waiting right outside the whole time."

"You really think something could happen here?" The princess entered the room.

"If you expect the worst, nothing can surprise you." Keys closed the door behind Adelaide, the lock clicking into place a second later. She took up position across from the door, propped up against the wall. Her own bags she let drop by her feet.

About thirty minutes later, their crew dragged their feet up the staircase.

"She's still in there?" Baxley asked.

"Are you really surprised?" she countered.

He sighed. "No, I guess not. Do you want me to wait for her?"

Keys shook her head. "Go get some rest." She passed the key to the women's room off to Arla and maintained her watch. Both their rooms were at the end of the hallway.

When another twenty minutes had passed, Keys knocked on the door. "Did you fall asleep in there?"

The answer was immediate. "Just a few more minutes," Adelaide squeaked.

The door opened within another ten minutes to reveal a very clean and refreshed princess. It was the most content Keys had seen her so far. Adelaide had changed into a fresh set of clothes — which seemed like a waste of time for the short walk down the hallway to their room, where she was just going to immediately change into her sleepwear. Her damp blonde hair dripped onto her shirt. Clearly, the princess was used to having a servant take care of it for her. Well, *she* wasn't going to offer to do it for her.

Keys picked up both sets of saddlebags and gestured for the princess to lead the way down the hall. "It's the last door on the left," she said, following behind her. A floral scent wafted off of her. Keys gagged on it, breathing through her mouth instead.

The princess reached her hand up to turn the doorknob once they arrived at the correct room, but it didn't budge. "It's locked," she stated the obvious.

"So, knock."

Her tiny fist tapped on the door. A black smudge on the side of her palm caught Keys' attention.

Keys head tilted to the side as she wondered: *Why is there a smudge on her hand after having just taken a bath?*

Arla opened the door for them, stepping aside to let them enter the room. Two extra cots had been squeezed into the small space for their use, barely leaving any room to walk. Keys plopped the bags down in front of one.

"You have the key still?" she turned and addressed Arla.

The soldier nodded, pulling it out of her pocket. "Here."

She took the key from her. "I have some things to take care of. Don't wait up," she said, closing the door behind herself.

Keys made a beeline for the bathing room, the door still hanging open. She closed it behind her, turning the lock. There wasn't much to search in the small room with only the bathtub, toilet, sink, and a vanity. Different soaps were on a shelf by the tub. Adelaide had left her used damp towels in a pile on the floor. Keys moved towards the vanity where some unused towels were still piled. When she lifted up the first towel, something fell out of it, plinking onto the floor.

Keys bent and picked up a bronze coin. What the hell was that doing here? She unfolded the towel and found two more within, along with a rolled-up piece of parchment. It was addressed on the outside to a Lord Bex, to be delivered to the palace at Gleyra.

What the fuck was this?

Keys shifted through the remaining towels, finding ink and a quill stashed beneath them. That would explain the smudge mark she saw on the princess' hand. But how did she get the —

The server! Scented soaps her ass.

Keys smacked her forehead. She had to hand it to her; the princess apparently did have a brain in that head of hers. But why would she be writing to someone in the palace from which she just escaped? Having no qualms against invading her privacy, Keys unrolled the parchment.

To my dearest Cal,

I don't know how to even start this. Baxley came for me. He said he never received my letter that I sent him. Instead, they received a demand for trade negotiations and that I was to be held as insurance. I don't know what to believe. I'm so lost and confused. None of this is what I wanted. It's not what we dreamed of.

I thought your parents agreed to this? I never would have made this decision knowing this is how it would turn out. We travel east. That's all I know. I still cling to hope that we can make this work, while also feeling like it's slowly drifting out of reach. The farther I travel from you the more desperate I become. Yet, I still can't find it in me to break his heart in person. If you come for me, know I can't go back there. I won't let myself be used against my own country or his.

Yours,
A

Keys read the letter twice. Maybe she'd been too hasty in deeming the princess smart. If this letter were to fall into the wrong hands, she could be tried for treason. The princess had, indeed, left on her own, then. Someone in the palace at Aglar must have helped her. Keys' bet was on the lady-in-waiting. It would be the only person she might confide in for a secret this ruinous. She'd run from her betrothal to one prince straight into the arms of another. But how did she and Prince Calbex even meet?

And Baxley had no idea. The princess was a coward—trying to take the easy way out of her engagement. For a second, her heart hurt for him. Once again, she wrestled with the idea of telling Baxley about what she'd seen and discovered of Adelaide and Prince Calbex. It would be the right thing to do—the moral thing. She would want to know if her betrothed had fallen in love with another and planned to run away with them…

Oh well. She shrugged. She was hired to rescue a spoiled princess, not meddle in the love affairs between two opposing princes and a princess.

Good thing her heart beat to a different set of morals. Baxley could figure it out on his own, or not at all. In the meantime, she needed to decide how to handle the princess. All she cared about currently was getting the princess back to Vesperis. After she was returned, Keys didn't care what happened to her. She wouldn't hand the letter over to Baxley, but should she use it as leverage against the princess now?

A drink would help her plan out how she was going to play this new development. Folding the letter and tucking it into her bra, she headed below for the bar.

***

As they left the village, many of the farmers were already out working their fields aided by their magic. The wielders worked together to water their crops, making the smell of damp manure permeate the air. It wasn't helping her current situation. Her head pounded to the beat of her horse's hooves. Last night, one drink turned into two. Two turned into three. Three became four. And soon there was number five, and with it a tongue—that belonged to a handsome man—down her throat.

She had passed on going back to his home to instead collapse in her cot in the early hours of the morning. Cain was quick to notice her hungover state when they set out after breakfast. He'd been relentless in his teasing, until she hit him in the face with a sphere of water. That seemed to shut him up—at least for now.

The floral soap the princess used was still clinging to her. Instead of only making her gag, it also made her queasy today. Several times she'd almost lost her breakfast. How the prince could stand it was beyond her. This day couldn't end soon enough.

The only positive was that the princess did seem to be in a better mood after staying at the tavern for the night. Or maybe her good mood was due to the letter she thought was on its way back to her prince. Keys scoffed at the thought. The village was so remote that it wasn't set up for air messages. They would have had to deliver it to a larger village first before it could be sent on to the palace. It never would have made it in time for Prince Calbex to catch up with them himself. The most he could have done was alert any soldiers this way to be on the lookout for them, which she was already expecting even with Peri's diversion.

The letter was still tucked safely in her bra. After finding the coins the princess left for the server, Keys had counted out the money she had stashed in her own saddlebags, finding several coins missing. Obviously, the princess couldn't be trusted not to go through Keys' things, so she'd have to keep it on her person. As long as Adelaide's newfound perseverance continued, Keys decided she wouldn't mention the letter. But if the princess started complaining endlessly and slowing them down again, she would use it as some...persuasion to bolster her along.

Rather than veering off the road again, Keys chose to keep them on their current path. It would eventually lead them where they needed to go, and if it did actually keep the princess in better spirits, then she would take it.

Today was the hottest day they'd experienced, signaling summer would soon be on its way. The sun beat down on them from overhead, roasting her alive. Or maybe it just felt that way as the liquor leaked out of her pores while she sweat. She used her magic to create a breeze, stirring up the stagnant air. Wind brushed over her sweat-drenched skin, helping to cool her down some. She breathed a sigh of relief just as a whiny voice rang out from behind her.

"What's that atrocious smell? It's repulsive."

Cain roared with laughter before answering the princess. "*That* is the smell of regret."

Keys sent another sphere of water shooting for him.

"Maybe you should save some of that water to bathe in," he snickered.

"It's making me nauseous," the princess moaned.

"Now you know how I feel," she muttered under her breath, but otherwise ignored her.

A few minutes later, the princess spoke up again. "Are we going to have to smell this the entire day? I'm going to be sick."

"Keys, just blow the air in another direction," Baxley called up to her from his position riding next to Adelaide.

She sent a huge gust of wind straight at him instead. He let out a cry of surprise as it nearly unseated him from his horse.

"Real mature."

She smirked, but did redirect the breeze to blow to the side.

The day dragged on, trying her patience. She didn't argue when the princess had them stopping every few hours. They passed over a small bridge in the early afternoon where she actually called for a break herself. It was only a shallow river, but it would still serve her purpose.

Dismounting from her horse, she fished out a bar of soap. She left the horse to graze as it pleased, not worried about it wandering far. There was no privacy to be found with the plains spreading out around them. That didn't bother her, though, as she began to strip off her clothes at the edge of the river.

"What do you think you're doing?" the princess shrieked.

"Bathing, since my smell was so offensive to your sensitive nose," Keys replied, wading into the water. The chill of it was a nice relief after baking in the sun all day. It came to about her waist once she reached the middle of the river.

"This is highly inappropriate."

Keys rolled her eyes, not seeing the problem since her underthings still remained on. She ducked down in the water, getting her upper body wet, and began scrubbing with the soap.

"Baxley, are you going to allow her to do this?" Adelaide huffed.

Keys turned around to regard them. Adelaide stood with her arms crossed, facing Baxley as he walked towards her.

"Yea, Bax," Keys called, sending a spiral of water his way. It landed short of his feet. "What're you going to do? Punish me?"

"I don't *allow* her to do anything. She just does. Come on, Adelaide." Baxley took her hand, trying to pull her in the opposite direction.

"She calls you *Bax*?" She heard the princess hiss at him.

"Not by my choice," was the response he gave back.

Cain provided a distraction by scooping up a squealing Sarja and charging into the river to join Keys. Sarja let out another shriek when he dunked her beneath the water.

"I'm still in my clothes, you idiot," she gasped, surfacing.

"Those needed washing, too," he laughed.

Keys snorted, tossing her bar of soap to Sarja.

"Come on Felix, Arla," Cain yelled. "The water is amazing." He sent a small wave at Sarja, which splashed her in the face.

She retaliated by throwing the bar of soap at him. He only just managed to dodge it, and then plucked it from the water before it could be lost. Pulling his sopping shirt off, he flung it to shore—nearly hitting an undressing Arla—and started scrubbing with the soap. His pants shortly followed.

Arla stripped down like Keys, but Baxley had managed to drag the princess far enough away by then, preventing her from commenting on it. Felix was the only one left standing on the bank, contemplating the ensuing madness in the water.

"Let's go, Felix!" Keys called out to him. She remembered his hesitancy to share a bed with her and wondered if this would be another situation in which he felt uncomfortable.

"Don't make me carry you in like Sarja," Cain added, grinning.

That got Felix moving. His shirt hit the ground, and when he started on his pants, Cain let out a wolf whistle. Arla joined in, hooting and hollering. Felix stuck a hand out, flicking off both of them. It quickly evolved into a three-way water fight.

Keys chuckled to herself and left them to it. She sank back, floating in the lazy current. Her head finally stopped pounding with the help of the flowing water after a tortuous day. It was blissful…

Her bliss only lasted so long when a wave of water splashed over her. She coughed and sputtered, turning narrowed eyes on the trio. Standing up, she gathered water behind her, letting it float in the air.

Cain was the first to notice. "Oh, shit."

And then she showed them what water could really do.

Chapter 25

SKELETON KEY

STILL NOT FEELING COMPLETELY HERSELF, KEYS allowed them to convince her to stop early for the night in another small village where there was an inn they could acquire lodging. Not wanting a repeat of the night before, she stayed glued to the princess' side while they dined, even escorting her to the bathing room when she needed to relieve herself.

The following day the princess' mood was sour once more, despite having a roof over her head and a bed. The steady stream of dissatisfaction with their circumstances renewed. It was made worse when they didn't come across another village, forcing them to camp for the night instead. They were already further behind schedule than Keys would like, so she pushed them until the last light of the day faded.

Adelaide's mood deteriorated more, if that was even possible, the next day when they reached the start of the Sutra Plains. The Cathburn Mountains ran almost the entire length of Vesperis' southern border with Voglar. The wind patterns blew in a southeast direction, which meant the Vesperis territory received heavy rainfall along the mountain range, leaving Voglar's territory with a semi-arid climate. Villages and cities sprang up around areas where people strong with water magic had been able to detect underground water sources. Those strong water wielders were treasured here. They were essential to help support life.

The city Keys aimed for now was situated on the edge of the Sutra Plains. It was a regular stopping point for her travels when passing through—the perfect place to trade any horses in for the better suited camels. Keys grew giddy with anticipation. Camels were one of her favorite animals, which was a surprise with how much she loved the sea. There was just something about them.

"Oh, thank goodness," the princess croaked when the city came into view ahead of them on the road. "We're stopping, right?"

It was only a little past noon, the sun high in the sky. "Only for supplies. Baxley, Felix, and Adelaide, you'll be coming with me. The rest of you head to the market. Tell them you'll need clothing to make the journey across the plains."

"And what will we be doing?" Baxley asked.

"Acquiring the camels." The smile that spilled across her face was the first real one since they began this whole mess. Baxley stared at her, his jaw hanging open. "What?" she asked, while Adelaide shrieked in the background about not riding a camel.

Before he could respond, the princess swept down upon them in a blaze of fury. "You can't be serious? I can't ride a *camel*."

"You said that about horses," Keys muttered to herself.

The princess continued, unfazed. "I won't. I refuse. This is ridiculous. *Insanity*. I've never been treated this way in my entire life."

"What do you want me to do, Adelaide? We have to cross the Sutra Plains," Baxley sighed, trying to explain to her. He looked like a man hanging on to his sanity by a thread.

"Find another way," she replied, crossing her arms and nearly toppling off her horse from the force.

"There is no other way!" he roared at her, his chest heaving with his breaths.

Keys' eyes rounded at the prince's outburst, which seemed to come out of nowhere. She was used to him being difficult with her, but never would have expected it to be directed towards his betrothed; no matter how taxing this journey had been so far.

The princess' face blanched, probably having never been spoken to that way—by anyone. She could add it to her list of firsts. Keys watched the pair, unsure what would happen next.

Adelaide recovered first, saying, "You will not speak to me in such a manner!" Her tone conveyed her anger, color tinting her cheeks.

"I will if you're being unreasonable."

Not the best thing to say to a woman when she's angry.

"*Unreasonable?*" Adelaide's voice reached a whole new pitch that had Keys flinching. "The only unreasonable thing here is you and this plan!"

"The best minds in my country came up with this plan to get you home and all you've been is ungrateful."

"Maybe I don't want to go home with you anymore!" the princess screamed at him, yanking her horse to a stop.

Baxley reined his horse up next to her. "Then go! Get home on your own!"

The pair glowered at each other, both refusing to concede, faces flushing. Angry tears filled the princess' eyes. None of the others stepped in to break up the fight, and she wasn't about to either. It was a long time coming in her opinion. Keys was just glad no one else was on the road to witness their showdown.

Finally, Baxley scoffed before he wheeled his horse to face the city, spurring it into a gallop.

A laugh burst from Keys at the shocked expression on Adelaide's face. She smothered it as best she could when the princess' angry gaze whipped her way. "Arla, Cain, Sarja, go after him. We'll meet at the market," she quickly spouted off orders. She turned to regard the princess after the three raced off down the road. "Are you coming along willingly, or do I need to force you?"

"Where else would I go?" The princess threw out her arms, gesturing to the landscape all around them.

"Exactly." Keys' eyes narrowed on her, finding her lacking in many ways. "You have no idea what he's given up to get you back." And she wasn't referring to the crown. She followed after the others before the princess could respond, leaving her to dwell on that thought.

***

The man who she was looking for owned stables on the farther side of the city, closer to the start of the plains. He had multiple fenced-in pastures for his animals to roam. She spotted him in one of the fields, sitting on a boulder and playing a ukulele to the surrounding camels.

"Wait here," she said to Felix. "Make sure she doesn't go anywhere."

"Again, where am I going to go?" the princess retorted.

Keys disregarded her and dismounted, tying her horse to a fence post. She hopped the fence, changing her face as she did. Her nose broadened, mouth widening—the teeth inside it becoming crooked. Her eyes changed to a dark gray while her brows thickened. Freckles sprang up, splashed across her face. The man—Tebak—only knew her as Ksenia.

His singing carried to her as she strolled his way.

"There once was a man who drank so much, they claimed he was part fish.

He travelled up and down the land wherever he might wish.

Amazing all who came to see how much he could fit.

Until one day he came upon a busy little town.

And there they dragged him in the bar to drink till he was sick.

"What's first?" they called. "What's first?"

The bartender pulled out some ale, pouring him a glass.

"A drink," they called. "A drink. Give the man a drink."

He drank that down. The crowd cheered loud till all the ale was gone.

"What's next?" they called. "What's next?"

The bartender pulled out the wine, pouring him a glass.

"A drink," they called. "A drink. Give the man a drink."

He drank that down. The crowd cheered loud till all the wine was gone.

"What's next?" they called. "What's next?"

The bartender pulled out the liquor, pouring him a glass.

"A drink," they called. "A drink. Give the man a drink."

He drank that down. The crowd cheered loud till all the liquor was gone.

"What's next?" they called. "What's next?"

The bartender just shook his head, having emptied his whole bar.

"The well," they called. "The well." And flooded out to the well.

He drank that down. The crowd cheered loud till all the well was gone.

"What's next?" they called. "What's next?"

The man shook his head, having no idea what they could give him now.

"The pond," they called. "The pond." And ran over to the pond.

He drank that down. The crowd cheered loud till all the pond was gone.

"What's next?" they called. "What's next?"

The man shook his head, wondering what they'd come up with next.
"The sea," they called. "The sea."

He drank that down. The crowd cheered loud till all the sea was
gone and the man fell over dead."

"Always a pleasure to hear your voice, Tebak," she called out
to him.

The man paused his playing, turning towards her. A wide
grin spread across his face when he recognized her. "Ksenia,
always a pleasure to be visited by you." He took up strumming
on the instrument again.

"Ah, is it me or my coin you enjoy?"

"You wound me, my dear. Can it not be both?"

She chuckled. "Yes, well, you'll *enjoy* me immensely this time.
I need seven camels and have seven horses to trade."

"Seven?" He missed a note. "You usually travel much
lighter."

"Circumstances are different this time," she said, shrugging.
"Do you have them or not?"

"For a price."

"Name it."

"Two gold pieces."

"May Death Adder take you." She clucked her tongue.
"That's steep, even for you. Especially when the camels are
trained to return to you."

"Take it or leave it."

There really wasn't a choice. "Is Vincent here?"

"In the field over."

"Have him and six others saddled in the stables in an hour
and you have a deal." She tossed him two gold coins and spun to
walk back to the others, her face morphing as she did.

"Pleasure doing business with you," he called after her.

She flicked him off over her shoulder. The man was a crook.

***

They found the others in the market just finishing up shopping. Baxley refused to look in the princess' direction at all, his gaze icy.

"Is this going to be a problem?" Keys asked, sidling up next to him.

"No." His jaw clenched.

"Good. See that it doesn't become one. Apologies go a long way, you know."

"*I* have nothing to apologize for."

"Right." Sarcasm dripped from the word.

Keys made them all change before leaving the market. The flowing linen clothing would help with the heat they were about to experience during the day. She made sure everyone had a head scarf, too. If the wind picked up and started blowing, getting sand in their eyes would be a real hazard.

By the time they returned to the stables, Tebak was gone. Keys found seven camels saddled and ready to go in the different stalls, Vincent among them.

"Hello, friend," Keys greeted Vincent. "It's been a while." She scratched down his neck, exactly where he liked it. Pulling some apple slices from her pocket, she slipped them to him, muttering, "Don't tell the others." Apples were his favorite.

They swapped all their bags and gear over and left their horses in empty stalls. Getting Adelaide to mount the camel proved to be a challenge—though not an unexpected one.

"They smell," she complained.

"You'll get used to it," Keys said, already annoyed.

"It'll be even harder to fall off them than the horse." Sarja tried to coax her on as well.

Keys grimaced. That wasn't always necessarily true, but if it got the princess on, then she wasn't going to correct it.

"They're two humped beasts," Adelaide grumbled.

"Bactrian," Keys stated.

"What?"

"They're Bactrian camels," she explained.

"I don't care what they are, I'm not getting on them!" the princess shrieked.

"Look how easy it is," Sarja said, waving to the others who were already mounted.

"I already told you I don't want to," Adelaide lamented, stomping a foot.

"And I told *you* there wasn't another way." Baxley directed his camel over to them. "Get on the fucking camel!" he yelled down at Adelaide, pointing to her camel.

"Not helping," Keys snapped at him. What was his problem today? "Go back with the others if you're only going to cause more trouble." This was not how she thought this trip was going to go at all. So much for the prince fussing over the princess. Turns out, he did have his limits on how much he could take with her attitude. By the end of this, their betrothal might lay in tatters — for more reasons than the obvious. She snorted. They were doomed. It was only a matter of time before he saw it, too. He couldn't be that dense, could he?

Snapping out of her musings, she turned to help console the princess with Sarja. Large tears streamed down Adelaide's cheeks.

Fuck's sake, this woman cried a lot.

"You're both just stressed." Sarja rubbed the princess' arms.

"He's never treated me this way before," Adelaide sniffled.

"While he might have said it like an ass, he is right. For us to bypass the plains would take at least a month and move us in the wrong direction. This is our only way forward, which means you need to get on the camel." Keys hoped spelling it out for her would make her more agreeable.

"Fine." She finally relented.

Glad one of them was starting to be reasonable, Keys helped the princess mount. While she wasn't above tying up Adelaide, it would still be much easier and more discrete to avoid that. Now if only Baxley would get his shit together.

Once they were all mounted, Keys led them out of the city. The landscape quickly changed along the road. Small shrubs and tall grasses replaced all the lush greenery through which they'd been riding. Only drought resistant trees survived the lack of rain here. They sparsely dotted the land, allowing them to see for miles around.

The first village they would come across would take almost a half day's travel to reach. With no hope of making it that far today, Keys stretched out her senses when the sun descended in the sky, searching for any underground water sources close to the road. Finding none, she settled with finding the most vegetation around, choosing to stop there for the night.

The princess must have accepted her fate, or else felt dejected from her argument with the prince, because she hadn't said a word since getting on the camel. Even after learning they'd be camping for the night, her mouth remained closed. She retreated into their tent as soon as it was set up for her and refused to come out for dinner. Sarja took pity when no one else would and took her a bowl of the jackrabbit stew Keys had cooked for them.

After eating, Keys hollowed out a hole in the ground by where the camels were resting. She reached out, feeling for all the water particles in the surrounding vegetation—and then she forcefully yanked on them. The plants withered and died as the water slowly trickled towards her. Her brow furrowed with the effort it required to go against the natural order of things. This wasn't simple redirection; it was bending nature to her will. Keys directed the water into the hole, filling it up for the camels to be able to drink. Her breath whooshed out of her when she finished, muscles shaking.

"How did you do that?" Felix asked from behind her.

She jumped, not realizing he had crept up on her while she was focused.

"Sorry," he chuckled. "Didn't mean to startle you."

"I wasn't startled."

"Sure, you weren't." He smiled widely at her.

"I wasn't," she said, glaring at him.

"I think this is a day to remember. Maybe I should celebrate it every year." He stroked his chin. "The day I scared Skeleton Key."

"Watch it. Unless you want to find a snake in your bedding as well."

Felix cringed. "Who's bedding did you put a snake into?"

"Cain's." She smirked. "Bastard didn't think I'd realize it was him pranking me."

"That's my tent! What if it slithers out of his bedding and into mine?"

"Don't be a baby about it. It's just a kingsnake. Not like it's a rattlesnake."

"I don't like snakes." His whole body shuttered.

"Then best not go to bed first."

"Back to this." Felix gestured to the small puddle behind her where one of the camels was now drinking. "How'd you do that?"

"Pulled the water from the plants. Simple."

"That's not simple. I've never seen it done before, or even heard of it being possible. Some can collect moisture from the air, but this…it's astounding. Can you do it to a person?"

Her brow arched. "Are you volunteering to find out?"

"Never mind."

"I assume I could, but expect it would be more difficult than plants. It's not the way nature works. Working against it is more strenuous," she explained.

"But you held off the waves for hours when we were on the ship."

She shook her head. "I *redirected* the waves for hours. There's a difference. To nudge them towards a new path is one thing, to force them the opposite way would have been another." Keys eyed his tattoo. "You could probably redirect a sand storm if you needed to, or at least parts of it, depending on how powerful you are."

"I've never even *seen* a sand storm."

"Hope you never do." It was a very real possibility while they traveled across the plains. "Do you use your magic while fighting, or only your gift?"

"Usually just my gift," he admitted.

"You should practice your magic more. It's not only useful for farmers, you know."

A scream interrupted them, coming from Cain's tent. A slew of curse words followed.

Keys doubled over with laughter. "Looks like you won't have to worry about that snake."

Chapter 26

BAXLEY

THE PAST FEW DAYS HAD BEEN ESPECIALLY TAXING FOR Baxley. His temper had gotten the better of him when it came to Adelaide. He had never seen her this malcontent—didn't know how to handle it. It felt like she pushed and pushed and pushed—until he finally snapped. Nothing seemed to make her happy. Nothing he did mattered.

As soon as he rode away from her towards the city, he regretted the words he'd yelled at her in frustration. But his pride wouldn't let him turn back. All of this was for her—for her safety. Why couldn't she see that? Why did she seem so angry? What more could he do?

Arla had cornered him while they had been at the market. "An interesting tactic you used back there," she said.

He had ducked his head in shame. "Not one of my finest moments. The way she's acting...she's not herself. I don't know what to do about it—how to react." His fists clenched by his side. "She's like a completely different person."

"Maybe to you she is, but..." Arla trailed off.

"But?" Baxley prompted her.

"She has a reputation around the palace of being *difficult* for the staff."

"No one's ever said anything to me."

"You think any of them would dare?"

"I would have hoped they'd bring any of their concerns to my attention," he replied, frowning.

"A spoiled princess is hardly a large concern."

They both paused for a moment. Maybe he didn't really know Adelaide well at all. Most of their time together was spent in their own respective countries. They relied on letters to communicate. Of course, he went to visit as often as his father allowed, but that was few and far between. The last three months she'd spent at the palace, before being abducted, was the longest period of time they'd seen each other in person. She could have been putting up a front this whole time, and he never would have known. The thought didn't sit well with him.

"Have you asked her what happened while she was in there?" Arla finally asked.

"She said nothing happened. That they treated her well. It doesn't make sense."

"And do you believe her?"

"I don't know. Fuck, I thought this would be easier once we had her back." He dragged a hand through his hair. "Now, I don't know what to think. What to feel."

"Whatever you do, maybe try yelling less."

They'd gone back to their shopping after that.

And not even an hour later, he'd found himself going against her advice, yelling at Adelaide over the camels. He was just so tired. Tired of her complaining. Tired of her whining. Tired of her not making the best out of a poor situation.

At present, guilt ate at him while he stared into their fire, turning the conversation with Arla over again in his head. Pride kept him away earlier; embarrassment kept him away now. He knew he should go and apologize to Adelaide. Try to talk about what happened between them. Try to understand more of what she's going through since being here. But he'd never had to deal with something like this before. He didn't know *how*. He wished his mother was here to ask for her advice. Or even his sister, so he could have someone to talk it out with who didn't report to him as the prince.

If he didn't do anything, would they return to normal once they were home? The perfect, in love couple. Would she stay, or would she call off their engagement? Did he want her to stay? This was ridiculous. He shook his head to stop his thoughts from spiraling further. He *loved* her. And she loved him. Of course they'd still be together. This was just a bump along the way caused by circumstances beyond either of their control. *Right?*

Dusting his pants off, he pushed himself to standing, resolved to go talk to her. A scream suddenly cut through the air from one of the tents. His hand went straight for the dagger stashed at his hip. Cain started cursing loudly—something about a snake. He noticed Keys bent over in a fit of laughter. Whatever was going on, Keys was definitely involved in it. His hand fell away from his dagger, body relaxing. Before Baxley could make it to Adelaide's tent, Cain emerged from his own, holding a wiggling snake by the tail. The soldier's eyes found the laughing Keys immediately.

"You put a *snake* in my sheets?" Cain thundered, stomping over to her while holding the snake as far away from himself as possible. The snake twisted up on itself while he was distracted, biting onto his hand. Cain squealed, yelling, "Get it off! Get it off!" He flung his hand around wildly, sending the snake flying. It landed a few feet away, unharmed.

Keys fell to the ground, gasping for breath in between her laughter. "I think I peed myself a little." She wiped tears from her face.

Baxley's mouth became a thin line. He'd told Cain not to mess with her. He could deal with the consequences on his own. Leaving them to their own devices, he ducked into Adelaide's tent. The food Sarja brought to her earlier sat untouched. She was curled up on her side, facing the wall of the tent.

"Are you not hungry?" he asked, not sure what else to say.

She flinched at the sound of his voice, twisting his way. Her face was red and blotchy; she clearly had been crying. The guilt he was feeling heightened at the sight. He'd done this to her.

"What're you doing in here?" she asked, voice nasally from being stuffed up.

"I came to check on you."

"Don't see why you bothered." She rolled back away from him.

"Adelaide," he sighed, sitting down next to her. "Please."

The silence stretched between them.

Evidently, she wasn't going to be the first one to talk, and he would have to try something unless he wanted to sit here all night. "I'm sorry for earlier. I shouldn't have said those things to you."

"You've never talked to me that way before." She sniffled.

"I know. Please, look at me."

She acquiesced to his request, turning back over.

"I don't know what to do for you right now. Nothing makes you happy. What do you need? What can I do?"

Tears filled her eyes. "I don't know." Her gaze lowered from his, staring down at the bedding.

"Would traveling slower help, even though it'll take us longer to get there?"

"I don't know," she repeated, whispering.

"Should I insist on us staying at an inn every night?"

"I don't know."

Frustration started to build within him. He fought to keep it contained. If she didn't know, then how the hell was he supposed to know? "Should we try and get you a horse again?"

"I don't know."

"Then how am I supposed to help you if you don't even know," he snapped, voicing his thoughts.

"I don't know!" she yelled, sitting up. "I don't know, I don't know, I don't know." The words spilled from her over and over. "I just can't be...here. I never expected any of this. I didn't want *this*." Her fists slammed down onto her bedding. "How did it even come to this?" A sob slipped past her lips. Once the one was out, more followed. Her face dropped into her hands, shoulders shaking with the force of her sobbing.

His temper cooled instantly. "Adelaide," he murmured, not sure how he should comfort her. He settled with scooting closer and trying to wrap his arms around her as best he could. She leaned in to him, but her tears didn't subside. Baxley started rocking her back and forth, making shushing noises.

It took several minutes for the tears to let up, her breathing finally returning to a normal pace.

"Are you sure nothing happened while you were in there?" Baxley whispered, squeezing her tighter. If someone had touched her—done something to her—he didn't know what he would do. "You know you can tell me anything."

"Nothing happened. I already told you that." She tried to shake him off.

He didn't relinquish his hold on her. "I find that hard to believe with the way you've been acting."

Adelaide stilled in his arms. "You think I'm lying?"

"I'm merely trying to understand what's going on with you."

"Nothing's going on with me," she grounded out, her tone dropping.

"Clearly something is. It feels like you don't want to be here."

"I *don't* want to be here." She pushed away from him again.

He relented this time, letting her pull away. Their eyes locked onto one another. The space separating them felt like an impassable canyon. "Like you didn't want me to come for you," he clarified, searching her face for answers. Something that Keys had said about Adelaide had been sticking with him; that it seemed like Adelaide didn't want to go back to Vesperis. Could that possibly be true?

She looked away from him, a strange expression flitting across her face for a second, making his heart drop. "You didn't want me to come for you, or you no longer want to marry me?" he choked out, the words getting stuck in his throat. His chest felt like a heavy weight was crushing him alive. He felt like he was going to be sick. His hand fumbled for his pocket watch, trying to ground himself.

Her gaze shot back to his. "How could you even ask me that?"

"What else am I supposed to think?" He was the one to look away this time.

Her hand slipped into his. "I'm simply overwhelmed. This all has been a lot to handle. Nothing has changed between us."

"You're sure?"

"Yes." Her hand squeezed his.

"You still want to marry me?" His heart was in his throat, waiting for her answer.

"Of course." Another tear slipped out from the corner of her eye.

"Then how can I help you?" he asked as a few more tears joined the other. He released his watch, reaching up to brush them away.

"Time. Give me time."

Something inside him still didn't feel right, but he nodded anyway.

"Will you hold me for a little while?" Adelaide tried to smile, though it appeared forced.

"Of course."

She laid back down, and he tucked in behind her, curling himself around her. Pushing his uneasiness aside, he whispered stories of their past to her. Like the time her one brother caught them kissing and nearly pummeled him to death. He'd returned to Aglar with a black eye; his father had not been pleased. And the time she took him to view the Falls of Bromier. Baxley had tried to coax her to go for a swim, but she refused. And the moment he'd seen her on the ship when she arrived at Aglar to stay until they were wed. He thought he'd died where he stood. He was the luckiest man in the world, and all his dreams were finally coming true.

When her breathing evened out, he whispered, "Adelaide?"

She didn't respond to him.

Easing away, he collected the bowl of food and returned to the campfire. Only Keys remained; all the others must have turned in for the night.

"You could have taken my tent."

"I was fine." She eyed the bowl he was holding. "Are you going to eat that?"

"Have at it." Baxley passed the bowl over, sitting down next to her.

He felt only somewhat better about where he and Adelaide stood before he had entered the tent. It could have gone worse he supposed. Maybe he was overreacting. Maybe everything was fine and he was so used to living in a state of anxiety that he was looking for problems where there weren't any. But why wasn't Keys driving him crazy still, then? The two of them were finally getting along, and he wasn't sure what to make of it. That smile he caught on her face earlier knocked the breath from him —

"Did you work out whatever is going on between the two of you?" Her question cut into his thoughts.

"We're fine." If he said it enough, maybe he would believe it.

"Be a shame if you did all this for her for nothing," she said around a bite of food.

He stiffened. "Even if something happens to us, it still would have been worth it."

"If you say so," she snorted.

"I could never leave her there. She doesn't deserve that." He still didn't know if he believed her when she said nothing was done to her. Maybe she was hiding it from him, hoping to save his feelings.

"A word of advice," she started, lowering her spoon, "at some point, you're going to have to put your country before her."

"I'll never let it come to that," he growled, ready to defend Adelaide no matter what was happening between them.

"It might not be your choice."

Baxley didn't reply, letting them lapse back into silence. Keys left when she finished the food, yet still he remained. His mind was too heavy for sleep tonight.

Chapter 27

SKELETON KEY

TENSION STILL RADIATED BETWEEN BAXLEY AND THE princess, but at least they were interacting with each other again after yesterday—even if it was in a very formal manner. Their conversations were polite enough, yet it seemed like neither knew how to truly move forward. It was exhausting watching them awkwardly skirt around each other throughout the day. They were acting like teenagers. Though maybe that was an accurate description. Surely nobility had very little dating experience. Hell, this was probably the first woman he'd officially courted and then became engaged to. No wonder they were a mess.

Keys took full advantage of the princess' distraction, pushing them as hard as she dared. They passed through one village well before lunch, but she didn't allow them to stop. With the pace she was able to set, they managed to reach another village come nightfall. It surrounded a lake, the buildings spiraling outwards from there.

She chose an inn, rather than any of the taverns, for them to stay at for the night. It was unlikely for them to come across any soldiers at this particular village, but if they did, they were more likely to frequent the taverns. Adelaide insisted on taking a bath again, to the point that upon learning there was no bathtub here, she wanted them to relocate to a different establishment. She was so vehement that Keys immediately nixed the idea, telling the princess that she'd have to make do with a shower. Considering the last time she took a bath, the princess wrote a letter to Prince Calbex, Keys wasn't about to go out of her way to give her a second chance.

Instead, she stayed plastered to the princess as best she could until they retreated to their bedchamber for the night. There were enough rooms available that the women didn't have to all squeeze into one. Keys kept Adelaide with her—not trusting that she wouldn't try anything else.

She didn't have to wait long to see what the princess had planned next. About an hour after they went to sleep, she heard the princess get up and head for the door. The door clicked open, letting the dim light from the hallway flood into the room.

"What're you doing?" Keys sat up immediately.

Adelaide slammed the door closed, plunging them back into darkness. "I—"

Keys sent a ball of light up to see her.

"Don't make me ask again," she warned.

"I was hungry."

"Bullshit." Keys narrowed her gaze. "Want to try again?"

The princess shifted on her feet, not saying anything.

"How about I take a guess?" She tossed back the blankets, swinging her legs off the bed. "You were going to try and write another one of these." Keys pulled out the folded letter from within her top.

Color drained from the princess' face. "I don't know what you're talking about."

"No?" She unfolded it. "Would you like me to read it to you?"

Adelaide didn't respond.

"To my dearest Cal," Keys started reading. Her voice higher and whiny, mocking the princess. "I don't know how to even start this. Baxley came—"

"Stop!" Adelaide jerked forward, hand outstretched towards the letter. "Give that back to me."

"I think not," Keys replied, folding it and tucking it safely away.

"How'd you get that?"

"You really thought you were being clever? I should take this to the prince. You let me think you'd been compromised against your will." Keys stood up, stalking towards her. "You make it worse for women who have been. Who no one believes." Her eyes blazed into the coward before her.

"Please," the princess begged.

"Here's what we're going to do. You cooperate for the rest of the trip. No more whining. No more trying to sneak away and write letters. You suck up whatever I tell you to, and he won't ever see this. You're coming back with me, one way or another. What you do once you get there, I couldn't give two shits about. You fuck shit up...I'll ruin you."

Adelaide stared at her for a second before responding with, "He won't believe you." Her chin raised higher.

"Then by all means, test it and find out. You're only hurting yourself."

After a moment, the princess asked, "You won't give it to him or anyone else?"

"As long as you hold up your end of the deal, no one will see it."

The princess' lips pressed together in a straight line. "I'll do what you say."

"Wonderful. Start by getting back in bed. I'd like to get *some* fucking sleep tonight."

***

The next few days were the smoothest they'd had since leaving Aglar. They were able to cover a considerable amount of ground as the camels plowed on ahead. The princess stuck to their agreement and kept her mouth shut, whether they were able to stay at a village or not. It was such a nice change of pace that Keys started to enjoy her time traveling with the group.

By the second day, Baxley became suspicious of the drastic change in the princess' attitude and confronted Keys.

"Did something happen between you two the other night at the inn, after we all went to bed?" he asked, riding up next to her later in the evening.

Her eyes darted to him and then ahead again. "She and I came to an…understanding."

"What did you do?"

"Does it matter what, if it worked?"

His jaw clenched. "If you threatened her—" he started.

"I merely made her aware of what's at stake." Keys raised her palms up.

"She already knows what's at risk," he fumed.

"Yes, well sometimes one needs it spelled out for them."

He didn't respond, but still stayed riding next to her.

"Your life is going to be very interesting if you keep her by your side," she said after a time. That might be an understatement. His life was more likely to be destroyed with her around.

"Going to try and give me more unwanted advice?"

"Sometimes the unwanted advice is the most helpful," she chuckled.

Silence fell between them again until Baxley said, "Well you've never held your opinion back from me yet. What else do you have to say about it?"

"She may be what you want, but is she what you *need*?"

"Is there a difference?"

"When it comes to your country, yes. Does she compliment you? Pick up where you lack? Push you to be a better leader? Show empathy to your citizens?"

He gazed out towards the horizon. "I love her. The rest of it, I'll deal with."

"You'll be a king one day; you can't afford to marry only for love." Her eyes stayed locked on him, assessing his reaction.

"My father married for love." His tone held a touch of yearning to it.

"And he got lucky that your mother turned into a worthy queen. Not everyone is up for the task. Is she?"

He turned to look at her with hard eyes. "That is none of your concern."

"It's a concern of your citizens. What kind of king are you going to be?"

He studied her before replying, "For a thief, you have a lot to say about politics."

"You'd be surprised how much it all comes into play for one with my profession."

Baxley rode away instead of saying anything else.

*****

Two days later, they finally reached Opora, a larger city that sat in the middle of an oasis. Several natural springs made the land lush. The land closest to the springs was developed for farming. Fluorite, gypsum, and feldspar magic all worked in tandem here to help keep the land fertile and prosperous.

Ideally, they would have been able to skirt the city as it was likely to have soldiers stationed at it; however, the next leg of their journey through the Sutra Plains would be traveling through the harshest part, and they needed to restock supplies, as food sources would become scarce.

Keys had them stay together, unwilling to separate in case there was trouble. The market was teeming with activity, people and animals everywhere. She spotted a couple of soldier uniforms amongst the crowd and steered the group clear of them. Merchants pressed in on them, trying to sell their wares. Children darted around, laughing and chasing one another. Several of their camels became unsettled by the forced close proximity. Not Vincent, though; he was the best boy. She patted him on the hump in front of her. Cain, Arla, and the princess had to dismount or risk being thrown as the streets grew busier. Baxley followed suit, not wanting to leave Adelaide's side.

Keys led them to several different stalls where they were able to restock everything they'd be needing in the coming days. They were just over halfway through the plains. A few more days and they'd be back in Vesperis.

"Mount back up. They should be calmer here," Keys said to the others, who were still not back on their camels when they reached the edge of the market.

Baxley helped Adelaide coax her camel into laying down so she could clamber up into the saddle and went to mount his own once she was seated. As her camel started to rise, it stumbled on its front legs. Adelaide lurched to the side with the movement, unable to right herself with her lack of experience. She tumbled to the ground, letting out a piercing scream.

"Adelaide," Baxley cried, having no chance of making it there in time to catch her.

Keys reacted on instinct, sending a gust of wind to help cushion the princess' fall. The princess plopped onto the ground, barely being jostled. Her screeching continued, others pausing to stare at her. The camel lumbered to its feet, moving away from the hysterical woman. Fuck, this wasn't good. Jumping down from Vincent, Keys started straight for the princess. Baxley got there first—right when Adelaide started screaming words.

"No! I'm done," she yelled, slapping his hand away. "I'm a princess. A *princess*! I should never have been forced on that bloody beast in the first place."

"Shut her up! Now!" Keys roared. She scanned the crowd around them, palming the dagger at her hip. Not spotting any uniforms, she whirled back to the pair.

"I said no." Adelaide pushed Baxley's hand away from her again. "I want a carriage, or I'm not moving." She settled cross-legged in the middle of the dirt road, crossing her arms.

"Adelaide, we need to leave," Baxley pleaded, his eyes glancing around them.

"No!"

"Now," he hissed, grabbing a hold of one of her arms.

"So help me, if you don't get your ass off the ground and back in the saddle this instance, I'll drug you and take you anyway," Keys interrupted them.

"You can't—" Adelaide began.

"Watch me." Venom laced her words. Her eyes were ice cold as they bored into the princess.

"Fine." Adelaide's lips pursed as she finally took Baxley's hand, allowing him to pull her up to standing.

Her camel hadn't gone far, and soon enough Keys had her back in the saddle, ready to go. Keys was just mounting Vincent when warning bells pealed in the distance.

"Fuck," she muttered. What were the odds the bells weren't being rung because of them? Someone must have alerted the soldiers about what they heard Adelaide screaming. "We need to move." She wheeled Vincent around, driving a path through anyone still milling about to watch the spectacle the princess had created.

"That could be for anything," Baxley called while still matching her steady pace.

"I don't believe in coincidences." Even if those bells weren't for them, nothing good could come of hanging around.

She pushed them as fast as she dared, winding through the streets towards the east side of town. Other bells sounded from different corners of the city. She should have split them up. Should have sent the princess on ahead with some of the others rather than dragging her into the market.

Stupid.

Her eyes scanned their surroundings, trying to spot any sign that they'd been detected. People still moved about the streets. Their heads also on a swivel, looking for the cause of the alarms. No one seemed to know what was going on. There—just a few more blocks in front of them and then they'd be clear of the city.

Keys felt a shift in the air. "Get down," she yelled, twisting in the saddle and blindly sending out a burst of wind. Too late— she was too late. Cain toppled from his camel, disappearing from her view with an arrow sprouting from his chest.

Chapter 28

BAXLEY

HIS HEART DROPPED STRAIGHT OUT OF HIS CHEST AS Cain fell from the saddle, their eyes meeting for a brief second. Eyes that were wide with shock. "Cain!" Baxley yelled. He couldn't see the soldier where he landed, but he heard the thump as he hit the ground. Everyone except for them scattered, scrambling for cover.

The world around him seemed to stop, everything freezing in place. Keys had warned them. He truly didn't believe anyone would find them, yet here they were. All their caution was for nothing. They were all going to be killed and Adelaide would be dragged back to Gleyra.

A horn sounded, dragging him back to the present, time speeding up around him.

"Sarja, get to Cain!" Keys ordered. She had the bow in her hands, an arrow nocked, ready to shoot. He watched as she scanned the tops of the buildings, waiting for the coward to show his face.

"What do we do?" whimpered Adelaide.

"Stay low," Baxley replied, not sparing her a glance as he held his breath. Where were they? Were there more than one?

Another horn sounded from close behind them. Others were coming. And almost there, by the sound of it.

"We need to move," Arla urged, her camel shifting beneath her.

"So they can shoot us in the back? I don't think so," Keys responded, her bow still drawn back.

The archer blew their horn again, returning the call, drawing the others to them.

Training her bow on where the sound came from, Keys said, "Get Cain back on his camel if you can." Somehow her voice was steady.

Not wasting time, Baxley leapt down from his own, racing around Cain's camel to find Sarja was still kneeling over him. She looked up at him, tears cascading down her face. Blood covered her shaking hands that were pressed around the arrow protruding from his chest. Cain stared up at the sky, his eyes unseeing. The sight stopped Baxley in his tracks, his breath sticking in his chest. Cain was dead. This was his fault. He'd chosen Cain to come along. His knees grew weak.

"It hit his heart. There was nothing I could do," she whispered, voice trembling.

"What's going on over there?" Keys called out to them.

Baxley forced air into his lungs, fighting against his body's reaction. "He's dead," he yelled back, not fully believing the words that left his mouth.

"Then get back on your camels. You need to leave," she commanded them.

"I'm not leaving him!" he roared. Cain was his responsibility. He wasn't about to leave him behind in this country.

"We don't have—"

Her response cut off as soldiers poured from around a corner behind them. There were seven of them to their four capable fighters, plus the archer on the roof.

"Focus on them!" Keys bellowed. "The archer is mine."

"Get back to your camel. Stay with Adelaide," he instructed Sarja, not waiting to see if she listened. Felix and Arla had already dismounted, moving to intercept the soldiers. Baxley charged after them, pushing away all thoughts of Cain plaguing his mind, needing to focus on the current threat.

Felix turned into a blur right before clashing with the first soldier. The man dropped to the ground, blood pulsing from his neck. Felix scooped up the man's sword, and then he was off again. Arla disappeared for a second when she reached her own soldier, popping back into view as her dagger plunged into his back. Two down.

One of the soldiers broke off to engage Baxley, and he lost track of where Arla and Felix were. The woman raised her hand, sending a blast of fire in his direction. He only just managed to dodge it, aided by a small gust of wind that he pulled towards himself. Not waiting for her to try again, he reached his palm out, ripping the sword from her other hand. Too close to make use of it now, he let it sail past him, drawing a dagger from his waist instead.

The soldier was ready for him and sent another stream of fire straight for his face. He ducked, twirling around her to cut her Achilles tendon on her left leg. The woman collapsed forward in a cry of pain. He left her there, not slowing his momentum as he moved to help the others where they still fought—

A burst of fire hit him squarely in the back, burning straight through his clothes, the thin linen providing barely any protection from the flames. Baxley screamed in pain, slamming to the ground. A suction of air surrounded him, not of his own making, suffocating the flames still scorching his skin. Gasping, he rolled over to face the woman he had thought was no longer a problem. She bared her teeth at him from her position on the ground, lifting her hand for another go. Without thinking, he sent his dagger flying, using his magic to drive it straight and true. It was faster than the fire, sinking into her chest. Her flames guttered out halfway to him as she fell over backwards.

"Stay there!" Keys roared at him as she bounded past towards the others. The archer must be taken care of, then.

Baxley couldn't even turn to follow her progress or see how many soldiers were left. His gaze stayed glued to the woman. A life. He'd taken a life. Stomach lurching, he crawled towards her, his back protesting the movement as it pulled at his fresh wounds. He needed to see for himself—needed to check if she was still alive.

The last few feet between them were the hardest, still Baxley compelled himself forward. The woman's eyes were closed, her chest unmoving. He collapsed to the side, puking up anything in his stomach. He retched until there was nothing left, the stomach bile searing his throat. It was an accident. When he threw the knife, he hadn't meant to kill her—simply subdue her. It happened too fast. His stomach heaved again, but nothing else came up.

"We need to go," Keys said, skidding to a stop next to him. "Can you stand?"

Baxley couldn't tear his eyes away from the woman. "I killed her," he muttered.

"We have to go." Keys shook his shoulder.

"I've never killed anyone before." He finally managed to rip his gaze away, looking up into her face. Blood splattered the sword she was holding. "I didn't mean to kill her," he whispered, eyes wild and unfocused.

Her head tilted to the side, a strange expression on her face — and then she plunged the sword into the woman's chest.

"What're you doing?" he gasped out, snapping out of the stupor.

"She wasn't dead yet," she said, shrugging. "Can you walk or not?"

"But you—"

"You didn't kill her. *I* did. Now, on your feet, Prince." Keys grabbed his arm, yanking him to standing.

He yelled as his wounds pulled even worse. Swaying, white spots danced across his vision.

"I'm sorry." Keys helped steady him, arm slung around his waist, dragging him back towards the camels. "You'll have to wait until you're well clear of the city before Sarja heals you."

"Until we're clear of the city," he corrected her.

"No. *You.* I'm going to draw them off."

"You'll be killed." He pulled her to a stop, eyes rounding, pain momentarily forgotten.

"They can try." Her smile took over her entire face. Like she relished this. Thrived in the chaos. She forced him to keep moving. Felix and Arla were just finishing putting Cain onto his camel. Sarja hovered around Adelaide, already prepared to go. Keys left him to round up his camel.

"Head east until you're out of view, then cut north," she told him after helping him mount, their eyes locking. "I will find you."

"Be safe," he replied, knowing arguing with her to come with them would do no good.

Keys gave him a small nod before turning and running towards her own camel. She leapt, adding some air behind it, and landed smoothly in the saddle. He finally noticed the horn slung across her body that she must have picked up from a fallen soldier.

"Go!" she yelled at them.

He tapped his camel to get it moving. Twisting in his saddle, wounds complaining, he watched Keys ride off in the opposite direction. If any of them could survive this, it would be her.

Within minutes, they were at the edge of the city, flat plains stretching before them. They'd have to travel several miles before the city would be out of sight. How did Keys have any hope of finding them again?

A horn sounded from farther away. Keys was really going to try and draw them away while they escaped. His gut clenched, uneasy with having left her behind, worry coiling inside him.

"Keep a steady pace," Felix told them. "We don't want to make it look like we're running."

When they wouldn't have been able to make out a single person back at the city, they urged their camels into a gallop. They pushed a little farther once the city was completely out of view, not wanting to risk it. Then they headed north, exactly like Keys had instructed. Still, something felt off to Baxley as they added more distance between themselves and the city. It felt like he left something behind. Something he may never get back. For hours they rode, the feeling only increasing in intensity. Not once did his gaze pull towards Adelaide.

***

They continued until darkness fell and then made camp. The Cathburn Mountains, which had loomed in the distance along most of their journey through the plains, were probably only a day's travel away now. A somber cloud hung over the group as they prepared to rest and wait for Keys to catch up to them.

Sarja had been silently crying for hours as they rode. He knew that Cain was interested in the healer, but he wasn't sure how far their relationship had developed. His heart hung heavy with guilt. It beat in time with his thoughts, over and over: *My fault. My fault. My fault.* They needed to decide what to do with his body. It wouldn't last for them to carry him all the way back to Vesperis, but he couldn't stomach the idea of leaving him here.

They relied on their supplies for a meager dinner, none of them having an appetite as it was. Sarja healed his back as best she could, needing time to rest before she could finish. It had been agony the entire time they were riding, every shift irritating the burns, but at least he was alive—unlike Cain. He didn't deserve to complain. She said it would likely scar some. Baxley would cherish the reminder for as long as he lived. He'd sent the others to get some rest after that. There was no way he'd be getting a restful night's sleep, anyway.

Adelaide lingered behind. "I'm sorry. I didn't mean—"

"Your apology won't bring him back," he interrupted, not interested in hearing her excuses. Baxley didn't turn towards her, his eyes watching the dancing flames of the fire. He couldn't stomach the sight of her. Anger surged through him—anger at her.

"Be that as it may—"

"Go to sleep, Adelaide." He clenched and unclenched his fists repeatedly, trying not to lash out at her.

"I'm sorry," she whispered again. He heard her walk away after that.

Baxley lost track of time as the night slipped past. Perhaps he should patrol the camp, yet he couldn't seem to force himself to move from his spot by the fire. His thoughts jumped and changed as fast as the flames he fixated on—from Cain, to Adelaide, to Keys, to the woman he killed—because even though Keys had stabbed her, he knew in his heart that she was already dead—and back to Cain again, and then to his kingdom.

Was this a foreshadowing of how his rule as king would be? Was he destined to make the wrong choices? Risk the lives of others for what he wanted? Be a selfish, unworthy king? Would his kingdom crumble around him like how he felt he was crumbling now? His grandfather had done all he could to secure peace. His father was doing the opposite, contesting all prior trade deals, driving them closer to war each year. Keys' question haunted him. What kind of king did he want to be?

"Even a child could have snuck up on you to slit your throat," a voice said from the dark.

Startled by the sound, he blinked his eyes, trying to adjust them after staring at the fire for too long. As Keys stepped into the light, Baxley's shoulders relaxed. He hadn't realized he'd been tense since they separated until this moment. "Are you okay?" he asked.

"Nothing I couldn't handle." She waved off his concern, taking a seat close to him. "Led them on a merry chase through the city and then disappeared."

He studied the thief. She was so nonchalant about all of this. Acted like it was a normal everyday occurrence. "You truly are amazing." The words slipped out before he comprehended what he'd said.

She flinched. "Don't go getting sappy on me, Bax."

He jerked, remembering who he was talking to. "Right, sorry. What now?" For once he wasn't asking because he wanted to know the plan; he was asking because he needed her direction. Needed her to take charge because he had no idea where they should go from here.

Keys didn't reply at first. He felt her eyes scrutinizing him before she said, "A little more than a day's ride from here, there's a secret pass through the mountains."

"She won't make it." They'd been over this; Adelaide would never make it across the mountain range.

"It doesn't go over the mountains—it goes through them."

"How is that possible?" It must have taken *years* to construct. And all done without either countries' nobility ever learning of it.

"*That* is a secret which will remain with me. Do you trust me?"

"Yes," he said with zero hesitation.

"Enough to let me blindfold you? I can't permit you to see the entrance."

"Are there any other options?" he asked.

"We'd risk being discovered again if we continued east. They'll be sending all their resources that way come morning when we still aren't found in the city."

"Then we have no choice," he replied.

Her tone softened. "What would you like to do with Cain?"

"Can we take him with us?" Heat built behind his eyes as they misted over.

"It'll take at least three days to get to the tunnel and through it. We could cremate him. Take his ashes back with us."

"Do we have time for that?"

"We can make time, if that's what you want."

"Okay." He cleared his throat, scrubbing a hand over his face. "We'll ask the others their opinions in the morning. They should get a say."

"Go try and get some sleep. Not like you were doing any good out here, anyway."

He scoffed, though she did have a point. "I still don't think I can sleep."

"Have you never lost anyone close to you before?" She hugged her knees, head resting on them as she faced him.

He dipped his head. "My grandparents on my father's side. I was particularly close with my grandfather. He called me his little shadow." Baxley let out a watery chuckle, recalling his childhood memories. "I used to follow him all around the palace. Hell, I might have been worse than Lumoz is. He died when I was nine. I remember...not understanding. Waking up in the mornings and expecting him to have come back from wherever he had gone.

My father was already hard on me, but he became harder still. Never happy. Always disappointed. I often ran and hid for hours around the palace, only coming out when I needed to eat. There's a small room in one of the towers. It has a window that overlooks the city. That was my favorite spot," he mused.

Baxley gave his head a hard shake. "But this feels different. Cain was under my command. I brought him here. I—" he choked, unable to finish.

"It wasn't your fault, you know," she said. "You may feel like it is now, but give it time. Some things are beyond our control."

"Who's getting sappy now?"

She grimaced.

"Maybe I will try to get some sleep." Baxley pushed to his feet, heading for his tent.

"Sleep well, Bax," he heard her murmur.

Chapter 29

SKELETON KEY

THE OTHERS AGREED TO CREMATING CAIN WHEN ASKED the next morning. Keys didn't want to risk doing it here. She'd covered their tracks last night, blowing away any evidence of them traveling this way, but it was still too close for comfort.

The entrance to the tunnel she'd told Baxley about was in the opposite direction, requiring them to backtrack to make it there. Despite running on little sleep, she drove them mercilessly. All of them were worse for wear. Baxley was almost dead on his feet, constantly nodding off in the saddle. More than once, she had to prevent him from falling using the wind. Sarja's face was puffy from crying. The healer was even quieter than usual, barely engaging with anyone. Arla and Felix weren't much better, though they hadn't been crying—at least not in front of anyone. Keys expected that Cain's death hit Felix the hardest. The pair kept by each other, casting glares towards the princess when they thought no one was watching. And Adelaide—well Adelaide was actually trying to be somewhat helpful whenever they stopped for a break. It was disconcerting and usually resulted in more harm than good.

As night fell, she called for them to halt. They were quiet as they set up camp, no one feeling like talking. She managed to shoot a jackrabbit earlier in the day and cooked it into a stew. There would be some supplies stashed throughout the tunnel, but they'd need to rely mostly on the preserved foods they'd picked up in the market.

After dinner, they prepared Cain's body. If they hadn't traded most of their prior wardrobe to lighten their load, Keys would have suggested dressing him in the sarong. They made do with a fresh set of linen clothes. Sarja was able to put together a paste that would serve well enough as a paint. Felix drew a mandala symbol on Cain's forehead and on each of his palms.

Keys hollowed out a shallow pit in the earth, pulling on the sandy soil to collect in a mound off to the side. Felix and Baxley placed Cain to rest there, and then joined everyone already circled around the edge of the pit.

"Would anyone like to say anything?" Keys asked, her eyes finding Sarja.

Sarja let out a gasping sob, her hand held over her mouth. "I'm sorry," she whispered, shaking her head.

"Thank you for being my friend." Felix stepped forward. "It meant more to me than you could ever know. You stood by my side when others wouldn't. Rest easy, brother." He pressed his fist over his heart before stepping back.

Arla went next. "You made the world a brighter place. A funner place. And you deserved the snake in your tent. I warned you Keys was on to your shenanigans." Her lips tilted up at the edges despite a tear running down her cheek.

Keys let out a soft chuckle. She'd been wondering what Cain's next move would have been. Now, she'd never find out.

"I chose—" Baxley tried to start, voice cracking. He cleared his throat to try again. "I chose you for this because of your gift, but more than that, I trusted your judgement to help guide me along the way. You were taken from the world too soon, and for that, I am sorry." He ducked his head. Adelaide reached out to take his hand, but he pulled away. Baxley raised his head to finish. "Thank you for your service. You will never be forgotten."

When no one else said anything, Keys stepped forward. "Be at peace," she said, pulling on the spark within her and setting his body alight. She'd need to maintain a high enough temperature for several hours. Everyone except her and Sarja dispersed to their tents for the night.

After a time, the healer wandered over her way. "I should have slept with him," she said. "I don't know why I didn't. It's not like we hold the same standards as Aswal. You would have slept with him." Sarja gave Keys a small watery smile.

"I would do a lot of things you wouldn't do," she replied with a smile of her own. "That doesn't mean either is right or wrong."

"No, but it's a regret I'll carry."

"It doesn't have to be. Let it be your reminder to embrace every moment, rather than a regret."

"I like that." Sarja let out a loud exhale, scrubbing at her eyes.

Keys reached out, squeezing Sarja's hand. "Go get some sleep."

The healer nodded and did just that.

Keys sank down cross-legged into the sand. Her eyes closed as she focused on increasing the temperature of the fire, making it burn hotter and hotter. She lost track of time while the inferno blazed.

Her eyes snapped open when she heard footsteps crunching through the sandy soil behind her. Twisting her head around, she found Baxley making his way towards her. "What're you doing awake?"

"Couldn't sleep," he replied, taking a seat next to her.

"Probably cause you slept all day in the saddle."

He rolled his neck side to side. "And I'm paying for it now. The real question is how you're still awake. You must be exhausted."

She lifted one shoulder, watching the flames burn. "Not like any of you could have done this."

"Is there anything you can't do?" he asked.

Shocked, she turned to meet his gaze. "There's plenty I can't do."

"Not from where I'm sitting," Baxley scoffed. "You're stronger than anyone I've ever seen using water. Not to mention all the air you've been working. Did you think Adelaide wouldn't tell me you had her *jump* off a balcony?"

"She didn't jump off," she snorted. "*I* did."

"No, no. I'm not finished yet." He held up his hand. "Now this," he continued, waving his hand at the fire. "Only someone who was powerful with fire could do this."

"Maybe I just practice more."

He ignored her, speaking louder. "And there's the whole you breaking into and out of the Gleyra palace as if you do it every day. Plus," he increased his volume more when she opened her mouth to interrupt again, "you escaping a city full of guards after drawing them all towards you."

"Is there a point you're trying to make?" she asked, her eyes narrowing on him.

"Why did you become a thief? You could have done almost anything you wanted. My father would have paid handsomely to have someone with your talents in his army."

Her stomach soured. "I'm no one's tool."

"Just because you work for the crown doesn't mean you're a tool." His eyebrows creased.

"Doesn't it? Are your soldiers allowed to tell him no if they don't wish to do something he commands?"

"Well, no, but—"

"Exactly. I live my life how I want and do what I want, whenever I want to."

She felt him studying her as their eyes locked and held.

"Why did you stab that soldier back there for me?" he whispered.

The abrupt change in topic threw her. "I told you already. She wasn't dead yet."

"You couldn't possibly know that."

"And you can't prove she was."

Their eyes narrowed on each other, waiting for the other to break.

Keys sighed, backing down first, letting him have this one. "I did it because—because taking a life is never easy. But the first one...that's the hardest. It stays with you forever. And if I could prevent you from having to go through that, why shouldn't I?"

"But why would you care?"

"Because, against my better judgement, I'm finding I like you, Bax. Even if you're starting to annoy me right now. And you were breaking, about to tear apart at the seams. I needed you to hold it together, at least a little while longer."

"I wasn't breaking," he murmured.

"You were and you know it. I thought we were going to have to carry you for a second."

"Fine," he conceded. "But what does that say about me? How am I supposed to make the difficult decisions once I take the crown if I can't handle killing someone?"

"It *says* you're a good person. Someone who cares about not just his own country and people, but others as well. You see a person as a person. Not everyone can do that."

Baxley's head dropped down. "My father would disagree with you on that. He would think I'm weak."

"And that reflects more on his character than yours."

He didn't respond. His finger drew patterns in the soil that he traced over and over.

"Healing," she blurted.

"What?" His gaze shot back to hers.

"I'm not great at healing," she admitted. "That's why I asked you to bring Sarja along."

He gave her a soft smile.

"What're you thinking?" she prompted when he didn't say more.

"I'm thinking that maybe thieves aren't so bad, after all," he said before returning back to his tracing. He drew a mandala pattern next before wiping it away.

"Do you know why we're always tattooed with mandalas? Why we paint them on our dead?"

"It's tradition," he replied, drawing another one. "It's always been done."

"But why a mandala?"

He paused his tracing. "I don't know."

"It came from when people used to practice religion. Back before magic was discovered. They first started using the symbols in tattoos because they believed the gods granted them this magic. And then they realized—why worship a god, when you can become one?"

Baxley looked over at her. "Are you saying you're a god?"

She laughed. "No. There's no such thing as gods." But there was a way magic wielders could become more powerful, stronger. A teaching that was forgotten here long ago.

Baxley resumed his drawings.

His words about thieves stuck with her for the rest of the night. Maybe princes weren't so bad either.

***

Baxley fell asleep sitting next to her while they kept watch over Cain, his head resting on her shoulder. He smelled of sweat and dirt, but Keys found she didn't mind. Her own eyes started to droop after several hours maintaining the fire at such a high temperature. When nothing was left but ash, she woke him.

"Sorry," he mumbled, shifting away from her.

"It's fine."

They collected his ashes together, placing them in a cloth bag. They'd be given to any remaining family once they returned to Aglar. Both of them retired to their tents to get any sleep they could before the sun rose.

Only a few hours later, Keys was up and moving again, her body lagging with the lack of sleep and excessive use of magic she'd been using within the last few days. Food helped, but she really needed to sleep longer.

They rode along the base of the mountain for several hours until she called for a break. The entrance she was looking for would only take about another hour to reach. It was as close as she was willing to get to it without having them blindfolded.

"Wrap your head scarf around your head to cover your eyes," she ordered everyone when they remounted. They all complied, and once satisfied no one could see, she got them on their way again. Not even the princess dared complain about being blindfolded.

Within the hour, Keys spotted the unique rock formation that formed an arch which marked the entrance. The tunnel had been built several hundred years ago by The Underground. They use it to shuttle black market items between Voglar and Vesperis faster, amongst other things. The opening to it was tucked in a little alcove, hidden from view unless someone already knew where it was. It was barely large enough to admit a camel.

Keys helped them dismount one by one before leading each camel inside and then helping them back into the saddle. The tunnel was just wide enough to pass another party if they came across them. She sent up several lights to illuminate the space for the camels to see. Once the entrance was out of view, she allowed everyone to remove the head scarfs.

"This is amazing," Felix marveled, eyes roving over the carved-out rock walls. "It must have taken years to construct."

"From what I've heard, it did," Keys answered. "If we come across anyone else, you keep your mouths shut and heads down. I'm breaking enough rules even having you here."

Fortunately, they didn't cross paths with anyone on the first day. They kept track of time using Baxley's pocket watch. Every so often, they passed recesses in the wall that held supplies, some water and food that wouldn't spoil. Keys had them restock their waterskins at one, but left the food. The camels she didn't worry about as they would be able to make the journey without drinking.

On the second day, two people traveling the opposite direction came into view. They had several horses loaded with supplies and merchandise.

"Cover your faces," Keys ordered the others, winding her own head scarf around the bottom half of her face. Her hand rested on the dagger at her hip as the pair came closer. She called out to them, "The sun sets in the mountains."

"And rises from the sea," one of them answered. A woman.

Keys released her dagger and nodded at them as they passed. They, too, covered their faces, though she suspected the second was a man judging by his size. Keys unwound her scarf when the two couldn't be heard anymore.

"What the fuck was that?" Baxley hissed.

She'd really been hoping they wouldn't come across anyone, so she wouldn't have to explain. "A code phrase. And don't bother trying to remember it. It rotates every few months."

"This is a smuggling route," Felix guessed.

Keys pursed her lips. "It has many uses."

"You're organized," Baxley noted. "How many people know about this?"

Between taking Felix into an Underground location and now this, Keys had revealed too many secrets to them. She couldn't add any more. They might start to poke around, trying to find things on their own. That could only lead to disaster—for them.

Keys needed to deter them from doing so. "Enough to cause you problems if you ever try to find it again," she warned. Wheeling Vincent around, her eyes pierced into them. "Your silence on everything you've seen will be considered payment for the passage. Should you break it, you'll pay with your life."

Baxley straightened in his saddle. "Back to making threats again already."

"I am not the only one you'd have to worry about should it come to that." There were many others she could think of that would react first and ask questions later should they find the prince wandering around where he shouldn't be. In this, Keys hoped Baxley would finally exercise some sense.

Chapter 30

SKELETON KEY

KEYS TIMED THEIR EXIT FROM THE TUNNEL TO BE AT nightfall the following day. She still made everyone stay blindfolded as a precaution, but soon the mountain range disappeared from view in the darkening forest. With little chance of the group knowing where they were, she allowed them to remove the blindfolds. They traveled for hours into the night, pushing northeast. It was drastically warmer on this side of the Cathburn Mountains. Even at this hour, humidity hung in the air. She'd missed this. Her skin had felt so parched after their time in the plains. She pulled moisture from the air, winding the small bands of water between her fingers, just because she could.

When Keys did finally allow them to stop for the night, she made sure to find a small stream for the camels to drink their fill. They decided to keep the camels rather than trying to trade them for more horses. Keeping them would make the party more noticeable, but Keys wasn't worried since they were out of Voglar. It would take almost a week for them to make it to the coast where they could hire a ship to sail them back to Aglar. Where the tunnel exited in Vesperis, it would have taken even longer to try and travel all the way back over land.

Their journey to the coast was blessedly uneventful—at least when it came to traveling. Baxley and Adelaide's relationship, on the other hand, was more chaotic than ever. One minute they were acting as if everything was fine—though still very formal—and the next they were bickering up a storm. The days grew monotonous watching the two of them interact. The fate of their relationship grew more uncertain with each passing day. She never wanted to be in a relationship like that. This whole ordeal had brought out the worst in the pair; they no longer fit together as they once had.

Keys still hadn't revealed the princess' letter to Baxley. She heavily considered it after the princess' stunt in the market, especially since it cost Cain his life. Some days it felt like it was burning a hole in her chest. At times, guilt ate at her for allowing him to continue living a lie, but she shoved the feeling deep down inside whenever it raised its head.

Nevertheless, she still thought it would be more useful to hold over Adelaide's head if the need arose. And Keys didn't want to deal with the fallout it would more than likely bring. If Adelaide's infidelity ever came to light, Keys hoped she was long gone by that point.

They arrived in a port city on the morning of the seventh day. On the outskirts of the city, Keys had them dismount.

"We'll leave the camels here," Keys explained.

"They'll be alright on their own?" Arla asked. She, too, had grown fond of the magnificent creatures.

"They know the way back. Don't you, smart boy?" Keys cooed, scratching up and down Vincent's neck. Tebak's training with them to return home, wherever they might travel, always paid off. It was how he made such a profit off of them. He "sold" them over and over, only for them to eventually return.

After unloading all their belongings and unsaddling the camels, Keys sent them on their way. Her heart was heavy, not knowing when she'd next see Vincent. They left everything they wouldn't need right there for someone else to find.

The city was buzzing with activity during this time of day. There were plenty of ships at the docks to pick from, and it didn't take them long to find one sailing north. Within a few hours, they were cutting through the water, wind filling the sails. It was decided before they set sail that they shouldn't send word on ahead via air message of their return, in case it was intercepted. The chances of that happening were low, but it still wasn't worth the risk.

The rocking of the ship soothed Keys. She stayed up on deck for as long as possible, soaking in the mist coming off the waves, wind whipping through her hair. Soon, this would all be over, at least for her. The princess would be returned, and she'd part from them much richer, so long as the king stuck to their deal. For his own sake, he had better. The consequences if he didn't would be catastrophic. It would be strange not seeing the others after having spent so much time in their company the past weeks. Most of them she found she would actually miss. Adelaide—well she wouldn't shed any tears over never laying eyes on *her* again.

At dinner time, she relented and went below deck, her hunger winning out over her want to stay above in the open air. The small galley was cramped as the crew and her group gathered together. The crew hurriedly grabbed plates and left, returning from wherever they came and leaving the table for their use. Baxley helped Adelaide, who was looking a little peaky, into a seat. He retrieved plates for both of them. Keys took up a place as far from the princess as possible.

"What's that?" Adelaide asked as Baxley slid a plate in front of her.

"Some kind of fish."

"I can't eat that," Adelaide groaned, shoving the plate away from her. Her hand clamped over her mouth.

"Are you feeling okay?" asked Sarja.

"I think she's a little seasick, but she's never had issues before." Baxley's eyebrows creased, his gaze locking on Adelaide.

"The smell of the fish isn't helping." Adelaide waved her hand in front of her face, trying to waft it away.

"Why don't you go back to your room? I can brew you some ginger tea and bring it to you. Hopefully that will help settle your stomach," Sarja offered.

"Too late," Adelaide choked out, leaping up and rushing towards the head.

Keys grimaced, hoping she made it in time. *She* sure wouldn't be cleaning up after her if she didn't. The others stared after Adelaide while Keys continued to shovel the fish and rice into her mouth. "Are you going to go help her?" she mumbled around her mouthful of food to Baxley.

He cringed. "Maybe I'll give her a minute."

"Coward," she taunted.

"I don't get it. As soon as we stepped on board, she started getting nauseous."

"It could be from stress. This hasn't been easy for her," Sarja reasoned. "Hopefully the tea helps."

***

The tea did *not* help. The princess remained queasy the next day and the next after that. Keys abandoned the cabin the two of them were given to share, preferring to bunk in a bed along the hallway—despite the lack of privacy—rather than listen to her moan about all day. Granted, it was only particularly bad when the princess caught a whiff of an especially strong scented food, which sent her immediately to the head. Otherwise, she was just a little green around the edges.

On the third morning, Baxley joined them a little later than usual, his appearance slightly disheveled compared to his normal standard. His black hair had grown longer in their time away. It was messy and sticking up in odd places like he tried pushing it up away from his forehead and out of his eyes. He had also stopped shaving when they arrived in Gleyra, trying to make himself less recognizable. The short beard made him look older than his twenty-seven years. While Keys thought the look suited him, she preferred him with only a few days' worth of stubble on his face.

"Rough morning?" Arla asked.

He sighed. "I'm just going to take her food to her." Baxley picked up the plate of bland food that had been set aside for Adelaide. "I'll be back," he said, trudging back the way he came.

"If I didn't know any better, I'd guess she was pregnant," Sarja commented.

Felix snorted. "Well, we know *that's* impossible."

Keys' eyes widened. *Oh, fuck.* It wasn't impossible. It was actually quite plausible. Why didn't Keys think of that sooner? The timeline would make sense. She could be in the early stages and being on the water was magnifying any morning sickness. Just when she thought the situation between Baxley and Adelaide couldn't get any more fucked up. Keys scrubbed a hand over her face.

"You okay over there?" Arla nudged Keys under the table.

"What?" Keys snapped out of her thoughts. "Yea, I'm fine." After all, everything with her was fine. It was Adelaide that was in a heap of trouble.

***

Keys waited until later in the day, when Baxley had gone up on deck to get some fresh air, to go confront the princess about her suspicions. It did occur to her that Adelaide might not have pieced it together herself yet, and she might not even realize that she was carrying a child. Opening the door, she slipped inside, closing it and locking it behind her.

The princess was laid out on the bed. She groaned when she saw it was Keys that entered. "What do you want? I'm miserable enough as it is."

"Are you pregnant?" Keys blurted, not wanting to beat around the bush.

"What?" Adelaide gasped, springing upright. "No. Why would you even say that?" she hissed. Her eyes shifted around the room as if someone could be hiding in the small, confined space that might overhear them.

"When was your last bleed?" Keys pressed her.

"It was…" The princess paused, thinking. "I don't know," she finally said, waving her hand. "But there's no way I'm pregnant."

"Are you on the fertility suppressing potion?" The potion needed to be taken monthly to properly prevent pregnancies.

"Of course not. It's against my culture for unmarried women to be on it, but Calbex said he was."

Keys always thought that part of the Aswal culture was backwards. They wanted their women to remain pure for marriage, forbidding them from taking the fertility suppressant to help encourage that. It instead resulted in many women becoming pregnant outside of wedlock—women who were then being shunned and looked down upon. The men, of course, had no consequences for their part in all of it. It was a messed-up system if anyone asked her. The men were equally responsible for their own actions.

"And you believed him?" Keys raised her eyebrows at the princess. "You should never rely on a man when it comes to that. You'd already lost your virginity—not to mention all the lying and scheming you've done—why not say to hell with this as well?"

Adelaide ducked her head. "I tried. He said I didn't need to since he was taking it. He didn't have a reason to lie about it," she said, straightening her spine.

"He had every reason to lie to you," Keys argued. "He's forced your hand. Even if you were where you had wanted to be, had you changed your mind, there would be no way out of it once you were pregnant. You're backed into a corner now. Baxley *will* find out. With or without your letter."

"I'm not pregnant," Adelaide barked. "I can't be."

"Time will tell. And if I'm right, then what are you going to do?" She left the princess to ponder that.

Chapter 31

BAXLEY

BAXLEY STUCK TO TAKING ADELAIDE HER MEALS. IT seemed to be helping, and she hadn't thrown up since the day prior, though she still felt nauseated from time to time. After dinner, he checked in on her, wanting to retrieve the dishes as well.

"Still doing okay?" he asked, stepping into the room. It looked like a little more color returned to her face.

"Better," she replied, giving him a small smile from her seat on the bottom bunk.

"That's good to hear." Baxley bent down to pick up her plate and wooden cup.

Adelaide reached out, taking a hold of his outstretched arm, stopping him. "Will you stay for a while?"

"Of course."

She scooted over, giving him space to sit down.

"I know you mentioned it, but I want to bring the wedding forward once we return," she said, reaching out and taking his hands. "Let's do it in a week."

"A *week*?" he squeaked. There was no way either of their parents would agree to that. They'd need at least a month to move all their plans forward. And her father and brothers would need to travel from Aswal to be there. "We'll never be able to pull it off in time."

"It doesn't need to be big. As long as the two of us are there, that's all that matters." She pulled her legs up underneath herself, fully facing him.

"Your father would have a fit if he's not there." His own mother would be beside herself if certain standards weren't upheld. He was a crown prince, after all.

"I don't care anymore. I want you. All of you. Completely," she whispered, her chest heaving. She rose to her knees, pulling her shirt off as she did.

Baxley froze. He forced his eyes to stay on her face, trying to ignore that she was wearing a very lacy—very revealing—bra. "Adelaide," he mumbled, "what're you doing?"

"I'm tired of waiting." Heat radiated from her eyes, and she crushed her lips to his.

He gasped, not expecting it. She took advantage, dipping her tongue into his mouth. When it retreated, he couldn't help but follow after it with his own. There would be time later to reason with her on why getting married in a week was an irrational idea. "I've missed this," he sighed, his lips ghosting over hers.

"Me, too." She claimed his mouth again, starting to tug at his shirt. Her hands roamed over his bare sides, moving towards his back, pushing the shirt farther up as they went. "Take this off," she demanded.

"Why?" he chuckled in between kisses.

"Because I want to feel close to you."

"If you insist." Baxley shrugged one shoulder, allowing her to pull the shirt up and over his head. He let her take control as their lips found each other again. He felt the urgency surging off of her. Her mouth was desperate, tasting as much of him as she could get. This was a new side of her he'd never seen, but he didn't mind. Her hands clutched his biceps, tugging him closer still.

"Touch me," she groaned into his mouth.

His hands found her thighs, caressing them, still trying to be respectful.

"Here," she said, guiding his hands up towards her naked sides before she resumed kissing him.

Baxley held her with clammy palms, unsure where he should touch. They'd never gone this far before. Sure, they'd kissed, but they were entering into new territory—forbidden territory. His throat bobbed as he swallowed, trying to push the uncomfortable feeling away.

Adelaide abandoned his mouth, nipping and licking down his neck. She reached around behind herself, unclasping her bra and letting it fall.

He caught a glimpse of her full breasts—her pert nipples begging to be played with—before he thrust his head up, gaze to the ceiling. "Maybe we should slow down," he muttered, blood heating his face.

"I need more," Adelaide begged. She climbed into his lap, straddling him. Her hands pulled his face back to hers. Her lips took what they wanted, nudging his mouth back open for her tongue to swirl in, searching for his own. Breasts pressed flush against him, she started grinding her hips down into him, but he couldn't seem to care—too perplexed with how she was acting.

She moaned, increasing her speed. Her one hand trailed down his body to find his waistband, fingers dipping beneath as their tongues twined together. Before he could stop her, she lifted off him slightly, allowing enough space for her to reach down his pants and take hold of his cock—his still soft cock.

"Adelaide," he gasped in surprise. He jerked backwards, unseating her and causing her to tumble to the side. Her hand slipped out from beneath his pants. "What's gotten into you?"

"Don't you want me?" Her brows creased. "You weren't even hard yet."

"Not like this." He blew out a huge breath.

"But we're getting married so soon." She crawled back towards him.

Baxley held a hand out to stop her. "We need to stop. I don't want to put you in a compromised position."

"What does it matter if it's now versus next week?" Her frown deepened.

"It matters to me. I won't do that to you. There's no rush. We have time."

"I don't want to take more time," she huffed. "I want this now." She tried to lean forward to kiss him again.

Baxley bent backwards. "Why are you pushing this?"

"Because I love you..."

"Adelaide," he sighed, resting his forehead against hers. "We've both been through a lot the last few weeks. We need time to decompress. To work through everything. I don't want this to be a regret—for either of us."

She pulled away from him. "Do you not love me anymore?" Her bottom lip trembled. He could see the tears welling up in her eyes.

"That's not what I said." He rubbed her arms. "We'll get back and then see how we feel from there. Okay?"

A few tears escaped from her eyes.

"Don't cry," he pleaded.

"Why don't you want me?" She sniffled.

"I do," he assured her. "But not like this." He wiped a tear off her cheek. "You deserve better than a hard mattress on a ship for your first time."

Apparently, that was the wrong thing to say, because she started crying harder.

"Adelaide, what's wrong?" he beseeched.

"Everything has felt so different between us. I feel like I'm going to lose you," she whimpered, the desperation clear in her voice.

He reached out to hold her face, making sure she looked into his eyes as he said, "I'm not going anywhere. I love you." More tears ran down her face. "Two more days and we'll be home. Just two more days."

Adelaide shook her head out of his grasp. Her expression changed in a blink, becoming stormy. "I don't want to wait two more days. I need this now," she demanded in a sharp tone.

"Why?" His eyes searched hers, looking for an answer.

"Because I do," she whined, her voice softening back to normal.

Baxley couldn't accept that. It didn't make sense why she was acting this way all of a sudden. Not when they were almost home. "I can't. I'm sorry." He snatched up his shirt, standing before she could stop him.

Her cry of "Baxley" followed him as he bolted out the door, dirty dishes abandoned—where he collided straight into Keys.

***

Baxley disentangled himself from Keys, who he'd wrapped his arms around when they came together to prevent either from falling. He stooped to pick up his shirt that he dropped. "Apologies," he said.

She raised her eyebrows at him as he straightened, eyes scanning his exposed torso.

"This isn't what it looks like." He struggled to put his shirt back on in his haste.

"I would hope not based on the way Adelaide called your name. Otherwise, I'd say you left her *very* unsatisfied."

His face heated further if that was possible. "If you'll excuse me..." Baxley did his best to squeeze past her, not that she made it easy for him in the small hallway. Fresh air. He needed some fresh air. To clear his head and process what just happened.

His feet hit the deck before his mind caught up with him. Baxley leaned on the railing, staring into the dark waters that reflected the rising moon. What the hell happened back there? Adelaide had always respected her culture. Always insisted they never go too far. What changed? He tugged at his hair. None of this made any sense. She was right in saying that things had been different between them. That didn't mean they should jump feet first into this and do something they could never undo. They needed time—*he* needed time.

The past few weeks had brought out a side of her he didn't like. Not that he was at his best either. They were both equal in the blame. Is this how it would be whenever a crisis arose? Were they doomed for discord rather than working in synergy? His stomach churned uneasily at the thought. He wanted the type of relationship that became stronger in the face of hardships, not one that was torn apart—and therein lay the problem. The cracks between him and Adelaide were starting to show and he couldn't unsee them. The man he had been before she was kidnapped would have gladly taken her virginity, traditions be damned. The man he was now couldn't for more than one reason. Reasons he could no longer ignore since his eyes were wide open.

"Do you want to talk about it?" Keys asked, flopping against the rail next to him.

He shouldn't be surprised she followed him. "I didn't sleep with her," he blurted.

"I'd be shocked if you did."

Baxley turned to face her, surprised. "Really?"

She nodded. "You wouldn't be you if you had. Besides, everyone's seen the tension between the two of you, and it's not the good kind." Keys snorted.

"Cause you know me so well."

"I know that you're honorable. You made the right choice — the good choice." She reached out, squeezing his arm.

"I know."

"So, then why are you up here moping?"

He turned back towards the ocean, pausing a moment before he admitted quietly, "Because I'm starting to question what I really want."

"Only you can figure that out."

"I know." And that was why he felt so unsettled.

What did he want?

Chapter 32

BAXLEY

TWO DAYS LATER, THEY WERE SAILING INTO THE PORT AT Aglar. Night had already fallen by the time they docked. Felix managed to flag down two carriages to take them back to the palace. Baxley took the first one with Adelaide and Keys, leaving the second for the others. It was the most awkward carriage ride he'd ever experienced. Baxley had avoided Adelaide as much as possible since the incident the other night, though he still dutifully took her all her meals. They stuck to basic pleasantries unless she tried to broach what happened between them, at which point he would make an excuse and leave. It wasn't the most mature course of action, he had to admit, but what else was he to do stuck on the ship with her?

He was extremely thankful for Keys' presence now. "What are you planning on doing after this?" he asked her. He hadn't considered it until this moment. It would be different not seeing the thief every day.

"There's always work to be done," she said.

"Very descriptive. With the crown in your possession, you'd never have to work another day in your life."

"Some may enjoy that kind of life. I fear I'd find it boring." She smirked.

"Typical," Adelaide grumbled. "Once a thief, always a thief."

"Careful princess," Keys warned. "Your privilege is showing."

Adelaide's expression soured, though she didn't respond, turning to look out the window instead.

"Are you going to send me an invite to the wedding?" Keys asked him.

Baxley laughed. "Would you even come if I did?"

She tilted her head to the side. "I'd at least consider it. After all, how many people get lucky enough to attend a royal wedding? The food alone would be worth it, I'm sure."

"And I bet a few of the guests would find themselves missing some personal items by the end of the night."

"It's not fun if it's too easy, Bax."

Before he knew it, they were at the entrance to the palace, the guards waving them through after realizing who was inside the carriages. Someone ran ahead to inform the king and queen of their arrival. They barely made it past the entrance hall when his family rounded a corner, racing towards them.

"Bax!" his sister cried, sprinting for him.

He opened his arms wide, preparing for impact. Lumoz flung herself into his arms, almost taking both of them down with her enthusiasm.

"I was beginning to think I'd never see you again," she mumbled into his shoulder.

"Come now. I wasn't gone that long." He squeezed her tight, cradling her head. "I missed you, my light."

His mother reached them next. "Adelaide, my dear, are you alright?" He watched as she took Adelaide's face between her hands, turning it left and right to check her over. "We've been so worried for you."

"I'm alright," she whispered. He could see her eyes watering from here.

"Oh, of course you're not, sweetheart," his mother cooed. "I can't imagine what you've been through." She wrapped her arm around his betrothed. "Come, come. Let's get you to your rooms. A nice bath will do you good." His mother directed her through the others, weaving past his father who had finally caught up to them.

Baxley rolled his eyes—not even the return of his son was cause for haste.

"We expected you days ago. Edwin's spy got word to us when you broke her out," his father said, shoving between Keys and Sarja who were exchanging their farewells. "Ouch." He rubbed at his arm.

"What happened?" Baxley's brows creased.

"Just a scratch." His father stopped in front of him. "You're missing a member of your party. Where is Major Hillcrag?"

"There was an incident on the return journey. He didn't make it." Baxley's heart still felt heavy thinking about it.

"Was *she* involved?" His father's eyes darted over to Keys, narrowing on the thief.

"*She* is the reason everyone else made it out," Keys interjected, clearly eavesdropping. Though his father wasn't being quiet in the first place.

His father ignored her comment, turning back to address Baxley. "And why isn't she wearing a cuff?"

"We needed her magic. Several times." Baxley kept his voice level, raising his chin. "It seemed ill-advised to cuff her again." Of course, his father would go straight to questioning his decisions.

"I'll be on my way as soon as I receive payment for my services rendered." Keys sauntered closer to them.

"Do you think she'd show me how to pickpocket someone?" Lumoz leaned closer, whispering in Baxley's ear.

"Not now," he hissed, his eyes staying glued to their father who was leering at Keys.

"Certainly. If you'll follow me this way," His father sneered, disdain dripping from every word. He waved over several guards who had accompanied the family.

The guards closed in around Keys, trailing behind her as she followed the king. Something felt off about it.

"Lumoz, where's the crown?" he asked, lowering his voice.

His sister shrugged. "I thought it was in the vault, but he wouldn't take her there."

Baxley's eyes narrowed. "No. He wouldn't." He took a step to follow them before halting, looking back at Lumoz. "Go back to your chambers."

"And miss all this?" Her eyes were lit up, brimming with excitement. "No way."

"Please behave," he sighed, rubbing between his eyebrows. What was he going to do with her?

They had to jog to catch up with their father and Keys, leaving his traveling companions behind. Their father appeared to be heading towards the throne room, but ended up veering off, taking them to his study instead. Throwing the door open, he stomped inside the room. Keys entered right behind him, flanked by the four guards. Baxley caught a glimpse of a velvet bag sitting on his father's desk before his view was blocked. Did he really keep it out in the open this whole time?

"I'm sure you'll find this satisfactory." The king scooped up the bag and its contents, tossing it towards Keys.

As she reached out, catching the bag, one of the guards standing next to her clamped a cuff onto her outstretched arm, the other three simultaneously all drawing their swords.

Her head slowly tilted down, examining the cuff. "So, this is how it's going to be." Her voice dropped low. It sent a chill down Baxley's spine.

"You really thought I'd give you that crown?" he taunted.

Keys opened the bag, revealing a silver crown. Very much not the crown of the first king. She chucked it at his feet. It struck the stone floor with a clatter, narrowly missing his father as it rebounded.

"Father, stop this. Let her go," Baxley demanded, stepping around the guards.

"You and your mother might have tied my hands before, but not this time." His lips curled back. "Seize her and take her to the dungeons," he commanded the guards.

"Stop!" Baxley yelled at the guards, but they didn't obey him. "This isn't right! We made a deal with her," he implored his father. Baxley's eyes widened as Keys didn't fight, allowing the guards to yank her hands behind her back.

"Deals can be broken when you're king."

"You'll remember this moment, Your Majesty." Keys looked down her nose at him, her eyes blazing with the heat of the sun. "For this is the beginning of your downfall."

"Get her out of my sight!" the king roared.

"Your kingdom will know what a backstabber you are," she growled. Keys dug in her feet, slowing the guards down who were trying to force her out of the room. "Our contract will be circulated to the public if I'm not released."

Baxley stiffened. He'd wondered what she'd done with her copy. It didn't surprise him at all that she managed to send it to someone she trusted.

"I do not care about a piece of paper!" A vein throbbed in his father's neck, spittle flying from his mouth.

"You should, for I am your judgement. And you have *failed*." She flashed her teeth; head bent backwards as the guards finally managed to push her from the room.

For some reason, Baxley believed her.

Lumoz stood smushed against the wall, her hazel eyes wide.

"What have you done?" Baxley asked, his tone haunted as he turned to his father.

"I am not scared of a thief," his father hissed.

Maybe he should be.

Chapter 33

BAXLEY

THERE HAD BEEN NO CONVINCING HIS FATHER TO change his mind the prior night. His mother promised to talk to him when he found her exiting Adelaide's rooms, but he had little hope. He slept uneasily, finding himself tossing and turning into the early hours of the morning until he finally gave up.

Baxley dressed and wandered aimlessly around the palace. Servants were about, beginning their preparations for the day. After a while, he found his feet led him towards the dungeons. Baxley hadn't set out to see Keys, yet now that he was here, he couldn't turn away.

The stairs to the dungeon took him deep into the earth, the chill biting into him as he went. They'd taken her to the lowest level, thinking it would be harder for her to escape from there. If she somehow gained access to her magic again, Baxley didn't think it would make a difference where they kept her. He found two guards posted at the bottom of the stairwell. Without acknowledging them, he walked past, coming to a stop halfway down the hall when he spotted Keys huddled on a small cot. At least they'd given her a blanket. Her shoulders rose and fell in an easy rhythm.

"Come to watch me sleep, Bax?" Her voice rang out in the quiet.

The corner of his mouth twitched up in a half-smile. Of course she knew he was there. "Actually, I came to apologize. I didn't know what my father had planned. I wouldn't have let you come to the palace if I had."

She sat up, swinging her legs over the side. "Have you come to let me out, then?" she asked, head tilting to the side.

"It's not that simple."

"Tool," she goaded.

He bristled. "I'll change his mind."

"If you say so." Keys laid back down, facing away from him.

Apparently, their conversation was over. He turned to walk back down the hall.

"Oh, and Bax," she called out.

He paused.

"The clock is ticking."

***

His father didn't join them for breakfast, their mother informing them that he had taken ill—a mild cold she assured them—and wished to remain in bed. Unfortunately, she hadn't been able to change his mind about letting Keys go free. Baxley was going to have to come up with something that would sway him. Potentially, she could provide them with more information on the palace of Gleyra that he could use to bargain for her freedom.

Adelaide was a no-show at breakfast as well. He was thankful he wouldn't have to fake being happy in front of his mother, at least not yet. At some point in time, he knew he needed to figure out what was going to happen between the two of them. It didn't need to be the day after they returned, though. Adelaide could settle back in, and he could focus on getting Keys out of here. Both of them could use the time apart to get back to normal—whatever normal meant to them at this point.

Lumoz needled him the entire time they were eating, demanding to know every single detail about their journey and how they managed to rescue Adelaide. He tried his best to appease her despite being distracted. When Lumoz asked what happened to Cain, he completely shut down, unable to look up from his plate.

"Leave him be," their mother cut in. "That's enough for one day."

Baxley was grateful, offering her a weak smile. He wolfed down his remaining food, fleeing after that.

By mid-day, it was clear that whatever the king had contracted, it was not a mild cold. His temperature spiked to dangerous levels, causing him to hallucinate. Baxley paced in the sitting area adjoining his parents' bedchamber suites, waiting for news. Multiple royal healers flitted in and out of the royal chambers, none pausing to give him answers.

He spotted a familiar face amongst them. "Sarja," he called out to her.

The healer's head snapped towards him at the sound of her name.

"How is he?" he asked as she made her way towards him.

"Nothing we've tried is helping reduce the fever. Ice baths are helping to manage it, but we can't find the cause. As soon as we take him out, it shoots right back up." He could see the uncertainty in her eyes.

"Should we be worried?"

"If it doesn't drop within the next day or two...I'd be concerned."

"I see."

She reached out, squeezing his hand. "He's strong. I'm sure he'll be fine."

He gave Sarja a small smile, trying to take comfort from her words. But something in the back of his mind still made him unsettled, though he couldn't pinpoint exactly what. The feeling stuck with him, tormenting him as he kept his vigil into the night.

***

The next day, his father's fever was lower, but he slipped into unconsciousness. Lumoz joined Baxley in the sitting area, trying to distract him with games of cards or chess. Adelaide even made an appearance at one point to express her well wishes. He appreciated the effort despite them being in a strange state of limbo. His mother refused to quit his father's side, even for meals. It was this that made him the most worried. What had the healers been telling her that had her concerned enough that she wasn't willing to leave him for short periods of time?

The day dragged on, the hands on the clock moving ever slower. By nightfall, there had been no changes. The healers seemed baffled, unable to determine why his condition worsened within the span of two days. That was the problem with healing. Mending was easy—broken bones, cuts, and burns could all be healed as long as the healer was strong enough. Treating an illness, however, wasn't as simple. Most needed to be treated with tonics and poultices, not reacting directly to healing magic when wielded.

As Baxley was nodding off lounging on a couch, chin tucked to his chest, he heard someone say, "Your Highness." His eyes cracked open to find a guard standing in front of him.

"Yes?" he asked, pushing himself up to sit. He noted Lumoz was asleep in an oversized chair.

"The prisoner is requesting to see you."

He sighed, wiping his eyes. Baxley had forgotten all about Keys. "Tell her I'll visit tomorrow if I have time."

The guard shifted. "You may want to hear whatever she has to say. She claims to know why the king is sick. She refused to talk with anyone except you."

His gaze narrowed. "How does she know he's sick?"

"That's the thing, Highness, no one told her that."

Baxley was on his feet in an instance, stomping for the door.

The clock is ticking.

What if she wasn't referring to the contract being released to the public like he assumed? What if she had something to do with his father falling ill?

What the fuck did she do?

Chapter 34

SKELETON KEY

THE GUARDS MARCHED HER DOWN AND DOWN, DEEPER into the dungeons. They tossed her into a cell with a small cot and a bucket in the corner to relieve herself. Keys grimaced, not looking forward to having to use that. All her daggers had been removed. They missed the princess' letter she still kept stashed in her bra and the set of lock picks she'd sewn into the hemline of her pants. Baxley might have been surprised by his father reneging on their deal, but she wasn't. And she came prepared. Now, all she needed to do was sit back and wait.

***

Keys was almost asleep — having nothing better to do — when a surprise visitor graced her with their presence. Princess Lumoz walked down the hallway, stopping out of reach of the bars. Her head turned towards the princess. "I don't think your brother would appreciate you being here," she said, smiling.

"What he doesn't know won't hurt him," the princess replied, her eyes gleaming with interest in the soft lights.

Keys studied Lumoz's tattoo on her neck. It was similar in style to Queen Mesra's, but it had a falcon in the center with its wings stretched out wide. She remembered that Baxley said her gift was walking through walls—there was so much potential for someone with a gift like that. Curious, she said, "Tell me, Princess. Can you walk through a person?" Keys sat up, leaning forward to rest her chin in her hand.

Lumoz's brows scrunched together. "I've never thought to try that."

"How about pulling someone with you through an object?"

"I haven't tried that either." The crease between her brows deepened until her eyes widened slightly. "You want me to break you out of here," she whispered, glancing towards the guards at the end of the hall.

"No, no." Keys waved her off. "I'm quite content where I am. Merely curious how much you've developed your gift."

"You can't develop it more. Everyone's born with their limits."

"If that's what you say." Keys laid back down on her cot.

"How'd you get through Gleyra's wall?" Lumoz asked.

"Not even the others know that. I certainly won't be sharing my secrets with you," Keys said, staring up at the ceiling.

There was a pause before the princess asked another question. "Can you teach me how to develop my gift more?"

"*If* I knew how to do that, I wouldn't be here long enough to make a difference."

"So, there is a way…"

"Like I said," Keys turned her head to face Lumoz, "*if.*"

"What's your gift?"

Keys snorted, but didn't respond otherwise.

Lumoz tried a different question. "What happened to Cain? Baxley wouldn't tell me."

"Then maybe you should respect that."

"I'm old enough to know," she huffed.

"It has nothing to do with your age. It's about respect for the dead."

"Fine."

Silence fell between them, and Keys thought the princess might finally leave until she posed another question.

"How old were you the first time you stole something?"

Sighing, Keys said, "You're exactly like your brother with all the questions."

"Is that a good thing?"

"No. Good night, Princess."

Lumoz gave up after that, leaving Keys alone for the night.

***

Apart from the earlier morning visit from Baxley, she saw no other person except for the guards who delivered her meals for the next two days. Surprisingly, they brought her breakfast, lunch, and dinner. It was the only way she was able to keep track of the time down here. The guards were all silent when they delivered her meals. And when she grew bored enough and decided to entertain herself by taunting the ones standing at the end of the hall, they never responded.

Sitting back and biding her time was easier said than done for an active person like her. Finally, a few hours after dinner on the second day—or what she thought had been a few hours—she went to the front of her cell. Keys leaned on the horizontal bar, draping her arms out the front. "Tell Prince Baxley I want to see him," she yelled to the guards. She couldn't see them from where she was at, but she knew they were there. None of them answered her. "I know what is making the king sick." It took a minute before she heard footsteps walking down the hallway.

A female guard stopped outside her cell, arms crossed. "What do you know about it?"

"I won't talk to anyone except the prince."

"The prince has better things to do than talk to the likes of you," the guard sneered, turning and walking away.

"Then let the king die for all I care," Keys called after her.

She saw the woman's shoulders stiffen before she was out of view. A smirk spread across her face. The prince would come.

Chapter 35

BAXLEY

BAXLEY'S HEAVY FOOTSTEPS ECHOED OFF THE STONE OF the long hallway. Keys was sitting up, waiting for him. She smiled as he grabbed onto the bars of her cell. "What do you know about my father?" he demanded.

"No pleasantries? *How've you been? Is the dungeon to your liking? Have they been treating you well?*" She pushed up from the cot, sauntering towards him as she talked.

"You seem no worse for wear," he said. Her clothes were a little rumpled and her hair not as sleek, but apart from that, she appeared the same. "You said you knew about my father, or were you lying?"

Her eyes flashed. "I have never lied to you." She reached up, clasping onto his hands. "I'm not going to start now."

Baxley flinched when one of her rings pinched him. "What's wrong with him?"

"Simple." She smiled, releasing his hands. "He's been poisoned."

He felt the blood rush from his face. "How could you possibly know that?" His hands clenched the bars harder, helping to steady him.

"Because *I* did it," she whispered in a deep voice, the one corner of her mouth quirking up into a smirk.

"You couldn't have," he reasoned. "You've been down here the whole time. How is that possible?"

He could have sworn a little sadness flitted across her face; there one second and gone the next. "The same way I just poisoned you."

"What?" he murmured, his stomach sinking. Her eyes looked down at his hands holding the bars. His own widened in understanding. Her *ring*. Why was he so stupid? They hadn't removed her jewelry because it didn't contain any minerals. He never would have believed it served another purpose. Baxley released the bars as if they were burning hot coals.

But when did she get close enough to his father to touch him? His mind raced back to the night they arrived at the palace. They'd been across the room from each other in the study. There was no way she could have — no, that wasn't right. His father pushed past her…and said he got scratched. Baxley felt like a damned fool.

"Why?" His voice hardened. Dread filled him, for his father and also for himself.

"When you set a trap, next time check to make sure you caught what you were hunting."

"I don't understand." His brows furrowed.

"*I* am not Skeleton Key."

"No," he said, shaking his head in denial. "You are. You said…" What did she say that night?

If that's what you choose to call me.

His breath stuck in his throat. He hadn't paid close enough attention to her wording. She'd never confirmed that's who she was. He swayed where he stood. "If you're not Skeleton Key, then who the hell are you?"

"I am judge, jury, and executioner," she ground out. "I am *Death Adder*." Her smirk grew to encompass her entire face, her dark nature shining through as the mask she'd been wearing the entire time lifted. He no longer recognized the woman standing before him.

His legs grew weak beneath him. "No," he muttered, stumbling back to hit the wall behind him, keeping him from falling over. He couldn't catch his breath, his lungs refusing to inflate. Something that felt oddly like betrayal rushed through him. His stomach gave a lurch, twisting with everything he just learned. "You can't be." They were *beyond* fucked if that was true.

The name reverberated inside his head: *Death Adder. Death Adder. Death Adder.* That name was the only thing known about Death Adder, and that was given to them by the people. There were rumors that Death Adder was very selective in who they killed, and they didn't always go through with the hit; hence, being named after a snake where one had a fifty percent chance of living after a bite, if they didn't receive the antivenom. Should Death Adder choose to kill someone, though, the person was dead before they knew it. Keys had said his father had failed, maybe the rumors were true. Did that mean Baxley failed as well?

"What did you use?" His mind snapped back to the more pressing problem.

"Something you have no hope of finding the cure for in time."

"So, we're both dead? Then why tell me this in the first place? To gloat?" His hands slammed into the stone wall in frustration.

"Bax, I'm hurt," she pouted, her bottom lip heavy. Her hand clutched her chest. "You should know me better than that by now."

"Don't call me that!" he snarled, lunging for the bars. "I don't know you at all!" His spit flew in her direction with his words.

Her eyes darkened. "Your father made his choice!" she spat back. "Had he kept his word, I would have sent the antidote to you, and he'd have been fine in a few days' time. He chose his own path. And now he must walk upon it as it leads him to death," she hissed, her tone icy.

"So, there is an antidote?" Baxley fixated on that word, hoping.

Keys dipped her head in acknowledgement. "There is."

"What do you want in exchange?" His heart thundered inside his chest, waiting for her answer.

"For you to choose to live."

"What?" He felt so lost. None of this was making sense.

"The antidote is more than a day's ride from here. It's stashed in the middle of a forest, so don't get any ideas about searching for it yourself. You'll never find it without me."

"Why would I have to choose to live if it's so close?"

Now he wasn't imagining it when he saw sadness in her smile. "Because there is only enough antidote for one of you—and I will not let it be for your father."

"No," Baxley whispered. "I don't believe you." His voice rose with the anger inside of him.

"I told you; I have never lied to you."

"That doesn't mean you haven't deceived me!" he yelled in her face. "I don't accept this."

"You must!" Keys yelled back. "Your father is dead by his own hand. You don't have to follow in his footsteps. You can right his wrongs. I've seen it in you."

"You don't know me." Baxley slammed into the bars, rage coursing through him. "No, there has to be another way." He began pacing back and forth in front of her.

"There isn't. You must receive the antidote within five days. The king only has three more before it's irreversible. By the sixth day—he'll be dead."

"I can't accept that. I won't!" He grabbed the bars again, leaning his head into them, his eyes closing. "Please, I'm begging you. He's my *father*."

"His fate is already sealed. Now you must choose yours," she whispered.

His eyes flicked open, finding hers immediately. They stared at each other for long minutes, neither saying anything. Something clicked in his brain.

"This was your plan all along, wasn't it?" Somehow his voice came out steady and calm.

"It was."

It was all starting to piece together now. Peri was right. "You knew the museum was a trap. Knew who we were hunting for."

Keys tipped her head. "Skeleton Key is my sister," she replied with a soft smile. "We were curious why you wanted to capture her—and I had been hired for a contract on both you and your father." She shrugged. "It gave me a way in."

"There must have been easier ways for you to kill us." Spending weeks helping him rescue Adelaide didn't make sense.

"I like to get to know my targets. Learn who they are. How they work. If they deserve to die…"

"Then why poison me only to offer to save me now?"

"Because I need a way out, and because you are a *good* person. And I don't kill good people."

"An assassin who has a twisted conscience." He snorted. Wonderful, but that still didn't help his current problems.

"We all have our own ways of living with ourselves. I did not lie. Had your father let me leave, I would have saved him—would have left both of you to live."

Baxley didn't have time to ponder what-ifs. He needed to get to the healers. Inform them to start searching for an antidote. Maybe if they had a sample of the poison, it would be easier for them to identify.

"Give me your ring," he snapped, holding out his hand.

"It will do you no good," she said, though she still pulled it off her middle finger, handing it to him.

He held it in between his fingers, examining it.

"Twist the top," she explained.

Baxley did as she said and a sharp needle-like point popped out from a hole that opened.

"You'll only waste time. The antidote isn't from this continent."

Not from *this* continent. Meaning it could be from one of the smaller islands down south or from the sea — at least it gave them a starting point.

"I can try."

"Then you will *die*." He caught a hint of frustration in her voice.

"If I am to die, then so shall you." His glare cut into her.

"I do not believe it will come to that."

"Either you save both of us or all three of us die. I will not bargain for anything less." Baxley gritted his teeth.

"You may not," she said, her voice softening. Her hand reached through the bars, and she trailed a finger down the side of his face. "But will your mother be willing to lose her son after just losing her husband?"

He jerked back away from her. "I hate you."

"Tick tock, Bax. Tick tock."

The words spurred him into action. He raced away, feet pounding on the hard stone floor. Baxley ignored the concerned looks of the guards, who surely heard the entire exchange. Up and up, he climbed the stairs, pushing through the stitch in his side that appeared by the time he reached the main level.

What did he bring upon them?

Death. He brought death herself.

The words taunted him as he flew up more stairs, heading for the royal wing. He was the one that insisted they capture Skeleton Key. He trusted her when he shouldn't have. He let her get too close. He was the one who had pursued Adelaide endlessly. If he accepted King Aariz's refusal in the first place, they wouldn't be in this position.

His breath came in short pants by the time he reached his parents' chambers. Baxley flung open the sitting room door, sending it crashing into the wall with a bang.

Lumoz jerked awake in the chair. "What's going on?" she asked him, eyes blinking awake.

Baxley didn't answer her, heading straight to the bedchamber. He burst through the set of double doors, gasping, "Poison. He's been poisoned. And so have I."

Chapter 36

BAXLEY

HIS MOTHER SPRANG FROM THE BEDSIDE. "WHAT'RE YOU talking about?"

"Keys, she—but she's not even Skeleton Key. We thought she was, but we were wrong. She did it—poisoned him—poisoned me. She's not—this is all my fault," Baxley rambled on, the words tumbling out of him.

"Slow down." His mother urged, cupping both sides of his face. "What happened?"

"Keys said she knew what was wrong with father. That she'd only tell me. So, I went. I was stupid—careless. I got too close. She pricked me with a ring and then confessed—she's *Death Adder*, not Skeleton Key," he said, hopeless. "This whole time—" The words stuck in this throat. "She wasn't who I thought she was." That feeling of betrayal returned, churning through his body.

"You saw only what she wanted you to see." His mother stared deep into his eyes, her grey eyes that were so different from his own. "That isn't your fault."

"Do you have the ring, Your Highness?" one of the healers present asked.

"Here," Baxley said, holding it out for them. "She said we wouldn't find the antidote in time. That it wasn't from this continent. Start with what's found on the southern islands or maybe from the sea. We only have three more days to administer the antidote to him." His eyes found his father. The king appeared to be sleeping, the only hint of his illness a brow blanketed in sweat.

"We'll do our best," the healer replied, taking the ring from him.

"Mother," Baxley whispered, only for her ears. "She has an antidote. Claims it's more than a day's ride from here...but there's only enough for one." He paused, taking a breath. "She wants me to honor the contract. She wants me to save myself and leave Father to die. I can't—" Heat built behind his eyes. He blinked them, trying to keep the tears at bay.

"How do you know she isn't lying? Isn't trying to deceive you again to be freed?" she whispered back.

"She insists she never lied to me. Her wording was always so careful that I'm inclined to believe her. If she isn't lying...if we really can't find the antidote in time..."

"It won't come to that. Give the healers time."

"If it does," he swallowed, "you execute her. You don't make a deal with her."

"You're not even going to try?" Lumoz snapped from behind him.

Baxley whirled around to face her. In his panic, he hadn't realized Lumoz had followed him into the room. He never would have let her hear what he just said. Would have tried to protect her from this.

"You'd rather the two of you die than take the chance that she's telling the truth and there really is an antidote?" she continued, her face flushing.

"If Father dies, it can't go unpunished," he tried to explain.

"So, you live and bring her to justice another day!" she yelled at him. "You don't throw your life away just because your pride is bruised."

"It's not that simple," he sighed, pinching the bridge of his nose. She was still too young to understand, too caught up in the righteous side of ruling to see the murky gray areas.

"It is!" Tears fell freely down her face. "I don't want you to die," she murmured.

It crushed him to say his next words, knowing how much they would hurt her. "He's the king. It shows we're weak if we let her go."

"And you're my brother!" Her eyes were wild. "I don't care how weak we look as long as you're still *here*. Don't let Father plant words on your tongue. To hell with what he thinks is a weakness. His own conceitedness has made him weak! Look at where it got him." She stabbed a finger towards the bed. "All his resentment and hate has put him there. A king is only as good as his word." Her chin lifted high.

"Lumoz," their mother gasped.

"Everything will work out," Baxley said, trying to reassure his sister. He took a hold of her hands, but she reeled away from him.

"Not if you're no longer here." A sob escaped from her mouth. Her distraught expression was so unlike her normal cheerful self that Baxley was almost ready to change his mind, but she turned and fled the room before he could say anything else.

Baxley took a step to follow her.

"Let her go," his mother said, catching hold of his arm.

The feeling of defeat settled over him like a dark cloud. Why was it so hard to please everyone? "Promise me." He turned back to face her, shoulders set and determined. "Promise me you won't give in to Keys' demands."

"I will do what I must."

He took no comfort from her words.

***

Exactly like his father, Baxley fell sick the next morning, none of the antidotes the healers tried making any difference. Even with the sample, they were having no luck identifying what the poison was. Lumoz, despite being upset with him, stayed by his bedside. She did her best trying to keep him distracted regardless of all the healers fussing about.

Someone must have eventually informed Adelaide, because she tore into the room at some point when his fever was setting in.

"Baxley!" she cried, nearly collapsing on top of him. "Why didn't you send for me?" She caressed his face, her hands soft against his feverish skin.

"Didn't want to worry you." He grimaced, trying to shift her weight off of him. Truthfully, it had slipped his mind to even apprise her of the situation when he had been poisoned.

He'd called all the royal advisors together in spite of the late hour, his mother even leaving his father's side to join them. They'd talked into the early hours of the morning, making plans should both he and the king die. Word was dispatched to his cousin, Favian, who was third in line for the throne, to travel immediately to Aglar. He would become regent until Lumoz reached the age of majority at eighteen. Baxley would potentially be dead by the time Favian arrived.

"How bad is it?" She finally eased off him.

Baxley breathed a sigh of relief. "I'll be fine." He hoped his smile looked reassuring. "The healers will figure it out."

"Don't sugarcoat things for her," Lumoz grumbled. "He's going to let himself die, because he's stubborn."

"If there's something we can do, then we should do it." Adelaide's eyes flicked between brother and sister, waiting for one of them to provide the answer.

"There's nothing." His eyes narrowed on Lumoz in warning. "I'm sure they'll have something by the end of the day." Baxley turned his head back toward Adelaide, taking her hand. If only he believed that himself. The more concoctions the healers dumped down his throat, the less hopeful he became.

His fever rose steadily as the day went on, roasting him alive. He swore there must be steam coming off of his skin at one point. The damp compress on his forehead seemed to be more of a comfort for Adelaide than himself. He wished she would go away. Her fretting was fraying his already stretched nerves, her screeching voice cutting into his skull. He couldn't even follow what she was saying.

Baxley thrashed his head from side to side, trying to drown out her voice. "Shut up!" he yelled when it didn't help, the words bursting from him.

"What?" Adelaide squeaked.

"Shut up! Shut up! Shut up!" His back arched off the bed, his head pressing hard into the pillow. He dug the heels of his palms into his eyes.

"Maybe you should leave…" he heard his sister say.

Yes, make her leave.

"But I want to be here for him," Adelaide whined.

"Get her out!" Baxley clamped his hands over his ears.

Everything was muffled now—better. He relaxed onto the bed.

When he finally cracked his eyes open, it was to find only Lumoz at his side. Adelaide was gone.

"Thank you," he mumbled, exhausted.

"I should have let her stay to torture you. Maybe then you'd agree to release Keys and heal yourself."

"Smartass," he laughed, which caused him to go into a coughing fit.

Even being prepared for the hallucinations didn't help him once they started. Cain haunted him, often appearing behind the people who came and went from the room. He never said anything—merely stood there staring with an arrow protruding from his chest, watching him with the same unseeing eyes he'd had back in Opora. Baxley wept, apologizing over and over for failing him. For not being able to save him. When he still didn't leave, Baxley yelled and threw things towards Cain, trying to get him to stop tormenting him.

Keys made some appearances, too; stabbing him in the back...in the side...in the heart. He relived her betrayal all over again—fought and thrashed against it. His fists often connected with physical flesh, though he couldn't tell who he actually hit, his mind too far gone.

At one point, he could have sworn he saw his father above him. He spoke of how disappointed he was in Baxley. How he'd never amount to anything. How he'd run the country into the ground.

When his mind finally went blank, it was blissful.

Chapter 37

QUEEN MESRA

A MOTHER WOULD DO ANYTHING TO SAVE HER CHILD. A wife would give up everything for her husband. A queen would put her king above all else.

Queen Mesra repeated those words in her head while she sat, listening to the advisors bicker amongst themselves. Hours. They had scant hours left until the king was beyond saving. She should be at his side, not here listening to these fools. He still hadn't regained consciousness. The healers had been useless. Both for Oren and for Baxley. Her son had joined his father in oblivion yesterday.

"Enough!" she shouted, slamming her palm down on the table.

Everyone quieted immediately, her uncharacteristic outburst snapping them back into the nobles they were and not the baboons they were behaving like.

"I need options." She quickly held up a hand when several mouths opened at once. "Viable options." The mouths closed.

"We have ways of extracting information," Edwin, their Master of Intelligence, said.

Queen Mesra grimaced. "You know how I feel about torture."

"Which is why I haven't suggested it until now. We are out of time, and I can see no other way to acquire the information we need."

She found the Head Healer, Gia, seated around the table. "Do you have any hope of finding the antidote by this evening?"

The older woman ducked her head. "No, Your Majesty. It seems unlikely we'll discover it by then."

"Is there truly no other option?" she asked the room at large.

No one responded.

Queen Mesra took a deep breath, driving away the despair that threatened to swamp her. Her gaze traveled around the table, taking in all the faces looking to her for direction. She repeated the words to herself again, this time with more resolve.

A mother would do anything to save her child.

A wife would give up everything for her husband.

A queen would put her king above all else.

"Do it," she whispered, her eyes meeting Edwin's. "Save my husband and son."

"It will be done," he replied, standing and quitting the room.

She closed her eyes, resting her head in her hands as the people around her also rose to leave. The room emptied until she was the last one left—or so she thought.

"What have you done, Mother?" Lumoz asked, stepping out from a dark corner.

Queen Mesra shouldn't be surprised her daughter snuck into the meeting. She encouraged her to further her knowledge, after all, while her father denied her. It was one of the only areas Oren and her ever fought about.

"What I had to do." She pulled back her shoulders, projecting the confidence she didn't quite feel.

"You would never have allowed this before. Have always encouraged Father to be better."

"Times have changed." Her jaw clenched.

"If we lose our morals, we lose ourselves. You taught me that."

Pride swelled in her chest for her daughter's convictions. If only she had been strong enough to hold to them herself. She faced down an impossible choice and now had to live with her decision. "I had no other choice," she explained.

"Except there was! We could honor the deal. We can save Bax!" Lumoz urged.

"That isn't good enough!" Queen Mesra shouted. She couldn't lose Oren—wouldn't lose him. He might have his flaws. Might not be the most humble and benevolent king—but she loved him in spite of it all. Death would have to pry him away from her bloody hands. For she would have blood on them after this.

"And instead, we may lose them both." Lumoz's eyes raged with molten fire. "You will have to live with that hanging above your head," she hissed, turning to leave.

Queen Mesra's shoulders drooped. A piece of her withered and died as her daughter walked out of the room. She hoped her sacrifice would be worth it.

Chapter 38

DEATH ADDER

MULTIPLE PAIRS OF FOOTSTEPS ECHOED DOWN THE hallway. Keys continued with her push-ups, waiting until they stopped outside her cell to look over. "I wondered if I'd be seeing your face again," she said, recognizing Edwin. He had two others with him. One of which was carrying chains. She shoved up from the ground.

"The great Death Adder. Look at you now," he taunted.

"You think I let myself end up where I didn't want to be?" Keys cocked her head to the side.

The man bristled. "I will ask you once, and then we will resort to other methods. What did you use to poison the king and prince?" Edwin asked, getting straight down to business.

"As I already told Baxley, you won't find the antidote around here."

"What is it called?" he demanded.

"It doesn't matter what it's called. Your healers won't know it." She rolled her eyes. When would these people learn?

"If you resist, this will be worse for you," he warned. Edwin withdrew a key, unlocking her cell door.

She tensed, preparing for a fight. Keys wasn't about to make things easy for them. Not when she knew what was coming. "I suggest you rethink what you're about to do." Her fists clenched at her sides.

When he swung the door open, she darted forward, ducking low to aim for his legs. Edwin was ready, sending out a blast of air. It sent her reeling, slamming against the back wall where she collapsed down onto the cot. It sagged against the force. Her head spun from the impact with the stone wall. Keys was no match for them while wearing the cuff, cut off from her own magic.

"I suggest you stay down," Edwin sneered, stepping into her cell.

The other two followed. The man carrying the chains let them fall to the ground. Blinking through the dots dancing across her vision, Keys saw one side had manacles, the other a large spike. He drove the spike up into the ceiling, embedding it into the rock. The manacles dangled down, hanging well above her head.

Edwin waved the two towards her once the chains were set. Keys' struggle was futile against them, though they still had to wrestle her into the chains. At least her feet still rested on the ground, letting her support her weight. "Remember who I am. You think you'll be alive much longer if you go through with this?"

"You won't be leaving this cell alive." He chuckled, pulling out a bundle from within his cloak. Edwin rolled it out across the ground, revealing different instruments. Instruments he would be using on her.

"We shall see," Keys spat, baring her teeth at him.

Edwin ignored her, selecting an instrument meant for breaking fingers and toes. "Major Lockridge here has a unique gift. She can amplify emotions, making you feel things more intensely. I've heard it's excruciating when used on pain." He prowled towards her. "How long do you think you'll last before you crack?"

"Longer than you will when I get my hands on you." She arched towards him as much as the chains would allow.

"Let's begin, shall we?" His gaze trailed down her body. "I think we'll start with the toes." Edwin leaned down to untie her boots.

Keys grasped hold of the chains, taking as much weight off her wrists as she could before hoisting herself up to kick him in the face. Her cackle as he went sprawling backwards rebounded around them. One of his lackeys stepped forward, punching her in the ribs from behind. Her breath whooshed out of her, cutting off her laughter.

Edwin sat up while she tried to catch her breath, his hand going to the bridge of his nose, smearing blood from a cut there. Unfortunately, she didn't think she broke it. His hand pulled away, fingers rubbing together while he examined the blood on them. "That wasn't very nice." He pushed himself up to standing. "We can start somewhere else if you're so eager to spill blood." Edwin dropped the tool back with the others and withdrew a scalpel instead. "I was going to work our way up to this, but since you're so insistent…" He paced around to the back of her.

Keys tried to turn with him as much as the chains would allow. "I will be your demise," she hissed as he ripped the back of her shirt away.

She felt his hot breath on her ear. "Not if I'm yours first."

The first cut into her skin took her by surprise. She couldn't contain the gasp that escaped. The second had her back arching. Her blood pulsed in her ears, drowning out all other sounds. Keys wasn't a stranger to pain, but this was something else — something more. By the fourth cut, she was howling in pain. And then it got even worse—

A strip of her skin landed on the floor in front of her. He was skinning her *alive*. Bile burned the back of her throat and she wrestled it back down, refusing to vomit. She wouldn't give him the satisfaction.

She.

Would.

Not.

Break.

***

They'd had to bring a healer in when she blacked out from the pain. Still, she only kept repeating the same things over and over:

The antidote isn't from this continent.

Their healers will never find it.

She refused to tell them where she stashed it.

Keys never changed her answers, no matter what Edwin threw her way. Her face was bloody and bruised, her right eye almost fully swelling shut. Her back was a patchwork of missing flesh, the pieces all strewn before her. He did eventually work his way down to her feet, where he broke each individual toe and then smashed a few bones in her feet as an added measure. Afterwards, she was unable to put pressure on them, having to hang from her wrists. She could barely feel her fingers anymore. There were burn marks, cuts, bruises, and stab wounds littered over her entire body. They had to give her blood replenishing potions twice already. And yet still, Edwin continued.

The hours crawled along, seeming to never end. It had to be nearing the mark where it would be too late for the king. But still, no one came to stop Edwin. No one came to help when her voice went hoarse from screaming. No one came when all she could do was hang there, no longer reacting to the pain. When her body gave out, and she wished for death, not even then did she give them the answers they sought.

Chapter 39

QUEEN MESRA

DREAD FILLED HER HEART, TWISTING AND CHURNING inside of it. Queen Mesra had never felt this helpless in her entire life. After meeting with the advisors, she hadn't left her husband's side. They were within the last hour before it would be too late for him. The healers had come up with nothing else.

Lumoz had joined her a little while ago despite their earlier disagreement. The pair sat in silence, holding each other's hand. Oren's skin had developed a waxy appearance. His eyes were sunken in, flitting behind his eyelids. Whatever was happening in his mind, it didn't appear restful. He would hate others seeing him in this state—appearing feeble.

The doors to their room opened, but Queen Mesra didn't even turn to look, assuming it was another healer.

"Your Majesty." A voice broke through the morose stillness permeating the room.

Her head swiveled to Edwin. Blood dotted his clothing, making her cringe. "You have news?" she asked, her heart poking its head up with hope.

"I'm sorry," he replied, shaking his head. "She has given us nothing else."

Her heart fell out of her body, that last hope gone. A sob burst from her lips, unable to be contained.

"Would you like me to continue?"

"No," she choked, brushing her tears away. Her gaze fell upon her husband. How much time would she have left with him? "Everyone out."

"As you wish." Edwin and the healers exited the room, closing the doors behind them.

"Mother," Lumoz said after a time. She'd almost forgotten she was still here. "We can still save Bax." When she didn't respond, Lumoz reached out, shaking her shoulder. "Let me save him."

"Do what you must," she heard herself say, her eyes only for the man she loved.

After she heard the door close again, she climbed into bed next to Oren. Her cheek rested on his chest as she wrapped herself around him. All she wanted now was some time alone with him before the end.

Chapter 40

DEATH ADDER

SUDDEN PAIN BROUGHT AWARENESS BACK TO KEYS. SHE cried out as someone lifted her up, freeing her wrists from the manacles.

"I'm sorry," a soft voice apologized.

Keys collapsed into the strong set of arms holding onto her, her eyes blurring with tears, preventing her from making out who was there.

"Set her on the cot," a different voice said. It sounded somewhat familiar.

The arms lowered her down, trying to place her on her side to avoid laying her on the wounds on her back.

Other hands quickly replaced the ones that held her, and she felt healing power sweep through her body. "My feet," she managed to mumble. If she was to be strung up again, she needed to be able to stand. She felt bones snap back into place, groaning through the pain, closing her eyes. It was nowhere near as agonizing as when it was first done, but healing was painful in a different way.

"Where else?" the voice asked after some time.

She cracked her good eye open to find Sarja above her. "Didn't think I'd be seeing you again." Keys gave her a small smile, her split lip reopening.

The healer returned the smile. "It appears our paths were meant to cross again. What else is the worst?"

"My wrists." She held them out before her. Some feeling was starting to seep back into her fingers. The pins and needles prickled.

Someone else stepped into her line of sight while Sarja began to heal her wrists. "Two visits, Princess. I'm touched," Keys said to Lumoz.

"If I give you the crown...if I let you go...you'll save my brother?" Lumoz asked, biting her lip.

Their eyes locked together.

"Does your mother know you're here?"

Lumoz nodded. "She's aware."

"He'll have to come with me. There may not be time to send it back." She gasped as whatever spot Sarja was healing sent a shock wave down her arm.

"Sorry," the healer murmured.

"Where he goes, so do we," Felix said, both he and Arla stepping into view.

Her smile widened, taking in the pair. "That is acceptable." Of course they were here as well. "We should leave as soon as possible." Keys groaned, trying to push herself to sit.

"You won't be going anywhere, unless you want to fall off your horse," Sarja said, stopping her and forcing her back down onto the cot.

"How long does she need?" Lumoz asked, wringing her hands together.

"At least a day to recover her strength, though I'd prefer longer."

"I'll give you until the morning," Keys moaned. "And can we get this cuff off me, please?"

"Right." Lumoz jumped, pulling a key out from her pocket. "Sorry." She stepped forward, fitting it into the cuff, twisting the key to unlock it. "I'll make sure everything is ready before morning."

"Thank you," Keys whimpered as her magic flooded back into her.

"Alert me, should Edwin return, though he shouldn't." Lumoz said, withdrawing from the cell.

"Princess," Keys called out before she could leave. "Baxley will not be happy when he wakes."

"At least he'll be alive."

***

Keys was as healed as she was going to be. Sarja worked on her until the point of collapse, her powers completely drained. The healer would need sleep and food to recover. Felix carried her away, leaving Arla to watch over Keys.

Sagging back on the cot, Keys closed her eyes. Her own healing powers would do her little good right now, as exhausted as she was. She hadn't been lying to Baxley about not being great at healing. Sure, she could do the basics—healing small cuts and bruises and mending fractures. Anything more than that was beyond her abilities. Her body was barely patched together after all Sarja's work. Sarja had only been able to focus on the largest problems—her feet, wrists, and back, along with a few cracked ribs. The next few days would push her to her limits.

She must have drifted off, because she jolted when someone nudged her. Felix had returned with food and water. Keys ate greedily until her stomach was bursting and then promptly fell asleep once more.

It felt like minutes later when she was shaken awake again. Everything ached.

"Lumoz is ready if you are," Arla said. The look on her face displayed her doubt that Keys could do this.

"I will manage," she groaned, struggling to even sit. She had to. Keys wasn't willing to risk waiting longer to leave. It was best not to give anyone time to change their mind, for one thing. And if she was honest with herself, she wouldn't feel relief until Baxley was given the antidote.

When she first accepted this job, she never expected it to lead her to where she currently stood. Yes, she was selective on who she assassinated. And yes, she learned all about them to set up tests for them to either pass or fail to determine their fate—but she didn't grow to care for them. She'd never started to consider that they could be friends under the right circumstances; and yet, with Baxley, *she had*. It would hurt more than she'd ever admit if he were to die. It would mark her soul in a way that couldn't be expunged.

Arla had a new set of clothes waiting for Keys to change into. She did so with haste before they made their way out of the dungeon, the guards at the bottom of the stairs no longer there. They encountered no resistance as Arla led her out to the stables. The sun hadn't begun to rise yet. Baxley was already tied to a horse, its reins connected to the horse Felix was mounted upon so it would follow. Two other horses were tied up, waiting for Arla and Keys.

As they made their way towards them, another person rode out from the stables.

"No," Keys said, noticing who it was.

"Felix never specified who exactly would be coming along." Lumoz smiled at her.

"It was implied." Keys clenched her jaw. She didn't have time to babysit. She'd already dragged one princess across two countries, and that was more than enough for her.

"Be that as it may, I'm coming." Lumoz nudged her horse forward, holding the first crown of Vesperis down to Keys. "As promised."

Keys took it, turning it in her hands as she examined it. It was the real thing; a basic gold crown with one large ruby set at the front. Her sister would be so excited; too bad Keys was keeping it for herself. After all, she'd earned it. "Keep up or you're getting left behind."

"I believe it may be you who will need to keep up."

***

Keys would never tell Lumoz she had been right. She would go to the grave before the words ever parted her lips. Being shown up by a teenager was beyond embarrassing, notwithstanding that she had been tortured the day prior. They pushed as hard as she could manage with her injuries, eating in the saddle and stopping every few hours to swap out for fresher horses. Luckily—for them—the others had been smart enough not to comment on her condition.

Despite traveling slower than she'd like, they made decent time. As the sun descended in the sky, she gave them the choice of continuing through the night at an even slower pace or stopping and racing again in the morning. She estimated it would take about three more hours with the horses pushing.

The group chose to stop for a few hours, deciding to make camp rather than taking the time to find a village.

Keys noticed the princess' mood dropped with the sun. "Is something wrong?" she asked as they dismounted.

Lumoz looked towards the fading light. "Is my father still alive?" Her voice was so quiet that Keys almost didn't hear the question.

She examined how much daylight they had left. "It's possible..."

"But?"

"If he is, it won't be much longer," she admitted.

Lumoz tucked her chin. "He should have let you go. *Why didn't he let you go?*" She slammed her fist into her thigh.

Keys wasn't sure what Lumoz needed. She eventually settled on saying, "Not everyone is noble. For what it's worth, I *am* sorry he didn't uphold our deal. I don't enjoy taking a life."

"Then why do you?" Lumoz turned toward her. Her face streaked with tears.

"My first—it was survival. And then"—her eyes darkened—"revenge. From there, I learned I was good at it. I could become someone from it, though I've always maintained certain boundaries."

"If you don't always kill everyone, why do people even hire you?" Lumoz swiped at her tears.

"Simple—I'm the best. And should I decide not to go through with a contract, which is rare to be honest, I return the deposit I've collected from them."

They stood in silence for a moment, the princess processing the information.

"I want you to teach me," Lumoz eventually said with a determined look in her eye.

"You want to learn to kill?" Keys raised her eyebrows. That was the last thing she thought the princess would ask of her.

"No." Lumoz crinkled her nose. "My gift. I want you to teach me to be better."

Keys narrowed her eyes, really studying Lumoz. "I will consider it."

Chapter 41

QUEEN MESRA

NIGHT HAD FALLEN A SHORT WHILE AGO AS SHE LAID beside her husband, watching his chest rise and fall. She'd barely moved from this spot since yesterday, not even leaving to say goodbye to her son. Her mind couldn't handle it if she were to lose him as well. Queen Mesra had refused to allow anyone else in the room. Refused any food or water left outside the door.

Her eyes were dry from trying not to blink, afraid she would miss something. His breathing slowed further, chest not rising quite as high. There was a stutter in it, as if he couldn't get enough air.

"Please," she murmured, "don't leave me." Her hand stroked down his face.

He took another breath—

And then his chest didn't rise again.

Queen Mesra sprang up, staring intently at his chest. "No," she whispered, willing him to take another breath. "No!" Her voice cracked on the word. "Please." She started shaking his shoulders. "I love you. You can't leave me," she cried.

The doors to their room opened. "Your Majesty?" Gia popped her head inside the doorway.

"Get out!" she screamed. "You can't take him from me!" She curled over him, freely weeping into his chest. She wouldn't let them take him; he was hers and she was his.

Queen Mesra was vaguely aware that the Head Healer walked over towards them. "I'm so sorry, Your Majesty," she heard her say, but everything sounded like she was under water.

She sobbed harder—clung to him tighter.

"Let us know when you're ready." The doors closed behind Gia.

How could he be gone? He was still in her arms. He couldn't just be gone. She couldn't comprehend how she would never hear his voice again—never see his eyes shining back at her again—never feel *him* again. Something within her broke, a chasm opening within her chest, and she fell into it, plummeting into a pit of despair.

Sometime later, the bells rang throughout the city.

The king was dead.

Chapter 42

DEATH ADDER

THEY WOKE WITH THE SUN AND WERE OFF AFTER A quick breakfast. Keys felt worse than she had the day prior, even with the extra sleep. Being on a horse all day yesterday had taken its toll on her already battered body. She used what little strength she had to heal her most pressing aches. After this, she vowed to sleep for a month.

It was before midday when they reached their destination — a small cabin in the woods. It clearly hadn't been used in a while based on the state of its disrepair.

"Settle the horses and get him inside," she ordered the others. She didn't wait for them to argue, dismounting and striding off into the woods by herself. Keys whistled a bird call while she walked. One answered her in kind. A soft smile spread across her face — her sister was here.

About forty paces from the clearing with the cabin, she stopped in front of a large tree. Reaching out with her gypsum magic, she directed two branches to lower to her. The two branches parted from each other, allowing her to pluck the vial that had been stashed there, a dark gray liquid sloshing inside of it.

"You have a few extra friends with you, Sister." A voice said from directly behind her.

Keys didn't even flinch, used to her sister's antics. "Plans changed," she replied, turning to face her.

"You look like death." El cringed, taking in Keys' bruised face.

"Hilarious," she said in a dry tone.

"Here," El said, reaching out for her chin.

"After." Keys pulled back before her sister could touch her. "I want to get this to him first. Then you can play nursemaid all you'd like." She started back towards the cabin. "And cover your face," she called over her shoulder. "You really need to start being more careful."

"It's fine, Juju," El groaned. "Don't be so paranoid."

"I can feel your eyes rolling from here."

"You sure took your sweet time on this one." El's voice sounded slightly muffled from the mask she no doubt tied around the bottom half of her face, despite her grumbling. "I've been waiting *ages* for you to return."

"Oh, please. You've probably been having a grand time lounging in the capital and stealing anything not nailed down."

"It's been too easy," El whined, catching up to her. "It's like everyone is asking me to steal from them."

"How awful."

"So…the palace of Gleyra?"

"Still as arrogant as ever."

"It's been a time since I visited them."

"Don't even think about it." She side-eyed her sister. "They might have finally increased the guards inside the palace after losing the princess."

"Exactly! Finally, something would present a challenge."

Keys snorted as they emerged from the trees. The horses had been tied up around the small clearing, left to graze. They headed straight for the front door, the cabin's deck groaning beneath them. She pushed the door open on squeaky, unused hinges. Felix and Arla sprang up from the small worn table at the sight of her sister, hands going straight for their swords.

"Relax," Keys told them. "She's not here to harm anyone."

Their shoulders stayed stiff as the two sisters walked past them, heading for the door to the only bedchamber. El waved her fingers at them in a teasing manner.

"Knock it off," Keys reprimanded her.

"Someone's got their panties in a bunch," El grumbled.

Keys walked into the chamber, finding Baxley on the bed with Lumoz sitting next to him.

"Who's that?" the princess asked, perking up in interest.

"The *real* Skeleton Key," El said before Keys could stop her. She took a bow. Always one for dramatics. El was going to get them into trouble one day. She didn't appreciate how much effort Keys put into keeping their identities a secret.

Lumoz's eyes widened. "You're both here," she said in awe, eyes flicking back and forth between them.

"Help me sit him up." Keys ignored the princess' comment. She wasn't used to anyone fawning over them. The princess was a strange one.

Easing Baxley to be propped up against the headboard with Lumoz's help, Keys uncorked the vial and tipped the contents into his mouth. She made sure he swallowed it all.

"That's it?" Lumoz asked.

Keys nodded. "And now we wait."

"How long before he's conscious?"

"He should wake sometime this afternoon."

"Plenty of time for you to start teaching me, then." Lumoz's smile stretched wide.

Keys' gaze narrowed on her. "Fine," she said. She supposed she did owe the princess something for killing her father. Lumoz's face lit up with excitement. "But no complaining." She pointed a finger at her in warning.

Keys led her outside, stopping briefly to inform Felix and Arla that Baxley would be fine now that he received the antidote, though it would be a few days before he was on his feet again and ready to head home.

She made her way towards a shaded area of the clearing, well away from the horses, and then sat on the grass facing Lumoz. "Our magic is like a muscle," Keys started to explain while Lumoz also took a seat. "The more we use it when we're younger, the more elastic it will be. The more *potential* you can achieve. If you accept the limits without ever trying to stretch it, you'll never grow. Once we hit adulthood, our magic becomes more rigid — harder to push or pull in any direction. It becomes fixed in what it already knows."

"Why have I never heard this before?" Lumoz gaped at her.

"Because it was forgotten centuries ago by most," El supplied, taking a seat beside Keys. She reached over and took her wrist, sending her healing magic into Keys. Healing was the only form of magic that required physical touch to work.

Keys let out a deep breath, not realizing how much pain she was still experiencing until her sister's powers flowed through her.

"Am I too old to still learn?" Lumoz asked.

"You still have a few more years, but it will be harder having not started when you were younger. Did you try any of the suggestions I gave you?" Keys raised an eyebrow at her.

"I can't pull someone with me. And I was too nervous to try and walk through someone." Lumoz cringed. "What if I hurt them?"

"What if you don't?"

Their gazes locked, Lumoz's swimming with desire. "What do I need to do?" Her excitement was clear in her tone.

"We'll start you working on control. I want you to be able to choose which part of your body can pass through an object. From there, we'll work with plants, which are living, after all. Just not as complex as a person or animal. Obviously, you can bring certain things with you already or you'd end up naked without your clothes. You need to expand on that. Work on pushing it outwards to encompass larger objects and eventually another person."

"It sounds easy enough." Lumoz shrugged.

"You won't be saying that after a few hours."

***

By the time the sun was sinking, Lumoz managed to make her hand pass through an object and nothing else. She was drenched in sweat, her muscles trembling from the effort.

"Why do I need to be able to do this again?" Lumoz asked.

"Are you whining?" Keys cracked an eye open from her reclined position in the grass.

"Merely *wondering*." Lumoz puffed out a breath.

"Because you need control first. Sometimes the smaller things are the hardest. If you don't have a strong foundation, you can't build on top of it."

El stuck her head out of the cabin. "He's waking up," she called to them.

Lumoz hopped to her feet, no evidence of her exhaustion lingering as she sprinted for the door. Keys took her time pushing up from her position to follow. The princess had too much energy for her own good.

The others were already crowded into the small bedchamber by the time Keys arrived, with Lumoz sitting on the edge of the bed. Keys leaned against the doorway.

"Can you hear me, Bax?" Lumoz reached out, taking his hand.

"Water," he croaked, eyes still closed.

Arla moved to pour a glass from the pitcher they'd placed on the bedside table. Lumoz helped him sit up so he could take a drink, his eyes blinking open, gulping the water.

"Where am I?" he asked after draining the glass, his eyes staying on Lumoz.

"We're in a cabin." She bit her lip.

"*Why* are we in a cabin?" His eyes turned to slits.

"Because I wasn't going to let you die," she huffed.

Baxley swallowed. "Father?"

Lumoz shook her head, eyes downcast.

His gaze ripped away from her, swinging around the room to settle on Keys when he spotted her. "*You*." He glowered at her. "What are you doing here?"

"That's not a very nice way to speak to the person who just saved your life," she chided him.

"King Killer," he spat at her.

"I prefer King *Maker*," she said, raising her hand and examining her nails.

Chapter 43

BAXLEY

KING. HE WAS *KING*. THE BLOOD RUSHED FROM BAXLEY'S face. He hadn't even thought about it. There was no outcome that he planned for where he lived and his father died. Either they both lived or his cousin would have become regent. That was it. Those were the two outcomes. Not this—

He swayed before slumping back onto the pillows.

"Are you alright?" Lumoz lurched towards him.

"I'm king," he mumbled.

"You are," she said slowly, her brows creased.

"Father's dead."

"He is." Her expression grew more worried.

"And I'm alive."

Lumoz looked towards Keys, asking, "Did the poison do something to his brain?"

Keys snorted at the same time Baxley muttered, "Rude."

"I believe he's processing everything," someone he didn't know supplied.

Baxley's eyes snapped to the newcomer, not noticing her before. He could only see part of her face with the mask she was wearing. She had curly, light brown hair that was tied back in a low bun. Her eyes appeared to be hazel, though he couldn't tell for sure from where he sat on the bed. Based on her appearance, he wouldn't have guessed Keys was related to her, but who else could she be? "You're the sister, I presume?"

"So, you've heard about me?" The woman turned to Keys. "My, my, Juju. How close did the two of you become?" She threw in a wink.

"You know princes aren't to my liking." Keys made a sour face.

Baxley didn't know if he should feel offended or not.

"Could have fooled me. I thought you went for anything with a pretty face and a cock between his legs."

"That's you, you ass." Keys tossed a dagger at her sister, who cackled.

The sister slowed the dagger down, pulling it straight to her hand. Magnetite. She was probably tattooed the same way Keys was.

"Why aren't they both in shackles?" he hissed at Lumoz.

"Because we had an agreement." She frowned at him.

"Which I told you not to fulfill."

"Technically, you told Mother," she sassed.

"You still knew my intentions. The agreement was already broken and should have stayed that way." Frustration grew in him. It felt like everyone was against him. First Keys and her betrayal, and now his sister.

"And breaking it is what got you into this state in the first place," she said, her voice rising in volume.

"It wasn't for you to decide." He matched her.

"Why are you so against living?"

"That's not what this is about!" he roared.

"Then explain it to me," she urged, her voice softening. "Don't push me away from these things like Father did." Her eyes pleaded with him.

His heart lurched, embarrassed with how he'd spoken to her. Baxley looked away, noticing that everyone in the room was listening intently. "Leave us, please."

"Don't mind us. It was just getting good," the real Skeleton Key replied, waving them on.

"Come on, El," Keys groaned.

"But I'm invested," she whined back.

"This is why I don't invite you to anything," he heard Keys grumble as they left the room. It was strange watching the two sisters interact—almost made Keys seem normal. And not like a killer.

When the door clicked closed behind everyone, Lumoz said, "Talk to me."

He sighed, trying to sort through his emotions. Where should he even start? He fumbled for his pocket, searching for his watch.

"Here." Lumoz held it out to him instead. "I kept it safe for you. Figured you'd want it when you woke up."

"Thank you," he whispered, clutching it hard, feeling better with it in his hand. "I feel like I've failed." And once he began, the words came easily. "At everything. Adelaide being kidnapped for one—and I'm not even sure what I want when it comes to her anymore. Things between us haven't been the same since we rescued her. Cain dying." He rubbed a hand over his face. "I let a goddamn *assassin* into our home for fuck's sake. And now Father's dead because of it. Because of my choices. I got our father killed. How am I supposed to live with that?" he asked, feeling helpless.

"It would have been easier if you had died with him," she whispered. It was like she could read his mind. Somehow, she always knew him, despite their age difference.

"Yes," he admitted. "And what kind of person does that make me for thinking that?"

"Human. You're human. You're my brother." She reached out, taking his hand.

"I have the entire weight of our country on my shoulders, looking to me with him gone. How am I to lead them when I've made a mess of all of this? I can't even trust my own judgement. How are they supposed to trust me? Where do I even go from here?"

"We take it one day at a time." She squeezed his hand. "You are *not* alone in this. I am here. Mother is here. The blame doesn't fully rest with you. Everyone had a part to play. You can't control everything. Only do your best to make the right choice."

"When did you get so wise." The corners of his mouth tugged upward in a small smile. His sister was growing into a strong young woman, leaving behind the silly little girl he remembered fondly.

"I've always been wise; *you* just never listened. Plus, do you think I wasn't paying attention and learning from all the meetings I snuck into?"

He chuckled. "Noted."

"Are you hungry?" she asked when he didn't continue.

"Starving, but I also think my bladder might burst." He groaned, trying to sit up again.

"I'll ask Felix to come in and help you." Lumoz stood, releasing his hand.

"Thank you," he said before she could walk away.

"I will always be here for you."

"I'm supposed to say that to you." As the oldest, he'd always looked out for her.

She shrugged. "It can't go both ways?"

"I suppose it can." Baxley really smiled this time. "I love you, my light."

Lumoz returned the smile. "I love you, too, Bax. I'm glad you're still here."

Hopefully, he would feel the same way soon.

Chapter 44

DEATH ADDER

IT TOOK TWO MORE DAYS BEFORE BAXLEY WAS TRULY back on his feet. Keys spent the time training Lumoz, driving her to her limits every single day. She'd found the girl's excitement refreshing. There was still a long way for her to go, but she'd made some progress on control. Keys tested Lumoz by throwing rocks or sticks at her and seeing if she could adapt fast enough for it to pass through that part of her body.

"I'm pretty sure you simply enjoy throwing things at me," Lumoz had muttered at one point when a small rock bounced off her forehead.

"And I'm pretty sure if you were actually concentrating, that wouldn't have hit you," Keys had sassed back. She pulled the rock back to her hand and sent it flying again. This time it passed through Lumoz's face. "Why are you so accepting of me after the death of your father?" she asked, giving Lumoz a break.

The girl chewed on her bottom lip. "My father has"—she flinched—"had," she corrected, "always been...difficult. I think he would have preferred another son, even though women are allowed to inherit the crown. He had little time for me while I was young. And it only grew worse when I started expressing interest in learning about the politics of our country. Mother snuck me into meetings when he refused to allow me to attend. He was furious when he caught her, though she didn't care. I think at first it was just a way for me to try and spend time with him; but overtime, I grew to love the intricate balance needed to run a country. Sometimes I joke with Bax that I willed my gift into existence simply so it was harder for Father to exclude me." She gave a watery chuckle, a tear falling from the corner of her eye.

"Not that Bax had it any easier than me," she continued. "I'm not sure which is better, being constantly criticized or completely ignored. Though how can a princess complain about having a pampered life?" She looked up at the sky as more tears tracked down her face.

Keys remained quiet, not sure if Lumoz was looking for an answer to her question.

After a few deep breaths, Lumoz wiped the tears from her face. "I know it was you that killed him. That if you hadn't poisoned him, he would still be here. And yet...I can't help but blame him instead." She paused for a beat. "Does that make me a bad daughter?"

"You're asking an assassin for their opinion?"

Lumoz played with a blade of grass. "Seems as good as anyone else's."

Keys let out a sigh. "My mother disowned both my sister and I when we weren't much younger than you. Being a parent doesn't mean they're always right. It doesn't make it right if they treat you poorly. It doesn't mean you must have the same views and opinions as them."

Lumoz's mouth popped open. "What did you do that was so bad?"

"My sister wanted to live her life how she was most comfortable, and I supported her in that."

"And your father?"

"He chose us." Keys swallowed around the lump in her throat, remembering the way he had vehemently defended both his daughters against their own mother, his wife. "We were lucky to have one parent to show us what unconditional love meant. Just as you are. It doesn't make up for the damage you've experienced at the hands of the other, but it's something."

"No," Lumoz agreed. "It doesn't."

They had gone back to practicing after that.

If Lumoz stuck to her training, she could accomplish incredible things. Hell, Keys might even be interested in hiring her—just think of all the possibilities with someone like her.

***

Keys found herself outside that night, staring up at the stars. Tomorrow, they would part ways. For good this time. Baxley was going to be fine. She was completely healed from being tortured. There was no reason for any of them to stick around—and yet, she felt like something was missing.

She rubbed at her chest, trying to dispel the strange feeling there. She and Baxley hadn't even talked to each other since the day he woke up. All he did was scowl in her direction anytime they occupied the same space. Keys tried to not let it get to her—it shouldn't bother her—but for some reason it did.

"Why are you out here brooding?" El plopped down next to her.

"I'm not brooding." Her eyes stayed locked on the stars.

"Sure, you aren't."

They fell into an easy silence.

"I don't know what it is," Keys blurted out. "Something doesn't feel right."

El turned fully to face her. "We could leave now. We don't have to stay here any longer."

"It isn't that." She shook her head.

Her sister frowned. "Don't tell me you actually did fall for him. I was joking about that."

"Fuck no. At least not in the way you're implying. Gag me." Keys made a puking sound.

"Then how?"

"He already seemed so lost before, and then everything with his father—I feel *bad* for him. His life is about to get worse before it gets better. I don't know. I feel like I should be doing something to help."

"So, you feel guilty?"

"No. It's not—" Her eyes widened, realizing there was something she could do. Something that she had wrestled with for a while. Keys drew out Adelaide's letter from her bra. Somehow it had made it through the interrogation without Edwin finding it. The parchment was well worn by now, covered in sweat and some blood.

"What's that?"

"Read it." Keys held it out for her to take, casting a small light for them to see.

El's eyes grew bigger the farther down she read. "Do you know what this means?" She scanned the letter again.

"I know."

"Holy hell. This could blow up three countries."

"I know."

"What're you going to do with it?"

"I *was* planning on throwing it away. Now…I think I might give it to him."

"You *do* care for him. My little Juju, finally growing a heart."

"Oh, stuff it, you asshole." Keys shoved her sister, pushing her over. El laughed, rolling back up to sit. "And if anyone's little, it's you. I'm older."

El suddenly became serious. "You think he'll believe you?"

"He doesn't have to believe me. There's proof other than this."

"What?"

"She's pregnant."

"What an idiot," El moaned.

***

She stayed outside even after El called it a night, heading for bed. Her mind listed out all the reasons she shouldn't tell him — and then all the reasons she should. It was well past midnight before she finally decided.

Groaning, she pushed up from her spot. The door to the cabin didn't creak quite as loudly with all the use it had seen lately. Keys crept through the living area, trying not to wake anyone. She found Lumoz in the bedchamber with Baxley. The princess had been sharing the bed with him ever since he woke up. Any moment she wasn't training, she was glued to his side. Keys couldn't blame her. If her own sibling had almost died, she'd probably be doing the same.

Walking to the side Baxley slept on, Keys gave him a nudge. When he didn't wake, she did it again. He still didn't rouse. Keys jabbed him, hard, in the side.

Baxley jerked awake, eyes wild. They narrowed when he spotted her. "What?" he hissed.

"I have something you need to see," she whispered, eyes moving to Lumoz.

"Nothing you have is of interest to me," he bit out in a harsh tone.

"You'll want to see this." She tried again.

He rolled over, ignoring her.

"It's about Adelaide."

That got his attention. He rolled back over to face her.

"What about her?"

She swore she could hear his teeth grinding together. "Outside." Keys didn't wait to see if he was following.

"Where are you going?" Lumoz's voice split the air.

"Go back to sleep. I'll be right back," Baxley muttered.

He followed Keys back through the house, coming to a stop in the clearing outside.

"Well?" he asked, crossing his arms.

"Here." Keys held the letter out to him, sending up a small light again.

Her heart beat faster in her chest as his fingers closed around the letter. Right or wrong, there was no going back from this. She watched as his eyes read over the words, darting from left to right. And then he read it again. And again, pacing as he did.

"I don't understand. Where did you get this?" His hands trembled.

"I caught her trying to send it while we were still in Voglar," she explained.

"No. That's impossible," he said in denial. "Did you forge this? Is this another one of your deceptions?" Baxley stomped over to her, getting in her face.

"I wish for your sake it was." She tilted her head up, meeting his gaze.

"I don't believe this. She wouldn't do this." He shook the letter. "She wouldn't throw everything away."

"And yet, she did." Keys stood firm.

"No!" he yelled, pacing away again.

"You don't need to take my word for it. There's other proof."

"What?" he snapped, not stopping.

"She's pregnant," she whispered.

Baxley came to a halt, his head twisting back towards her. "Say that again," he growled.

"She's pregnant."

He crouched down, tugging at his hair. "The seasickness. Trying to sleep with me—"

"She didn't know, if that makes you feel better. Being on a ship probably exacerbated any nausea she'd been feeling before then. And she most likely thought she could cover her tracks by sleeping with you."

"It doesn't." Baxley stayed crouching for several long moments.

"You knew," he eventually whispered. "This whole time, you knew. You let me act like a fool." He stood, turning to face her. "What? Were you laughing at me behind my back? Did you think it's funny?" he yelled, coming at her again. "The stupid prince who risked *everything* for a princess who doesn't even want him."

"I don't think that makes you stupid," she replied, keeping her voice calm.

"My father is dead. And for what? All of this—all of it was for nothing." He raged and she let him, weathering his storm.

"There was a time you said that even if you didn't end up together, it would be worth it."

"And I was stupid! This"—Baxley threw his arms out wide—"none of this has been worth it." His chest puffed with the force of his breathing. His shoulders fell. "How could she do this?" he whispered. "How could she throw it all away?" He choked on a sob, more soon following.

She let silence fall between them, giving him time to process.

When he eventually pulled himself back together, he said, "Tell me." Determination in his voice.

"What do you want to know?"

"Everything—anything you know."

So, she did. She laid it all out for him. How she found Calbex and Adelaide in bed together. How she found the letter. How she blackmailed Adelaide with it. How she confronted her when she suspected her of being pregnant. Keys held nothing back.

"Is this all connected?" he asked when she was done. "Her running away. The assassination of my father…and me."

"I'm not sure." Her brows creased. There were some missing pieces that she intended to find—for her own curiosity, of course.

"Who hired you?"

"I can't tell you specifically—"

He cut her off, asking, "Can't or won't?"

"Won't," she admitted. "If it got out that I turned in a client…well, bad for business, you know."

He opened his mouth to interject something—

"However." She held up a finger before he could speak. He closed his mouth, watching her. "I will tell you the person was from Voglar. You should be wary. I'm not sure how far this goes, but only one path seems likely."

"What is that?"

"War."

They regarded each other. She could almost see his thoughts racing behind his eyes.

"Why tell me all this? Why now?"

"Because I didn't want this on my conscience," she explained. "It felt like what I needed to do."

"I'd like to be alone," he muttered, turning away from her.

Keys started to walk past him, heading towards the cabin, but paused, resting a hand on his shoulder. Surprisingly, he didn't shrug her off. "You are a good man," she said. "Even if you hate me now, you are still a good man. Don't let this change that. Be a good king. An honorable king."

"Look at where being good has gotten me," he scoffed.

She squeezed his shoulder before continuing. Keys rubbed at her chest again, a different feeling there now. Her heart ached for him, for the tough times he was about to face. And she wished it didn't.

***

Their parting was short in the morning. Dark circles hung beneath Baxley's eyes. He was quiet, not speaking to anyone.

Lumoz bound up to her, full of life as always. "I'll keep practicing, I promise."

"Remember what I told you."

The young princess nodded. "I will. Can I contact you somehow if I have questions?"

"Start one of those rumors you're so good at that you're looking for me. But I'll be watching from time to time." She winked. Sometimes she did find herself in Aglar, after all. She might even be willing to travel a little out of her way if there was a reason to visit.

"Your Highness," Arla called to Lumoz. "Time to go." Everyone else was already mounted on their horses.

"Goodbye," she said quickly to Keys before rushing to her own horse.

Keys and her sister watched the group ride out of the clearing. Baxley never looked back.

"Ready, Juju?" El asked when they were out of sight.

She nodded. "Let's go home." Keys walked over to the one remaining horse, leading it in the opposite direction. No one ever asked *how* her sister had gotten there.

"What are you going to do next?" El walked along beside her as they weaved between the trees.

"Take a very long bath and then sleep until I wither away. After that…we'll see."

El stopped, looking around. "This is far enough."

A swirling portal opened before them, and they stepped through, disappearing from view.

Chapter 45

BAXLEY

NUMB. HE FELT NOTHING BUT NUMB. BAXLEY DIDN'T even remember the ride back to the palace. Everything blurred around him. Lumoz fretted over him endlessly—especially the one night that they had to stop—yet he couldn't even make an effort for her. How did his life become this? Any food he managed to choke down tasted like ash on his tongue.

Before he knew it, they were riding up to the palace. He stormed into the entrance hall, striding away from the others.

"Bax," Lumoz called after him.

He ignored her, pushing on through the halls. His thoughts were consumed by one thing—Adelaide. He needed to find Adelaide. Baxley took the stairs two at a time. His blood heated, pulse rushing through his ears, growing louder and louder the closer he got to her rooms.

Baxley burst through the door, slamming it into the wall. Adelaide started from her position in the sitting room. His eyes immediately locked onto her, piercing into her.

"Baxley," she cried, standing up from the couch. "You're alive." Relief flooded her face.

"What the fuck is this?" He drew the letter from his pocket. It was even more worn now with how much he had folded and unfolded it, rereading the damning words written there.

Her eyes grew large, face paling. Adelaide collapsed back onto the couch. "I can explain," she croaked.

His heart dropped into his stomach. So, it was true. All of it. He could see it plastered all over her face. The fire within him built to an inferno. "You fucking traitor."

Acknowledgements

First to my readers, if you made it this far, thank you! I couldn't be writing if it wasn't for your support. It means more to me than you could know that you took a chance on an indie author just starting out. I hope you enjoyed it as much as I loved creating this world! I can't wait to dive deeper into these characters with you. Buckle up for the next two books. The Scales of Annihilation is already in the works!

To Mandy, thank you again for making me brave enough to share this story with everyone! You're stuck in this with me now, whether you like it or not.

To my sister, Janel and mom, Sharon, thank you for your support and excitement! Sorry you had to read the smut scenes. I'd say there won't be any in the following books, but that would be a lie. If you black out those chapters in Dad's copy, I wouldn't be mad.

To Marisa, leave my commas alone! Just kidding. Thank you for making my book better! I couldn't have done it without you. Glad I could teach you what a negligee was.

To my husband, Aaron, thanks for putting up with me adding yet another time-consuming hobby to my life. At least this has kept me distracted enough that I haven't added more animals to our family...yet.

About the Author

Meredith C. Armolt recently started writing after being an avid reader for years. She currently lives in Florida with her husband and two dogs. In her free time, you'll find her doing home improvement projects or practicing yoga. After working as an animal trainer at zoos for eight years, she made a career change to an office job, which has allowed her to expand on her hobbies outside of work. She hopes to continue writing and creating in the coming years.

Follow her on Instagram: @meredithcarmolt
Follow her on TikTok: @meredith.c.armolt